T0315633

Happy
Ever After

Adèle Geras

This volume contains:

The Tower Room

Watching the Roses

Pictures of the Night

DEFINITIONS

HAPPY EVER AFTER
A DEFINITIONS BOOK 9781849417709

The Tower Room first published in Great Britain 1990
by Hamish Hamilton
Definitions edition published 2001

Watching the Roses first published in Great Britain 1991
by Hamish Hamilton
Definitions edition published 2001

Pictures of the Night first published in Great Britain 1992
by Hamish Hamilton
Definitions edition published 2002

5 7 9 10 8 6 4

Copyright ©Adele Geras, 1990, 1991, 1992

Verse from *'Upon a Gloomy Night'*, taken from *St John of the Cross: Poems*,
translated by Roy Campbell (Harvill Press, 1951), by permission of
William Collins Sons & Co. Ltd.

The right of Adele Geras to be identified as the author of this work
has been asserted in accordance with the Copyright, Designs
and Patents Act 1988.

Definitions are published by Random House Children's Books,
61-63 Uxbridge Road, London W5 5SA,
a division of The Random House Group Ltd.

Addresses for companies within The Random House Group Limited
can be found at: www.randomhouse.co.uk/offices.htm

THE RANDOM HOUSE GROUP Limited Reg. No. 954009
www.kidsatrandomhouse.co.uk

A CIP catalogue record for this book is available from the British Library.

The Random House Group Limited supports The Forest Stewardship
Council® (FSC®), the leading international forest-certification organisation.
Our books carrying the FSC label are printed on FSC®-certified paper.
FSC is the only forest-certification scheme supported by the leading
environmental organisations, including Greenpeace. Our
paper procurement policy can be found at
www.randomhouse.co.uk/environment

MIX
Paper | Supporting
responsible forestry
FSC® C018179

Printed and bound in Great Britain by Clays Ltd, St Ives plc

Contents

The Tower Room   5

Watching the Roses   133

Pictures of the Night   249

The Tower Room

For Jean Ure who read it first

En la noche dichosa
En secreto, que nadie me veía
Ni yo miraba cosa,
Sin otra luz y guía
Sino la que en el corazón ardía.

Upon that lucky night
In secrecy, insructable to sight,
I went without discerning
And with no other light
Except for that which in my heart was burning.

From *Saint John of the Cross: Poems*
Translated by Roy Campbell

Up in the tower, nothing seemed real
Except the sky, and you, at night, calling.

from *Letter to Rapunzel* by Frances Wilson

ONCE upon a time, the linoleum was green. I remember it clearly from my first day at Egerton Hall. I was not quite eleven then, and of a fanciful turn of mind, and I imagined it as a ribbon, streaming down the three storeys of Austen House, snaking all along the corridors and winding round the stairwell, slipping down over the stairs and along Study Passage until it met the brown linoleum that marked the beginning of School Corridor. Of course, it's not like a ribbon at all, and it isn't even properly green any more. All those shoes: regulation lace-ups, Sunday-best brown ankle-straps, the Staff's Cuban heels, muddy lacrosse boots, grass-stained tennis shoes and, more recently, Saturday night Sixth Form stilettos (officially forbidden but still worn) have left their mark. The lino is cracked, pocked and scuffed and looks pallid from the attentions of a thousand mops.

*

London *April 6th 1962*

THERE it is: a beginning, and exactly the way a beginning ought to be. Once upon a time. I miss Bella and Alice. I miss the Tower Room, even though we're high up here as well. I am alone almost all the time, and these words are company. It's my eighteenth birthday today and I've hardly noticed it. I told you about it, of course, and tonight we will go to the pictures to celebrate, but there are no cards from Bella or

Alice or any of my friends, and nothing from Dorothy. I will send them all this address today, just to let them know where we are. I want to be seen to be behaving responsibly. I can't decide what to do, what ought to happen now, but I feel that if I write the whole story down, try and analyse it all in a way that even Dorothy would approve of, then everything will become clearer. I hope it does, and more than that, I hope that you read this one day, because in all this time, we've never spoken very much, or if we have, then they haven't been the right words.

*

I came to Egerton Hall for the first time in January 1955, just over seven years ago. My father had already left for Africa, and I used to enjoy imagining him in a jungle surrounded by heaps of bananas, with monkeys swinging from creeper to creeper round his head. We'd driven from the station in a taxi, my mother and I. It was five o'clock and snowing heavily. Fat flakes broke against the windscreen and drifted and blew outside the cab like ghosts. Up and up the drive we went, and as we turned into the gravel courtyard in front of Main School, I caught sight of a huge building, even darker than the dark sky, with rows and rows of lighted windows set into the black. Like topazes lying on black velvet, that's what I said then. What a peculiar child I must have been, but even now I can recall how comforting it was to see that yellow shining out in the night. The whole place looked magical to me, like a castle in a toy snowstorm, the kind you pick up and shake so that the flakes will fly about. What else can I remember? My mother's face, very pale, both of us trying hard not to cry, and Dorothy standing beside a polished table that seemed to stretch for miles and miles. Dorothy waiting to receive me.

I had been hearing about Dorothy since infancy. She was a friend of my parents and particularly of my mother's. I didn't know her age exactly, but she must have been in her late thirties when I first arrived at Egerton Hall. She had been our neighbour long ago, while my mother was pregnant with me and just after my birth. When my mother had confessed to a craving for asparagus, Dorothy had provided it fresh from her carefully laid-out garden. Shortly after my birth, however, she had taken up her teaching post at Egerton Hall, and after that, my mother had spoken of entrusting me to her care.

'Dorothy will see you're properly educated,' she used to say, or, 'You'll be well looked after with Dorothy,' and now here she was, just as I'd seen her in my parents' photograph albums: small and grey-haired (had she always had grey hair, even in her twenties?) with startling light blue eyes, dressed in a suit of greenish tweed.

'Hello, Dorothy,' I said.

'Welcome to Egerton Hall,' she answered, almost but not quite smiling at me.

After my mother had gone, I tried imagining her in the fantasy jungle with my father, but it was hard. For a long time after that night, when I thought of her, I thought of her face in the taxi's back window, a small, ivory shape, disappearing into the snow and out of sight.

I never saw her or my father ever again. They died that spring on a trip upriver, and Dorothy adopted me legally. It was a very straightforward matter. She was already my guardian while my parents were abroad. I can hardly remember my sadness now, but the feeling I had of being completely alone in the world was very strong. No brothers, no sisters, no aunts or cousins, only Dorothy, and no home apart from a small room at Egerton Hall. Everything I possessed was capable of being packed into my school trunk. For a while after my parents died, I used to dream at night of places in Africa and Asia that I had lived in with them when I was a very young child. I dreamed so much that what I actually remembered about each place became blurred and misty and all the different scenery ran together in my mind, and soon all that was left to me was an unfocussed image of somewhere full of sunshine and blue water and very green trees heavy with purple, scarlet, crimson and vermilion flowers.

'Welcome, child,' Dorothy said to me, that first night. 'As soon as you're ready, we'll walk across to Junior House and find your dormitory. I want you to regard Egerton Hall as your home as well as your school.'

Which of course it was, until a few weeks ago.

*

IT's difficult to know how far back to go. I think I shall start just before the beginning of last term, the last day of the Christmas holidays, and if I have to refer to things that happened further back than that, then I can do it as I go along.

'Be sure that what you write, that *everything* you write, is relevant, germane to the issue.' Oh, I can hear you saying it, Miss Doolittle, and I'll try. I will try.

*

THE Christmas holidays were nearly over. I liked Egerton Hall with no one in it. Of course, I missed Bella and Alice, missed the laughter and the noise and even quite looked forward to lessons, but there was something especially quiet and more than a little eerie about a building that was accustomed to being full of people and loud with voices, and that found itself, all of a sudden, empty. It seemed to me sometimes as I walked along the corridors in the holidays listening to the squeak of my own shoes, that everything was holding its breath, waiting for something. Desks looked at me as I passed, lockers in the cloakroom hung open expecting shoes, pianos in the practice rooms hummed quietly under closed lids, and curtains hung at windows, looking out. I decided to go and have a look at the Tower Room before everyone arrived. I hadn't been up there since getting back from my visit to Alice's house where I always spent a part of the holidays.

The Tower Room was the highest room of all, right at the top of Austen House, and the only room with three beds in it. It had sloping ceilings and a large window that looked down over the front drive and the fountain in front of Main School. From it you could see past the sweep of lawn that stretched to the lacrosse pitches, and beyond those, to the trees. Even more important, from the Tower Room window you could get an uninterrupted view of the sky and, living there, I became a sky-watcher in the same way that other people become bird-watchers. It didn't matter to me what the weather was like. I loved the massed, bruise-coloured clouds of a storm, and the little cotton-wool puffs of early spring. I admired the high blue dome of summer and the low grey ceiling of rainy November. Best of all, I liked the way the light left the sky after a day full of sunshine: bleeding out of it slowly before the darkness came.

Bella, Alice and I regarded the Tower Room as ours.

'But Sixth Formers have never shared a three-room before,' Miss Herbert, the Housemistress of Austen House, had said when we'd been to see her at the end of the Fifth Form. 'You'll all be House Prefects next term, you know. Besides, you've had the Tower Room for a year and perhaps there are others who would like it. I'm sure you'd all get used to single rooms . . . and anyway, your A-levels will be coming up soon . . . hours of private study . . .' On and on she had gone, but we (mostly Bella, it was true) had wheedled, cajoled, and persuaded, pointing out how the rest of the House could be accommodated in single, double, and four-bed rooms, saying that everyone knew ours was the only threesome, etc. etc. In the end, Miss Herbert had given in. She was a thin, dark woman with her hair bobbed ('Just as it must have been in the Twenties,' Bella used to sigh. 'Desperately unfashionable!') and she had the face of a well-bred and quite pretty horse. Her clothes tended towards the brown, and her shoes Bella regarded as unspeakable: thick-heeled, high-laced clodhoppers. Still, she had long fingers which Alice said were aristocratic-looking and I admired her exquisite jewellery – a magnificent amethyst brooch pinned to her tweedy lapel, and a half-hoop of opals the size of small peas on the fourth finger of her right hand.

'It's not bad luck for her,' Alice had said when she saw it. 'Her birthday's in October, so it's her birthstone.' Alice is the sort of person who knows about such things. Miss Herbert taught Latin and I liked to think, during weary translations from Cicero, about who it was who had placed the opals on her hand. Perhaps it had been intended as an engagement ring, and Miss Herbert's fiancé had been tragically killed during the Second World War, and since that day Miss Herbert had stopped thinking about men at all, but had devoted herself instead to looking after the girls of Austen House.

'You can tell from her ornaments and things that she

has taste,' Alice used to say. 'I'd love to see her house. It must be very elegant and refined. Not a bit like Miss Doolittle's.' Miss Doolittle was Assistant Housemistress. She taught English and lived in a room of spectacular chaos. She looked like nothing so much as the figurehead on a galleon: golden-haired, with slightly protruding eyes and an enormous swelling bosom that curved in front of her as she walked. She favoured tight dresses of mauve crepe with draperies about the hips and high-heeled shoes of black patent leather.

'You can tell how plump she is,' Alice said once. 'Have you ever heard the deafening noise of her nylons rubbing together as she walks?' We collapsed into giggles on the candlewick counterpanes of the Tower Room.

I looked around at the empty white walls cleared of pin-ups, the white painted chairs, chests-of-drawers, cupboards, and the beige squares of carpet material pretending to be warm, comforting rugs beside each of the beds.

At the end of the Fifth Form, Miss Herbert had said:

'Of course, if you have the Tower Room as Sixth Formers, I shall trust you not to abuse the privilege.'

Bella had looked innocent, Alice really didn't know what she was talking about, and I answered for all of us:

'We'll be very sensible about talking late and so forth. Really we will.'

So it was settled. The Tower Room had been ours for two years and one term, and the three of us were still in it.

'The really good thing about this place,' Bella used to say, leaning too far out of the window, 'is the view. And the fact that it's up so many stairs that no member of staff is going to be bothered coming up here, are they?'

'Hope not, for your sake,' Alice answered. 'Do you truly like those horrible cigarettes or do you only pretend?'

Bella stopped leaning out of the window and turned to laugh at Alice.

'Oh, I love them, Alice . . . You're such a goody-goody at heart.'

'I'm not a goody-goody at all. I just don't like the smell. It's awful. The taste's horrid as well. I had one at a dance once and I was practically sick.'

'Just make sure you don't get caught,' I said. 'I don't trust some of those Third Formers out there.'

'They'd never dare tell on me, would they?' Bella's eyes looked very dark in her face. 'And anyway, I'm careful as anything.' And she was careful, in a reckless sort of way. She'd found a wonderful hiding-place for her cigarettes and matches under the floorboards of one of the cupboards, hidden by about a foot of tangled games equipment: shorts, boots, balls, racquets and lacrosse sticks. No one would ever look there, and (I supposed) one cigarette smoked after lights out every few days couldn't really be considered wicked.

'There are girls out there of our age,' Bella said once, waving her hand in the general direction of the outside world, 'who are married with children. We are not kids any more. We are almost eighteen years old. That's grown-up.'

'I'd hate to be married at eighteen,' Alice said, wrinkling her nose.

Bella laughed. 'And we all know why that is, don't we, eh?'

Alice's eyes filled with tears. 'Don't be so beastly, Bella. I told you and Megan all that in deadly secret. You don't have to tease me about it. I can't help it.'

Alice's deadly secret (one the three of us had discussed long and vigorously under the sloping ceilings of the Tower Room) was that, as she put it, she was not 'all that keen on kissing boys'. She admitted to us that she had never yet met one boy who made her heart beat faster, and she used to listen with wide eyes while others (well, mostly Bella, in all honesty) regaled her with tales of open-mouthed kissing, fumblings with brassières in the back seats of various cars, and once, some nervous fingers on an upper thigh, above a stocking-top.

'I promise you,' Bella said, 'nearly fainting wasn't in it. I can't tell you how delicious it felt. Waves of warmth sort of rushing over you.'

Alice was unimpressed. She told me one day when Bella was in the bath: 'I think she makes up half that stuff just to annoy me. I think she gets most of it out of books. Remember *Lady Chatterley's Lover* last year? How she carried it round covered in brown paper? It was all she ever talked about. I could never get into it myself.'

I agreed with Alice about *Lady Chatterley's Lover* but Bella and I had agreed between the two of us that Alice was definitely afraid of sex.

'I regard it as my mission in life to find Alice a boy she *will* be excited by,' Bella used to say, and I'd answer:

'How, stuck away in Egerton Hall with three hundred girls and an almost completely female staff?'

'Love will find a way,' Bella would mutter mysteriously.

'You sound like a book,' I'd say, and laugh.

I remembered that conversation now as I walked over to the window. The beginning of January, and no snow. The sky was whitish-grey and there was no colour anywhere. The whole landscape had taken on the appearance of a photograph. There were two magpies on the chimneys of Eliot House, and my heart lifted. Two for joy. I was superstitious about these birds which seem, in their colouring and shape, almost too dramatic to be quite real. Their cry is like the noise of a mechanical toy, and one magpie, so they say, brings sorrow. If I ever saw a solitary magpie, I would scan the heavens for a long time looking for another, and if I couldn't find one, I would salute the bird and say: 'Magpie, magpie, where is your mate?' to ward off harm. Many birds liked Egerton Hall, and so did I. It was built in the shape of an E with one extra prong, or a comb with four evenly-spaced teeth. I knew its history backwards. In the eighteenth century, an enterprising and newly-rich Egerton had built the hall in acres of expensively landscaped garden, and it is to be hoped that whoever had laid out the plan was not turning in his grave over the lacrosse pitches, tennis courts, netball courts, open-air swimming pool and other such monstrosities that had been added much later. There was still the terrace, and the fountain in the middle of the courtyard with its statue of nymphs and seasnakes intermingled so that you couldn't really tell where the ladies ended and their fishy friends began. There were still lawns and a kitchen garden, and there was the San, where we were sent when we were ill. A house had been built for the younger girls near what we called 'The Rim of the Known World'.

After that, there was the forest.

'Jolly clever of old Egerton to put his house here,' Bella had said, long ago. 'Think how useful for nature ramblers, botany freaks, mushroom collectors, etc.'

'It's romantic,' said Alice, thinking of *Babes in the Wood*, *Robin and Marian* and other well-known tales of that kind.

'It's not a frightfully foresty forest, though, is it? More like a large wood. And a bit too near civilization to be wild or anything,' I said.

Bella had snorted loudly. 'I don't call Egerton Parva civilization and I'm not altogether sure that Coleston counts either, for all that it's a town and a famous eighteenth-century watering place or whatever.'

Foresty or not, I thought, looking at the tops of black branches just visible behind the Chapel, there have been stories. I suppose it's natural for children to make things up. Once there was a rumour about an escaped lunatic hiding in there, then there was the time when Josephine Graham ran away and wasn't found for ages . . . There had been a very strong 'the forest has got her' gang at work then, but in the end she was discovered behind the bar at the pub in Egerton Magna. Still, whichever way you look at it, there's something strange about trees, and especially so many trees together. They do so often seem as though they are nearly alive, and it's easy to imagine that they are about to move, or have only just stopped moving, or even (like in the story of Daphne who was forced to turn herself into a bay tree to avoid Apollo's lustful embraces) that the bark is a covering for some kind of body.

The nineteenth-century Egerton sisters, Phoebe and Louisa, inspired by Miss Buss and Miss Beale of Cheltenham Ladies College, and Miss Lawrence of Roedean School, decided an educational establishment was just the ticket, and proceeded to organize one the moment their father was safely dead. They had no tiresome husbands to put down feet in the way nineteenth-century husbands were wont to do, and so they had a grand time remodelling Egerton Hall. Apart from defacing the grounds with various sporting facilities, they built a chapel (all white marble and Victorian stained glass) and had the stables converted into an art studio, decorated with Art Nouveau tiles of lilies in bronze and eau-de-nil and murky pinks and mauves. They installed a science laboratory, and called each 'wing' of the original building a House, naming them after famous lady writers: Eliot,

Austen, Brontë, Browning. Each House has a long passage called Study Passage where the prefects' studies are to be found, three floors of bedrooms and bathrooms in assorted shapes and sizes, a Junior Common Room (J.C.R.) complete with gramophone, small fiction library, and copies of the *Daily Telegraph, Punch* and the *Illustrated London News,* and a Senior Common Room (S.C.R.) for senior girls who are not prefects. The younger girls do their prep. in the J.P.R. (Junior Preparation Room) with a prefect to supervise them, but Fifth and Sixth Formers are left to their own devices in the S.C.R. A great deal of toasting of crumpets by the gas fire goes on, and much reading of novels and writing of letters. Each House also has its own dining room and kitchen. Miss Herbert has three well-appointed rooms to herself: a drawing room, a study, and a bedroom. Miss Doolittle has a drawing room and a bedroom. Then there's Matron's Room, like a cross between a hospital and a nursery in an old-fashioned children's book, full of cupboards packed with Virol, bandages, iodine, Friars' Balsam, packets of sanitary towels, an impressive array of pills and potions, and a phalanx of fearsome silver instruments of a medical nature.

The Egerton sisters had clearly been of the opinion that luxury was wasted on the young, and so the girls' rooms are uniformly spartan. We have candlewick counterpanes in shades of pink, blue, yellow or lilac, and curtains with a flower pattern made almost invisible by countless washes, and that's that. Everything else is added by whoever's living in the room: posters, books, photographs of parents, or pets, or (later) boyfriends, and ornaments of all descriptions. There are crazes for things. I remember an especially disgusting statuette of a cat I had, which was supposed to turn blue when it rained and pink when it was fine. Everybody had one at this particular time except (typically) Alice.

'I can see what the weather's like just by looking out of the window,' she'd said. 'And besides, they're hideous, those things.'

She wrinkled her nose. It was remarks like that, made in the calmest and gentlest of voices, that gave Alice a reputation for taste and refinement and earned her the nickname of 'Princess Alice'.

'That,' Bella used to remark, 'and the fact that you live in the palace next door.'

'It's not a palace!' Alice always rose to the bait. 'Only a biggish house. And I don't call five miles away next door, either.'

'Biggish!' Bella would roll about and clutch her sides. 'Fifteen bedrooms: biggish! Listen to her!'

'It's not my fault,' said Alice. 'It's where I was born. And you don't live in a hovel either, so there, Bella Lavanne!'

'Keep your hair on,' Bella smiled. 'You're a very nice, kind princess and we don't care at all how rich and grand you are. We forgive you.'

'I'm not grand!' Alice would start to wail again, and I'd end up throwing a cushion at her.

I sat in the Tower Room and wished that the holidays were over and that it was tomorrow already, and then they'd be back. During the time I'd spent staying with Alice, gales had blown away much of the roof of Austen House, and now there was scaffolding around most of the brickwork that faced over the main courtyard. This cat's-cradle of metal pipes came right up to the window of the Tower Room, and in places there were planks balanced between one bar and another, so that the men (who were, it seems, replacing the whole roof bit by bit) could walk about comfortably.

Dorothy had said: 'Of course, it will take the whole term to complete the work.'

'Surely not!' I answered. 'There must be a whole crowd of them, isn't there?'

'Yes, of course, but they can only work after you girls are safely in lessons and, naturally, they have to finish before it gets dark. We don't want any nonsense about the men looking at the girls in their bedrooms. As it is, Miss Herbert will have to warn all of you to be particularly vigilant about putting away your pyjamas in pyjama cases, or neatly under the pillow, and not leaving your belongings lying about your rooms.'

Stockings drying on a towel hung over the towel rail, a few hair rollers left out on the chest-of-drawers, fluffy slippers peeping out from under the bed: I imagined these things driving the poor workmen into frenzies of unrequited lust, so that they plummeted off the scaffolding and down to the gravel below. Bella would be sure to try and talk to them. Alice would be nervous . . . they'd be so rough. It would all be immensely interesting.

I went to look out of the window, and there, suddenly, was Dorothy, looking up at the Tower Room. It's freezing, I thought, but still, I'd better, just the same. I opened the window.

'Hello, Dorothy!' I called.

'Hello, dear,' said Dorothy, craning her neck. 'You look extremely . . . medieval.'

'I'm jolly cold.'

'Then close the window and come down. We'll have some tea. I've a piece of news you may find interesting.'

Dorothy smiled and waved and strode off towards Brontë House, where she had a small flat, being not only Head of Science, but also a kind of caretaker as well. As always, it seemed to me that, Cheshire-cat-like, a faint impression of her smile hung in the air after she had gone. I shook my head to get some sense into it. As I closed the window, I noticed that my hair, which I wear in one long plait down my back, was wet at the ends from brushing against the windowsill.

*

London *April 9th 1962*

WE were lucky to find this place. It's a bed-sitting room near Gloucester Road tube station. It's very high up, on the fourth floor, but I, at least, am used to that after the Tower Room. We've tried to make it as nice as possible, but, as you often tell me, we haven't got much money to spend on posters and things and I didn't have a chance to bring much with me. A letter came today from Miss Herbert. She must have asked Bella or Alice for the address and written at once. She says:

> 'I would ask you to consider most seriously, Megan, what you are in danger of losing. All the efforts of the last seven years (yours and your teachers') will come to nothing if you persist in the path you have chosen. At least keep the work going in case you do return to Egerton Hall. You know, of course, that there have been voices raised in favour of your expulsion, but Miss Donnelly, Miss Doolittle, Miss Clarke and I have carried the day, I think, and should you decide to come back, I'm sure it could be arranged.'

I have brought my books. I read them all the time when I'm not writing, and not doing my shift at the coffee bar. I can't believe my friends and I ever thought that being able to work for a few miserable pounds a week was glamorous. I think I was very spoiled at Egerton Hall, even in the matter of views from the windows. Here, there are red-brick semis in every direction as far as the eye can see, and the people look like insects, so far below me that I cannot make out their faces at all. The sky at night is a kind of mucky gold because of all the street lights, and during the day it resembles old dishwater, but perhaps that's only my mood. There are some sunny days, from time to time.

*

IN Dorothy's room, I drank my tea in silence. Silence was one of the things I'd had to get used to since my parents had died. Dorothy only spoke when it was necessary to do so, and then as economically as possible. I filled in the time that hung between one sentence and another by looking at the room and at Dorothy in it. There was something cool about her. I decided that it wasn't just the pale blue walls of her sitting-room, nor the bone china teacups that were so white they seemed luminous, like ice. It was Dorothy herself who made everywhere she went less warm. It was hard to know her age, and she never referred to it, but the iron-grey helmet of hair had remained unchanged for as long as I could remember, and above the fireplace there was a photograph of her in a gown and mortar board at her degree ceremony, which showed the same pale eyes and the same sharp features that I had known most of my life. There was only one picture in the room: a view of mountains capped with snow, and even the armchairs had straight backs. Good posture was something Dorothy believed in, along with economy of speech, hard work, early rising and prose. She had never said so directly, but I knew Dorothy felt there was something soft and squashy and not quite correct about poetry, because it often dealt with feelings and emotions and these were squashy, soft and not quite correct either. Or perhaps it was only my poetry she didn't approve of . . . she'd never have dared to speak out against Keats or Byron or Shelley. That would have been Philistine. Still, I knew Dorothy's opinion of 'adolescent scribblings'.

'They are usually,' she had said once, 'a morass of sentiment, and couched in words that are of the most violent purple imaginable.'

I didn't argue. One didn't lightly bandy words with Dorothy. I had been fourteen at the time, and I vowed then and there never to show Dorothy another poem of mine, not ever.

She was clearly in no hurry to break the silence. I thought about words, and came to the conclusion that that was why I liked them so much: because Dorothy was so stingy with them. Azure . . . translucent . . . iridescent . . . viola . . . antique . . . they're like jewels, I thought, all different colours. I liked taking them all out and arranging them this way and that, and putting them in lines and making patterns with them . . . ineffable . . . scarlet . . . peonies . . . wine . . . leaf . . . japonica . . . gardenia . . . camellia.

'Are you,' said Dorothy, 'feeling confident about the examinations?'

I put my cup down, feeling irritated suddenly by her maddening behaviour. No one else would invite you to hear an interesting piece of news and then not tell you . . . but the rituals had to be re-enacted over and over again.

'Yes, I think so,' I replied. 'Of course, I shall have to revise all next week.'

'Of course.'

'But I think I've got it mostly under control.'

'Excellent.' Dorothy continued taking small bites from an apparently never-ending biscuit, and said at last:

'I have a somewhat unusual item of news. I only heard finally today . . .' she paused, and looked at me. 'I have found a replacement for Miss Bristow.' Her eyes shone and a small, enigmatic smile touched the corners of her mouth.

'That's good,' I said. 'You must be very relieved.'

Privately I thought: why is Dorothy finding a new laboratory assistant so exciting? Miss Bristow had left suddenly last term, no one quite knew why, although naturally there had been rumours. There were always rumours.

'A young man called Simon Findlay is arriving tomorrow to help us out. Only a temporary appointment, I'm afraid, as I believe he has other plans for next term, but still, it will be a help to me.'

Dorothy leaned forward to put her cup back on the tray. Young probably means thirty-five, I reflected, but it was best to be sure.

'How old is Mr Findlay, exactly?' I asked.

'He's twenty-two,' said Dorothy. 'I do hope some of our more frivolous girls can be persuaded to curb any silliness.'

I took a biscuit from the plate. I could hardly ask how handsome he was. Dorothy would definitely class that as 'silliness'. In any case, I thought, I hardly ever go near the labs, and so will probably see very little of him. I decided to stop thinking about him, although of course Dorothy was right, and there was almost bound to be 'silliness'. In her magic kingdom of silver instruments, glass beakers, and phials of unnaturally blue and red and yellow crystals, where white light shone down on luminous and non-luminous flames of Bunsen burners, where everything was capable of measurement, analysis and description, such things as the feelings of one person for another were out-of-place and incomprehensible. The younger girls were often 'keen on' one of the prefects, although so far I had escaped such adoration. Bella and Alice had their share of admirers, though, who brought them bars of chocolate after they'd been out with their parents, sent them sloppy cards for their birthdays and watched them hungrily in chapel, on the games field or in the dining hall.

'There's nothing sexual about it,' said Bella once, last year, in the cloakroom, of all places. Bella was the expert on such matters. 'It's simply that everyone needs someone to love and admire and these kids pick the nearest and most glamorous creature they can. If it can't be Elvis or somebody, it's got to be someone near at hand.'

Alice smiled. 'Are you saying you're glamorous, then?'

'The most glamorous thing you've ever seen,' said Bella, and started to do a belly dance in her netball shorts and gym shoes.

'Bella, they're waiting for you on the court,' Miss Robbins called out, and that was the end of that conversation. I recalled it now and thought: this new young scientist chap will probably fall for Bella. Or perhaps he's engaged.

'I'm sure most of us,' I said, 'have too much work to do to trouble our heads with young men.'

Ten out of ten! That was precisely the sentence Dorothy had been waiting for. She rewarded me with one of her rare and beautiful smiles and rose to her feet.

'Good girl, Megan,' she said. 'He is a very talented young scientist, far too talented for such a relatively menial position. I wonder whether I might not entrust him with some teaching . . . only the lower forms, of course . . .' Her voice slid away into silence and she became lost in her thoughts for a moment. Then she gave an uncharacteristic laugh, almost as though what she'd been thinking about had embarrassed her. It seemed to me that she was blushing, but perhaps she was only feeling warm. She stood up and went over to the window.

'I know I can rely on you.' She pulled the curtains across. 'How very early the dark comes down at this time of year, doesn't it?'

'Yes,' I said. 'Yes, it does.' I stood up too. 'I should go now, Dorothy. I'd like to go and see Miss van der Leyden. I'm sure she must have arrived by now.'

'By all means, dear,' said Dorothy. 'I have some work to do before supper. I shall see you at half past six.'

Miss van der Leyden still lived in her little room right at the top of Junior House. I could have gone straight up the stairs, but I never did. Every time I visited her, I made a point of walking through the dormitories. Blue and Green, Violet and Rose were the biggest, and as I strode along the narrow strip of appropriately coloured carpet, I glanced in at the quiet cubicles and remembered all the sounds: the giggles and whispers, the squeaks and crashes, and often, especially on the first night of term, the sounds of homesickness – muffled sobs and sniffs and the padding of slippered feet from those who had undertaken the task of cheering people up. I couldn't remember crying much. I paused at the cubicle nearest the door in Violet which used to be Bella's, went in and sat on the bed. I tried to look into the mirror that stood on the chest-of-drawers, but had to bend my head right down.

'I can't ever have been this little,' I said aloud, and my voice rang through the empty space, and the mauve curtain that formed a kind of flimsy front door for the cubicle stirred slightly.

Bella had been as nosey then as she was now. I

remembered the conversation perfectly. It was more of an interrogation than a conversation, but I hadn't minded. Bella was so beautiful. I had stared and stared at her, and thought: her hair is so black, it's almost blue . . . and her skin . . .

'Hello,' Bella had said. 'Come in. Isn't this a funny place? I haven't really got used to it yet, even though I've been here for a term already. It isn't a bit like I imagined. Have you read the *Malory Towers* books? I have. They're super. I'd hoped we'd have midnight feasts and things, but we didn't last term. I'm Isabella Lavanne, but you can call me Bella. What's your name?'

'Megan Thomas.'

'Why have you only come in January? Everybody else came in September. Oh, except for someone called Alice Gregson. She's new this term, too. I think she's in the cubie next to yours. Yours is over there. Look!'

'Cubie?' I was lost already.

'Short for cubicle,' said Bella, 'which is what this teeny-weeny little bit of space with wooden partitions all around it is called.'

Bella had evidently forgotten all about her question. Why had I only come to Egerton Hall in January? I really had no idea at all. Perhaps it was something to do with my eleventh birthday. Maybe you could only come in the term during which you had your birthday. I would ask my mother in my first letter home. I thought with pleasure of my red zip-up writing case, complete with a little book of stamps. There was a compartment for the air-letter cards I had to use to write to my parents, but I couldn't imagine who I was going to write to on the pad of azure Basildon Bond. Bella interrupted my daydream.

'Where do you live?'

'I live here.'

'No, silly. I mean where do you live in the holidays?'

'Here.'

This had silenced Bella for about five seconds, but then she'd said:

'Why?'

My parents were still alive then. I said:

'Because my father works abroad, and my mother's gone to be with him, and there aren't many schools where they are . . .'

'Who will look after you?'

'My guardian.'

'What's a guardian?'

'Someone who looks after you when your parents aren't there. My guardian is the Chemistry teacher in the Upper School. She's called Miss Dorothy Marshall.'

'My mother's dead.' Bella put a picture in a leather frame on the chest-of-drawers next to a china pig decorated with pink flowers. 'That's her.'

'She was very pretty.'

'Yes, she was. My stepmother's quite pretty, too, but not as pretty as my mother. My mother wanted me so much, and then she died while she was having me.'

'That's sad.' I had had trouble keeping back the tears that sprang to my eyes.

'I don't feel especially sad about it. What I mean is, it was ages and ages ago, so please don't cry.'

Bella was taking handfuls of clothes from her trunk and pushing them into the drawers. 'Actually, I think it's rather romantic. Like something in a story. Have you got any brothers or sisters?'

'No,' I said. 'Have you?'

'No, but I wish I did have. Sometimes I think I should make up a brother and pretend to have him. I don't see how they'd find out, do you? Shall we do that? Yes, let's . . . Go on, it'll be our secret.'

I laughed into the silence, recalling the Danny episode. Bella had invented a brother so plausibly that everyone believed her for ages, and it was only when Miss Baker, the Housemistress of Junior House, had asked Bella's father how his son was that the story fell to pieces.

I left Violet and went upstairs to Blue and Green. Walking through them, I thought of Mack, who had been Matron then. Miss van der Leyden had only been Under Matron, second-in-command in those days to Miss McLaren, who was an elderly, thin, sandy-beige person with 'a shortbread look about her' as Alice had once put it, and an iron will. Mack would stride through the dorms on sheet-changing days calling out: 'Top to bottom and bottom away!' which sounded vaguely nautical, like 'Avast the mizzen mast!' or whatever it was that sailors shouted from the rigging. Miss van der Leyden would clump along behind her, reminding us to change our knicker linings, and collecting all the laundry bags to put in the big wicker basket outside on the landing. I thought: I wonder if the Juniors still wear knicker linings or if they call them knickers now? Maybe those heavy-duty navy bloomers we all wore over our ordinary white knickers are a thing of the past . . . and do the poor little Juniors still have to wear those horrible, scratchy, knee-length socks made of wool?

'What I want more than anything else in the world,' Bella used to say in those days of Liberty bodices and elastic suspenders for keeping the dreaded socks up, 'is a roll-on and some stockings. We can wear them on Sundays when we're in the Upper School. I shall have American Tan stockings, and a lace brassière.'

Bella had been the first to wear roll-ons and stockings and

now she's the first to wear tights . . . always racing ahead, Bella was, rushing into things. Unlike Alice, who never saw any good reason for change, and was nearly fifteen before she went into stockings, and then only did so because of Bella's constant nagging.

At last, I reached Miss van der Leyden's door and knocked.

'*Ah, ma petite fleur!*' cried Miss van der Leyden as soon as the door was open, and hobbled over to enfold me in her arms. I closed my eyes and let the fragrance of mint, face powder and rose-geranium toilet water wash over me. Miss van der Leyden's smell was the smell of childhood, of safety, of home. For the first time that day, I felt warm. I sank down into a small armchair beside the gas fire and looked around at this room which I liked almost better than any other at Egerton Hall.

'I love your room,' I said. 'There's so much to look at. I love all the photos, and knicknacks and bits of wool, and the cushions and the lovely china with blue pictures on it . . . oh, I love it all.'

'It is, how do you say, "a filthy mess",' said Miss van der Leyden, 'but it is my home.'

'Really? Do you think of it as home? What about Belgium?'

'No, no, *chérie*, I have told you many times before. From there I am . . . what is it you say? Exiled.'

'But you don't have to be. No one exiled you, did they? No one said you couldn't live there, did they? You could go back, couldn't you?'

'But there is nothing to go back for. I have been here so long.'

'What about your family, though? Don't you miss them?'

'Well, I still see them, of course. I visit. But they all have lives, concerns of their own. Also, I am not a relation of whom one would boast, *n'est-ce pas*? Like you girls say: the ugly mug!' Miss van der Leyden's laughter filled the small room.

It was undeniable. Miss van der Leyden is the ugliest person I have ever met. Long years ago we had all called her 'Quasimodo' and speculated late into the night about the causes of such ugliness. Celia Hammond, who read spy stories, thought she was a foreign agent. Mary Gillis thought she was a witch, and at first no one could look her straight in the eye. The fact that she was Belgian and spoke English with a strange accent did not help. But it didn't take long for us to grasp the main fact about Miss van der Leyden. She loved us. We were her children. Oh, the other staff were dutiful and caring and conscientious all right, but Miss van der Leyden loved us. Mack would slap the plaster on a cut knee, and Miss van der Leyden would hug us and cuddle us and give us a surreptitious sweet. If you were sick in the night, she would sit with you and sing to you and hold your head over the basin and clean you up beautifully afterwards. If you were homesick, she would take you up to her room and show you photographs of Belgium and tell you stories about her childhood, about her grandmother teaching her to make lace, oh, about all kinds of things. She was a mother to us and better than a mother: completely uncritical and undemanding. Provided you kept your cubicle tidy, that was good enough for her.

I said: 'Do you remember how you taught us knitting?'

'Agony!' said Miss van der Leyden. 'That is what it was. Oh, I was in despair sometimes with you. How clumsy you were! And how dirty the wool became . . . and how you could never count properly and above all how you did not grasp the – how do you say – the principles of knitting.'

'But you had Alice, didn't you?'

'La petite princesse! The little angel! Now she . . . she was dainty, and careful and so neat. Do you remember how she used to embroider those traycloths printed with flowers?'

'She still does embroidery and tapestry and knitting. Most people think she's mad.'

'Mad? Because she is not jumping to the Elvis music and sitting in cafés her whole life? Ah no, she is not mad at all. She is above all that.'

'But what's she going to do when she leaves?' I asked. 'She can't sit in a room and embroider all day. She's going to have to go into the world, isn't she?'

'So are you all, *cherie,*' said Miss van der Leyden. 'So are you all. You will have a cup of coffee?'

'No, thanks. I've just had tea with Dorothy.'

'I will have coffee alone, then.'

As she busied herself with cups and jugs and spoons, I began to think about Alice.

Of all the people I have ever met, it is Alice who always seems to me vulnerable. The very first time I saw her she was crying. It was our first night in Egerton Hall, and after lights out I soon became aware of sniffing and weeping from the cubicle (cubie) next door. That's the other new girl, I thought first, and then: why aren't I crying? I felt strange, and I think also a little sad, but I was somehow frozen. It was as though I knew that crying was going to be of no help. Perhaps I had some kind of premonition that this was going to be the only place I would see for years and years. Anyway, I was dry-eyed and the misery I could hear next door distracted me still further from my own feelings. I got out of bed and went to see if I could help. Bella was already there, sitting on the bed with one arm around someone who looked, even in the dim light from the landing and with her nose bubbling and her eyes streaming with tears, like a princess from a book of fairy tales. Her hair fell in an undulating cascade down her back until it touched the pillow, where it lay spread out and shining in waves of reddish-gold. I had never seen hair like that in my whole life, and it was all I could do not to put out my hand and touch it.

'This is Megan,' Bella whispered. 'Alice, look. Megan's new today, too, and she's not crying.'

Alice held out her hand as if she were being introduced to someone at a garden party. I noticed how frail her arm was, and how I could almost feel each separate bone in her hand as I squeezed it.

'Cheer up,' I said, somewhat inadequately. 'Bella and I will look after you.'

Bella nodded vigorously, but corrected me nevertheless.

'I'll look after you both, Megan. Show you where to go and what to do. Everything. We'll be friends,' she decided, and perhaps it was the firm way that she said it that made it so, from the first. Ever since that night, we have been friends, but our relationship has always had at its heart the shielding of Alice from the harshness of life. At times, over the years, I've been jealous when Alice has been nicer to Bella, or when I've thought she has, and I'm sure Bella is sometimes secretly peeved that I spend so much time staying with Alice during the holidays.

I've realized, also, that the way other people treat you has a great deal to do with how you look. I, for example, am tall and fair and placid-looking. In the mirror I see what I regard as a moon-face and a long plait of hair which I call 'dirty yellow' and Bella, kindly, calls 'corn-coloured'.

'You look,' she's often said to me, 'like a Scandinavian milkmaid.'

I think she means it as a compliment. I do not look like

the kind of person others will rush to protect or cherish, like Alice, nor do I look exotic, flamboyant and faintly dangerous, like Bella. What I look is strong and healthy and calm and reliable.

Miss van der Leyden's coffee was ready.

'How is Dorothy?' she said. 'Did she have . . . did you both have a pleasant holiday?'

'We're fine. She's got a new lab. assistant. A young man of twenty-two called Simon Findlay. He's coming tomorrow.'

Miss van der Leyden began laughing. She laughed so much she had to put her cup down and wipe her eyes with a lace-edged handkerchief.

'*Oh, là, là,*' she cried. '*Que ça va être amusant!*'

'What?' I asked. 'What's going to be so "*amusant*" as you call it?'

Miss van der Leyden sniffed and the laughter subsided gradually.

'*Mais, figures-toi,* Megan, all you young ladies . . . your parents, they pay the money, much money, to remove you from the real world to here, a little fantasy world where there is only girls and more girls and lessons in things you can find only in books, and where you are far, far away from life . . . and now, look what happens. A young man will come from the outside, and he will be a cat among the doves.'

'Pigeons . . . a cat among the pigeons.'

'Pigeons, doves, what does it matter? You know what I mean.'

'You mean, we're all going to go soppy over him. What Dorothy calls "silliness".'

'*Précisément.* Only silliness I do not call it. I call it *tout à fait naturel.* If a young woman is locked away, as you are locked away, at the top of a tower for years and years . . . imagine what can happen.'

34

'I'm not locked away. I can go whenever I like. And I do go. Look. I spent a week at Alice's during the holidays, and I'm going to university next year.'

'But you are still . . . how do you want to say it? Removed from life. You know nothing, in spite of having read so much and in so many languages. You should try and guard it, this ignorance.'

'But I'm *not* ignorant!' I was indignant. 'I know all about things . . . poverty, unhappiness, hunger. I read the newspapers. I know what's happening.'

'But love,' Miss van der Leyden said. 'Do you know about love?'

'No,' I said, biting back a rude remark that I'd been ready to make about Miss van der Leyden's looks not leading her to many experiences in that direction.

'You think,' the ugly face smiled at me, 'that I know nothing about such matters, with my beauty, no? But you will be surprised if I tell you, and this proves what I am saying: you know nothing of the world outside. Nothing of real life.'

I saw a chance to direct the conversation on to a more interesting topic.

'Tell me about your love life, then . . . Go on, you've never told me. I'd love to hear.'

'Perhaps another time. Now, I wish to hear all about your time with Alice.'

So I started to tell her.

I never slept well the night before term started. Most of the time during the holidays I forgot about what Egerton Hall was like when it was full of people. It was almost as though it were quite a separate place from its holiday self, linked only by a similar geography. But the night before last term began, I felt restless and ill-at-ease. It was as though I were an actress in a play – some huge production with a cast of thousands – and I'd arrived early for that night's performance, and no one else was in the theatre at all. I was waiting for the others to appear, put on their costumes and take up their roles. I, too, was waiting, to be myself, my school self, which differed from my home self by much more than a uniform put on and discarded. At home, alone with Dorothy, I think I would have described myself as introspective, shy, hardworking, and alone. When the others arrived, all my friends, but especially Bella and Alice, I seemed to change quite dramatically. For one thing, I talked. Not quite as much as Bella, it's true, but then there were few who could match her torrents and waterfalls of speech. For another, I became steady and reliable, one of Miss Herbert's right-hand girls. I was efficient, and good at seeing to things like the composition of the Table List each fortnight, making sure that sworn enemies weren't sitting next to one another, and that prefects took turns to have at their tables girls whose table manners were enough to put you off your Jam Roly Poly. Alice, for example, had firm preferences when it came to her table:

'I'm not having Joanna Burton and that's that,' she told me. 'Have you ever looked at the front of her tunic? All egg stains and spots of marmalade.'

She shuddered delicately, and I promised her I'd do my best. After all, she had had me to stay so many times during the holidays that I owed her more than one favour.

I loved staying with Alice. Quite apart from the luxury of 'the castle next door' as Bella called it, there was the great advantage of Alice's family.

Alice, like myself and Bella, was an only child but she did have the A.A. 'The Assembly of Aunts' (not Alcoholics Anonymous or the Automobile Association) was our name for the simply enormous Gregson tribe, although we also called them 'The Flower Fairies of the Forest' sometimes, because all their names were either flowers or plants of some kind.

'However did you escape?' Bella used to ask Alice.

'I expect they ran out of garden names in the end. I mean, after thirteen of them . . .'

'It's very unimaginative of them,' Bella said. 'They could have called you Magnolia or Japonica or Tulip or something. Not to mention things like Poppy.'

I made all the names into a rhyme, partly because I like doing things like that and partly to help us remember them all. It went like this:

> Rose and Lily, Marguerite,
> Petunia, Daphne, Myrtle sweet,
> Fleur and Marigold and May
> and we're not finished yet.
> There's Ivy, Hortense, Daisy
> and the dreaded Violette!

'Why "dreaded Violette"?' asked Bella, when I first showed it to her. 'I mean, I know it needs something there for the rhythm, but why not "lovely Violette"?'

'Because I don't think she *is* lovely,' I said. 'Alice says she's the black sheep of the family. And she lives in France.'

'And what kind of flower, pray, is a Hortense?'

'It's the French for hydrangea, I think.'

Bella sighed. 'It sounds just like a gardening catalogue to me. Poor old Alice!'

Alice's mother and father were wonderful people to stay with because we hardly ever saw them. They were much older than most parents. Alice's mother's hair was quite white and she made no effort to disguise it. Her father spent much of his time in the garden, communing with his roses. Roses grew everywhere on Mr Gregson's land: he had beds of them laid out in formal patterns, he had bushes of them lining the drive. Every available wall had a rose trained to grow up it, and he had small trellises and arbours here and there in the grounds which you could walk in and the roses would meet over your head. Of course, the Gregson garden was not at its most spectacular in December.

'But wait till June, my dear,' Mr Gregson said to me at dinner one night. 'Wait for the night of Alice's eighteenth birthday party. That,' he winked at me, 'will be something to see.'

'As a matter of fact, I like it like this,' Alice told me as we trod the chilly gravel paths, 'only don't tell my father. I like the black branches and the thorns. You can see them so clearly when it's winter. In the summer you forget, and the leaves cover them up and all the flowers puff out so you never see them, but they *are* there all the same.' Alice paused. 'I like to see the thorns. Look how sharp they are!' She bounced the tip of a finger on one, to show me. 'They can really hurt, you know. You do have to take care how you touch the roses. That's the best thing about them: how dangerous they are without looking dangerous. I love that.'

*

London *April 10th 1962*

WHO do I know here? Mr Scarpetti, my boss. Patsy and Janey, the other waitresses on my shift. Miss Hills, my neighbour downstairs, and Mr Steele, my neighbour across the passage, but these last only to say 'good morning' to. The lady in the tobacconist's, the man in the grocer's, the ticket collector on the Tube, the milkman – all these I just nod and smile at, unless I'm actually buying something from them. I'm alone in this room for most of the day, and then after my early evening shift at work, we two are alone all through the night. In one of the most densely populated cities in the world, why do I feel as though I'm in a desert?

At school, I had circles of friends: that was how I imagined it. Bella and Alice and I were like a stone thrown into a pool. There were a few people in a small circle around us, then a bigger circle after that, and still another. Bosom friends, friends, people you were quite friendly with, the rest of your class, the other people in your House, the rest of the school. And the teachers: I must not forget the teachers. They took the place of my parents, and Dorothy more than anyone. I suppose she must have loved me in her own peculiar way. I wonder whether she will ever be able to forgive me?

*

BELLA arrived on the school coach with all the shrieking Third Years and Fourth Years. I was waiting on the terrace outside Austen House and saw her waving frantically out of the window. She was talking, calling over the heads of the younger girls almost before the doors of the coach were opened:

'Marjorie made me come down on the train, can you imagine? With all the hoi-polloi and positively no one to talk to. Oh, Megan, how lovely to see you . . . Come on, let's run away to the Tower. Is Alice here? Are there tons of duties we have to do?'

'Hearts and Lungs, Fleas and Lice, Weights and Measures,' I answered. 'The usual stuff. But let's go and put your case in the Tower Room first. Alice never arrives till later. I don't think she enjoys supervising all those queues of people being checked by the doctor and weighed and as for Fleas and Lice . . . you know Alice. She'd be afraid of some kind of contamination.'

'I do see her point,' Bella panted up the stairs behind me. 'It's all frightfully undignified – all that standing around in dressing gowns being checked. We've only just been done. I can't think why once a year couldn't be enough. Oh, blissful Tower Room!'

Bella sank on to her bed and looked as though she might stay there for the rest of the afternoon. I went over to the window and looked out.

'I say,' I said. 'Look at this.'

'Don't tell me,' Bella said. 'You say it every single term: doesn't everyone look small, just like a crowd of beetles, so on and so forth.'

'No, Bella, it isn't that . . . look . . . it's a man.'

Bella bounded off the bed. 'A man?' She adopted her African Explorer tones. 'Good Lord, Frobisher, I thought they were extinct . . . are you ebbsolutely sure?'

'Yes, I am, and I also know who it is.'

Bella peered out of the window. 'Is that him? He looks a bit weedy to me. Very thin and what a long scarf he's got on.' She leaned out as far as she could and started to wave. 'Hardly Marlon Brando, is he? I mean, he's wearing glasses, of all things.'

I said: 'He's more refined than Marlon Brando. More intellectual looking. The Dirk Bogarde type. I can't think why you're waving if you think he's so awful.'

'Beggars,' (Bella went on waving) 'can't be choosers. He is of the opposite sex, and moreover he is here, in the purlieus of Egerton Hall. Look, he's seen me. I think he's coming over here.'

'Oh, gosh, Bella, whatever have you done? What if someone sees you? A member of staff?'

'They're busy checking people's heights and weights and
things. Did you say you know who he is?'

'He's the new lab. assistant. His name is Simon Findlay.
He's twenty-two. Dorothy told me.'

I leaned out of the window and looked down with Bella.
The young man was standing at the bottom of the scaffolding, looking up.

'Hello,' he said. 'Can you tell me how I get to the Science
Block? My name's Simon Findlay.'

I could see Bella's Number 2 smile (open and welcoming)
spreading over her face.

'I'll be down in two minutes,' she called. 'If you want to
wait there, I'll take you over. My name's Bella, by the way.'

'Thanks,' Simon shouted. Bella had flown out of the
room. She'd left the door open and I could hear her clatter-
ing down the stairs. He remained looking up, and said:

'What's your name?'

'It's Megan. Megan Thomas.'

Then a dreadful silence fell. He stood at the bottom of the
scaffolding, staring up at me. He was very like Dirk Bogarde,
only thinner, younger and with hair that wasn't quite so
dark. Even behind his glasses, I could see how blue his eyes
were. I didn't dare move away from the window and besides,
I didn't want to. I just wanted to stay there, looking at him.
Then Bella appeared and started chatting away. This seemed
to break the spell. He said:

'I expect I shall see you about,' and waved up at the Tower
Room window as he was dragged away. It looked to me as
though Bella had actually put a hand on his arm to guide
him. I didn't know how she could touch him, just like that.
I would never have dared. After they'd gone, I sat on the bed.

The room seemed altered. It was as though seeing Simon Findlay's face at the bottom of the scaffolding had shaken pieces in a kaleidoscope, so that all the individual physical features of the landscape, the room, the known universe, had been changed in some way I didn't at all understand. Or perhaps (and this is hindsight, of course) the world remained the same and it was *I* who was different. That, in any case, was the beginning. I didn't feel like going down and supervising queues. I didn't feel like checking that the Third Years were unpacking their trunks tidily. I took out the private notebook where I wrote my poems and wrote this:

> I am in the window
> and you've turned,
> looked up to see
> the frame around my face.
>
> You are too far down
> and leaving. Walking
> towards the fountain
> where the fish spring
> silver from the nymphs'
> encircling arms.
>
> I am still waiting,
> a portrait of myself
> in the frame of the window.

If this was falling in love, it seemed too quick to me. I thought and thought about it. I was surprised and a little shocked at myself. Was it allowed, this strength of feeling, simply because I had looked at a person? I knew nothing about him. He might turn out to be boring, or unkind, or stupid . . . and somehow none of this seemed to matter. I wanted to be near him, with him forever. Perhaps I was not normal. Perhaps being on my own such a lot had addled my brain. I waited for Bella to come back with every separate part of me vibrating, like violin strings under the sweep of a bow.

We, Alice, Bella and I, always talked for a long time after Lights Out. As we were prefects and the ones in charge of ringing bells to tell everyone else when it was time to go to sleep, Miss Herbert assumed that at 10.30 we would, naturally, turn our own light out without any need of supervision. And turn it off we usually did, not because we were especially obedient, but because it was such fun to lie there chatting in the dark, with the square of the window letting in the dim glow of the lamps along the drive, and a thin, yellow line of light shining under the door from the passage outside.

It's much easier to talk frankly in the dark. You can say things that you would never dare to say in the daylight, even to your very best friend. Any blushing that went on was unseen. You could even let the odd tear slide out of the corner of your eye and on to your pillow, although Bella had a kind of sixth sense about that and could always tell when one of us was miserable, however we tried to inject courage into our voices.

Lying in bed at night we spoke about everything. We analysed everyone, from the Headmistress (a glamorous widow called Mrs Castelton, whom we rarely saw except on ceremonial occasions) down to the annoying little pipsqueak of a Second Former who'd given Alice some cheek. We discussed food. We worried about exams. We put together any information we had about the private lives of members of staff and considered long into the night the probable effects of a new hairstyle or a new pair of shoes. We mourned the fact that we weren't eligible to audition for the School Play 'because of those boring old exams', as Bella put it. Most of all, though, we talked about boys. Bella said that night:

'I can't think why I bothered with that Simon Findlay. I don't think he's up to much. I mean, he looks all right, but a bit weedy, and he hasn't got much to say for himself. A scientist! How boring!'

Bella considered that only artists were interesting. It didn't much matter what the art was, but she did insist on pallor, squalor, beards, dirty fingernails and general suffering. Jazz musicians were best, because of the deliciously late hours they kept.

'As it happens,' she went on, dismissing the subject of Simon Findlay (and leaving me to try and work out how I could get the conversation back to him. I wanted to know exactly what he'd said and done every second he was with Bella), 'I did meet these absolutely amazing men.'

'Were they really men?' Alice wanted to know. 'You always call them that and then they turn out to be about fourteen.'

'No, no,' Bella was so excited that she sat up in bed. 'Honestly! Men is what they are. There's not one of them under twenty-five. Some must be nearly thirty.'

'Why are there so many of them?' I said.

'Because they're a band, silly!' Bella laughed. 'Don't you want to hear all about how I met them?'

'Go on,' I said, 'get on with it. Is it a good story?'

'Tremendous. Listen to this. D'you remember Nigel Warren? That cousin of Jennifer Black's . . . you must remember . . . Anyway, he'd taken me to this amazing dance. Some friend of his had a sister who was having a coming-out party. That bit's all boring so I'll skip to where a whole group of us went off after the dance to The Establishment.'

'What's that?' asked Alice. 'It sounds like a bank.'

'Alice, I despair!' cried Bella. 'How can anyone not know

what The Establishment is? Don't you read *Private Eye*? Haven't I told you about *Beyond the Fringe*? The Establishment is a nightclub. They have a satirical cabaret. Everyone goes to The Establishment.'

'Oh,' said Alice quietly. *Private Eye* was beyond her. She'd told me so herself. She couldn't understand it properly, she said, and anyway the ink it was printed with came off on your hands. And it looked so messy.

'Anyway,' Bella said, 'there we were at The Establishment and Nigel was getting a bit . . . you know . . . demanding.'

'Tell us,' I said.

'Well, you know, pressing up close during dances and saying these flirtatious things into my beehive, and I just knew that he was going to dance me into a corner and kiss me, and quite honestly, I hated the thought of that.'

'I thought you quite liked Nigel Warren,' I said.

'Enough to go to a dance with, but not enough to kiss. So, I excused myself and said I had to go to the Ladies and then I left him. He went back to where all the others were sitting and I went to find a lavatory.' Bella paused. She often paused at moments of special drama. We knew our cues, though. We'd been having this kind of conversation for seven years.

'Then what happened?' said Alice.

'Then,' said Bella, 'I bumped into Pete. Literally. I opened the door of the Ladies and walked straight into him. It was almost as if it were meant. Destined.' Bella sighed.

'What does he look like?' I asked.

'Tremendously dark. Bearded. Kind of sunken eyes. He was wearing jeans and a checked shirt and he had a cigarette burning . . . oh, he was so *thin*!' There was yearning in Bella's voice.

'He sounds awful,' Alice said. 'He could have been drunk or anything. He sounds . . . dangerous.'

Bella laughed. 'That's what I like about him. Anyway, it turned out that he was just leaving for what he called a "jam session" with his band, and would I like to come and hear them? And so I did. I went off with Pete and met the other six members of the band in this little club called The Black Cat.'

'What about Nigel? Didn't he mind?' You couldn't leave anything out when Alice was listening. She did like all loose ends to be neatly tied up.

'I just said goodbye and thank you and that I'd met this really old friend, etc. etc.'

'Gosh!' Alice was impressed. 'Weren't you scared? I'd have been terrified.'

'You haven't met Pete. He is so clearly gentle and unterrifying.'

'But the black hair and the beard and the sunken eyes!' I said. 'You do make him sound like a pirate.'

'Well, he isn't,' Bella said. 'He's kind and plays the saxophone. Anyway, don't you want to hear what happened next?'

'Go on,' I said. I was getting a little bored. Bella's story didn't seem to be very exciting and it was getting late. I wasn't going to be able to steer the talk back to Simon. My eyelids drooped from time to time but I heard the gist of Bella's story, the main parts . . . the band, and how nice they'd all been and how she had sung with them.

'Imagine!' she said. 'Me singing! "Sweet Georgia Brown" and "Danny Boy" and "Blue Moon" with a *real* band! I've never had such fun in all my life and the very best thing about it is: they want me to sing with them again. They're playing for a dance at Coleston next month . . . for St Valentine's Day. On a Saturday night. Will Herbie give me permission, d'you suppose?'

'To go and sing with a gang of bearded jazz musicians? You must be joking!' I said.

'That's what I thought,' Bella said. 'Well, I shall have to sneak out and sneak back . . .'

'You can't!' Alice shrieked. 'You'll be expelled.'

'They won't catch me. I'll get Pete to wait in the van at that road just through the forest. When I come back I can get through a downstairs window. The J.P.R. or something. You'll have to make sure to leave one open for me. We'll arrange it all most awfully carefully, don't worry. But isn't it exciting? Me, singing with a band?'

'What about Pete?' Alice asked. 'Are you in love with him?'

'No,' Bella said. 'At least, I don't think so. But I shouldn't mind him kissing me. He hasn't got a soft, round, pink, rose-buddy kind of mouth like Nigel had. He's got a straight, firm sort of mouth.'

'But the beard,' Alice shuddered. 'Ugh! Wouldn't the hair sort of get in the way?'

'I'll tell you,' said Bella, 'when I've done it. In Spain they say: a kiss without a moustache is like an egg without salt. It's true. Miss Clarke told us last year.'

A silence fell while I wondered what I could say to turn the conversation back to Simon Findlay. Then Alice said into the darkness: 'I've met a boy too,' and Bella and I both almost jumped out of bed.

'Oh, Alice,' Bella said. 'How could you let me go on and on! That's marvellous! Who is he? Where did you meet him? Have you kissed him? Tell us what he looks like. Tell us everything.'

'There's not that much to tell,' Alice said. 'I've only just met him. The day before yesterday. He was staying with my Aunt Lily. He comes from France, but he speaks such good English. He had an English nanny or something. He's called Jean-Luc. He's very fair. He's got blue eyes. I can't describe people like Bella, so that you can see them. All I know is, he's jolly handsome.'

'How many times did you see him?'

'Once.'

'And did he kiss you?'

'No, of course not. Don't be silly. How could he possibly have kissed me with Aunt Lily and his mother sitting in the drawing-room with us?'

'Would you have liked him to kiss you?' Bella persisted.

'Oh, yes. Yes,' Alice said and although I couldn't see her, I felt sure she was blushing. 'I keep thinking of what it will be like. I think about it over and over. What it will be like when he kisses me.'

'So when is this kissing going to take place?' Bella asked. 'When are you going to see him again?'

'I don't really know. He's gone back to France. But he'll write to me. He said he would. And I will write to him. We did swap addresses.'

'Oh, hurray!' said Bella. 'Honestly, Alice, you are slow! Couldn't you have kissed him goodbye or something?'

'No, but I could see from the way he looked at me that he wanted to. I might get a letter from him tomorrow. I shall ask him to my dance in the summer . . .' Alice's voice was fading. She would be asleep in seconds. Bella hadn't said anything for a few moments, which almost certainly meant that she was asleep too. I was left alone, to wonder when I would see Simon Findlay again. Would he come to Chapel in the morning? Perhaps I could go and see Dorothy in the labs. at break. Perhaps.

*

London *April 13th 1962*

EVERY day, you get up early and go to your work in the laboratory. I can't really imagine it very clearly and you never describe it. When I think of it, I think of the labs. at Egerton Hall. If I'm all alone here, which I am for the most part, I just stay in bed. It's perfectly comfortable for writing and also for reading, and it does save money. The meter that provides gas for the fire seems to gobble up the shillings. Or sometimes, after I've finished my shift at the coffee bar, we go to the pictures. It's so lovely and warm there in the dark. Occasionally, we share a choc ice. *The Hustler* is on, with Paul Newman in it. I'd love to see that. Maybe we can go tonight.

Alice and Bella have both written to me. They're coming to visit me next week, but not together. Bella thinks what I've done is romantic – flight, escape, the search for freedom. Her letter is full of stuff like that. Also, love. As if love were the most important thing of all, more important than anything in the world. I used to think that, but now I'm not so sure. Perhaps love needs a whole arrangement of other things to support it, to keep it standing: a kind of scaffolding without which it simply falls to the ground in little shards and splinters. The scaffolding around Austen House, the pattern of metal bars and wooden planks between the ground and my window . . . how differently everything would have turned out if it hadn't been there!

*

ENGLISH, French and Spanish: those were (and maybe still are) my subjects. Bella's are the same as mine, and Alice's are nearly the same, only she's doing Art instead of Spanish.

There were only six of us in Miss Clarke's Advanced Spanish Class. We thought of ourselves as different, special, a cut above the others who were studying mundane subjects like Geography and Biology. Spanish most definitely had a touch of the exotic about it. Bella used to say she only did it because she could imagine herself so well in a red skirt covered with lace-edged flounces, and with a black mantilla cascading down over her hair. Part of this was Miss Clarke's doing. She assumed a good knowledge of the language because she had striven for four years, and made us learn lists of words, and recite verbs, and do exercises in translation from one language to another until we were more or less proficient. Now that we were in the Sixth Form, she, of all the staff, treated us as entirely grown-up and discussed everything with us as though we were equals. She was a stout, grey-haired lady who dressed in clothes more appropriate to a slender young girl: beads and floaty chiffon scarves and shoes in ridiculously light colours. Still, Bella and I (and Prue, Joanne, Nicola and Alison), were agreed that Miss Clarke was a Woman of the World and well-versed in sexual matters. She was, Bella asserted, 'certainly not a virgin', or how could she possibly discuss Saint John of the Cross in the way she did?

'Most of these poems,' Miss Clarke told us, 'were written by Saint John during his imprisonment in Toledo in 1567. In a tiny prison cell. Imagine that, girls! A cell so small he could hardly turn round in it. And of course, in a poem such as the one beginning "*En una noche oscura*" . . . translate, please, Megan.'

'Once, on a dark night,' I said.

'Good, good,' Miss Clarke continued. 'It is clear, is it not, that although Saint John is speaking of the mystical union of the Soul with God, the *language* he uses is that of human, physical love. This is the only way he can convey the sheer ecstasy that losing himself in God brings, do you see? Of course, you do have to remember that he is writing from a man's point of view. Now,' she swept a stray end of wispy scarf over her shoulder, 'Alison, find me two examples of physical images in the poem.'

'Um,' Alison murmured. She was a careful girl, and Bella said she wasn't altogether sure that Alison knew the meaning of the word 'ecstasy'. 'I think . . . "*El rostro recliné sobre el Amado . . .*".'

'Good,' Miss Clarke said. '"I laid my face upon my Lover." That's clear enough. Another, please.'

'"*Con su mano serena . . .*"' Alison began, and Miss Clarke interrupted her.

'Yes, yes, yes, *of course*. Listen to the whispering s's, the gentle stroking of them! Read the lines aloud, please, child, so that we can all thrill to them.'

Alison sounded dreadfully embarrassed.

'"*Con su mano serena*
En mi cuello heria
Y todos mis sentidos suspendia."' she stammered.

'No, no, no, child!' Miss Clarke cried. 'You make it sound like a laundry list. Can't you *hear* the music? It's even there in the English. I shall read it in Roy Campbell's translation. He, of course, is a poet in his own right. Now listen.'

Miss Clarke stood up and her hand fluttered in the air. She seemed almost to be swooning as she said the words in English:

'"With his serenest hand
my neck he wounded and
suspended every sense with its caresses."'

Later, we all agreed that what with burning hearts, and love flowering in his breast, and the Lover and the Bride transfigured each into the other, Saint John of the Cross was certainly putting forward a very convincing picture.

'I don't know,' Joanna said after the lesson. 'There's an awful lot of it about in poetry and things. I mean, are we supposed to mention it in essays in the exams? I'm not sure

I actually know what he's going on about all the time. Maybe because of what Miss Clarke said about him being a man. Perhaps it's different for women.'

'It isn't all that different,' Bella said. 'I know exactly what he means. I've had lots of caresses that have suspended every sense!'

'But what's all that about wounding your neck with his hand?' said Prue. 'That doesn't sound too pleasant.' She giggled.

'It's just like that, though.' Bella was always glad to enlighten us lesser mortals, the ones with no experience to draw on. 'It honestly is. Sometimes when they touch you . . . you know . . . in certain places . . . well, it feels as though you're being burned, set on fire.'

'How frightful!' Prue didn't like the sound of that at all. Bella sighed. 'There's no hope for you, Prue Simpson,' she said. 'Go down to the lacrosse pitch and chuck the ball about.'

'Lots more fun than fainting away among the lilies.'

Prue smiled in a good-natured way and went off to her healthy activities. The rest of us stayed in the classroom for a bit, discussing whether or not Saint John of the Cross could possibly have known what he was writing about from personal experience. Bella thought he must have done, but I thought he could have made it all up. After all, I'd written pretend love poems by the dozen, and had never been near a boy in my life. Now that I really loved someone, though, the usual love words wouldn't appear in what I was writing. I think I was shy of making the marks on the paper. That would be like putting up a sign for all to see. That afternoon, I was alone in the study I shared with Alice and a no-nonsense pony-lover called Marion Tipton, who just happened to be a brilliant mathematician as well. Our study was always full of people. Bella, for instance, was almost always in there, bringing her radio with her.

'Radio Luxemburg is too noisy for some people,' she would sigh. 'Some people think themselves too high and mighty for rock 'n roll.'

This was a reference to Mary-Ellen Walker, who was, in our opinion, snobbish and silly and had won our undying contempt in Junior House, when she would never answer to 'Mary'.

'My name is Mary-Ellen,' she would simper to girls and staff alike. Bella always called her 'Our Ellie' to her face, and Mary-Ellen had grown used to this over the years, but she and Bella had never grown to like one another, and it was a stroke of bad luck that had them sharing a study. What it meant was that Bella did most of her prep. sitting in an armchair wedged between my desk and Alice's, and quite often there'd be Jerry Lee Lewis in the background telling us (as if we didn't already know) that there was a whole lot of shakin' goin' on. But that day, Bella was taking prep. in the J.P.R. and Alice was in the Art Studio, 'getting the draperies right' as she put it, on her clothed figure drawing. I was revising my French: reading through *Phèdre* and making notes on her character. The light of what had been a bright, frosty day was disappearing, and the sky was exactly as I liked it best: turning all sorts of beautiful colours – blue, and pearly-mauve, and finally an opalescent grey just before the dark fell, against which the outlines of Eliot House stood out like black paper cut-outs. In the Eliot House studies, lights had been switched on. Some people were quick to draw their curtains, but some had left them open and I could look in and see what they were doing. Marcia Willis was putting up a bull-fighting poster. Someone I couldn't see had their feet, still wearing lacrosse boots, up on the windowsill. Out of the corner of my eye I saw two figures coming down the steps of Main School and turned to see who they were. It was Fiona Mackenzie and Simon Findlay and they were walking directly towards my window. Where were they going? What were they talking about? I drew the curtains across the window and sat down, trembling. Then I stood up and turned the light out, pushed my fingers between the curtains to make a tiny gap and looked out. Fiona had her face turned towards Simon Findlay all the time and he was looking at her. They disappeared round the corner of the building. Was Fiona going to take him to her study in Browning House and give him shortbread from a tin? I sat down at my desk in the dark and felt like crying. If Fiona was interested in the new lab. assistant, then he certainly wouldn't notice me, wouldn't even know I existed. Fiona was tall and slender with an abundance of dark curls spilling over the collar of her school blouse. She was Deputy Head of Browning, Captain of Netball and Lacrosse, and had the whitest, straightest teeth you ever saw outside a Macleans advertisement.

Moreover, she was doing three sciences for A-level and scarcely had a lesson outside the labs. I was no competition for Fiona. It wasn't until I'd said that to myself that I realized how much I wanted to be the one that was loved, the special one, the one to catch the attention of this, the most beautiful young man I'd ever seen.

'You're a fool,' I said aloud and then again just to make sure I'd heard myself the first time: 'A bloody stupid, idotic fool!' I simply wanted to be in love, that was all, and it probably wouldn't have mattered a bit what he was like. I'd made up my mind to fall in love the moment Dorothy had told me about him. I could see that now. It was almost as though I had become a cave: dark and empty and all ready to have the first wave rush up the beach and flood me, fill me up with love like foamy sea-water. That was what he was, this Simon Findlay: the first wave. The first man I had ever seen, the first person who wasn't a school boy or someone's spotty brother, and he had looked up at my window, and that was that. I thought of telling Bella how I felt, but I knew what she'd say:

'You don't get out enough. You don't meet enough people. You're practically as bad as Alice.'

I switched the light on again and turned back to my work. Forget him, I said to myself. Fiona has got him and you've got exams. Concentrate, I said to myself. Think of poor Phèdre, also suffering the torments of love . . . but I couldn't. I took out the poem I'd written the night before and tinkered with it a little, and added a bit to it. It made me feel better, doing that. By the time the bell went for supper, the poem looked like this:

> I was in the window
> and you turned, looked up
> to see the frame around my face.

> You were too far down
> and leaving. Walking
> towards the fountain
> where silver fish rise
> from the green circle
> of the nymphs' arms.

> I waited,
> a portrait of myself
> in the frame of the window.

> Now,
> the solid brick of roof and wall,

gable and chimney, have thinned
to paper cut-outs, stuck
on a pearl-grey sky.

You passed my darkened window
and didn't know
that it was mine,
that I was watching you
and that I stood against the wall
trying to disappear.

By the time I turned the light on,
the dark had covered you.

The next afternoon, Alice and I were walking along the paths between the lacrosse pitches and the netball courts. Bella was playing netball, which, for some reason I couldn't really understand, she enjoyed, but Alice and I were going for a short walk instead. Games were mostly optional now that we were in the Sixth Form, and as far as I was concerned, that was almost the best thing about not being in the lower forms any more. I shuddered when I remembered how I had hated it: the cold, the pointless running through mud, my total inability to manage that ridiculous contraption of wood and leather called a lacrosse stick and the scorn of everyone trying to play the game around me.

'Buck up, Megan! Pass, for goodness' sake, Megan!' the other girls used to shout, and Miss Robbins used to steam up behind me, her leathery cheeks flushed, her silver whistle bobbing about on the front of her Aertex shirt, and shriek:

'Run, Megan! Faster! Pick your feet up!'

Tears of rage would spring into my eyes at this. Did she think I *could* run faster than I was running already? Couldn't she see that I was practically exploding? I hate her, I hate her, I used to think. I wish it would rain. I wish I could twist an ankle, break a leg, anything.

It was only about two years ago that I suddenly realized that Games didn't matter. I could be good at something else. There was no disgrace in not being very athletic, and a snail-like runner. We were allowed to sign the Health Book, as it was called, when we were having a period, and be excused from Games. In the Fifth Form, the gap between my periods became shorter and shorter until it had disappeared altogether. Miss Herbert had summoned me to her study.

'You have, Megan dear,' she said, 'a somewhat unusual pattern of menstruation.' She smiled. I couldn't think of a word to say.

'I take it,' she continued, 'that you are, in fact, quite well?' I nodded.

'Then this is clearly a ploy to be excused from Games.' I nodded again.

'Very well. I shall have a word with Miss Robbins and her staff. You will go for walks during Games lessons in future. Is that more agreeable to you?'

'Oh, yes, Miss Herbert. Thank you very much.'

Miss Herbert smiled again: 'Fresh air, my dear, and some small movements of the limbs . . . far more ladylike than all that rough and tumble in the mud.'

'Oh, far more ladylike,' I agreed, and bounded out of the study to tell the others.

I thought about this interview as Alice and I listened to the shouts of the players rising into the frosty air. They were running up and down on the churned-up grass, their thighs pink from the cold, the white ribbons of their breath curling up out of their mouths and flying in the air. Alice wrapped her cloak tightly around her and shivered.

'Only another three days and then it's exams,' she said. 'I really don't know if I've done enough work. I'm so worried.'

'You don't have to worry, Alice, honestly,' I said. 'You're one of the hardest workers I know. You always have been. You do everything so carefully, so methodically. You always have, ever since Junior House. Everyone knows that.'

'Yes, but . . .' Alice looked at the ground. 'I find it all . . . I don't know . . . hard. I don't know how to make a good answer out of what I know. I mean, I know I know it all, because I've learned it, but when the time comes to put it down, I can't somehow seem to get it all into the right size. I feel as if I'm cramming a huge lump of squashy dough into a little bin. I push a bit down here and another bit swells out there. I have nightmares about it, honestly.'

'Oh, Alice, don't worry!' What could I say? I knew Alice was terrified of exams, but I didn't know what the right words were, the ones that would cheer her up. 'It's only because we're friends with Bella that we notice it so much, but Bella's . . . well, she's different. Most people are more like you. Frightened. Or nervous at least. I know I am.'

'Are you really?' Alice looked a little more cheerful. 'I don't know how Bella does it, do you?'

'No,' I said, 'she's amazing.'

It was true. For seven years, I'd come close to hating Bella at exam time. She'd be putting her hand up for more paper before you'd covered two sides, and she regularly finished ten minutes before the time was up, and generally sat there staring round the room, smiling if you happened to look up at her. When she was younger, she used to use the point of her compass to clean under her nails, but that habit had mercifully been dropped. The really galling part about it all was how well Bella always did with what was the minimum of effort. I did well too, I know, but I had to work for it. I suppose I should have been thankful that Dorothy had brought me up to study carefully and to organize my time, and that my own teachers had made me love what it was that I was working on for the most part, but still, I agreed with Alice, it was difficult not to feel resentful of Bella when exams came round.

'Anyway,' I said to Alice in an attempt to cheer her up still further, 'exams aren't everything. You have talents. Gifts for all sorts of things . . . and beauty.'

'Do you think so, really?' Alice looked so grateful. It always astonished me that someone as artistic and lovely as she was should be so unsure about almost everything.

'Yes,' I said, noticing how her golden-red hair was blowing in strands across the perfectly pink and white skin of her face, how her grey eyes weren't really grey at all, but like the sea on a stormy day: grey and green and blue all at once. 'Yes, you have all the gifts, Alice, and it is quite clear to me that exams or no exams, you will live happily ever after.'

'I feel a lot better now, Megan. You *are* nice!'

'I feel as if I've been blown inside out,' I said. 'Let's go in.'

I'd managed to steer us to the back of the Science Block. In order to reach School Corridor for the next lesson, we would have to pass behind the labs. The labs. had enormous windows and Simon might be there, pouring sinister-looking liquids into round-bottomed flasks or something. Maybe we would see him. I would have to look without Alice noticing that I was looking. I would tell them about it, I thought, if there were anything to tell, but just this great, damp bundle of unrequited and unrequitable love – why should anyone, even my best friends, want to know about that?

'I think,' said Alice, 'I'll just go into the Studio for a minute. You go on ahead, and I'll see you in English.'

This was a stroke of luck. I wouldn't have been able to

look at Simon Findlay as carefully, as lovingly as I wanted to, if Alice had been there. I took my time walking along. Two labs. seemed to be empty. Dorothy was teaching Fourth Formers in a third, and Simon Findlay was nowhere to be seen. I felt ridiculously disappointed, realizing that it had been my intention all afternoon to walk along this path at this time solely in order to catch a glimpse of him. I was in a worse condition than ever. I watched myself sliding deeper and deeper into a pool of feelings that were threatening to overwhelm everything else. The proof was that I had hardly given my work or the exams any thought at all. But where was he? With Fiona, I said to myself, and felt jealousy rising in my throat like bile. There was a ten minute break before English. If I went into the labs. and walked around, I could at least be in the place where he worked, touch the things that he touched, look at his lab. coat, perhaps, hanging on a peg on the back of the door.

I've never thought of laboratories as particularly romantic places. When I was younger and doing Chemistry, I regarded them as chilly and smelly and unwelcoming, but oh, the transforming power of love! This lab., where Simon Findlay's coat was indeed hanging on the back of the door, seemed to me to be a kind of fairyland, an enchanted place where the glass bottles, jars of crystals and powders and liquids the colour of jewels, dishes and pipettes and retorts and clamps and Bunsen burners all glowed with a radiance I'd been too stupid to notice before. I walked over to the sink where a rack of test tubes was standing on the draining-board. They had only just been washed. Drops of water still hung like small pearls along their sides. Maybe Simon Findlay himself had washed them.

'Hello,' said a voice suddenly, and I turned and in spite of looking for him, planning to see him, wanting to speak to him, going over and over in my mind the exact words I would use when I *did* see him, I was still so surprised that I nearly knocked the test-tubes into the sink.

'Oh, gosh, I'm so sorry,' I said, catching them.

'That's quite all right. No harm done, is there?' Simon Findlay walked right over to where I was standing. He was no more than a foot away from me. I suppose it must have been my imagination but I thought for a moment that I could feel a warmth coming from his body. Certainly I could smell him. He smelled differently from anyone else I'd ever been near. Part of it was cigarette smoke in his clothes – a smell I recognized from being near Bella and Marjorie. Part of it was probably a laboratory smell of one kind or another, but not unpleasant: rather sharp and astringent. Maybe it was also his clothes, the tweedy smell of his jacket, but most of it I knew was him – his skin, the blood going round in his veins, his flesh. I almost fainted.

'Haven't I seen you before?' he said, looking at me rather carefully. I didn't dare look into his eyes, and pretended suddenly to find a deeply intriguing speck on the linoleum.

'Look at me,' he said. 'I'm sure you're familiar.'

I fixed my eyes on his face. I could see every pore of his skin. I could have counted his eyelashes.

'Got it!' he said. 'The damsel in the Tower. The one with the golden hair falling over the windowsill. I knew I'd seen you. Hang on, I even remember your name. Mary. No, May . . . no, I'll get it in a sec. It's just on the tip of my tongue . . .'

I put him out of his misery. 'Megan. Megan Thomas,' I said, and because I didn't know exactly what to say or do next, I started babbling on about Dorothy and how she was my guardian and how I lived here during the holidays as well. On and on I went and even as I spoke I wondered how I was ever going to stop.

But he stopped me.

'So you're what Dolly Dragon . . . gosh, I'm frightfully sorry . . . that's my name for her . . .'

I giggled. 'That's all right. It's a jolly good name, actually. It suits her.'

'She calls you "her charge". She did tell me all about you. She seems to be very fond of you.'

I was immediately ashamed. 'I know. I shouldn't really giggle when you call her a dragon. It's disloyal. She's been very kind to me. She's looked after me for years and years and I'm being ungrateful. It's just . . .'

'That she's not exactly . . .' he said, and paused.

'What you'd call lovable or cuddly,' I finished his sentence.

This started a new paroxysm of laughter. In the middle of it, I noticed that a queue of Second Formers had lined up outside the door.

'Look,' I said, 'I have to go now, or I'll be late for English and there's a class waiting to come in here.'

'This is an absolutely impossible place in which to have any kind of civilized conversation, isn't it? No sooner do things become interesting than a bell goes, alas, alack . . . but I do hope we'll have a chance to chat again sometime?'

'Oh, yes,' I said, 'I hope so too.'

I left the laboratories and floated down the stairs that led to School Corridor. Then I walked along it as quickly as I could to English, Simon's words (he had magically been transformed to 'Simon' in my head) lingering sweetly in my ears. 'No sooner do things become interesting.' That means he thinks I'm interesting, or was he only being polite? He didn't have to say that, or the bit about wanting another chat, and he remembered who I was. He forgot your name, said another, more sensible voice in my head. But he knew *me*, I answered this sensible voice firmly. He recognized my face, which he only saw for a minute, and right up there in the window of the Tower Room . . . far away, and he recognized me.

Miss Doolittle had started the lesson and was not best pleased at my lateness.

'Really, Megan, if this is the attitude to your classes you're displaying a few days before the examination, then it's most regrettable.'

'I'm sorry, Miss Doolittle. I had to go back and fetch my Keats. I'd left it behind, you see.'

'Very well, Megan. Sit down now and let us continue. We are discussing Keats' appeal to the senses: sight, sound, touch and so on, in "The Eve of St Agnes". Please go on reading, Susan.' Susan Martin, a silent, rather plump girl started to read:

> 'And still she slept an azure-lidded sleep,
> In blanchèd linen, smooth, and lavender'd,
> While he from forth the closet brought a heap
> Of candied apple, quince, and plum, and gourd;
> With jellies soother than the creamy curd,
> And lucent syrops, tinct with cinnamon;
> Manna and dates, in argosy transferr'd
> From Fez; and spicèd dainties every one,
> From silken Samarcand to cedar'd Lebanon.'

I looked at Susan as she read and wondered if she was imagining herself to be Madeline and someone she knew to be Porphyro. Bella pushed a note into my hand. It said: 'D'you think Dooly realizes what's going on in stanza 36? Is it right to feed such sexy stuff to impressionable girls? Great balls of fire! Pant, pant!' I looked at the lines in question:

Ethereal, flush'd and like a throbbing star . . .
Into her dream he melted, as the rose
Blendeth its odour with the violet,
Solution sweet . . .

I winked at Bella. She was right, though. Between Keats and Saint John of the Cross, it did rather look as though the examiners were conspiring to make our young hearts beat faster. I spent the next few minutes in a dream of myself as Madeline, running along the tapestried halls with my lover:

'The arras, rich with horseman, hawk, and hound,
Flutter'd in the besieging wind's uproar;
And the long carpet rose along the gusty floor.'

Susan finished reading the poem. Miss Doolittle pushed her gold-rimmed glasses more firmly on to the bridge of her nose and stood up.

'Well, girls, are we agreed that John Keats is a poet who appeals to the senses?'

Nods and yeses came from every corner of the room.

'Very well, then. Now it is up to us to discover exactly how it is he achieves these effects . . .'

I tried to do two things at once: to listen and learn so that perhaps I could borrow some of Keats' recipe for luscious poetry and put it into lines of my own, and also to shut my ears so that knowing how he put it together would not spoil the magic, break the spell that those words in just that order were capable of casting over me. I wondered briefly if Simon ever read poetry. I blushed when an image of him reading my poems came into my mind. A peal of laughter broke into my dreams.

'No, Bella,' Miss Doolittle was saying, ' "azure-lidded sleep" does *not* mean that Madeline has failed to remove her eyeshadow. I would urge you to be serious, girl. What *does* it mean? Yes, Angela?'

'It means her skin is very white and you can see the blue veins on her eyelids.'

'Precisely. Thank you. And why do you think he uses these place names: Fez, Samarcand, Lebanon? What sort of image do they conjure up in your mind?'

The lesson continued. At the end of it, I walked along School Corridor with Bella. She said:

'I think we ought to have a sort of practical English lesson. Male volunteers to show us what it means, all that stuff about blending the rose and the violet. We'd be able to write much better about Keats, if we knew about all that.'

The following day, Bella and I walked back to school from the Games pitches with Fiona Mackenzie. Simon drove past us in his car and waved cheerily.

'There's that rather divine young lab. assistant,' said Fiona.

'D'you think he's divine?' asked Bella. 'I thought he was a bit feeble, actually. Not my type.'

'Oh, no, he's not feeble at all,' Fiona was quick in her defence. 'He's most awfully nice. Friendly. I see quite a lot of him in the labs., one way and another. He walked all the way down to my study with me the other day and I was going to give him a cup of tea and a biscuit when Miss Bates came bustling down the corridor behind us and scared him off . . . but I really like him, and,' she winked at me and Bella, 'I think he quite likes me.'

I had kept quiet during this conversation, but this was too much for me. I said:

'Did he say anything? To make you think he likes you, I mean? Or do anything?'

I could feel, as I waited for Fiona's answer, my heart fluttering about like a bird beating its wings against my ribs.

'No, nothing in particular,' said Fiona, turning into the Browning House Study Passage. 'Still, it's only the first week of term, isn't it? Lots of time . . .'

After she had gone, I went over my earlier conversation with Simon. What I had thought of as something glorious and shining and hopeful had been reduced to a tarnished little scrap of nothing very much.

*

London *April 15th 1962*

I WONDER how grown-up you have to be to stop thinking of a year as being divided up into terms and holidays? The word 'week' when I say it to myself, brings to mind a printed timetable such as we filled in at the beginning of every term, with the times of the lessons printed down the left-hand side, the names of the days at the top of seven columns going from left to right, and two thick black lines separating the morning from the afternoon. We always started exams on a Monday morning (top left-hand corner) and by the time we'd reached the bottom right-hand corner, they were generally over. Those were school exams, though. Public exams, A-level exams, will be dotted about all over the sheet, will go on for weeks. There will be whole days between one paper and another, and the sun will shine as it always does during exams, and we (they?) will lie around on the grassy slopes leading down from the terrace and pretend to be revising. I remember it from other years, from watching other girls doing it, summer after summer. When Bella, Alice and I first came up from Junior House, we couldn't really believe that we would ever be quite as grown-up as that. And now, here I am, exactly the same as those girls were when I admired them and wondered at them. I can't think why I feel so childish and ignorant and bewildered. There are days when I would be relieved to see Dorothy marching in here and saying: 'Enough of this nonsense, child, you're coming back home with me.' On other days, I fear that she might actually do it. But she won't. She'll say nothing and write nothing and just wait for me to . . . what? Come to my senses? Disappear without trace? Sometimes I wonder if she'll ever forgive me, and at other times I wonder whether I actually need to be forgiven, whether what I've done is so dreadful after all. Dreadful or not, Dorothy is hurt by what we did.

*

IT seems to me miraculous that I managed to pass the exams, let alone do quite well. That week (which is actually only about eight weeks ago) seems to belong to another lifetime, and when I think of myself then, it's as though I'm looking at a stranger, someone I hardly know. What I mainly remember is a feeling of being two quite separate people, all the way through the week before the exams started.

'Schizophrenia,' said Bella knowledgeably. This was the night before the first exam, and up in the Tower Room after Lights Out. I had just told Alice and Bella about my longing for Simon, and how thinking about him seemed to have cut me in half. I used to crane my neck in Chapel to see where he was sitting and could he see Fiona and were looks passing between them. I used to go for long walks along the Rim of the Known World, peering into the spaces between the trees,

67

expecting at any moment to see him come sauntering out, his arm around Fiona's waist . . . it was a lover and his lass, with a hey and a ho and a hey nonny no. I would go and see Dorothy in the labs. on almost any pretext in the hope of bumping into him. I don't know what Dorothy thought of this, because she always said so little. Still, she must have wondered, because over the years an understanding had grown up between us: during the term, I was just another girl in the school. It was only during the holidays that Dorothy turned by magic into my adopted mother. In my heart I regard her as only a guardian, and never think of her as a real mother, and I don't know whether this is my fault or hers, but I do feel a certain guilt about it. She did try to be like a mother to me during the holidays but it was as though she were copying maternal behaviour she had seen in other people, and not quite succeeding. She was clumsy at domestic things, like going shopping together for clothes and shoes, and when we were alone, we talked or discussed or argued, but we almost never laughed. Small smiles were more Dorothy's sort of thing, and she seemed frightened of displays of emotion. There were times when I used to think that if she had had someone noisier, sillier, bouncier and more loving than me to look after, she would have been different, but it's futile to wonder such things after all these years. We visited a great many museums during the holidays, and Dorothy was a wonderful guide. She knew so much and explained it so clearly, and was so happy to see me interested that these visits remain in my mind as the most pleasurable occasions of my childhood. Dorothy was as contented as I was in the long, quiet corridors. We could become a teacher and a pupil again: roles in which we were well-rehearsed and confident.

Anyway, there I'd be, hanging round the labs. and

sometimes I'd be rewarded by a glimpse of Simon. There were always droves of giggling girls around his bench, or helping him to clean up the labs. after a lesson, so I never had a chance to speak. Once or twice, though, he saw me and waved and smiled and on these occasions I went about in a dream of bliss. Once, however, I thought I'd caught sight of him going down the Browning House Study Passage and for the rest of that afternoon I was in agonies of grief and longing in my study, imagining him and Fiona doing all the sorts of things we'd read about in *Peyton Place*, and (oh, what anguish!) *Lady Chatterley's Lover*. I explained all this to Alice and Bella at last, unable to bear it on my own,

'It's not only the love,' I said. 'It's everything else as well . . . working for the exams all the time and reading about all these other lovers . . . I can't concentrate properly. It's awful. I don't know how I'm going to keep my mind on what I'm writing for a whole three hours. I keep daydreaming.'

'You must speak to him,' Bella said. 'Just march straight up to him and ask him to go for a walk with you, or something.'

'She can't.' Alice looked up, shocked. 'Everyone'll see them. Dorothy would soon find out and then what would she say? She'd probably send Simon away.'

'That's being feeble, Alice. I bet I could find a way. What about writing him a note? Invite him to Study Tea.'

'What would I say in the note?' I asked.

Bella laughed: 'Oh, I don't know . . . something informal and cool, like you're burning with love for him . . . your thighs are throbbing, your breast is heaving . . . that kind of thing.'

I threw my pyjama case at her. 'Fat lot of use you are!' I groaned and punched my pillow into a more comfortable shape before lying down. 'There's nothing to be done. I shall just have to languish. Languish and hope for the best.'

'Maybe,' said Alice, 'the exams will take your mind off it a bit. I haven't even had time to answer Jean-Luc's letter.'

Bella and I giggled. Jean-Luc's letters we privately thought of as disappointing. Alice obviously regarded them as real love-letters, so we never disillusioned her, but to us they seemed very faint and lacklustre in the Shining Words of Love department. As Bella put it:

'You can hardly count "*mes amitiés*" or "*bien affectueusement*" can you? I mean, there's not even a "*baisers*" to be found, much less a "*gros baisers*". I don't think this Jean-Luc is up to much.'

'Don't for heaven's sake tell Alice,' I said. 'She thinks they're marvellous. Haven't you seen how she peers at the pile of letters by Herbie's plate all through breakfast?'

It was true. Alice could hardly eat, so busy was she scrutinizing the pile. Miss Herbert always gave out the letters after she had eaten

a) cornflakes
b) a boiled egg
c) one triangle of brown toast, thinly spread with butter and an almost invisible glaze of marmalade.

If Alice's name was read aloud, she would blush furiously and collect her missive with trembling hands. I sometimes thought Alice would eat more at breakfast if the letters were read out first, but then there would be the torment of waiting until she was on her own to open it.

Bella had been getting letters from the band. The dance they were playing at was on Saturday, February 17th.

'It's a Valentine's Day Dance,' Bella told us. 'I've got it all arranged. They're going to wait for me just the other side of the forest. The van'll be parked on the main road to Egerton Magna and they'll bring me back the same way.'

'It'll be the Valentine's Day Massacre if you're caught,' I said.

'But I won't be. Listen, I've got it all worked out. I'll say I've got a headache and I'm going to have an early night. Then I'll sneak out while you're all in the Hall for Saturday Night Dancing. No one ever comes up here, Megan, you know that, and I'll be back before morning. You leave the J.C.R. window open and I'll close it behind me. Don't look so worried, Alice. I'll leave pillows in my bed, just in case someone looks in. It'll be a jolly jape, just like the ones in those old school stories we used to read.'

Alice and I didn't argue. It was no use arguing with Bella once she'd made her mind up. In order to sing with a real band at a real dance, she would have risked almost anything. Bella didn't even notice our silence. She went on:

'And, I say, can you both come out with me this Sunday? I forgot to ask before. I had a postcard from Marjorie . . . they're coming to take me out and would I like to bring Megan and Alice? Do say you'll come. I can't bear going out with them all by myself . . . there's nothing to talk about. Go on, say you'll come.'

Alice and I both said we would, and then we all stopped talking. Soon the others were asleep, but I stared at the ceiling, going over my *Phèdre* revision in my head, imagining Simon in a toga.

> *Je sentis tout mon corps et transir et brûler,*
> *Je reconnus Vénus et ses feux redoutables.*

Me too, I thought. I'm fainting and burning too, and I may not be a seventeenth-century version of an ancient

Greek queen, but I can recognize Venus' redoutable fires when I'm feeling them, just the same as anyone else.

Next morning, the prospect of a week of exams made the whole Upper Sixth subdued. Even the knives and forks at breakfast were quieter. All the younger girls seemed to catch the nervousness, and didn't dare address a Sixth Former at all. After breakfast, there was much last-minute consulting of notes, sharpening of pencils and tucking of good luck mascots into pencil cases. Alice and Bella had received good luck cards from the Third Formers who admired them, and would have to reward these kids with radiant smiles at lunch time. Alice was pale and tense. I was tired. Only Bella seemed exactly the same as usual, humming Buddy Holly songs under her breath as she searched unhurriedly through her desk for a missing pen. I was in her study with her, helping her to look.

'Honestly, Bella! That's the kind of thing one ought to prepare in advance, one's pens and things. It's frightfully important,' said Mary-Ellen. She, Mary-Ellen, had everything neatly organized and was only waiting for the bell.

'Not as frightfully important, Ellie, me old fruit,' said Bella in the stage Cockney she always adopted simply to annoy Mary-Ellen, 'as actually having something interesting to write with one's pen when one has found it! All the stationery in the world, Mary-Ellen, will not make up for your startling mediocrity.'

'You're simply foul,' said Mary-Ellen. 'I don't know why I should have to sit here and be insulted.'

'You don't,' Bella answered calmly. 'You can stand in the middle of Study Passage and I'll gladly insult you there . . . and here's my pen! What a stroke of luck!' She sailed past Mary-Ellen. 'Don't be late for the first paper, now, will you?'

Mr Page, the caretaker, and his assistants had been busy in

the night, like the elves who helped the shoemaker. The Hall had been transformed. Scores of wooden desks had been brought up from the Nether Regions under the floor, and arranged in long rows. The Invigilator's desk was up on the stage, and on it there were alarming grey envelopes containing the question papers, and high piles of foolscap paper with blue lines and red margins. Each sheet of paper had a hole in the top left-hand corner, through which we had to thread a small piece of string. Miss Peacock, a Geography teacher, was walking up and down in between the rows of desks, even as we came in, putting out a little bit of string for each person. Miss Hardy, head of Maths, was following her with paper, four sheets each. Bella would be putting her hand up for more before I'd finished the first question. I looked round the Hall at the windows set so high up that no one could possibly see out of them; at the velvet curtains that had once, probably, been bottle-green, but had now faded to the colour of pea soup; at the wooden boards painted with the golden names of past prefects, Head Girls, and other school worthies. I was a prefect. It was strange to think that after I'd left school, someone would sit here, at this very desk and read my name: Megan Thomas, (1955–62). Portraits of Phoebe and Louisa Egerton, in puce and grey respectively, gazed down benignly on us from the back of the stage, and more visible than anything else in the room, a huge clock hung above the Founders' heads. Its face was as wide as a crater on the moon, and as each minute passed, the big hand moved with a click that was audible to everyone in all that silence.

Exam week passed. What a luxury to be able to dismiss it like that, in three words! All through that week I slept badly, worried by dreams of Simon, and of turning over a question paper only to find algebra questions on it that I could never begin to answer. It was because I was tired that Miss Herbert excused me from Saturday Night Dancing and told me to go and rest quietly on my bed instead:

'With a relaxing rather than an invigorating book, perhaps.'

I was delighted. I hated Saturday Night Dancing, and so did Alice and Bella, although most of the younger girls enjoyed it, and we were all expected to go.

'It's so frightfully depressing,' Bella used to moan. 'All these middle-aged women, dressed up in their best – and it *is* their best: full-length brocade and tatty fur stoles and Lord love us, even a bit of lipstick – all of them sitting there on stiff chairs up on that stage doing what? Watching a whole lot of lumpy girls dancing around together, and not very well, either, cos they haven't quite worked out the steps and should the girl being the man be going forwards or backwards . . . oh, it's dreadful!'

'Then, sometimes,' I'd add, 'they actually *dance*. As Herbie herself would say, "*horresco referens:* I shudder to relate." Some brave soul, or someone who's been dared to, goes up there and asks one of the staff to dance. What do they talk about as they go round and round? The results of last week's test? Yesterday's netball match? World current affairs? It's embarrassing, that's what it is.'

'It must be even worse for them than for us,' Alice said. 'I mean, they are grown-up . . . old, really. Don't you think they get reminded of dances they went to when they were young? They probably feel most awfully sad. I feel sorry for them, actually.'

'Well, I don't,' said Bella. 'It's their own fault. They don't have to have it. They could invite some boys' school over here, or they could let us play Radio Lux. and dance around on our own. I wouldn't mind that nearly so much.'

But boys and Radio Lux. were both regarded as disruptive, if not downright evil, so Saturday Night Dancing remained.

I was delighted, that night, to be alone in the Tower Room. It was a beautiful evening, with the full moon floating in a wide pool of its own light. I opened the window, even though it was cold, and looked at the silvery limbs of the nymphs and the fish. I could hear fainter music lying over the music I was listening to on my transistor. It was coming from the Hall, but it sounded distant and sweet and unconnected with undignified shuffling around on the parquet floor. Then I heard the scrunch of gravel, and I sprang away from the window, and felt a tremor of something like fear. Surely no one should be walking around at this time? Perhaps it was one of the maids, going home after washing up hundreds and hundreds of dirty plates. Yes, that was the most likely explanation . . . but I'd better have a look just in case.

If I hadn't thought in this way, if I hadn't gone to see, that night, whose were the noisy footsteps on the gravel, then . . . what? Would everything have been different? Would all that has happened in the last few weeks have taken place at all, let alone in exactly the way it did? I often think about that now, but then, I didn't hesitate. I went back to the window and looked down. The noise had stopped. Simon Findlay was standing at the bottom of the scaffolding.

'Hello,' he said. 'I saw the light on in your tower. I wondered if it was really you, or if the light had been left on by mistake. I was just about to call your name . . . I saw Dorothy doing it the other day.'

'Yes,' I said. (Oh, such brilliant, sparkling conversation from someone who has lived and breathed for just this chance of a private talk!) 'It is me. I've got a bit of a headache.'

'Gosh, I am sorry.'

'No, it's practically gone now, honestly.'

'Good-oh! I say . . .' Simon hesitated.

'Yes?'

'This is a bit stupid, isn't it? Me down here and you up there. We can't really talk. Not properly.'

(Did he want to talk 'properly'? What did that mean? My heart had jumped into my throat, so that I had some difficulty in answering him at all.)

'It can't be helped, I suppose,' I stammered.

''Course it can be helped. I'll come up,' he said, and before I could say anything to stop him, he had begun to climb up the scaffolding. I watched him coming nearer and nearer. Soon, I could see the individual hairs on the top of his head, and then his face was level with mine.

'Aren't you going to ask me in?' He was grinning. 'After I've come all this way to see you?'

'Come in,' I said, and he climbed over, into the Tower Room, and stood next to me. I could feel myself trembling all over.

'I say,' he said, 'you're not scared of being caught, are you?'

I was, but I wasn't going to admit it. In any case, it wasn't the fear that was causing the trembling so much as his nearness, and the fact that the three beds were the only places in the room where we could sit. I shook my head.

'Don't worry,' he said. 'First sign of trouble and I'm down that scaffolding like a cat-burglar.'

'They won't be coming back for at least an hour,' I whispered. 'It's Saturday Night Dancing.'

'What's that?' Simon said. 'May I sit on this bed?'

'Yes, do.'

He sat down on Alice's bed, and I sat down on my bed facing him. The tips of his brown suede shoes were only inches away from mine on the mauve rug. Our knees were almost touching. I began to tell him about Saturday Night Dancing and why Bella and Alice and I found it so depressing. On the transistor, Bobby Darin began to sing 'Lazy River'.

'May I have the pleasure?' Simon said, and stood up. 'This is one of my favourite songs, and I don't see why you shouldn't have a dance, even though you've got a headache.'

'What? Here?' I'd have given anything to have been able to take back the words. How silly they were! How completely and devastatingly unromantic!

'Absolutely,' Simon said, and took hold of me in just the way we had been taught the gentleman takes hold of the lady. How strange we must have looked, dancing in between the beds and around the chest-of-drawers! I can see that now, but at the time I thought I was going to die of pleasure. He was holding me very close to him. Every bit of my body from my head down to my knees could feel a part of his body touching it. The thought flew into my mind: how am I going to tell Bella and Alice exactly what this feels like? I didn't have to talk. Simon was humming along with Bobby Darin. I could feel his lips moving softly in my hair. What does this mean, I kept thinking. Does it mean anything? Everyone has to touch when they dance, don't they? This is what the gentlemen do . . . this is what the ladies do . . . it doesn't need to mean anything at all. Then the music stopped and Simon didn't let me go. I was dizzy. I was going to faint. I felt a blush spreading up all over me, all over my face. I stared down at the floor, but he put his hand under my chin, and forced me to look at him. I knew what was going to happen next. He was going to kiss me.

'I'm going to kiss you,' he said. 'If you don't mind, that is.' I couldn't speak. I just closed my eyes and waited. He kissed me very softly on the lips, so that I could hardly feel it, but I smelled his smell in my nostrils, and his hands were on my shoulders. I opened my eyes.

'I've been wanting to do that,' he smiled, 'ever since I first saw you at the window.'

What could I say? Yes, and I've been longing, longing, longing for you to touch me?

'Was that the first time that you've been kissed?'

I thought about lying for one wild moment, but in the end I said:

'Yes.'

'And how old are you?'

'I shall be eighteen in April.'

'Tsk, tsk. Whatever have you been doing for the last couple of years?'

'Nothing. I've just been here.'

'Up in your tower,' he smiled. 'Come and sit down beside me on the bed. I want to kiss you again. Properly.'

I think perhaps I had not been kissed enough in my life. My parents, even in my earliest childhood, were not much given to touching and hugging, and Dorothy had hardly ever kissed me at all: a peck on the cheek for goodbye and a similar one for hello each time I went to stay with Alice or Bella. Therefore, I was unprepared for what Simon meant by kissing. Listening to Bella and others whom I thought of as 'more experienced' and reading all the right books with particular emphasis on the 'good bits', I had always thought that kisses came rather low on the scale of possible excitement. But as Simon began to place small, fluttery kisses on my neck and eyelids, and deeper, longer kisses on my lips; as he persuaded my lips to part and touched my tongue with his, I began to feel as though every single one of my nerve ends was singing with pleasure. I was aware of nothing but Simon. It was as though I were drowning: drowning and falling at the same time. I could hear my own heart hammering in my body – or was it his? All sense of where I was, or what time it was, or other people, disappeared. The whole universe was now entirely contained in my body, and every beautiful feeling in the world was blossoming and uncurling under my own burning skin, over my flesh and in my mouth made moist and tender by his kisses.

'I think,' I gasped when Simon stopped for a moment, 'I must have died and gone to Heaven.'

'It gets better,' he answered. 'This is only the beginning . . .' oh, I shall show you such things . . .'

That means, I thought to myself, that he wants to see me again. That this isn't just a momentary aberration.

'It's going to be awfully difficult,' I murmured. 'I don't think a girls' boarding-school is the ideal place for . . . this sort of thing.'

'How unadventurous you are!' Simon smiled. 'It's absolutely perfect. There is an added element of mystery and danger. Keeping things secret rather adds to the fun, doesn't it?'

'Yes, but where can we meet? It's too cold to go out for long walks, and you couldn't come to my study. I share it.'

'What's wrong with this room?'

'Here? But however would you get here?'

'Silly! Up the scaffolding, just like tonight.'

'I can't have a headache every Saturday night, though, can I? They'll catch on, become suspicious.'

'We'll find times. Evening prep. You can creep up here when you're meant to be in your study, and I'll meet you. Daytime's no good because of the workmen . . .'

'And you don't want anyone catching sight of you on their way back from Games or anything.'

'Don't worry. I'll find a way to reach you. I must reach you. Oh, Megan, we're wasting what little time we have. Come here. I'm going to unplait your hair.' I turned my back to him and closed my eyes. I could feel his fingers threading through my tightly-braided hair, loosening it, shaking it out, then stroking it as if I were a cat, down from the crown of my head to where it hung nearly touching my waist. I could have gone on sitting like that for hours, but he pulled me round so that I was facing him again. He took me in his arms, and we forgot ourselves, and wallowed in our kissing to such an extent that he had to leave in a great hurry. I leaned out of the window and watched him climbing down. I wanted to call out: 'Come back. I love you. Stay with me. I want you,' and other soppy things, but all I said was: 'Goodnight.' He didn't even answer properly, just waved and smiled. My hair fell in a stream over the sill as I leaned forward. I gathered it hastily into an elastic band. I almost never wore it loose, and Alice and Bella would be here soon. I looked into the mirror to see if I looked different, to see if it showed, the fact that I had been altered, all the atoms of my body rearranged into new patterns. Apart from the fact that my eyes were very bright, almost as if I'd been crying, and my cheeks were flushed, I looked just the same. I lay on my bed and waited for the sound of footsteps on the stairs. The stairs . . . I closed my eyes and imagined myself tiptoeing up them, up and up while everyone else was bent over their work. The main staircase of Austen House would be the secret hidden stairway of the heart that Saint John of the Cross describes: '*la secreta escala disfrazada*', the one the Soul goes up on its way to Union with God:

> *En una noche oscura*
> *con ansias en amores inflamada . . .*

Well, the night would be dark when I went up, and all *my* cares would be blazing into love, and just as Saint

John describes, the only light in all that darkness and silence would be the one burning, shining, leaping in my heart.

*

I SHOULD go to the launderette, otherwise we will have no clothes to wear tomorrow. It's amazing, the things that are organized for you when you are a child, and that you have to attend to all by yourself as a grown-up. Bella, so eager, so much wanting to be grown-up, let me tell you: it's not easy. Bella even gets taken to the hairdresser's by her stepmother at the end of every holiday, so as to be neat for school. I went with them once, when I was staying with Bella, and now, when I look in the mirror and see my hair in the same style I've worn since I was six years old, I am reminded of it. It was on that day, too, that I understood how little Bella had exaggerated when describing her stepmother to us.

I shall write about it first and attend to the dirty knickers later. How real life does get in the way sometimes!

*

GOING to Armand's was one of the treats, one of the best things about staying with Bella during the holidays. In front of every seat there was an enormous mirror in an ornate, gilded frame, and the hairdressers, all robed in pink, wafted between the chairs like a cloud of butterflies. Bella, of course, was always attended to by Monsieur Armand himself. Marjorie, Bella's stepmother, had ensconced herself in one of the velvety armchairs in the reception area, but I sat in the chair next to Bella's and listened to everything that was going on. Monsieur Armand's eyes had lit up when he saw my hair;

he had such dreams of snipping and curling, you could almost see the scissors twitching, but Bella said:

'It's no use, Armand, looking at that plait. Silly old Megan insists on the Rhine-maiden look and there's nothing to be done about it.'

Armand sighed deeply, making me feel as though I were letting the side down.

As he combed out Bella's hair, she said:

'Come on, Armand, just a bit more bouffant . . . just a weeny bit.'

'But, mam'zelle, she say . . . your mother say . . .'

Bella put her tongue out and she and Armand giggled together.

'She's not my mother, she's my stepmother. Go on, while she's not looking. A tiny bit more backcombing should do it.'

Armand shrugged and picked up his comb. Bella, I thought to myself, will never be able to put her school hat on top of that. She wouldn't mind. She'd simply not wear it. Bella had strong views on lots of things, and one of her strongest views concerned school uniform.

'It's cruelty,' she used to explain to anyone who would listen and frequently to those who wouldn't. 'It limits our freedom. Our individuality. Our style.'

'But it's a great leveller, dear,' people (teachers, mothers etc.) used to say. Bella would snort in reply. She was a great snorter. Who wants to be level? she was thinking.

I glanced into the mirror. I could just see Marjorie. She was hidden behind the *Tatler* and only her hands were visible: long, dark red fingernails and very white fingers scarcely able to move about for the weight of rings, heavy gold-link bracelets and other assorted baubles. Bella didn't like her much, and enjoyed the fact enormously.

'Whatever's the point of a stepmother,' she'd say, 'if she isn't wicked?'

Marjorie wasn't exactly wicked. Not really. Even Bella admitted this. But she was small-minded, critical and jealous of the relationship between Bella and her father, between this friend and that, and especially of the relationship that had once existed between Bella's father and mother. Well, she was a jealous person and that was that. She was also vain. Bella, it's true, was forever prinking and preening and admiring herself, but, as she had once told us, me and Alice:

'Marjorie's worse. Much worse. Once she tore up a dress which made her look fat. Honestly. Didn't even bother to let me try it on, to see if it suited me. I bet it would have done, too.'

'*Voilà, mam'zelle.*' Armand stepped back, pleased with himself.

'*C'est formidable!*' Bella cried, and turned to me. 'Wouldn't Miss Donnelly be proud of me? Well, whatever's the point of French A-level, if I can't chat to Armand?'

Marjorie was summoned. She put down her magazine and came over to the mirror. Then she leaned down so that her face was near Bella's in the glass.

'Very nice, dear,' she said after staring for a long time. 'But don't you think a little . . . too much for school, perhaps?'

I could hear the voice growing thin, sharpening a little.

'Oh, no,' Bella said. 'Not at all. Truly. It'll be fine.'

'Very well, then.' Marjorie patted her own sleek, golden-brown pageboy hairstyle. 'But honestly, Armand, tell us what you think. Which do *you* think looks prettier?' Marjorie was smiling now through glossy lips. Armand threw up his hands in a gesture of defeat.

'That is of the most difficult, such a choice. Of course, Madame is chic itself. This we all know, *naturellement*. And yet, I have to say, mam'zelle's style is . . . how do you say? The latest. *Le dernier cri*. Utmost modernity. *Enfin, Madame, c'est la jeunesse . . . qu'est-ce qu'on peut dire?* He folded his arms in a gesture of resignation.

Marjorie hurried away to gather her furs from where they'd been hung up, and Bella said:

'One in the eye for her, then. Silly old thing.' She stood up to take her robe off. The mirror reflected no faces now, nothing but the movements of the butterfly-hairdressers and the row of silver driers on the opposite wall. I thought about their faces, Bella's and Marjorie's, nearly touching in the mirror, and about the look in Marjorie's eyes when she compared her skin (golden with make-up, but beginning to coarsen and wrinkle in spite of the best efforts of Elizabeth Arden) with Bella's, which seemed, in the rosy light of the salon, almost incandescent. And had Marjorie noticed the grey streaks just visible near her hairline? The almost blue sheen on Bella's hair, newly washed, set and backcombed, must have struck her like a warning. She walked out of the salon so abruptly that we had to run to catch up with her.

That day was almost two years ago now, and I remembered it because the next day, a Sunday, Alice and I were going out with Bella and her father and Marjorie. We found it hard to wake up when the bell went because we'd spoken so late into the night, analysing every word and gesture of what Bella was calling, with capital letters in her voice: 'Megan's Initiation'. Alice always found it hard to wake up, and Bella and I were quite used to throwing wet flannels at her, or stripping back the blankets or tickling her feet.

'There's another aspect to all this,' said Bella, pushing Alice's shoulder, 'and that's the brilliant idea your Simon has given me. I shall climb up the scaffolding to this very room after the dance on the 17th.'

'Bella, you can't! You'll fall and kill yourself.'

'What rubbish! I could climb up that scaffolding as easy as winking. It's just never occurred to me before.'

'But you're not seriously going to go and sing with this band, are you? I mean you could be expelled if you're caught.'

'Look who's talking. It's absolutely allowed, of course, to let young men have their wicked way with you in one of the school bedrooms.'

'He hasn't had his wicked way with me . . . and anyway, I do wish you wouldn't put it like that.'

'He will. Give him time. He's only been up here once. I bet you anything you like you'll be the first one of us to lose her virginity.'

'I won't.' I was blushing.

'Yes, you will,' Bella said. I shook my head vigorously, but she went on: 'Actually, I don't see anything so frightful about it. They can't expect us to read all these poems saying gather ye rosebuds and things like that, and then say, no, sorry, there won't be any rosebud-gathering after all, ducky, at least not until after you're married and quite respectable.'

'But, what if you were to get pregnant?' I asked, suddenly terrified. What if Bella were right? Was I ready for this? Did I even want it?

'There are ways of preventing pregnancy, you know,' Bella said.

'But no one tells us anything about them,' I said. 'It's not fair. They make us study all these love poems and then they don't tell us what to do about it.'

'You should ask Simon. He's sure to know. He's a scientist.'

'I'd die! I'd die of embarrassment. I mean, I don't really know him well enough.'

Bella had stopped listening to me, and was trying to lure Alice out of her sleep by murmuring things about Sunday breakfast into her ear. We had rolls and honey on Sunday mornings and bananas, too. We used to ask our banana a secret question, and then cut the end off it with a sharp knife. Sometimes, you could see a black 'Y' shape very clearly and that meant the answer to your question was 'yes'. Sometimes the fruit produced only a dot or an indeterminate blur, and that was a 'no'. Over the years, I'd got quite clever about my bananas and I knew just where to cut them in order to have the best chance of a 'yes'. At breakfast I would ask the question: does Simon love me? but meanwhile I was busy pondering the paradox of feeling that I hardly knew this person who last night had been so close to me that I had felt almost absorbed into his flesh.

'Oh, oh,' cried Alice from the bed. 'I'm coming, Bella. Stop tormenting me . . . I'm waking up now, honestly.' She swung her legs down on to the floor. 'Oh, I hate the mornings! I hate getting up. I wish I could sleep some more.' She shuffled off to the bathroom, moaning and shivering in the chilly half-light.

Bella's father and Marjorie were in the front row of the Parents' Gallery in Chapel that morning. Marjorie, whatever her other faults, was not a person who would miss an opportunity to impress the entire population of the school.

'You can't exactly accuse her,' Bella whispered to me, up in the back row of the choir, 'of not making an effort, can you? I mean, look at that fur hat, and the quite unnecessarily sparkly diamonds in that brooch on her lapel.'

'Maybe they're not diamonds. Maybe they're only glass.'

Bella shook her head sadly. 'They used to belong to my mother. They're real. The really ghastly part is, Daddy's plastered them all over her, or maybe she just helped herself and wheedled Daddy into agreeing to it afterwards . . . but anyway, they're all my mother's jewels, and they should be mine, by rights, I mean. I bet my poor mother's turning in her grave.'

'But do you like them? I think diamonds look a bit vulgar.'

'That's not the point,' said Bella. 'Golly, look what Dorothy's just walked in with!'

I watched Simon sit down in the Staff pews next to Dorothy, and felt confused and envious. Had Dorothy met him accidentally in the cloisters and had they wandered in together? Had she arranged to bring him? Why did it matter, anyway? Dorothy was my guardian, for goodness' sake. It was completely irrational to be jealous of her, particularly after last night. Nevertheless, I didn't like them sitting next to one another, nor did I like the way Dorothy helped Simon find his place in the hymn-book and prayer-book as though he were a small child.

'You're turning slightly green,' Bella murmured, 'and I can't say I blame you. Why do you suppose Dorothy has touched up her lips with the dreaded, scorned and totally reviled lipstick? Why is she wearing a dress I've only ever seen her wearing at Speech Day? Egad and gadzooks, madam, methinks you have a rival for your beau's affections!'

'Ssh! What rubbish! Dorothy and Simon? She's more than twenty years older than he is . . . It's disgusting. Ugh!'

'What about Phèdre?' Bella was relentless.

'What about her?'

'She was older than Hippolyte.'

'But not forty-five,' I said. 'And anyway, Dorothy isn't Phèdre. You're just trying to worry me.'

Bella giggled. 'It's fun, that's why. You always believe everything and take everything so seriously. It was *you* he was kissing, wasn't it?'

I nodded. The day before I had watched Dorothy and Simon leaving the labs. together. At the time, I hadn't been in the least worried. I don't think I even looked at them properly, but now, remembering it, I could see again the way the whole of Dorothy's body seemed to lean towards Simon's, almost to sway against him. Did she put her hand on his arm for a moment? I couldn't remember. What I did know was that when he had walked away, Dorothy had stood looking after him for a full minute. Was it only my imagination that made her gaze appear both loving and greedy? I couldn't decide. I looked at Simon, staring at the back of his head. If you stared at someone long enough and hard enough they would sometimes glance up at you, but it didn't work on this occasion. I was reduced to watching him and Dorothy, Bella's father and Marjorie and all the assorted parents waiting to take their children out for the day. In the old days, we used to give people's mothers marks out of ten for their appearance and dress, but today I didn't even feel like doing that. I gazed morosely at the stained-glass windows, full of angels with solid-looking arms and hefty legs standing around trying to seem mystical and transcendent. 'They're about as ethereal, those angels,' Bella remarked, 'as the lacrosse team.' Their plaited tresses hung down and very conveniently hid any breasts they may have had. They were draped in cunningly-arranged sheets and wore no shoes. You could see their pinkish, feathery wings sticking up over the edges of their shoulders. I sat there wishing that Chapel were over.

We went to lunch at the Royal George Hotel in Coleston. Parents, taking their daughters out from Egerton Hall for the day, often came to this dining-room, decorated in pale green and cream, with discreet little chandeliers dotted here and there over the high ceiling. There were many Egerton Hall girls in their navy-blue regulation Sunday suits, looking like a flock of dark birds pecking away at their tasty lunches in the midst of the normal residents, who were all uniformly ancient and seemed to favour beige or sage-green jersey, and rows of pearls. We, however, being Sixth Formers, were allowed to wear our own clothes.

'Darling, do pass Alice the mint sauce,' said Marjorie, 'and Bella, dear, I should go easy on the roast potatoes, if I were you.'

'Pass the potatoes, please, Daddy,' said Bella, and helped herself to four, deliberately choosing the crispiest and oiliest.

Marjorie sighed audibly. 'You young girls,' she said, 'just have no idea how easy it is to let your looks go. One has to be so careful.'

'Bella doesn't,' said Alice. 'She eats a frightful lot, honestly, and it never makes any difference at all.'

Alice's punishment for springing to Bella's defence was a pitying smile from Marjorie. She said:

'You, Alice dear, look very thin indeed to me. Positively unwell. Are you sure you're getting enough vitamins?'

'Oh, yes, thank you,' said Alice. 'I'm much stronger than I look, really.'

'Well, you must make sure that Bella shares her fruit out with you. I've given her simply bags and bags of apples, so do have some, and please, Alice and Megan, make sure that Bella has apples rather than those dreadful Mars bars to which she's addicted. We don't want her turning spotty, now do we?'

'No danger of that,' said Bella's father, who up till now had been silently munching through his lamb. 'Skin like untrodden snow, Bella's got. Always has had. Always will have.'

Marjorie flashed him a look of pure hatred and her mouth tightened. She changed the subject at once.

'And how have you all got on with the examinations?' she said.

Before leaving the hotel for the cinema, we went to the Ladies, Alice and Bella and I, to repair our make-up and fiddle with our hair and enjoy the luxury of thick pink carpets, bowls of plastic flowers, and mirrors lit with pink lamps.

'I used to hate going out in uniform,' said Bella, 'when we were in the Lower School. I hated everyone in Coleston knowing we were from Egerton Hall.'

'It's all right for you,' I said. 'Your home clothes are lovely. Mine are all . . . I don't know . . . wrong somehow. I'd rather be wearing uniform. Then people say: oh, she looks like that because of the uniform, and they imagine how nice you'd look in real clothes.'

'You need someone to go with you when you're trying on,' said Bella.

'I go with Dorothy, generally,' I said.

'And it shows,' said Bella.

'Don't be beastly,' said Alice. 'Megan can't help it. And anyway, she always looks nice.'

'I'm not beastly, Alice,' said Bella. 'I know Megan looks nice, but for your party, for instance . . . well, she's going to need something special and I think it'd be better if she let me or you choose it, and not Dorothy.'

'The party's not till June,' I said. 'I can't think why you're so worried about it in January. It's only Alice who's going to be the Belle of the Ball, and who's had silk worms in China nibbling themselves into a frenzy for years.'

Alice laughed. 'It's silk and lace, my dress, and the only

reason you know about it is because Aunt Ivy goes on about everything so much. She's making it, so of course, she has to keep having these conferences with Aunt Lily, who designed it, and we keep having to have these fittings.'

'Is the dreaded Violette coming to the party?' I asked. 'I'd love to meet her, after all your tales.'

'After the fuss she caused at my christening,' said Alice, 'I don't think they'd like to risk *not* inviting her.'

'Not inviting whom where, darlings?' trilled Marjorie, pushing herself into the room with a majestic swing of the pink door.

'Nothing, Marjorie,' Bella sang out as she swept from the room. 'Don't pick up fag ends!'

Alice followed her. Marjorie turned to me and wrinkled her nose slightly. A true grimace was hard for her. It would have made too many creases in her smooth, beige foundation.

'I can't think where Bella picks up such language,' she said to me. 'We pay enough to send her to that blasted school, Heaven knows, and then it's fag ends all over the place!' She shuddered delicately, and turned up the fur collar of her suit.

'We all say things like that, Mrs Lavanne,' I said to placate her. 'Much worse things than that, sometimes.'

Marjorie appeared to have lost interest in Bella, and in our conversation. She was staring into the mirror as if mesmerized by her own reflection, pulling with a dainty finger at the skin under her eyes.

'This *is* a kind mirror,' she smiled. 'I expect it must be the pink lights. I wonder whether I shouldn't put some in at home. What do you think, Megan? Don't you think it's effective? I can hardly see the crow's feet at all, can you?'

I bent down so that our faces were in the mirror together. 'What are crow's feet?' I asked.

'The little lines . . . wrinkles around the eyes one gets as one gets older. Haven't you heard of them before?'

'No, no, never. But cheer up,' I said. 'I can't see any, anyway.' I was lying, of course, but you couldn't tell unpleasant truths to someone who'd just bought you a really delicious lunch. I couldn't have lied very convincingly, however, because Marjorie said not a word. Dark furrows appeared on her brow, and you could almost see the anger rising from every line of her body, like steam. I had never met anyone who was so anxious about their appearance. Every sign of age she noticed seemed to make her more and more desperate. She opened her crocodile-skin handbag, and began a ferocious attack on her mouth with a lipstick whose colour was uncomfortably like the scarlet of freshly-spilled blood.

We always had to be back at school in time for Evensong. Between the end of Evensong and bedtime on Sunday night, there were a couple of hours that were a kind of limbo, an emptiness when it seemed to all of us that one week had ended and the next had not yet properly begun. It was a time I always thought of as sad, probably because so many people had seen their parents during the day, and felt homesick on Sunday nights. There was always, in the Junior House anyway, more cheering up to do on Sunday nights than at any other time.

'I'm never sad on Sunday nights,' said Bella. 'I love coming back from going out with Her. It's no hardship at all.'

For the Sixth Form, after Evensong was when we all crowded into the S.C.R. together. Prefects left their studies and we all lolled about, devouring the goodies devoted sets of parents had given us, and which were meant to last us until the next time we saw them. Pippa Grey was toasting a crumpet in front of the gas fire, having previously impaled it on her compass, and Marion Tipton was doing her best to divide a Fuller's walnut cake into seven pieces.

'I don't see why you can't have a bit, Sally,' she said. 'Then it'll be eight pieces and much easier to cut.'

'Because I'm slimming.'

'Well, why don't I cut a piece for you and then you can give it to someone else?'

'No.' Sally was adamant. 'If you cut it, I shall want it. If there are only seven bits there anyway, then I can say there's not enough for me and that's that.'

Marion sighed and continued to measure and calculate.

'Here, Sal,' said Bella from the depths of the armchair into which she had slumped, 'have an apple. Marjorie's best, I promise you, and all home-grown. They look positively slimming, don't they?'

She took one out of a paper-bag that lay beside the chair, and held it up for everyone to see.

'In fact,' she said, 'it looks so marvellous that I think I shall have one too.'

'Does that mean,' said Marion, 'that I can cut this blasted thing into six?'

'No, you can't,' Bella said. 'So there. I shall have both. Cake first, and apple later.'

'There you are, then,' said Marion, 'and if anyone feels hard done by, then I'm sorry. That's the best I can do.'

After the cake had been finished, after every morsel of gossip from the day had been thoroughly chewed over, after a few frantic searches for work that was due to be given in the next day and a major hunt behind desks and sofas for Rowena Menzies' copy of *Renny's Daughter* without which she refused to go to bed, Alice, Bella and I began the long trudge up to the Tower Room. Bella had the apple in her hand.

'The question is,' she said, 'can I wait till I get into bed to eat this, or is it too tempting? Shall I succumb like Eve? Look how red and shiny it is! I wonder if it *is* plastic? I wouldn't put anything past Marjorie.'

She opened her mouth wide and took a huge bite out of the apple. The next moment, she was choking. Alice noticed first.

'Megan! Look, Bella's choking . . . oh, goodness, Megan. What shall we do?'

Luckily, we were almost at the landing where Matron had her room. I shouted at Alice:

'Quick! Get Matron. Tell her it's urgent.'

Alice flew up the stairs. Bella's eyes had grown enormous in her face, and her arms were flailing about. I tried everything I could think of: banging her on her shoulder, holding her arms above her head . . . and all the time she was growing blue under my very eyes. It seemed like years till Matron arrived, although it couldn't have been more than a few seconds. I was so relieved to see her, I hardly noticed what she did, but she seemed to give Bella a punch in the chest. Whatever it was, it worked. A lump of apple the size of a golf ball flew out of Bella's mouth and she sank down on to the stairs like a rag doll. Matron put her arms around her.

'There,' she said. 'That's better. Now, Alice, stop crying at once. You and Megan behaved very sensibly. It was your speed, Alice, that quite probably saved Bella's life.'

'I'd never have thought to get you,' sobbed Alice, 'if Megan hadn't told me to.'

'Quite so,' said Matron. 'Well done, Megan. And you, young lady,' (she turned to look down at Bella) 'will have learned to eat a trifle more daintily. How are you feeling?'

'Fine,' Bella tried to say, but her voice had almost entirely disappeared.

'I think that apple must have hurt your throat. I shall

drive you to the San. and then Dr Murray can have a look at you tomorrow. Does your throat hurt?'

Bella nodded.

'I thought so,' said Matron. 'Megan, you and Alice go into my sitting room and make yourselves a cup of cocoa before bed. You both deserve it. You can go and visit Bella tomorrow. Come on, now, child.'

Bella tottered to her feet. She and Matron staggered downstairs together.

In Matron's room, over the cocoa, Alice said: 'She could have died, Megan, couldn't she?'

'It'd take a lot more than a bit of apple to kill Bella,' I said.

'But she could have, couldn't she?'

'I suppose so. But she didn't. So shut up about dying and drink your cocoa.'

We drank in silence and then went up to the Tower Room together.

*

London *April 20th 1962*

SOMETIMES, when I wake up, you've gone. It's not your fault of course, because you have to travel right across London to get to your lab. in time for 8.45. I like to lie in bed late, though. It's the only thing about Egerton Hall that I really don't miss – that hideous seven o'clock bell. Oh, I was used to it, of course I was, and never quite like Alice, having to be physically pulled by the hair from a deep, deep sleep, but still, I shudder to remember the horror of waking up on cold dark mornings, when the lino was like a sheet of ice, and there was frost on the inside of our windows. One tiny radiator that was only ever luke-warm was all we had: no gas fires, naturally. Was it any wonder that we used to put most of our clothes on under the blankets?

Here, the gas fire is always already on when I wake up. You know how much I like its apricot glow. There's sometimes a note on the table: 'Late back tonight on acc. important meeting. Love, S.' or 'Could you get some toothpaste – Macleans pref.' It's a far cry, isn't it, from Keats to Fanny Brawn in July 1819: 'I will imagine you Venus tonight, and pray, pray, pray to your star like a heathen.' Still, the first time I ever saw your handwriting on a piece of paper, I nearly died of bliss. Just the shapes of the letters on the page, the idea of your hand, your pen, making my own name appear in black on all that white – oh, it was wonderful! And at the time I had no quarrel with the content, either. You wanted to see me again. You mentioned a time, and I knew I would be there. You had taken the trouble to find out (how? whom did you ask? Fiona?) when I was free, and I knew how I was going to spend the time between the moment of finding your note (Sunday night) and Wednesday evening at five o'clock. I was going to press your small, neat words close to my heart, fold them up and tuck them into my bra, so that I could at least be touching something *you* had written. I was going to take your note out twenty times a day, and look at it. Its words would become an enchantment, a rune. What did it matter to me that you weren't Keats? You were you: a scientist and not a poet. I was writing enough poetry for both of us, great unstoppable spurts of the stuff. I felt as though a lid had been taken off a steaming cauldron. I have to admit, though, that maybe Dorothy was right, after all. Looking at it now, I see that most of it *is* a morass of sentimentality and all of it is so purple that you could use it on cut knees instead of gentian violet.

*

ALICE and I went to see Bella in the San. on Monday at lunchtime.

'I'm a fraud,' she said. 'There's nothing whatsoever wrong with me. I'm just lying here being spoiled.'

'But you nearly died, Bella,' Alice wailed.

'Oh, Alice, do stop being so melodramatic. I'm not, dead, am I? That's the point. It's useless to say: "you nearly died". I mean, we don't know how near death we are at any time, do we?'

Alice thought about this. I said:

'Oh, shut up about death, you two. Alice, you *do* keep going on about it. I've got something much more interesting to show you. Look.'

I fished inside my blouse and took a note out of my bra.

'What on earth is that and why are you keeping it there?' Bella asked.

'Because it's precious and it's private. It's from Simon.'

Bella read it.

'Gadzooks, sirrah,' she giggled, 'an assignation! How smashing! Wednesday at five . . . uhm . . . I think I'm just going to creep up to the Tower Room and . . .'

'Don't you dare, Bella,' I shouted. 'Oh, you wouldn't, would you? Oh, please, please don't spoil it.'

''Course I won't. I might even station myself on the landing below and keep *cave*. Never let it be said that Bella Lavanne stopped the course of true love running smooth . . . and in return you'll lie like mad for me on the 17th.'

'I suppose so,' I sighed. 'But look at the note. Don't you think it's blissful?'

'I don't know that I'd necessarily call "Dear Megan, How

97

about Wednesday at five, Tower Room? Love, Simon." blissful.'

'But he said "love". And "dear". "Dear Megan" . . . I mean, he didn't have to put my name at all, or "Love, Simon", if it comes to that.'

'And,' said Alice, 'he went to the trouble of finding out when she was free. And he must have taken a risk coming right up to the Tower Room and putting it on her chest-of-drawers. The window was shut, so he couldn't use the scaffolding.'

'I'm bored with this conversation,' said Bella. 'Guess who's in the San. with me. You'll never guess.'

'Tell us,' I said.

'Miss van der Leyden. Sister told me.'

'What's the matter with her?' I said. 'She's never ill.'

'I don't know.'

'I'll go and ask Sister,' I said, 'if I can visit her before we go back to afternoon school.'

Sister was exactly like a series of cottage loaves enclosed in a starched, white overall. She had a round face topped with a round, grey bun, and a mound-shaped bosom that seemed stuck to the front of her body. Her cheeks were pink and shiny. She wore a watch pinned to her breast pocket, and it bounced around as she walked, sometimes bumping into a thermometer in a silver case.

'Miss van der Leyden,' she told me, 'simply needs to rest. She's not been feeling quite herself lately.'

'May I say hello to her? Just for a second?'

'Creep in, dear, and see if she's awake. I don't want you waking her up, mind you . . . not if she's asleep. She's in Room 4, up the stairs and to the left.'

I opened Miss van der Leyden's door as quietly as I could. At first I thought she must be dead, because her hands were folded on the counterpane, her head was lolling and her mouth gaped open. Then she let out a small, snoring kind of breath, and I jumped back. Her fingers, thickened, knotted and twisted like the hidden roots of trees, lay so still. I'd never seen them idle before. Always Miss van der Leyden was making something: little 4-ply cardigans for other people's babies, and gossamer lace mats to sit under the perfume bottles on the dressing-tables of prettier women. I closed the door, hoping that I hadn't disturbed her. Perhaps, I thought, I'll come and visit her tomorrow . . . but I knew I wouldn't. I would leave it until she was back in her little room at the top of Junior House. Seeing her lying there frightened me. I remembered the curtain of the room blowing a little in the draught, and thought it could have been a corner of the wings of the Angel of Death . . . haven't I said I'm of a fanciful turn of mind? I put my hand on my heart to feel the crackling of Simon's note and promptly forgot about everything else. If the Four Horsemen of the Apocalypse had galloped into the San. on skeleton mounts, I wouldn't even have seen them.

*

London *April 22nd 1962*

I NEVER did return to the San. to visit Miss van der Leyden. Bella came back into school that evening, and in the fever of waiting for Wednesday and our second meeting, I forgot all about her. Now she is in hospital in Coleston and it nags at me that I can't go and visit her every week. Nobody has said what's the matter with her, but she must be quite old, and I can't help feeling she may have something terrible and be dying of it. Alice goes, I know, and I feel about this a mixture of relief and resentment, even jealousy. Miss van der Leyden has always had a special place in her heart for Alice, because Alice, of all of us, was the child who knew immediately and instinctively how to hold her knitting needles, how to make that length of wool running between her fingers twist effortlessly into smooth expanses of fabric and intricate patterns. The rest of us produced tatty, uneven pieces of stocking stitch, full of holes, and with edges that went in and out like rocky coastlines. Mine was one of the worst in the whole class. Only Alice, at the end of a term, had made a little yellow mateneé jacket, complete with ribbon trimmings. Golden hands, Miss van der Leyden said she had, and it was true.

'*Tenez, mes enfants,*' she would say, 'the back of Alice's embroideries is as neat as the front, do you see?' She would hold up the work to show us.

'The front of my embroidery,' said Bella under her breath, 'is just as messy as the back. Isn't that the same thing?'

'You know it isn't, stupid,' I said, trying not to laugh.

Bella, Alice had written to me, refused to go to the hospital 'and so I go on my own, but I hate hospitals. They smell so awful, and everyone looks so ghastly, especially Miss v.d.L. Her face is quite grey. I wish you were here to come with me.'

Whatever happens, whatever I decide to do, one thing is certain: I shall have to visit Miss van der Leyden in hospital. I don't want her to think I've forgotten about her. Also, it's not fair that Alice should have to keep going to a place she hates all on her own. I wish sometimes that Alice were not such a good letter-writer. She's had so much practice. Of the three of us, she was the one who was always writing letters to this aunt or that; sending cards to cousins, and during the last few weeks, writing letters to Jean-Luc. This had become almost a daily event and it was lucky for me that it had. Alice swapped with me and took prep. in the J.P.R., happily attending to her correspondence while I climbed the stairs to the Tower Room and waited for you.

*

AT half past five, I was sitting on my bed and there was no sign of Simon. I went over to the window and looked out, my heart still beating very fast from the terror of creeping up all those stairs as quietly as I could, and trying at the same time to look nonchalant. I had worked out a plausible story in case anyone (Matron, Miss Doolittle) was unexpectedly patrolling the corridors: I just had to run up and fetch my Spanish Lit. file that I'd stupidly left in the Tower Room. But I didn't meet anyone. As Saint John of the Cross puts it in his poem, the whole house was hushed, but my heart sounded as loud as a drum in my own ears. I left the window and glanced round the room to make sure that everything was tidy. Absurd notions filled my head: I should have brought up something to eat . . . been able to offer Simon a cup of tea . . . and then, quite suddenly he was there, tapping on the glass of the window. I went over and let him in.

'Hello,' he said. 'Frightfully sorry to be so late, but I had to wait until the coast was clear . . .'

'It's all right,' I said, and then couldn't think what to say next. I didn't know how to act, how to be. I didn't know where to put my hands, or what happened next. My mouth felt dry.

'Are you glad I'm here?' Simon said, sitting down on Bella's bed.

'Oh, yes,' I said, and because I felt I had to say something, almost anything else, I added: 'I'm just a bit nervous. I mean I *was*, coming upstairs during prep. What if we're caught?'

'We won't be caught. Everyone's busy. No one's going to come looking for you now, or me, come to that. Oh, Megan, don't look so terrified! Come over here and sit by me. Let me loosen your hair again. I love to touch it, to smell it. Have you forgotten the last time?'

I shook my head, meaning 'no' because I simply did not trust myself to speak. I was sure that if I so much as opened my mouth, words of love would pour out of it before I could stop them, and spill into the air. I went silently to sit beside Simon, and he put his arms around me and kissed me and undid my plait and I felt as though every part of me were also being unravelled: as though my body had turned into liquid, rushing gold.

It seems that in kissing you don't need an awful lot of practice before you become rather good at it, and not only good at it, but also able to sort out in your head the different kinds of kisses, the feelings behind them. Last time, maybe because it was the first time for me, everything was trembling, tentative, shivery. My legs felt weak, I remembered, and my head swam. Now, I could feel an urgency, a force running through both our bodies like a fever, a need to be close, to merge, to sink one into the other. I could feel Simon's hands undoing the buttons on my school blouse.

'No, please . . . please don't,' I said.

'But why not? Don't you want me to? I want to see you . . .'

'No. Not here.'

'But there *is* nowhere else. Please, Megan.'

'No, I'd feel funny. I couldn't.'

Simon smiled. 'I'm rushing you. I'm sorry. I really am

sorry. I won't rush you again. Come and kiss me and we'll forget about it.'

So I went and I kissed him and maybe he forgot about it, but I didn't. I felt torn in half. Part of me wanted him to touch me and wanted to touch him. What would his back be like? His legs? I could hardly bear to imagine how his skin would feel. Another part of me said: but you hardly know him . . . you've hardly spoken. You know nothing about him. I pulled away from him in the end and tried to speak, tried to have a conversation, but it was difficult to concentrate in between kisses. He left after an hour, and I lay on the bed and waited for the bell to call me to supper.

That night, Bella interrogated me:

'Don't you two ever talk at all? Did you find out anything at all about him?'

'He's got two sisters. His mother is a widow. They live in Brighton. He met Dorothy at some scientific party. He's only helping out because he's waiting to start a job in some school in London next term.'

'Did you ask him about Fiona?' Bella wanted to know.

'What about her?'

'Well, is he kissing her as well? You on Mondays, Wednesdays and Fridays, and her on Tuesdays, Thursdays and Saturdays, rather like the Bath Rota. Maybe he has to fit in Dorothy as well. They do so often seem to be having a chinwag and a smile together. Almost whenever one sees them.'

'Simon's very polite,' I said. 'He has to be polite to Dorothy.'

'Not that polite, I shouldn't have thought.'

'Oh, Bella, shut up! You are awful!' Alice said. 'He couldn't possibly be doing something like that. No one could.'

'Don't be so naive,' Bella laughed. 'He could easily. I should think it would be very easy for him.'

'I'm sure he isn't,' I said, although I wasn't as sure as I tried to sound. 'I mean, he kisses me so . . . well, so very passionately. I'm sure he loves me. I'm sure he wouldn't be kissing someone else.' My voice trailed away. Suddenly I was full of doubts, worries that hadn't been there before.

'Has he said he loves you?' Alice wanted to know.

'No, but that doesn't mean anything. I haven't said I love him.'

'Do you love him?' Bella asked.

'Oh, yes, I'd do anything for him. Anything at all.'

'You wouldn't even let him touch your breasts,' said Bella. 'You've just told us.'

'Well, I was frightened. I wanted him to, really, but I didn't dare. It seemed so strange, all that sort of thing happening up here, in this room. I mean, what if someone came in? There isn't even a lock on the door.'

'Cowardy, cowardy custard!' Bella grinned. 'He'll have his wicked way with you before long, though. Bet you anything.'

'Do you *have* to call it that?' I was suddenly irritated, annoyed at Bella for reducing feelings that were nearly overwhelming me to the status of something from a cheap romance. 'I love him. Maybe you've never been in love and can't understand how I feel.'

'Oh, sorry I spoke!' said Bella. 'I shall treat your precious Love with the respect it deserves in the future, never fear.'

'Oh, for goodness' sake,' said Alice, who hated any kind of row and was always smoothing over situations like this, 'don't start fighting over nothing. Go to sleep, both of you.'

Bella sighed. 'I didn't mean to laugh at you, you know, Megan, but you shouldn't take everything so seriously. Just because he's the first, doesn't necessarily mean he'll be the last. He'll be gone in a few weeks and you'll probably never see him again.'

'Oh, don't say that, Bella,' Alice groaned. 'You're making Megan sad all over again.'

'No, she's not,' I said, 'it's OK. I'm sure she's right, Alice, and I shouldn't make so much of it. As a matter of fact, that's probably exactly what'll happen at the end of term: I'll stay and he'll go and that will probably be that. Actually, I don't know what he sees in me, if you really want to know.'

'It's your sterling character,' said Bella. 'Your integrity, honesty, etc. etc. Or your brains.'

'Don't be stupid,' I said. 'I don't think people get attracted by sterling qualities.'

'Maybe he thinks you're pretty,' Alice suggested.

'But I'm not,' I said. 'Not especially.'

'There must be something about you,' said Bella, 'that appeals to him. Something physical that drives him wild with desire. Something deep and secret that no one will ever know which thrills him to the core . . .'

'What a lot of rot you do talk, Bella,' I said lightly, but I smiled into the darkness, thinking of the way Simon's hands had trembled in my hair, of how he had covered his face with its strands, twined it in his fingers, and breathed endearments into it. I felt weak thinking these thoughts. I lifted the plaited weight of it and felt the silkiness and intricacy of the braid in my hand like a smooth rope.

The others fell asleep shortly after this conversation, but I stayed awake, imagining a life in which Simon and I would share a house that looked very much like Alice's. Alice's parents had a wide, wide bed covered with a maroon satin counterpane. I closed my eyes and imagined myself and Simon in such a place, lying on those crisp, white sheets with our bodies entwined. I must have fallen asleep in the end.

Perhaps because of what Bella had said, I seemed to see Simon and Fiona together a great deal during the next couple of weeks. It wasn't that he had stopped coming to the Tower Room. Those meetings had continued and increased in frequency, so that by the middle of February, I almost knew what it was like to live two totally separate lives. In one, I was a prefect, a schoolgirl. I did my duties, supervised Junior Prep., studied for my lessons, took part in class discussions, sat around in the study listening to Radio Lux., went to Chapel, sang in the Choir, gossiped with my friends. No one seeing me could have guessed that almost every other day, as if by a kind of magic, I would change, transform myself as I went up that staircase to meet Simon, and that in the Tower Room I would lose myself in sensations, feelings, agonies of love and desire. For hours, we lay on the bed (my bed . . . I made sure of that) and explored one another. I thought each time that I would faint away from the strength of my love, that it would, eventually, drown me, carry me away completely like a wave. I hadn't, as Bella rather crudely put it, 'gone all the way' but that was because I was frightened, terrified of becoming pregnant. Still, each time we met, I feared that this would be the time that I wouldn't be able to resist . . . I would allow myself to be engulfed by love and lose all grasp of common sense. But there was the matter of Fiona to be dealt with. One evening, I asked him directly:

'Are you meeting Fiona Mackenzie like this, Simon?'

He threw back his head and laughed so much I had to cover his mouth with my hand because he was making such a noise.

'Don't be silly, Megan, honestly! It's a full-time job clambering up here all the time, I can tell you.'

'Well, no one makes you,' I said huffily. 'You don't *have* to come.'

'But I *want* to, can't you understand? I'm in a complete tizz over you, Megan, you must know that. I can't bloody think straight for dreaming about you all the time. Can't you feel how much I want you, Megan, when we're together like this, in this room? Fiona Mackenzie's nothing, truly. It's hard to avoid her, that's all. She's in the labs. all the time, isn't she? I don't see any point in being unfriendly.' He beamed at me, pleased with himself.

I believed him. I had to believe him, and needed to believe him. Nevertheless, late that night I lay in bed and went over his words. Words are very important to me. They mean something. They carry associations. 'I'm in a complete tizz over you' somehow didn't have the force or the weight of 'I love you'. They seemed frivolous, purely physical. 'Can't you feel how much I want you?' Yes, that was exactly what I *could* feel, but it was more than that I wanted. I made a silent resolution: if Simon ever says it, sincerely and truly, if he ever says the words: 'I love you' and really means them, I will let him make love to me. If he says them, those syllables will be an open sesame, an enchanted password.

The next day, Dorothy met me in the corridor, and stopped to talk.

'I've been meaning to send for you, dear,' she said. 'It has been such a long time since we've had a good chat. I was very pleased with your examination results, by the bye.'

'Thank you,' I said. I thought to myself: exams! what ages ago they were, and how trivial and silly they now seem compared with what I'm feeling. I had almost forgotten I'd done well . . . and why did Dorothy have to say 'by the bye' when everyone else in the world said 'by the way'? Dorothy continued:

'I'm having a small tea-party on Saturday, in my room. Just Simon . . . Simon Findlay I mean, of course, and you and Fiona Mackenzie. Do come, dear.'

'That'll be very nice, Dorothy. Thanks tons. I have to go to French now. See you on Saturday.'

Was there a tiny flutter in Dorothy's voice as she said Simon's name, or was I imagining it? I rushed along School Corridor, cursing the malign fate that had made Fiona good at science. Just my luck. How was I going to be able to eat sandwiches and drink tea in the same room with Fiona, Simon and Dorothy? I was meeting Simon on Friday night. My neck and arms would be bruised from his kisses, and I'd have to sit there making polite conversation . . . oh, it would be dreadful!

That afternoon, Bella came into the study just as Alice and I were settling down to our work.

'Is Marion not here?' she said. 'Goody goody. I can use her desk. The Walker creature is slowly killing me, and besides, we have to have a planning discussion.'

'What are we planning?' I said. 'You are a nuisance, Bella, honestly you are. How am I ever going to finish this essay and give it in by suppertime?'

'It won't take long and then I'll shut up, I promise. Only I want to arrange the Drop. I think that's what it's called.'

'I don't know about you, Megan,' said Alice, 'but I haven't the foggiest idea what's going on. What's a drop? What are we planning?'

'Oh, Alice, don't be so feeble!' said Bella. 'You know jolly well that I've thought of nothing else for weeks. Saturday is the day I'm climbing down the scaffolding and doing my singing with Pete and the band. You must remember.'

'Yes, I do now,' said Alice. 'Of course I do.' She sighed. 'It's just that I hate the idea of it so much – you climbing down in the dark and running through the forest . . . I mean the forest, Bella, and at night!' Alice shivered. 'I'd be petrified. I would, truly. And that's not to mention worrying about getting caught, and getting expelled. I do wish you wouldn't go.'

'But I've got to, can't you see that? I've been living for it. You just haven't a clue how marvellous, how splendiferously gorgeous it feels to be up there, with everyone looking at you and listening to you and your voice, your music just floating out of your mouth and over their heads like a . . . like a beautiful white bird.'

'I think I'd faint,' said Alice. 'I think you're fantastically brave. I wouldn't do it for anything. It's almost more terrifying than the forest at night.'

Bella laughed. 'It's not a forest, Alice, it's a wood, and anyway, where's your *Malory Towers* spirit, gels? Don't you remember Alicia and Darrell Rivers? Whatever would they think if they saw you trembling at the thought of an adventure? This is a real-life, school story kind of adventure and all I'm asking is a tiny bit of help from you, my chums, and you're turning into . . . into drips, that's what.'

'It's all right, Bella,' I said. 'We'll help you, of course we will. What do you want us to do?'

'The main thing is, could you put my party clothes somewhere safe, just inside the forest? There's that little shed. You know . . . you go up behind the San. and there it is: hardly in the forest at all, really. I mean, I'd do it myself, only I don't want to leave my stuff there too long and on Friday I'm doing netball at Games time and lessons all afternoon, then I'm taking prep. I'd leave it till Saturday, but you've got Dorothy's tea-party, Megan, and Alice, you're going on this Art Gallery outing, aren't you? So it's got to be Friday. You two can wander over to the San. on your walk, can't you? Please?'

'I suppose so,' I said. 'But what on earth are you going to put your clothes in?'

Bella smiled triumphantly: 'My sack, of course.'

Sacks were the large, shopping-bag shaped things that we all carried our books around in. They were tough, made of a canvas that was as thick as tarpaulin, and held an enormous amount.

'You should take my sack,' said Alice. 'Mine hasn't got any writing on it at all. Even my name tape's fallen off. If anyone finds yours, they'll know immediately whose it is.' Bella's sack had slogans, names, and huge red hearts drawn in biro all over it. She had written 'Bella Lavanne' in italic capitals and green ink down one side, had stated that she loved: Buddy Holly, Elvis Presley, The Everley Brothers, Jerry Lee Lewis, Connie Francis, and a few other people whose names had been rained on, and had run into blue and red messes here and there.

'Good thinking, old sport,' she said to Alice. 'You'll get quite good at all this adventure stuff in the end. So, you'll do it, will you?'

'I suppose so,' I said. 'What are you wearing?'

'My red circular skirt, and high heels. And I've got a pair of black stockings. And I thought I'd wear (if you'll be an absolute angel and lend it to me) your black cardigan. I'll wear it with the buttons down the back, of course.'

'Where's Pete meeting you?' Alice asked. 'Why don't you ask him to come to the hut?'

'Too late now,' Bella said, 'and anyway, I don't mind about

the forest at night. I shall have my torch and it's only five minutes' walk to the road. I'll be fine.'

'Just be careful,' I said. 'You are taking a risk, you know. What if you're caught?'

Bella burst out laughing. 'I like that! You're a fine one to talk about risk! All that spooning in the Tower Room. Asking for trouble, I call that.'

I think I blushed. Then Marion came back from a lesson, and we changed the subject. Bella sat down in between the desks, and I turned to my essay, wondering how I was going to write intelligently about the role of Fate in the short stories of Guy de Maupassant in the half hour left before supper.

Spooning in the Tower Room: that's what Bella called it. That's, I suppose, what it was, only I used to think of it so differently. I made the room, in my mind, into an enchanted place, not part of the real world at all. And we changed too, Simon and I. I felt it every time I went up the stairs, every time I heard his movements on the scaffolding outside the window. We were transformed into more beautiful, more amusing, altogether better people. Our silliest remarks and giggles became brilliantly witty, our most trivial words profound and moving, and when we spoke of the future, of what our lives would be like, it was as though we were describing Heaven, as though our futures were very distant from us, and not in any way connected to the present. The whole of time and the world and everything in it shrank each time we met until it was us, us, us and nothing but us existed.

'I feel,' said Alice on Friday afternoon, as we walked along the path towards the San. and the forest, 'like a criminal.'

'I know,' I answered. 'Me too.' I was carrying Alice's sack full of Bella's stuff hidden (I hoped) under my cloak. 'I feel as if I'm carrying a body . . . going to bury it somewhere.'

'Don't,' Alice shivered. 'I can't bear the forest.'

'But why ever not? It's only trees, when you come right down to it. No animals, apart from the odd rabbit, I'm sure. Nothing to be scared of, really.'

'I know,' said Alice. 'I know that *really* but . . . well, I had this book when I was little. I can't even remember what the story was. It could have been *Red Riding Hood*, I suppose, but the pictures were horrible: these tree trunks which had human faces and all the branches like arms reaching out and twig fingers at the ends . . . ugh. And it's worse in winter when there are no leaves.'

'But they were only pictures in a story. You shouldn't let your imagination run away with you. You'll be saying this old wooden hut is like the witch's sugar house in *Hansel and Gretel* in a minute.'

Alice giggled. 'Nonsense, Megan! It's just an old gardening shed. It's where Mr Carter keeps the roller for the cricket pitches and the lawnmower and things. Now *you're* being silly.'

'I know I am,' I said, as we put Bella's clothes in the appointed spot, just inside the door. I glanced back at the shed as we walked away from it. The two small windows looked like eyes, the ramshackle roof was a hat, the door separating the windows, a nose, and there was even a scratch in the battered paintwork of the door just where the mouth should be on a face . . . and I was daring to accuse Alice of having too much imagination.

'Come on,' I said, 'it's nearly time for Prep.'

Alice nodded, and we hurried away and the trees vanished behind us as twilight gathered in their branches. Alice may still have been worrying about Bella for all I knew. My mind had run ahead of me, and I was already halfway up the stairs to the Tower Room, hardly able to catch my breath, longing for the moment when Simon's face would appear at the window.

'Do have another slice of Battenburg, Simon dear,' said Dorothy. 'And you too, of course, Megan and Fiona.'

Dorothy was beaming. I don't think I had ever seen her beam before. Her cheeks were either very flushed or (amazing thought!) she had put on some rouge. It must have been for Simon's benefit. Her behaviour could only be called 'flirtatious' and I found this new, strange Dorothy that I had never seen before very embarrassing, even worrying. Dorothy, after all, was my guardian, and I had no desire for Simon to think she was a fool.

So far, the party had gone as well as I could have expected. Fiona had batted her eyelashes, just as I had warned Simon she would when I was lying in his arms last night.

'Shut up about Fiona. I'm not interested in Fiona . . . it's you. Oh, Megan, come away with me! We could live together all the time, and never have to be apart, not for a minute, and never have to worry all the time about being found out, and I could use the stairs instead of climbing up walls like a spider . . . Come on, leave all this . . . let's run away. Now.'

I'd laughed. 'Don't be silly,' I'd said. 'I've got my A-levels.'

'Gosh, you're unromantic . . . come here . . .'

I thought about all this while the tea-party was going on. Dorothy had provided scones, and cucumber sandwiches, and shortbread, and Battenburg cake, which I hated more because of its nasty colouring than because of its taste. The conversation had covered such thrilling topics as The Arts v. The Sciences (in which I was outnumbered three to one), single sex schools v. coeducational establishments, the forth-coming lacrosse match against Benenden (well, all right, Fiona was Captain of Games) and, of course, A-levels.

'I have great hopes of Megan,' Dorothy said in tones that could only be described as 'skittish'. 'I know I'm only your guardian, dear, but I do have a mother's feelings in this. Megan's mother, you see,' she turned to Simon, 'entrusted the child to me, before she died.' Simon nodded solemnly. Dorothy continued: 'It is my responsibility to see that she . . . fulfills herself. Lives up to her potential. She has done rather well in these Mock Examinations.'

'Yes, I know,' said Simon. 'They were jolly good marks, weren't they?' He smiled happily at Dorothy. I froze in my chair and clutched my saucer so hard that I nearly spilled Earl Grey all over Dorothy's pale blue carpet. Oh, Simon, I thought, after what I told you last night about watching your tongue you have to go and make a mistake like that! I was considering spilling the tea on purpose and creating a diver-sion, but it was too late. Dorothy, exact, methodical and sharp, wasn't going to miss something like this. Her fluttery, girlish demeanour disappeared into thin air.

'How do you know what Megan's marks were, Simon?' she said and each word as it emerged from her mouth hung in the air like an icicle. Simon went on nonchalantly munch-ing his Battenburg.

'You told me, Dorothy, don't you remember?' he said, and flashed Dorothy a smile of such brilliance that you could almost see her thaw. The stiffness that had set in around her mouth and neck dissolved in the warmth. She said:

'Did I? I *am* a forgetful creature! Getting quite absent-minded in my old age . . .'

Simon knew his cue. 'Absent-minded, perhaps,' he twin-kled, 'but old, never.'

Dorothy forgot about me, about Fiona, about her tea-party, and simpered. That was the only word to describe what she was doing. I was more relieved than I can say when the tea-party was over. I felt I'd been holding my breath under water for a long, long time. Fiona walked down School Corridor with me.

'I call it absolutely revolting!' she said. 'She's old enough to be his mother.'

'She *was* being a bit silly,' I agreed weakly.

'Silly? I call it worse than that. Did you see how she was pawing him? Walking round behind his chair and resting her hand on his shoulder, pulling his arm through hers as she walked to the door with us . . . patting his *cheek*, for goodness' sake . . . oh, just playfully, of course. But I ask you, you're her child, practically, so you know what I mean. When is Dorothy ever playful?'

'No, she isn't. She isn't ever.'

'She is now. You should just see her in the labs. Honestly, she's a laughing-stock! "Simon, could you come here a second," or "Simon, I wonder whether you'd mind . . ." Seriously, she doesn't leave him alone for five minutes. It's pathetic, that's what it is. Got to dash now, though, Megan. See you later.' Fiona ran down Browning House's Study Passage before I could ask her the really important question: how did Simon behave when Dorothy was 'being pathetic'? I remembered looking at them in Chapel, coming out of the labs., walking along School Corridor. I paused now, wondering why Simon hadn't left Dorothy's room at the same time that Fiona and I did, my heart contracting at the thought of the two of them alone together.

Alice and I found it harder than usual to go to sleep that night. We'd arranged that Bella should tap on the window three times when she got back, and I would wake up and let her in. The alternative was not to be contemplated in this weather: sleeping with the window open till morning. We would have been frostbitten by dawn.

'I wonder what she's doing now,' Alice said at about midnight.

'Bopping . . . jiving . . . whatever they call it . . . with Pete or one of the others. Or maybe it's what she calls "her spot": the bit where she gets up and sings.'

'I hope she got there all right. I hope Pete met her and everything.'

'Well, of course he did,' I said, sounding more cheerful than I felt. 'And anyway, if he hadn't turned up . . . I mean, let's just say, then Bella would have come straight back here, wouldn't she?'

'Oh, yes,' agreed Alice, 'of course she would.'

The unspoken words 'if the forest didn't get her' stayed in the air over our beds and practically glowed like neon lights.

'There's nothing to fear in the forest, Alice, seriously. I know people tell lurid stories and so on, but they're none of them true.'

'I know,' said Alice, 'only sometimes I think that's where Angus must be . . . where he must be living, or something. It's ridiculous, really. I know it is.'

'Alice, you are the end,' I said. 'You are so *irritating* sometimes. Who is Angus? You've never said one word about anyone called Angus before, and I've known you since we were eleven. Are you a dark horse? Or crazy? Or what?'

'I've never told anybody about Angus, ever,' Alice whispered. 'I shouldn't have said anything now, either. Forget it, Megan.'

'Oh, no I won't,' I said. I'd been drifting off to sleep, but I was wide awake now. 'You're not getting away with that.

Now that you've said this much, you'll have to spill the beans. I do believe you've got a Past, Alice Gregson. Fancy not telling us!'

'There's nothing much to tell,' Alice said.

'Don't try and wriggle out of it,' I told her. 'I want every detail.'

'Angus was just a boy. He used to work for us, helping Mr Foster do the gardening for Dad. He lived in Egerton Parva with his mother. Then my dad sacked him.'

'What for?'

There was such a long silence that I had to ask the question again.

'What for, Alice? Come on, let's hear it.'

'For trying . . . for trying to kiss me.'

'Is that all?'

'He was . . .' Alice was groping for the words. 'Rough with me. He . . . he tore my dress a bit. He . . . I don't suppose he meant anything bad, but I couldn't bear him. He used to follow me round and look at me in a horrible way.'

'What do you mean, horrible?'

'I can't explain it, as if he was seeing me without my clothes on. I felt . . . all slimy whenever he looked at me, and then he kind of grabbed me one day, to kiss me, and I just screamed and ran away, but he was holding me so tight that a bit of my dress was torn. Oh, Megan, I was terrified! What if he'd touched me with that great, slobbery mouth? Oh, I couldn't have borne it . . . and then after my father told him he mustn't come back, not ever, then I felt guilty because I'd made him lose his job.'

'It wasn't your fault. If he'd wanted to keep his job he should have behaved himself. He sounds ghastly, like some kind of sex maniac. I think your father was quite right to get rid of him.' A thought occurred to me.

'Alice, when was all this?'

'Oh, ages and ages ago. I was thirteen. Nearly thirteen. I don't think of it for months at a time, and then suddenly something happens to remind me . . . like Bella going off in the dark.'

'What's Bella got to do with this foul Angus creature?'

'Nothing. Only, sometimes I think he's going to come back for me. I have this nightmare where I'm somewhere dark and he's there, waiting for me. It's horrid.'

I laughed, to cheer myself up as much as to comfort Alice, and said:

'I don't fancy Angus's chances if Bella gets hold of him! She'll give him such an earful, he'll run away and never be seen again.'

I was rewarded by a faint laugh from Alice and after that we slid into sleep.

It was six o'clock the next morning when Bella tapped on the window.

'Leaving it a bit late, aren't you?' I said. 'It's breakfast time in a couple of hours.'

'Oh, but Megan, it was so super! Absolutely the best thing ever! A real, proper dance . . . and I was such a hit, honestly. You'll never believe how much everyone loved my songs. And I've danced till my feet are worn down to the ankles. It was blissful. Completely divine. And the food! Look, I've even brought back some lovely little marzipan whadyoumacallits . . . *petits fours* . . . for you and Alice . . . oh, Megan, don't you even want to hear about it?'

'Later, Bella,' I groaned. 'Later. Please let me sleep now. I'll listen after breakfast.'

I tried to get back to sleep, but it was difficult. Bella was singing her favourite song under her breath, but it was loud enough to disturb me . . . love was getting closer . . . going faster than a roller coaster . . . every day. Blast Bella and blast Buddy Holly! I pulled my pillow over my head, and closed my eyes.

*

London *April 25th 1962*

BELLA came to visit yesterday. She was just up for the day, going to have something done at the dentist's. She asked how we were getting on, and I told her 'Fine' and we are, in a way, aren't we? It was difficult at the beginning, I'm not denying it. It became clear to me during those first days, as I dragged round London from one distressing little bedsit to the next while you travelled about looking for work, that love gets very easily pushed to the margins of one's life when it's a question of a roof over your head and the next meal. I'm not saying we ever starved or slept in the street, only that it's easy to have love as your major preoccupation when you have no other urgent problems to think about. It's been much better since we found this room and since you found a job, but oh, how small and unlovely this place is during the long hours when you're not here! I look at the cracks in the ceiling and the blistering paintwork of the windowsill. I consider the ghosts of flowers in the greasy carpet. I get into the rusty bath, uncomfortably suspicious that I haven't made it properly clean however hard I've scrubbed it. I cook baked beans on our one gas-ring and we eat on a table branded with the circular marks of other people's cups of coffee. It's hard to feel romantic.

*

THE next time Simon came to the Tower Room, I was still feeling aggrieved about what Fiona had told me. It wasn't so much that I was jealous, as that I resented not being told what a chummy relationship he had with Dorothy. I felt excluded. Simon noticed immediately. Well, it wasn't difficult. Usually, I'd run into his arms the minute he came through the window. On this occasion, though, I sat stiffly on my bed, with my face turned away from him.

'Megan, are you all right?' he asked, coming to sit beside me. 'Megan, look at me, please. Why aren't you saying anything?'

'There's nothing to say,' I answered in a whisper.

'Oh, come on, Megan! There's obviously something troubling you. Is it something I've said? Something I've done? Do tell me, Megan . . . this is just a waste of time. We have so little time together. Don't let's quarrel.' He took off the elastic band that held my plait, and shook my hair free.

'I'm not quarrelling, as far as I can see.'

Simon sighed and stood up. 'If you won't talk to me or tell me what's wrong then I might as well leave.' He turned towards the window. I couldn't, simply couldn't bear for him to leave. I felt as though I were being slowly torn apart from the inside.

'No, Simon, stay. Please stay. I'll tell you everything. It's not that I don't want to tell you, and it's nothing you've done, only it's . . . it's embarrassing. I shall feel such a fool even saying it.'

'Say it. Go on. Get it over with.'

'Very well. It's Dorothy. I've never seen her like that in all the years I've known her. She . . . she was flirting with you, Simon, at the tea-party. It looked as if she were . . .'

'She's a bit keen on me, it's true,' said Simon, 'only Megan, you *must* believe me, it's nothing I've said or done.

Honestly. I'm just normally friendly, that's all, and she . . . well, it started with a sort of motherly kind of thing . . . she'd give me tea, and we'd talk about my work and so forth, but now I have to make excuses. I feel funny going to her flat. I think she's fond of me, and well, I don't really know how to behave. I mean, I don't want to upset her or anything, but I don't want her getting the wrong idea, either.'

'I see. But, Simon, what does she *do*? I can't imagine it. Has she kissed you?'

'Oh, no, no,' Simon frowned. 'It's nothing like that. It's just . . . she comes and sits next to me if I'm on the sofa, and touches my hand if she gives me a plate – that kind of thing. In the labs. she's always coming in for little chats. It isn't anything I can't cope with. I just wish you hadn't seen it.'

'I don't mind,' I said, 'if you promise me, cross your heart and hope to die, that you're not keen on Dorothy.'

Simon started laughing. 'You must surely be joking! She could be my mother. Oh, Megan, you are an idiot! Haven't you got the foggiest idea about what I feel? Am I that tongue-tied that I haven't made it clear to you? It's you I love, Megan. You and nobody else. I don't know how much more plainly I can say it: listen. I love you.'

'Say it again.'

'I love you. Love you and love you and love you.'

'Really?'

'Truly.'

'And I love you,' I said. I had never said the words out loud before. They floated in the darkness of the Tower Room like stars. My mouth felt full of sweetness.

'Don't turn the light on, Megan,' Simon whispered. 'Come here.' So I let him make love to me, and I was glad I did.

Afterwards, all alone again, I lay trembling in the dark. I felt as though I were no longer contained within my flesh, but spread out like a piece of shining satin on the bed.

One day a couple of weeks after that night, I came into my study after lunch and found Dorothy sitting in one of the arm chairs. She hardly ever came into Austen House.

'Dorothy!' I said. 'Has something happened?'

She was looking rather pale, I thought, and all signs of that flirtatious manner I'd caught a glimpse of had disappeared.

'No, dear,' she said, 'I was simply passing the study on my way to see Miss Herbert and thought I would give you your pocket money for the month. You appear to have forgotten all about it.'

'I'm sorry, Dorothy, only I've been so busy, you see.'

'Indeed. Well, here's £5. Will that be enough until the end of term do you think?'

'Oh, yes, thank you, Dorothy.'

My pocket money, which bought me such things as stamps and stockings and bars of chocolate from the Tuck Shop came from the same fund as my school fees: the money my parents had left me when they died. There wasn't an enormous amount, but it was enough to allow me to finish my education. Dorothy handed me five one-pound notes and left the room, nodding goodbye rather frostily, I thought. I put my books down on the desk, and it was then that I saw the note. It wasn't even in an envelope, just hastily folded over and put on my desk, but I recognized my name in Simon's writing. My legs suddenly felt very weak, and in the split second before I opened it, I imagined all kinds of dreadful things were going to be contained in it: just as it said in all the magazines I'd read, he'd lost his respect for

122

me, now that we were lovers. He'd had second thoughts. He didn't really love me. This is what it actually said:

My Megan,
What about Sunday? Can you possibly miss the lecture? If you can, 7.00 p.m.
   I love you.
      Simon.

I was so happy, I burst into tears, and when Bella and Alice came into the study, I was sobbing from pure joy. I had meant, honestly and truly meant, to keep my secret to myself, and I had been successful for quite a long time, but now Bella read the note and guessed at once.

'You've done it,' she said. 'I knew you would in the end. I told you you'd be the first. When did it happen?'

'Bella, shut up and don't be coarse. Can't you see Megan's upset?' said Alice.

'I'm not upset,' I sniffed. 'I'm radiant with happiness, can't you tell?'

We all subsided in helpless giggles after that.

'Was it wonderful? Was it like Saint John of the Cross?' Bella wanted to know.

'Exactly!' I said. 'Like Saint John and Keats and everybody else.'

'And Buddy Holly?' Bella continued.

'Naturally. And Elvis and Racine and Shakespeare, oh, everybody you can think of!'

'Are you going to tell us what it was like? I'm dying to know every detail.'

'Bella, you're disgusting,' Alice shivered delicately. 'How can you be so matter-of-fact about it? I don't understand you.'

'It's a very matter-of-fact event, Alice, and in case it's escaped your notice, it's going on all over the place all the time. It's what's responsible for human life on the planet, no less, so you'd better stop being so prissy and stuck-up about it. It's not an awesome mystery, it's a fact of life!' Bella's cheeks were flushed with passion.

Alice was unrepentant. 'I don't care if it *is* a fact of life. It's private. You've got no right to go poking and prying all over the place. Fancy asking when it happened! It's none of your business.'

'Stop it!' I said. 'Just stop fighting, that's all. I won't tell you anything I don't want to tell you. It isn't worth quarrelling about, honestly.'

'Then we won't,' said Bella promptly. If she was quick to lose her temper, she was even quicker at forgetting all about it. She grinned at Alice. 'We'll be the best of friends.'

Peace was restored and eventually the conversation strayed away from my love-life and on to other things.

Lectures at Egerton Hall were supposed to be special treats. All kinds of interesting people came to talk to us about every subject under the sun. There were Geographical lectures (Up the Amazon with Notebook and Camera), Careers lectures (My Days as a Junior Policewoman), Cultural lectures (Poets I Remember, by a Famous Publisher) and sometimes lectures turned into recitals, and the grand piano would be played by ladies with dancing fingers, or we would be sung at by plump tenors who were never anywhere near handsome enough. Some of the lectures were interesting, some were entertaining and others were dreadfully boring, but you could always daydream if the worst came to the worst while the long, wooden pointer stabbed at the white canvas screen and the colour slides clicked into place, sometimes upside down. It was quite easy to miss a lecture if you were in the Sixth Form. You simply had to ask Miss Herbert.

'It's not like you, Megan dear . . . you're usually interested in everything. Still, if you feel you *must* work . . . but would you still see everyone into the Hall quietly for me? I'd be so grateful.'

'Yes, of course,' I said, but my heart jumped in alarm. It would be at least ten past seven by the time everyone was sitting quietly and the lecture had started. Would Simon wait for me? I had no way of telling him. I would have to be patient and hope. I stood at the bottom of the steps leading to the Hall, assuming that everyone was behaving themselves and marching in fairly quietly. They could have done the Conga or a tap dance up the stairs for all the attention they were getting from me. I was somewhere else. I was with Simon, climbing the scaffolding, looking up and up towards the lighted window of the Tower Room. I was already, in my own mind, making my way up the stairs, past Matron's room and Miss Herbert's room and into his arms. Oh, if only he would wait for me! Surely he must? As the doors of the Hall closed, I looked at my watch. 7.15 exactly. I flew down School Corridor and along Study Passage and up the stairs, silently praying that I wouldn't bump into anyone, that I wouldn't have to stop. Austen House was quiet. Perhaps Simon and I would be the only ones stirring. I reached the Tower Room and opened the door. Simon was standing near the window and beside him, in front of the chest-of-drawers, was Dorothy.

'Ah, Megan,' she said in a voice like steel wool. 'We have been waiting for you. Come in and sit down.'

I wanted to turn round and run away. I wanted cracks in the floorboards to open and let me through, out of reach of Dorothy's pale eyes, but I went into the Tower Room. What else could I have done? I looked at Simon but he wouldn't meet my eyes. Dorothy spoke in a flat, even tone that nevertheless managed to sound . . . what? Disgusted? Angry? Hurt? Perhaps a little of all of those. She said:

'You will doubtless be wondering, Megan, how it is that I am here, in your –' she paused – 'love nest.' I could hear the quotation marks in her voice as she said that. The phrase reminded me of sordid stories in the *News of the World*, which, of course, was Dorothy's intention. 'If you will leave notes to Megan half open on her desk, Simon, then you must not be surprised if people read them, must you?'

Simon stood up straight and looked at Dorothy. 'I don't mind who reads my notes,' he said bravely. 'I have nothing to hide. The fact is, I love Megan.'

It was as if those three words had ignited something in Dorothy. Suddenly, she began to shriek at us, every feeling she had ever had that had lain concealed for so long rising and bubbling out of her lips like burning lava from the centre of a volcano.

'Facts! You dare to talk to me about facts! I'll tell you some facts, if that's what you enjoy. Fact One: you no more know what love is than two pigs wallowing in your own filth. All that kissing and pawing and yes, far, far worse, I've no doubt, has got nothing to do with love. Fact Two: you have been dishonest, both of you. Deceitful and underhand and wicked, creeping up here for your disgusting little sordid pleasures when other people are going about their normal lives. This is a school, Megan, not a brothel. Bedrooms are out of bounds to visitors, did you know that? And how dare you betray *me*? After all these years . . . all I've done for you. What would your parents say if they could see you crawling upstairs to meet this . . . this . . .' She burst into tears then and fell weeping on to Bella's bed. I didn't know what to do, what to say. I had never seen Dorothy like this. She seemed to be disintegrating, unravelling before my eyes.

'Dorothy,' I said finally. 'I couldn't help it. I wanted to, but I couldn't. I love Simon. We love one another.'

'And me?' Dorothy said. 'What about me? What about what I feel?'

'Oh, Dorothy,' I said, thinking that she felt somehow that I'd rejected her, that I no longer loved her. 'I'm sorry. Of course I love you too, and wouldn't hurt you for anything.'

But she wasn't even looking at me. She was staring at Simon, tears streaming out of her eyes, and her mouth all twisted up. She stood up and walked over to him. He backed up against the window, but she kept getting nearer and nearer to him, until she was standing right up next to him, pressing her body against his. He flinched backwards, but Dorothy was now out of control. I watched, frozen with terror, as she beat against his chest, with her hands fixed into claws.

'Didn't I mean anything? Didn't you care, not even a bit? All my help . . . why do you think I brought you here? Simon, Simon, answer me . . .' she moaned, and writhed against him and then brought her hands to his face. His glasses flew on to the floor and Dorothy turned and stamped on them with the solid heel of her shoe. She stamped and stamped until the lenses were ground to dust on the Tower Room floor. Then she slumped on to Bella's bed again, as though the destruction of Simon's glasses had exhausted her.

'Dorothy, listen,' said Simon. 'Megan and I are both very fond of you. This . . . this isn't like you. Shall I take you back to your room and make you some tea?'

Dorothy looked up at him. Then she visibly pulled herself together. By the time she spoke, some of the steel was back in her voice.

'I wish to have nothing more to do with either of you. You have betrayed me. Simon Findlay, you are dismissed. I shall write you a cheque for any money the school owes you, and not only that. I have to warn you that a carefully worded letter will be on its way to your next employers tomorrow. I think,' she smiled, 'you will have to set about finding yourself another position. You must leave Egerton Hall tonight, both of you.'

'We have nowhere to go,' said Simon.

'I can't help that,' said Dorothy. 'Megan, go to my flat and bring a suitcase. I want you packed and out of school before the end of tonight's lecture.'

'But Bella and Alice are in there!' I said. 'Can't I wait and just say goodbye to them?'

'Certainly not,' said Dorothy. 'I shall inform them. I shall also inform Miss Herbert.'

'Can I . . . will you give me some money?'

Dorothy laughed. 'Your parents' money,' she said, 'is put away for you until your 21st birthday, as you know very well. It is, until then, to be used for your education.'

'I have enough money for us both,' said Simon. 'Come on, Megan, let's go and pack.'

I followed him out of the room, leaving Dorothy there alone. I wanted to say so many things, wanted to try and explain so much, but the words wouldn't come out, and whatever I did, I couldn't bring myself to look at Dorothy. In a darkened Study Passage, Simon said:

'I'll meet you in front of Main School. It won't take me more than half an hour to pack.'

'Oh, Simon,' I cried. 'What will happen to us? What will we do?'

'We,' he said, 'will live happily ever after. But first, we'll drive to London and find somewhere to live.'

'How can you drive? She smashed your glasses.' I put my hand out and stroked his face. In her heart, I thought, she wanted to blind him. I stood on tiptoe and kissed his closed eyes and we clung together for a moment, trembling.

'I've got,' he murmured, 'a spare pair.'

I hadn't realized until I started packing that night how very little I owned. A few clothes and a few books, that's all. I left my uniform behind and filled up the space in the suit-case with text books and exercise books full of my essays. I hid a note to Alice and Bella in Alice's nightdress-case. It said:

'Can't write more than this. Dorothy found out about S. and me. S. has been sacked, and I think I've been expelled. In any case, we're leaving. Don't know where we're going. I'll write and tell you my address.
  Megan.
P.S. She wouldn't let me stay and say goodbye.'

There was no one about at all as we drove away from Egerton Hall. A thin, sleety rain was falling, blowing against the windscreen in a flurry of drops like tears. The last verse of 'The Eve of St Agnes' came into my head:

> And they are gone: aye, ages long ago
> These lovers fled away into the storm.

I sat in the front seat of Simon's car and Egerton Hall shrank into the darkness as we went down the drive towards the forest and what lay beyond.

*

SIMON, I love you. I don't want you to think there's any doubt about that. I love you and I always will, probably, but what worries me is this: I want more. Is that greedy? I don't mean more of your love, or more of you, not really, because I know you have to work and be away all day, and I know (I think I know) that you love me, but I want . . . what? My friends, my lessons, to take my A-levels and go to university. I want to travel, and go to parties and meet lots of different people, do all kinds of things and above all, be able to go back to Egerton Hall. That may sound strange to you, but you have to remember it's my home, the only one I've known since I was eleven. Also, I would like to make my peace with Dorothy. How, I have no idea, but I would. I know her shortcomings, but still she is my guardian and has done her best for me all this time. I want to visit Miss van der Leyden in the hospital. I want to go to Alice's birthday party in June. I know what you'll say: why can't I do all those things and still stay with you? The answer is: there isn't enough money if I don't work, so I have to spend my days in that dreadful coffee bar, and then where does all the time go? I can't study, or read, or see my friends. All I'm capable of when I'm not working is writing this. And doesn't our love outweigh all this? I don't know, Simon, truly. I don't know. Sometimes I feel I've spent years and years in one room at the top of a winding flight of stairs, looking out of the window at life, instead of taking part in it like everybody else. And I get the letters, Simon, all those siren voices saying 'Come back, come back to us!' From Bella, Alice, Miss Herbert, Miss Clarke . . . everyone has written except Dorothy. And even Dorothy, if I returned . . . if I could explain, there is a chance that she would speak to me again now after all this time. I can't say I love her as one should love a mother, but she is still responsible for me, and I, for my part, feel nothing but sorrow for her, understanding how much she must have wanted you. She is, in that respect, no different from me, so how could I hate her?

I can't think what my future will be if I stay, Simon, and that's the truth. If I go back, we can write to one another, see each other in the holidays. There's no need to part, not really. Not for ever. If our love is real, and I think it is, then it ought to survive. And from your point of view, Simon, if you are without me to look after, you can go anywhere, get any sort of job at all. Admit that that's a very tempting prospect.

I hope you read this, my dear love, by the time I return. I have made an appointment with Armand, Bella's hairdresser. He is going to cut my hair. I know you will be angry with me. I know how much you love it. Sometimes it's seemed to me as though you want to splash in it as if it were liquid, cover yourself with it, drown in it, almost as though it were separate from me. I shall miss your hands on it, and through it and in it, and how your face buried in it makes me feel. But whenever it's done up in a plait, which it is most of the time, I think of it as a rope that's hung down my back for years, tying me together, tying me down, tying me to Dorothy and my childhood. Soon, it will be gone. I will return to Egerton Hall with hair as short as any boy's. Bella will think me fashionable at last, but I will know that what I am is free.

Watching the Roses

For Frances Wilson

ONCE upon a time, I was a good girl and no trouble to anyone. Now, everyone is worried about me, although I don't think there's really anything that dreadful or strange about my behaviour. I do not want to speak, not at all, not to a single soul in the whole world, and therefore, I'm not speaking. I decided not to speak a week ago, and since then not one word has passed my lips. I stay in this room. I do not want to leave it. They bring me food on a tray and when they've gone, long after they've gone, I eat it. Then at least they don't have to worry about me starving to death. I truly don't want to worry anyone by what I'm doing, although already I can see signs that I have.

A week ago today was June 20th, and it was my eighteenth birthday party. It should have been a perfect day and it was spoiled, oh, horribly spoiled. They all try to get me to say something and I won't. In fact, every time I hear footsteps in the passage outside my door, I get on to the bed and arrange my hands over my body as if I were a medieval stone princess carved on an ancient tomb. I close my eyes. I become as stiff as I can and as still. As far as they're concerned, I won't speak and I won't move. I would like my mother to think that I am sleeping.

The doctor has been and examined me and shaken his head and gone, 'Tsk! tsk!' and whispered in a corner of my bedroom to my mother and father. I couldn't hear what he told them, but my mother (who quite often comes in to talk beside my bed, not really knowing whether I can hear her or not) said:

'You're exhausted, Alice. Nervously exhausted, that's what Dr Benyon says. He says we must let you rest and rest. First the exams, he says, and then . . . well, what happened at the party . . .' (she blinks very quickly in case I notice the tears in her eyes) 'you're simply worn out.'

That's a very good way of describing how I feel: worn out. As if I were a piece of cloth, or a sock or something that's been rubbed thinner and thinner until it's almost transparent. I am writing in an old notebook that must have belonged to my father when he was younger than I am now. I found it under a loose floorboard in my wardrobe. This was my father's room when he was a child. I'm quite used to the fact that my father is an expert on roses, and writes books about them and articles in magazines and newspapers telling people how best to take care of them, but now I can see the beginnings of this passion. In this notebook, he has copied down names of roses and a brief description of them, perhaps from an old catalogue. I like seeing what he wrote. I like the look of his young handwriting on the page and I feel as though he's provided a kind of decoration, an ornamental border for my own words. Perhaps, also, I will add something to what he has to say about the roses. I can see so many from this room.

When I was a very small child, my father used to take me for walks through the gardens. They seemed enormous then, laid out in elaborate patterns of flower-beds and terraces and arbours and lawns dotted with trees. The drive seemed to go on for ever, and the gates at the end of it rose up above my head as tall as cliffs. I couldn't reach the big ring that you had to twist to open them until I was seven years old. Now, although I can reach it easily enough, turning the ring to lift the latch would take all my strength. The gates usually stand open, but my father has closed them now. He closed them after all the guests had left the party.

As we walked about the garden, my father used to explain the roses to me: Damasks, Gallicas, Bourbons, Albas and the rest. I loved their names. So many of them were called after French-sounding ladies that I imagined them sweeping along the gravel paths in crinolines made of brocade and tall, powdered wigs: *Honorine de Brabant, Madame Lauriol de Barry, Comtesse de Murinais*, . . . there were scores of them, and I knew every one of them personally because my father did. He loved them and cared for them. I loved them and looked at them and inhaled their fragrance every summer, and felt saddened and betrayed when, year after year, having been so beautiful, they faded and grew brown along the edges of their petals and died.

'There'll be more roses next year,' my father used to tell me, and that was supposed to console me for the loss of these flowers, this particular beauty. In the end I grew suspicious of all the coloured glory and began instead to admire the winter skeletons of the plants. I liked the filigree pattern made by the dark stems, and the way the thorns stood out clearly, unhidden by any foliage or blooms.

Every evening, when I finish writing, I lock this notebook in a drawer of my desk, a secret drawer. Sometimes I imagine myself completely gone: dead, vanished, faded away, quite rubbed out, and then no one will think of looking in this hidden place for years and years, and these pages will just lie there, becoming yellow and dry like old petals. Someone will find them long after my death, and they won't know who I was or who anyone I've written about was, and they'll toss the whole notebook on the rubbish heap or put it on a bonfire.

Since the party, my dreams have been different. Before the night comes, I drift and slide into what I suppose are daydreams, because I know that I'm not fully asleep. I'm still conscious of my room all around me, but the edges of everything become fluid and soft, and the thoughts I'm thinking seem to turn into scenes in a play. All the figures are misty, like ghosts, and their words come to me from very far away. My dreams at night are quite different. When I'm fully asleep, I go into strange rooms, move in strange landscapes, and the people are like real people, but twisted somehow, contorted. In my dreams at night, everything looks as if it were being reflected in a fairground mirror.

FANTIN LATOUR. 1900. Large spreading shrub. Very palest pink.
These bushes are in a round bed at the front of the house. The flowers this year are so abundant that the tips of the branches are weighed down, sweeping the ground.

How melodramatic I've become, just lying here! It's this house. I wish I could be back at school, at Egerton Hall. I wouldn't want to speak there either, but I could lie on my bed in the Tower Room and Bella and Megan, my friends, would be there. I wonder what my parents have told them. That I am ill? That I must not be disturbed by letters or visits? I cannot even ask these questions. If I were in the Tower Room, Megan and Bella would chat away, and I could listen and everything would be plain. The food. The clothes. The decoration of the room. I like thinking about all the brown wooden desks in the classroom, lined up so straight in their rows that it makes you feel safe.

At first, when I was sent to Egerton Hall, I didn't feel safe at all. Everything there was so different from what I'd been used to. The building was terrifying: big and dark on the night I arrived, exactly as I imagined a prison to be. Then, inside, everything was so . . . I can't think of the right word. Empty? Clean? Unadorned? All three, perhaps. I can remember being taken down corridors where the walls were painted green up to the level of my shoulders, and then white up to the ceiling, and the green and white unrolled like two smooth ribbons with not one single picture to interrupt the flow. In my dormitory, the strip of carpet stretched on and on past ten identical cubicles on the right and another ten on the left. I cried in my bed to think of myself in these deserts, these vast, pale spaces, and I longed, longed, longed for the clutter of my home, and the houses, like those belonging to my aunts, that I had been used to.

I *do* have an awful lot of aunts. Bella and Megan could never get over it.

'Wherever do they all come from?' Bella said once. 'I mean, Alice, honestly, it's indecent. No one has thirteen aunts.' They aren't all real aunts, of course. Some are great-aunts, or aunts by marriage. There are aunts of all shapes and sizes and ages, although I can see that to Bella and Megan, who were not used to them, they must all have looked very old and doddery. Not one of them has a child, therefore all their maternal devotion is focused on me.

'But,' said Bella, 'they're frightfully aristocratic and romantic and exciting as well. Maybe that's because some of them are foreign.'

That was true. Long ago, my father's grandparents came from Russia and my mother's from France. My great-grandfather's real name was Gregorovitch, which he changed to Gregson.

'It's how they dress,' said Megan. 'They don't dress like aunts.'

'How do aunts dress?' I asked.

'Well,' said Megan, 'I don't know really. Suits, I suppose, in tweed or wool.'

'And felt hats,' Bella added. 'Usually beige or brown.'

'And dreary shoes.' Megan was laughing by now.

'Crepey stockings,' Bella giggled, 'and knitted gloves.' Anything less like my aunts it would be difficult to imagine. Most of them went in for lace collars and cameo brooches the size of belt buckles, amethyst chokers, chiffon scarves and high-buttoned boots. Daphne, one of the younger aunts, was tremendously smart, always dressed in the latest styles as laid down by Vogue.

'What about uncles?' Bella wanted to know. 'There seems to be a marked shortage of uncles.'

There were photographs of men wearing monocles and moustaches on various mantelpieces in my aunts' houses, but most of the uncles, it's true, had either died or been divorced. This didn't seem to worry my aunts at all. Some of them lived together in a big house in London, some had cottages scattered around the Home Counties, and then of course there was the detached Violette, who lived in Paris.

'What's the matter with her?' Bella asked.

I said: 'Well, she's a bit strange. Bohemian. According to Aunt Myrtle, she never washes and lives in a hovel with an impoverished painter and does nothing but complain about how well off the others are while she's starving, etc. And Aunt Daphne can't forgive her for wearing nothing but black. "One cannot help being ugly," Aunt Daphne says, "but one has a duty to be smart at all costs."'

'She sounds super,' Bella said. 'Let's get her to take us out one Sunday. She could come to Chapel and scare the living daylights out of the Juniors.'

'I've never even met her,' I said. 'I don't think she's been to England since my christening.'

Bella and Megan cheered me up on my first night at Egerton Hall and decided that I needed looking after. I suppose in a lot of ways I still do. I was hopeless at all the ordinary things when I first went to school, like getting all my dirty clothes into the laundry bag at the right moment on the right day. I always forgot, and then Bella or Megan would have to go chasing round to find me (in the long grass in front of Junior House, usually, at least during the summer term) and get me to do it. I wasn't very good at piling up plates and taking them to the serving hatch at the end of meals, or carrying huge silvery bowls full of watery stew from the serving hatch to the table.

'It's because she's a princess,' Bella would explain. She and Megan always teased me like that. They call this house 'The

Castle Next Door', but it isn't a castle really, only a rather large house, with a very big garden. Over the years, I've got used to the teasing, but it still annoys me sometimes. Once Bella gets an idea into her head, she'll go on and on about it, so I suppose I'm stuck with Princess. Bella's house is almost as big as this, even though it's got a much smaller garden because of being in a town.

My room runs the whole depth of the house. One large window faces south, and I can see almost the entire garden, right up to the gate at the foot of the drive. The window at the other end of the room faces north, and from it I have a good view of the terraces, the rose arbour, the kitchen garden and the beginnings of the orchard, which marks the furthest part of the property.

I can also see the summerhouse, but I don't look at it.

From a small round window near my bed, I can see the front of the house, looking like a yellowy-grey cliff with seven enormous windows set into it. The roses that climb along the walls are overgrown. No one has dead-headed them, and they have all become straggly, wilder. That's how they seem to me. It's as though my father has done no work in the garden since the night of the party. I can't speak of it though, and when they come to visit me, I lie like marble and can't bear to open my eyes to look at them.

The dormitories in the Junior House were called things like 'Rose', 'Violet', 'Blue' and 'Green', and the strip of carpet running down the centre of the room matched the name. So did the curtains that you could pull across the entrance to your cubie. That was what we called them. In each one, there was only room for a bed, a chest-of-drawers and a cupboard as narrow as a coffin standing up. There was a swing mirror on each dressing table. Everyone put pictures in leather frames on top of their chest-of-drawers. I had one of my father and mother taken in front of the house. There was also a photograph taken at my christening. I kept it because it included every single aunt, except for the dreaded Violette, of course. We used to pore over it, Megan and Bella and I, comparing hats and dresses, giving each aunt a mark out of ten for beauty, or sex appeal, which Bella insisted was something quite different. I was on my mother's lap in the photograph, wearing a christening dress which spilled over her knees in a white waterfall of lace.

I have slept in this room ever since my birth. I love this room. I don't care if I never leave it again. Because of the wide windows at either end, I feel as if the garden and the sky and the weather outside are drawn into it, are a part of it. It was newly decorated last year. I helped my mother to choose everything and it's almost as if I'd known I would be here for a long time. There is embroidery on the edges of my pillowcase. In one corner, there's my wardrobe, which is too dark for the room. Its doors are carved into strange and complicated patterns. Sometimes I think I can see something I recognize: an animal or a plant, but when I look again, it's gone and what remain are wonderful curves and lines and whorls chiselled out of the wood. When I was a little girl, I think I was frightened each night of what might be hidden in the black spaces behind the wardrobe door. My mother used to look inside it, to reassure me, but still, once she'd turned the light out and gone downstairs, I sometimes worried that it (whatever it was) had tricked her. Perhaps it was still there, rustling among my dresses, lying flat behind my shoes, preparing itself to pounce.

I'm not afraid of that any more. On the contrary, I wish occasionally that I could put myself on a coathanger and hide in there, flanked by my dresses, behind the carved, black wood of that comfortingly solid door.

*OEILLET PARFAIT. 1841. Pink, carnation-like
flowers.*
The neat bushes above the terrace have lost their shape,
and the roses are spilling over the rims of the stone
urns in which they grow.

My Aunt Daphne came with me and my mother to a shop in
London called Daniel Neal's to 'help' with choosing my
school uniform.

'But there's no choosing to do, Daphne,' my mother
insisted. 'I've got the school list. It's all down here in the
minutest detail.'

Daphne sniffed. 'It won't do any harm. At least I shall see
that the poor child's hideous things fit properly. It's amazing
what a difference a well-fitting garment makes. Not so many
people realize that . . . it's the great secret of true chic.'

Aunt Daphne's 'great secret of true chic' changed every
day. Sometimes it was colour, sometimes cut, sometimes fit.
On occasion, she'd branch out and then it would be black
court shoes, or a certain perfume, or spotted veils on hats, or
pure silk or cashmere. With the Egerton Hall uniform,
though, fit was the only comfort she could find.

As the afternoon went by (formal blouses, games blouses,
tunics, a cloak, a suit for Sundays, tie, hat, fawn socks) Aunt
Daphne became more and more gloomy, but I thought it was
wonderful. All these things were to be marked with my name
and folded in my very own trunk with my name painted in
shiny black letters on the lid. I knew about the trunk because
we'd bought it already, and it was waiting at home. My
father, I remembered, patted it rather nervously the first time
he saw it, and said:

'My word, Alice, this is something, isn't it? All these brass
clasps and wooden bands all over the place. One would think

you were going to sea for a year, and not a couple of miles down the road till Easter.'

He was right, in a way. The first time I went to Egerton Hall, I did feel it was an adventure, and for the first few nights it was a little like being marooned on a rather crowded desert island. Me and my trunk full of named and neatly folded clothes were off by ourselves in the world outside Arcadia House.

Bella was impressed with my school cloak. Aunt Daphne had insisted on sewing in a silky lining.

'Crikey!' she said when she first saw it. 'This is grand, isn't it?'

'My Aunt Daphne says . . .' I paused, not wanting to insult Bella's cloak with my aunt's pronouncement.

'Go on, tell us.'

'She says unlined wool looks poverty-stricken and besides, it isn't nearly as warm . . .'

'I'm sure she's quite right,' said Bella. 'And it looks tons nicer. I shall get my wicked stepmother to line mine next hols.'

When Bella came back the following term, her cloak had been transformed. My lining was discreet navy blue that matched the wool, but Bella's was a purply-maroon – not at all a uniform colour.

'They can't say anything,' she said. 'There's nothing in the rules about colours of linings.'

No one ever did say anything, although some of the staff frowned slightly whenever they saw it.

BOTZARIS. Damask. Pale green leaves. White, fragrant flowers.
This grows in the bed outside the drawing-room.
Someone should have removed the dead heads, but they haven't. There are only a few flowers left.

*

Last term, I told Megan something about Angus, about what had happened when I was thirteen. I couldn't help it. But I told her only a version of the truth. For one thing, I implied that he was much older than me, but there was only a year between us. I also said my father had dismissed him from his job when the truth was he didn't have a job of his own. He only followed his father around, helping from time to time. I told Megan that I hadn't thought of Angus for ages, but that wasn't true, even then. I often used to dream about him. He never actually *did* anything in these dreams. He just stood there, but it was the way he looked at me that I didn't like. It frightened me. It felt as though he were looking at me with a mixture of hunger and loathing: as though I were a thing he was going to eat, but which he knew would make him ill, once he'd eaten it. It's difficult to explain. Angus's dad used to be a gardener in Arcadia House. Not the head gardener, who was called Mr Harris, but one of the under-gardeners who helped my father tend the roses.

'Worse than babies,' my mother used to say when I was small. 'Your father's garden babies are more troublesome than you are.'

Is that why I feel for the roses, I wonder? Do I really think, did I ever really think, even when I was a child, that they were somehow related to me? All I know is, Angus's dad helped with the roses, and Angus came with him sometimes. I saw him picking the flowers when he wasn't supposed to, and I told my father. I was only about seven or eight. I ran along the gravel paths shouting:

'Daddy, Daddy, Angus is picking the roses! You're not supposed to pick the roses, are you? Are you, Daddy?'

My father and Angus's father would frown and go, 'Tsk! tsk!' and Angus would stare at me with his wet mouth hanging open (it always looked open, red and horrid) and his eyes flashing a message at me that only I could understand: 'You'll be sorry,' they said to me, clear as clear. 'You just wait and I'll see to it that you're sorry.'

Oh, I only told Megan part of the story.

At the beginning of the Lent Term Megan fell in love with Simon, the new laboratory assistant. There was scaffolding up around our part of the school then, and Simon used to climb up and meet Megan until Dorothy, Megan's guardian, found out and made the most terrible scene, and Megan was expelled from Egerton Hall. Simon lost his job. They went to live in a bed-sitting room in London. Bella and I stayed in the Tower Room and missed Megan. We wrote to her, of course, but she never said anything in her letters about coming back to school. It was such a shock to see her, and when I did, when I noticed that all her beautiful hair had been cut off, I burst into tears. I couldn't help it. It was frightfully embarrassing, because it happened on the platform at Victoria Station, in front of flocks of Juniors and their parents and Miss Runciman and Miss Biddulph, who were the teachers on school train duty. I had never been back to Egerton Hall on the train before, because this house is only a few miles away. Last holidays, though, I'd been visiting Aunt Daphne and Aunt May in London and so I arranged to meet Bella at Victoria. I wasn't expecting to see Megan and neither was Bella, and we didn't recognize her at first. Bella said:

'I say, do look at that frightfully pale girl with the short fair hair . . . doesn't she look like . . . oh, heavens, Alice, it is! It's Megan!'

She started rushing up the platform towards this stranger, shouting: 'Megan! Oh, Megan! You've come back!' at the top of her voice. Startled second-formers and third-formers cleared a path for her, pushing to one side their weepy, fur-coated mamas, and clutching their school hats to their heads.

I followed in her wake, crying because Megan looked so different, and so ordinary now. She could have been anyone. Behind me, the crowds of uniformed bodies went on with their pushing and shoving and no one paid attention to Megan and Bella and me.

'It's so glamorous, Megan,' Bella was squealing. 'It's really' (she looked into the air for just the right word, waving her hands about as though to summon one down from the iron-work above our heads) '*avant-garde!*'

'What do you think, Alice?' Megan smiled at me. 'And why are you crying? Not on account of the hair, I hope?'

'Oh, no,' I lied. 'Just, I'm surprised to see you. And . . . *pleased*. I thought . . .'

It was impossible to speak. Miss Runciman approached us from one side, Miss Biddulph from the other, like a pair of well-trained sheepdogs.

'Come along, gels, if you're coming,' they said, shoving us along with their hands, sweeping us up into the tide of bodies. It took us ages to find somewhere to sit. We stepped over lacrosse sticks and cases and teddy-bears fastened on to the sides of satchels, and came to rest eventually in a crowded compartment full of lumpy girls who must have been from other houses because I hardly recognized any of them. By the time the train started and everything had settled down a little, the subject of hair had been dropped. I was glad. I didn't want to upset Megan, but I hated the new short style. Megan's plait . . . it was as much a part of her as an arm or a leg, and I thought of its loss as though it were an amputation.

That evening, in the Tower Room, she told us why she had come back, and how chilly Dorothy had been towards her.

'She was pretty chilly to us while you were gone,' Bella said. 'I can't think why, can you? Almost as if she blamed us . . . anyway, you're back now, although I can't imagine why. Don't you and Simon love one another any more?'

'Yes, we do,' Megan said. 'At least, I do. I don't know about him. I,' – she blushed – 'I ran away while he was at work. I couldn't bear to face him. If he'd been there, I couldn't have done it.'

'Did you miss Dorothy?' I asked. 'Is that why you've come back?'

Megan laughed. 'I missed you two, that's all. And Miss van der Leyden. And a few other things. The place. And I want to do the exams. That's the main thing.'

'How can you actually want to do the exams?' I said. I could never understand the way Megan and Bella felt about exams. Bella treated them as a kind of performance. She was going to be the star and that was that. A sort of glittery excitement filled her while she was doing them, a sparkle of achievement. Megan worked steadily and thoroughly, and when exams came she was calm and placid and well-organized. I used to feel cold and sick at the thought of them. Sometimes, worrying about them even stopped me from sleeping and there's very little that can do that.

'If I don't do them,' Megan said. 'I will have wasted all that work. And I want to go to University, to try for Oxford and Cambridge. I want to leave Egerton Hall. I need a new home, a new life.'

'But you and Simon had a home,' Bella cried. 'A love nest, high above the city.'

Megan giggled. 'You should have seen it! Honestly, Bella, a dingy bedsit is not a love nest, I promise you.'

'Well, I think it's jolly mean of you to leave Simon. His heart will be broken and he'll run away to sea or join the circus and you'll never see him again. Years from now, when you're an old, old lady he'll return, looking like a wizened and ancient gnome and he'll find you and remind you of your young love. You will then spend the sunset of your days together.'

'What nonsense!' Megan was putting her school blouses

very matter-of-factly into her chest-of-drawers. 'I expect,' she said after a short silence, 'I expect we'll write to one another.'

After breakfast, every morning, Miss Herbert used to read out the names of girls who had letters. Silence would fall over the dining-room. All the noisy munching of toast would stop while the roll was called. Some people's parents had distinctive writing paper. I always recognized Marjorie's nearly royal-blue envelopes, but as Bella used to say: 'There's no fun in her letters, so what's the point of looking out for them especially?' I was waiting for letters from Jean-Luc, who lived in France. When I first started writing to him I used to peer at the pile from wherever I was sitting to see if I could see a corner of French stamp sticking out. Things were better when he was sent to Senegal in Africa for his military service. His letters then came in air-mail envelopes that had red and blue flashes all round the edges. I could spot those sometimes even as Miss Herbert was walking to her place carrying the mail, but of course, such letters weren't always for me. There were an awful lot of girls whose parents lived overseas.

Sometimes I take Jean-Luc's letters out of my drawer and reread them. They comfort me. I scratch around in them looking for all the affectionate words.

'I wish,' he wrote in one of them, 'that you could be here in Africa with me. Imagine for yourself the sun. The sky all day is blue. There are real baboons near the camp. A family: *Monsieur, Madame, et tous les petits enfants . . . et ils parlent français*. Yes, monkeys who speak French! I speak to them each day. I tell them about you. They say: "*Oh, la belle Alice! Quelle chance que t'as!*" and I agree.'

CRISTATA. 1890. Clear pink flowers. Well-scented. Prickly bush.

This rose grows on the orchard wall. The petals will have fallen to the ground and no one will have cleared them away.

This is the real story of what happened when I was thirteen, the story I didn't completely tell Megan. Sometimes I feel that if I'd said nothing, if I hadn't run to my father in floods of tears, Angus may have been so relieved that he would have left me alone out of gratitude instead of doing what he did. Instead of coming back. My father questioned me very closely and carefully at the time: what did he say? What did he do? How hard had he pulled at my skirt? Had I said anything to him? Had I *ever* said anything to him in the past that allowed him to assume that we were in some sense, friends? I remember the wrinkles of disgust in my father's face as he said this. He winced and recoiled as though the thought were too much to bear. I started crying again.

'We're not friends,' I sobbed. 'We're not! We're not! I hate him . . . he's always followed me round, ever since he came here. I hate him. Make him go away. Please. Please make him go away.'

And my father *did* make him go away, at least from the house and garden. I felt as though some dreadful wild beast had been locked up, after roaming the grounds for a long, long time. A wild beast with me as its prey. No, that's not quite right. There's something splendid, noble, admirable and graceful about the wildest of beasts. Angus was more like a reptile, a snake of some kind, sliding up behind me silently when I wasn't looking, hiding behind things as I passed, watching me with his bright, flat, dark eyes, waiting for his moment to strike. He was always there, just on the edge of my vision, wherever I walked in the garden. He had never spoken to me till that day, when he followed me into the greenhouse. I didn't know he was behind me.

'Miss Alice,' he said, and the s's hissed around my head. I looked over my shoulder and saw him standing close to me. I felt myself freezing up with terror, turning to stone.

'Miss Alice,' he said again and took a step towards me. 'You're so pretty.'

All I could think was: the door. I had to get to the door. I moved slightly to my right, thinking, if I can get past him, then I can run out, back up to the house. He put his hand on my arm to stop me. It was dry and rough, his hand, but I felt as though slime had touched me.

'Let go,' I managed to blurt out. 'I want to go. Leave my arm alone.'

'Aar, Miss Alice, just a little kiss now! That's all I ask.'

What I heard was hissing: Alisss . . . kisss . . . thass all . . . asssk. I thought: if he kisses me, I'll die. If he puts that horrible, wet mouth anywhere near me, anywhere on my skin, I shall die. I shook off his fingers, which were still on my arm, and lunged towards the greenhouse door.

'Aar, Miss Alice, don't go yet . . . please,' came the whining voice, the hissing. He moved to stop me, but I was gone. His hand closed on the fabric of my skirt, and he pulled, wanting to draw me towards him. I pulled as well, and instead of letting go, he clung on and the dress tore at the waistband. The noise of ripping was as loud as a pistol shot. Angus let go of my skirt at once. I ran up to the house, trembling. I've heard those words so often in my dreams . . . Miss Alice . . . please . . . kiss. Hissing and hissing in my ear, and his mouth drooling and slack, filling all my worst nightmares.

My nightmares were full of the scene for many months, but that was long ago. Now I dream more and more about what happened on the night of my party. At least, I think that's what my dreams are about. Last night, I was upstairs in her room with Miss van der Leyden, the Belgian under-matron at

Egerton Hall, but in dreams people can be who they are and someone else at the same time, and Miss van der Leyden looked like herself but acted and spoke like my aunt Daphne. I was supposed to be having my party dress fitted, but I was naked and Miss van der Leyden/Daphne didn't seem to realize this. She, they, fussed around my body as though it had a dress on, taking tucks in imaginary fabric and marking them with lines of silvery pins. It didn't hurt at all, having my skin pinned like that, but tiny drops of blood began appearing all over where I'd been pricked and Miss van der Leyden said in Aunt Daphne's voice:

'Oh, we can't have that! Blood is quite out this season. Take that blood off at once!'

That was when I woke up.

Megan must have been quite desperate to have had her hair cut like that. She's always been fussy about her plait. Most of us like to fiddle about with our hair, try different things with it, but Megan can't stand it. Two years ago, during World Refugee Year we were all trying to think of original ways of raising money. I made cards, with drawings of cats, and dogs and horses on them and people bought them to send for birthdays and things. Bella spent ages making toffee so hard that all our teeth felt as if they were coming out by the roots when we chewed it. But a girl called Katie in Brontë had the best idea of all. She started her own hairdressing salon. At first, people were nervous of going, but then it became clear that Katie was a dab hand with the rollers and the setting lotion, and everyone in Brontë was walking round with beautiful bouffant hairstyles.

'We're going,' said Bella. 'Did you see Jenny Martin's hair in Geography? It hid half the map of Scandinavia we had to copy from the board, it was so high! I can't wait.'

Megan didn't really want to go, but Bella can be such a nag.

'It's for a good cause, Megan,' she said, and Megan, haunted by a vision of thin children dragging heavy suitcases on to crowded trains, gave in, of course. Bella and I came away from Katie's salon looking tremendously glamorous, but Megan's hair was so long that all Katie could do with it was put it up in a French pleat and backcomb the front into the new shape called a beehive. We all told her she looked lovely, but she didn't, really. She looked quite wrong, like someone in fancy dress of some kind, and straight after Prep. she disappeared into the bathroom for ages and ages. When she came out again her plait was restored and she was back to normal.

MARIE LOUISE. 1913. Spreading bush. Large flat pink flowers. Strong, sweet scent.
This bush covers an enormous area now and all the flowers are crushed against the grass.

Arcadia House: it's the name embossed on every sheet of the notepaper my mother has sent from Harrods in London. Egerton Manor was what it was called in the old days, but my father renamed the house when he inherited it from his father. Arcadia, he told me, was an ancient classical paradise, and that was what he intended to turn the house and all its gardens into: a kind of Eden of his own, filled with roses.

There is a wall built round the garden and my father has trained climbing roses along every inch of its length so that now it is almost impossible to see the brickwork.

Since the day of the party, the air has been heavy and the afternoons thick with warmth. It is the time of the very longest days, when the yellow light lasts and lasts and turns mauve towards nine o'clock. Also, since the party, everything seems so quiet. Perhaps that's for me. Perhaps the doctor has said to them: Alice is sick and needs quiet. She needs the healing power of sleep. The whole house is hushed on my account. The stones in the wall are filled with sunlight. I can hear bees through the glass in my window, and their humming makes my eyelids heavy and I lie for hours on my bed, drowsing, while bars of sunlight find their way across my bed, striping my body with the heat. Then, suddenly, I remember and start up out of my sleep and feel cold and ill, and try to push the memory of those horrible hours out of my mind. I think of other things. I think about school, or Miss van der Leyden, or my parents.

My mother has stopped playing the piano. All my life, I have lived in a shower of notes: waterfalls of music cascading into the spaces of the house as long as I can remember. My mother loves – loved? – what Bella calls 'the watery composers': Schubert, Debussy, Chopin.

'But only nocturnes and waltzes,' Bella noticed at once. 'Never the marches and mazurkas.'

'She plays Bach,' I said in her defence.

'That's lucky,' Bella retorted. 'You'd all be entirely drowned otherwise.'

Now there's nothing. A dense, almost tangible silence seems to have fallen over the house. Or perhaps it's only in my head. Little children cover their eyes up and then they think they're quite invisible. Perhaps, because I have become silent, I think there is a universal silence all around me. Maybe.

Art is my favourite subject. I am good at it. I can draw things so that you can recognize them. That's not what good art is, according to Miss Picard. Good art, she says, is when you can see the thingness of a thing. It sounds like something from 'Alice in Wonderland' to me, but Miss Picard insists.

'The essential quality of a person or an object or a landscape – that's what we're after. The very soul of objects.' Miss Picard has dark hair and a pale face like the moon. She wears her hair in a bun and looks nothing like an art teacher. She teaches Still Life and Drawing. Miss Whittaker teaches Life Class and Lettering. She is tall, with wild, dark hair flying loose around her face. She concentrates not so much on the thingness of things as on harmony, order, symmetry, pattern. She points out the Art Nouveau tiles around the sink in the Studio, and follows the line of a lily with the tip of her finger, showing me how it curves and twists away again into a spiral of decoration unrelated to the object except by the needs of the pattern. She speaks of colour: obvious colour, subtle colour, muted colour, noisy colour. Colour is a star actor, she says, in the drama of life. Her word is: 'Look.' Look at everything, she tells me. Look at the underneath of things, and the backgrounds and the way objects sit together in a space. Look for asymmetry and sharp contrasts. Look at everything that's amazing, wonderful, not like life. She shows me pictures of teacups made out of fur, and watches melted and hung over bare branches in a kind of desert. I don't like some of the things she shows me.

I could draw in this book, but I'm not going to. If I drew this room and the objects in it, I would be bored very quickly. If I drew what I could see out of the window, I'd feel sad, because I want to walk about outside, and yet when I think of doing it, fears grip me and I feel sick. If I drew my thoughts, my fantasies, the things I think about when I'm not writing this, they would be ugly. People are impossible as well. My mother and father have become sad and quiet, and I don't want to draw them like that. I would draw Jean-Luc, but I've forgotten what he looked like. The whole of the inside of my head is taken up with another face, which leers and grunts at me when I'm not on my guard. It's a face like a twisted mask, and it fills me with dread and loathing. I can't draw, can't draw, mustn't draw.

*

For the Advanced Level exam, for my Free Choice, I chose to do a kind of portrait of Arcadia House: the front façade of the house at the bottom of the picture and stretching out behind it a kind of three-dimensional map of all the gardens, the summer house, the orchard and so on. I put a border round it and in the border I drew and coloured as many roses as I could remember. Miss Picard showed me all kinds of botanical volumes, so that the flowers would be correct. Miss Whittaker spoke to me about scale and perspective and ornament. We looked at every imaginable border from all over the world. I had a dream about my picture of Arcadia House last night. In my dream, Miss Whittaker and Miss Picard had asked to see me. They wanted me to change the picture.

'I don't think, dear,' said Miss Picard, 'that this is at all what the examiners will be looking for. Do consult your reference books more carefully.' She opened the same volumes I'd been studying and all the roses in it were black and withered, with unnaturally large thorns.

'And,' Miss Whittaker added, 'you've left out the maze.' I said: 'We haven't got a maze at Arcadia House.'

'Nonsense, child,' she laughed and her lips stretched wider and wider till her face seemed split in two. 'Everybody's got a maze.'

I wondered for a moment when I woke up whether my dream had really happened, but I'm almost sure that my real picture was sent off with all the others to the examiners.

LA FOLLETTE. 1910. Tea climber. Needs warmth and sun.
This year the stems have spread sideways, so that a fan shape of tangled wood hides nearly all the brickwork of the kitchen garden wall.

My mother and father, according to family legend, were perfectly happy before I was born. I was told this by my aunt Myrtle. She is the teller of stories, the one who knows the secrets, the feelings, the jealousies and loves and all the entanglements of relationships going back generations. A holiday with her is an education. She lives in a small cottage in the country and her lounge is a delightful clutter of papers, small bones from this or that animal skeleton and forgotten cups of tea sitting in chipped saucers that don't match. She smokes incessantly, putting her cigarettes out in the saucers, or throwing the stubs in the grate, where they smoulder briefly.

'Can't be bothered with a real fire,' she says. 'Not now that one can simply turn on a switch and Bob's your uncle! In my young days, the poor maids would have to get up before dawn and lay the dratted things. I always thought it was frightfully unfair, even as a child.' She snorted loudly. 'Is it any wonder Daisy calls me a dangerous Bolshevik?'

'Do go on about Mummy and Daddy,' I would say, guiding her back to the subject. Like many story tellers, she enjoyed the digressions, the asides, all the little bits and pieces outside the main narrative, the things (she would say) that spiced it up and made it interesting. That was all very well, and I enjoyed it too, but I did also want some information.

'Tell me,' I used to instruct her, 'about before I was born.'

'Your mother and father,' said Aunt Myrtle 'were as happy as two small kittens in a basket.'

I laughed. My mother, white-haired, shy, with her long, blue dresses and her long, pale hands, and my father, red-faced, thick-set, jolly . . . kittens in a basket.

'Your mother,' Aunt Myrtle went on 'was very beautiful. You are very like her, in fact. Your red hair and that fair, yet unfreckled skin – that's just what she was like. Of course, when your father met her and fell in love, there were voices raised against the match. Your mother was . . . well, let us simply say not too well-connected.'

'Poor, do you mean?'

'Yes, and with all those strange relatives. Well now, we're all used to Hortense and Ivy and Fleur but in those days . . . well, connections with those sorts of people – Bohemians, musicians, painters, writers and the like – were considered . . . shall we say a little daring. But nothing would stop your father, and besides, your mother and he were both of age. So in spite of all objections, they were married. It was actually during the ceremony that I heard Lily whisper: "I believe she has posed in the nude. That's what Daisy says, and she should know . . . at that Art school of hers . . . well, you can imagine the sorts of things that go on in such places!" and she shuddered with horror.' Aunt Myrtle looked steadily at me. 'I've never had any time for that sort of nonsense. Why shouldn't people with passable bodies display them for the purpose of encouraging artists? How is one to learn about Art except from Nature? You do Life Studies in your classes, don't you, Alice? You agree with me, I trust?'

I sighed. 'Of course I do, Aunt Myrtle, only do go on about the kittens in a basket.'

'Your father took her to Arcadia House. It was all quite different in those days. The first few months they were there, your father and an army of gardeners worked on the outside, cutting, pruning, uprooting, replanting and landscaping, and your mother and an army of painters and decorators, plasterers and glaziers worked on the inside, knocking holes through walls to make rooms larger, choosing fabrics, laying parquet, hanging lamps and mirrors everywhere, installing sinks and baths and basins and stoves and beautiful, beautiful central heating, which was by no means as commonplace then as it is today. There were those (naming no names, you understand) who muttered things about central heating turning you soft, and eroding your moral fibre, and yet the truth of the matter was that your parents made Arcadia House so comfortable that all of us went back there again and again and stayed for ages when we *did* go. There were times, my dear, when the house was so full of all of us, chattering and carrying on, that it resembled an hotel . . . perhaps one of those discreetly luxurious and tasteful "pensions" often found near Swiss lakes. They, too, I believe, are full of women with not enough to do and too much to talk about.

'So the years went on. The roses that your father planted grew and flourished and became quite well-known. One of the earliest articles about him and the garden with photographs appeared, I remember, just before the War.

'We were all beginning to be a little concerned that your mother (who by this time was not as young as she was) had not become pregnant . . . She and your father had been married for fourteen years . . . surely it was time.' Aunt Myrtle lit another cigarette and paced about the room. Then she looked at me.

'Your mother herself told me what happened then,' she said. 'I don't know whether anyone else knows the full story. I don't know if I should . . .'

'I shan't tell anyone, Aunt Myrtle. Do tell me. Please.'

'Very well.' She sighed and blew from between her lips a plume of smoke which curled up and up into the still air of the cottage and disappeared.

'This is what your mother told me while she was pregnant with you, remember. I haven't, as you know, had children of my own, but I do believe that all kinds of hormonal changes occur which make people a little bit . . . well, unreliable.'

'Do you mean,' I said, 'that my mother was lying to you? When she told you this story, whatever it was.'

'Oh, no, Alice. Never lying. No, all I'm saying is that in such a condition one's imagination is bound to be, well, altered, extended. What I'm saying is, your mother's fancy had probably been at work by the time she came to tell me about it.

'One afternoon late in September 1943,' Aunt Myrtle began, 'your mother took a train to London to meet your father. He was to have a 24 hour leave before being posted abroad. 6 p.m. to 6 p.m. He had been away, training and so forth, for some months. Your parents had arranged to have a quiet dinner together and spend the night in an hotel. I can understand that. They wanted to be alone during the very short time they had. It's difficult to convey to someone of your generation, Alice dear, how we felt in those days when there was the very real possibility that our loved ones might go to war and never come back.'

'It must have been dreadful,' I said. 'I *can* imagine how it felt. Exactly.'

'Can you, dear? Yes, perhaps you can. You do have, after all, the gift of imagination from me. Now, where was I? Ah, yes, your mother on the train . . . She told me that when she got on, all the carriages were crowded. There were soldiers leaning out of the windows and waving, she said, as the train left the station. She told me she had to step over people as she made her way down the corridor, looking into each compartment to see if there was a space for her anywhere at all. After what seemed to her miles of train, scores of rattling carriages, she found a compartment that had, miraculously, only one person in it. Emily went in at once and sat down on the opposite side of the compartment from the only other occupant: a woman. Your mother assumed this person was a widow, because she was wearing sober, greyish clothes, and a hat with a veil. A blue veil, thick as mist. I think your mother must have started the conversation – perhaps asked for a window to be opened – and before long the two ladies were talking like old friends. Emily told me – but *do* remember the hormones! – that it seemed to her as though the rest of the train had vanished away and that outside the closed door of the compartment there was nothing but the purple evening, rushing by. Because the lady's face was hidden (so your mother said) it was easy to talk to her, to confide in her, and what Emily confessed was her longing for a child, and the lengths to which she and your father had already gone in order to find out why they had not succeeded in conceiving one. Of course, they hadn't told anyone in the family about the doctors, the consultations, the specialists, the medical examinations. Can you imagine Rose and May sniffing around, waiting for results? They had gone through everything entirely on their own. All this and all her anguish your mother told the stranger. She wept and raged and apologized for her tears. The woman in the veiled hat said nothing. Then she stood up.

'"By this time tomorrow, there will be no more need to cry," she said, and then she left. Your mother thought that perhaps she was getting off the train at the next station, but she looked all along the platform and saw no sign of her at all. The compartment filled up almost at once with still more men in uniform, laden with kit bags, all very jolly on their way to London for some leave. Your mother forgot this woman whose face she'd never seen. She met your father that night and you were born exactly nine months later!'

'That woman predicted my conception!' I said. I loved the story. It didn't matter how many times I heard it, I still loved it. It made my birth, my whole existence, something special and wonderful.

'Well, dear,' said Aunt Myrtle, 'maybe she did and maybe she didn't. Maybe your mother was lulled by the motion of the train and dreamed it all. Maybe there was such a woman, and your mother misheard or misinterpreted what she said. Haven't you noticed how one quite often hears what one wants to hear and not what's said?'

'Nonsense, Aunt Myrtle. I was predicted and here I am! I refuse to believe all that stuff about beastly hormones and things.'

Aunt Myrtle laughed. 'It's certainly a better story the way Emily tells it. Let's leave it at that.'

Thinking about that now, writing about it, makes me feel sad for my poor mother. Would she have been so happy, I wonder, to discover she was pregnant, if she'd known that eighteen years later she would be tiptoeing round Arcadia House like a sleepwalker? Last night she told me that the piano had been covered in the dust sheets normally kept for those times when we're away from home. It won't wake up until my mother decides she wants to play again. That, I know, will depend on me. I have the power to bring Arcadia House back to life again, and I won't. Why should I, when this non-life, this dream-state, is so peaceful, so hushed? Oh, nothing, nothing can harm me here. I am safe, lying on my bed, on the apricot satin of my quilt. I am safe from everything.

Miss van der Leyden is still staying with us. She is better now, but she was ill for a long time. I was the only person in the whole school, I think, who ever went to visit her in hospital. Perhaps some of the staff went but I never saw them. I had to get special permission from Miss Herbert to go by myself. Bella was always too busy to come with me and in any case, she didn't really like Miss van der Leyden.

'All that needlework of hers bores me,' she'd say. 'It's not that I dislike the old girl, not really, but I've never been a special favourite like you, Alice.'

I went to see Miss van der Leyden because I remembered how kind she'd been to me when I first came to Egerton Hall. She'd taught me to knit and to crochet and she understood how much I missed my home.

'Like a little angel banished from Paradise,' she'd say, 'but concentrate on the yarn, *ma petite*, and watch the patterns grow. It does become possible after a while to console yourself with beauty, with things you have made.'

Miss van der Leyden's room was full of things she had made. She must have needed a lot of consolation.

I hated the hospital. I hated seeing her in that bed, her skin a kind of dirty yellow against the sheets. She looked shrunken. Her hands lying on the blankets looked like twisted roots of an old tree. The other old women in that long ward seemed crazy to me: toothless, drooling, snoring. One old lady was nearly bald. Another mumbled and picked at pieces of imaginary fluff. I came home and told my parents. I couldn't stop crying, every time I thought about it. I couldn't face the thought of visiting her again.

'We'll bring her here,' said my father. 'She can convalesce in Mrs Thanker's room.' Mrs Thanker had been the cook in Arcadia House long ago, and her room was right at the top of the house, under the cupola that crowned the opposite wing from the one where my room was. Mrs Thanker's room was practically an attic, but large and pleasantly-furnished with a good view of the garden.

It made me happy to have Miss van der Leyden here. She took to doing all the small sewing tasks around the house: mending curtains, sewing on buttons and seeing that clothes were in good repair. She also began making lace. She had a cushion and a lot of little wooden bobbins and silky white thread and lots and lots of tiny, golden pins, stuck into a felt pin-cushion I had made for her in the Lower Third. It was supposed to be a strawberry, but the green leaves I'd sewn on had long ago fallen off, and now it looked like a small, misshapen heart, pricked all over with little spears. I was learning to make lace. I don't know if I'll continue with it now, after what happened. I hope Miss van der Leyden is still making lace. My mother said, a few days ago, that she spends all her days unmoving in her chair, looking out of the window. Her hands are still. Her eyes are closed. She has done no mending or darning. Sometimes she comes down to look at me, but never stays. It hurts her to see me, my mother says, stretched out on the bed looking as though I were dead.

Bella and Megan teased me about Jean-Luc, right from the very first time I ever told them about meeting him. Megan wasn't quite so bad, but I could see that Bella thought the whole romance wasn't anything at all remarkable, just a boy writing to a girl. Lots of us, even in the junior forms, used to get the odd letter from time to time from a boy we'd met in the holidays. On Valentine's Day, the girls who'd received cards were gazed at by the rest of us with envy. If ever a real love letter did appear, it was passed around from hand to hand, and we'd all sit round in the S.C.R. or someone's study and look at it and ponder it, and debate the exact meaning of 'love from', or 'with love from' or 'very much love', and the precise weight on the emotional scale of 'Dearest' or 'Darling' or (best of all, we thought) 'My darling.' If Miss Doolittle, our English teacher, had heard us discussing all this she would have been thrilled, I'm quite sure. She was always trying to get us to see the difference that the placing of a word had in a line.

'"The rainbow comes and goes,"' she declaimed in one lesson. '"And lovely is the rose."' Then she looked at us intently and said:

'Can you see the resonance and accuracy of that "lovely"? Can you see how the whole weight of the line would be different if it were changed to, say, "The rose is lovely"?'

Bella's hand shot up.

'Yes, Bella?'

'You couldn't do that. What I mean is, Wordsworth wouldn't do that. The rhyme would be lost.'

'Quite right.' Miss Doolittle nodded and smiled enigmatically at all of us. 'The rhyme *would* be lost, and with it some of the magic, but if you were to change the word . . . say . . . "pretty is the rose" or "beauteous is the rose" that wouldn't have quite the same quality, would it?'

Bella wasn't going to give up her teasing of Miss Doolittle quite that easily.

'What if you were to say: "And lonely is the rose?" That sounds almost the same and the rhyme's still there. What's wrong with that?'

Miss Doolittle closed her eyes and sighed.

'That, Bella dear, would alter the *meaning*. Words, however evocative, do have to mean something, don't they? A lonely rose is quite different from a lovely one, don't you think? Lonely suggests that all the others are gone. Dead, perhaps. It gives a very autumnal feel to the line . . .' and so on and on they would go, while the rest of us lost interest and began looking out of the window or cleaning under our fingernails with the sharp edge of a page.

Jean-Luc's letters were in French sometimes and sometimes in English. Occasionally there was a mixture of languages. I only showed them to Bella and Megan. I never passed them round. Bella and Megan grew bored with them quite quickly. Megan was so taken up with Simon last term that she scarcely noticed what was going on, and Bella soon realized there weren't going to be what she called 'good bits' and got fed up with reading them. Bella liked 'good bits'. There were lots in *Lady Chatterley's Lover* but I didn't get far enough in the book to find any. I thought it was dreadfully dull. I did read *Peyton Place*, though, as Bella said there were masses of 'good bits' in that. It lay around the studies for ages with everybody reading those few pages so often that the book fell open at just the places everyone was looking for.

I never said anything to anybody, but I found the words

embarrassing. I could feel myself blushing when I read them and sometimes hot shivers would come over me at night when I thought about them. Sometimes I wished I didn't know Bella quite so well or like her quite so much. She was a real mine of information on matters sexual, and had no hesitation in handing out her knowledge whether you wanted it or not. Some of the things she told me, especially when we were very young, frightened me. I remember one frightening thing very well. It was in our first year in the Junior House. We were eleven, nearly twelve, and we were reading 'How Horatio Kept the Bridge' by Lord Macauley in English. We all liked it. 'Lars Porsena of Clusium by the nine gods he swore' swung along with a brave rhythm, and we enjoyed stories of courage. Then Miss Henry, our teacher, who was round-faced and fluffy-haired, happened to mention Shakespeare's poem 'The Rape of Lucrece'.

'What's a rape?' Bella wanted to know.

Miss Henry blushed and searched the four corners of the room for ages before she answered.

'It's . . . it's an attack, Bella. That's all. Now turn to page 89, please, all of you, and let us read "Mary, go and call the cattle home".'

Miss Henry avoided looking Bella straight in the face. Bella sensed immediately that Miss Henry was hiding something and so she began her researches, looking things up in dictionaries and thick books in the library. One night, after Lights Out, when she and I were sitting on Megan's bed, she told us the results of her enquiries.

'Rape,' she whispered, 'is not just an attack, like Miss Henry said. It's forcing someone to have sexual intercourse with you.'

'What's sexual intercourse?' Megan said. I was glad she had, because I wasn't quite sure either. Bella groaned.

'Don't you know anything? Don't you know how babies are made?'

'Of course we do,' said Megan.

'When it's in a book,' said Bella, 'it's called sexual intercourse.'

'But how,' I wanted to know, 'can you be forced . . .?' My mind, which hadn't really sorted out exactly what actually happened when babies were made, how everything fitted together, gave up completely. Bella, however, was never lost for an idea.

'Well,' she said, 'I expect the man hits the woman . . . frightens her . . .' Her voice faded to silence. 'I'm not altogether sure, actually.'

'Is that someone talking in there?' The dormitory prefect in her pink candlewick dressing-gown was standing in the doorway of the cubicle. 'Get back to your own beds at once or I'll send you to sit on the stairs.'

Sitting on the stairs was a horrible punishment. It was cold outside the dormitory and silent. The only thing that stopped you from being bored to death was fear: fear of the dark bit outside the bathroom, fear of something you couldn't put a name or a face to creeping up out of the darkness downstairs, and above all, fear of being found by a member of staff on her way to bed. No one ever sat on the stairs for more than twenty minutes or so, but it always seemed like half the night. I was only sent out there two or three times, and on those occasions, Megan and Bella both developed amazingly weak bladders and waved comfortingly at me on their way to the lavatory. How well they have both looked after me! How badly I'm now rewarding them!

I've never thought about it before, but perhaps that long-ago conversation with Megan and Bella is one of the things that has made me so fearful of men. Apart from my father, who is kind and loving, but a little remote from me, I've not known many boys or men in my life, only Jean-Luc. All my days seem to have been spent with women and girls. Men are different. Boys are different. Bigger, thicker, hairier, rougher, rather like large shaggy animals that might be quite nice when you get to know them, but are a little daunting at first. I used to think of the nice ones as big dogs, and the nasty ones I imagined as wolves. When I was a very small child, the story of Red Riding Hood gave me nightmares . . . the big, sharp teeth, and that tongue on her flesh, slimy and scraping at the same time, those furry arms round her, the breath like steam, the red eyes . . . I used to wake up screaming, and my mother would hug me and soothe me and say, over and over again:

'It's only a story, darling. Only a fairytale,' as if that made it any the less true or horrid.

At school, during the junior years, there was a Bath Rota. In the Junior house, each bathroom had three tubs in it and three washbasins, so there were always six girls in the room whenever it was time to have a bath. I used to dread it. I couldn't bear the idea that everyone was looking at me, at my body, and it amazed me that no one else seemed to mind all that much. They were quite matter of fact about it, even Megan. Bella actually liked it. Dressed only in a bathtowel, she would wiggle her hips and pretend to be a strip-tease dancer, or someone in a harem.

'And it's so interesting,' she'd say. 'Everyone's such a different shape from everybody else, and all their bits look different.' I'd burst out crying and say:

'I can't stand the thought of everyone discussing me or comparing me,' and Bella tried to cheer me up.

'They don't care a fig, Alice, honestly! They don't even notice. Half of them wouldn't notice anything that wasn't shaped like a pony. It's only me, truly. I'm just naturally curious, that's all. But I swear I shan't look at you.'

After a bit of swapping around, we managed to arrange it so that Megan, Bella and I all had our baths at the same time.

In Austen House, each bathroom has only one tub in it and a door that closes but does not lock. I always put the bathroom chair against the door so that no one could come in by accident.

I don't have baths any more. My mother gives me sponge baths in bed, as they do in a hospital. She lays a waterproof sheet down over my quilt and rolls me on to it. Then she takes off my nightdress and washes me and dries me. After that, she rolls me off the sheet and takes it away and folds it. Then she puts on a clean nightdress and brushes my hair. I lie there with my eyes closed and enjoy it. This is what it must feel like to be a tiny baby.

My mother leaves a chamber pot in my room, but I can't use it. The lavatory is next to my bedroom, and I wait until I know both my parents are somewhere else before I go there. I'm clever about it. I wait till they've just gone downstairs. I know they'd never come up again at once, so that's when I get off my bed and tiptoe out of my room. My parents know. I heard my mother say to my father across my bed in the early days:

'She must be leaving the room . . . sometimes. Isn't that a hopeful sign? It means she's conscious. Alive, not dead.'

My father, grey-faced, weary, answered:

'It means she doesn't want to speak to us, or see us, or anybody else. Isn't that a kind of death?' and he sighed.

It's funny how things you haven't thought about for ages just slide into your head when you lie on the quilt and let your thoughts drift. I remembered Prue Scott this morning. She left last year. After Junior House, she went into Eliot House and we hardly ever saw her. But I've just had a kind of vision of her as she used to be when we were juniors. I used to sit behind her in Scripture and she would spend the entire lesson constructing a tiny box out of paper stuck together with

Sellotape. She did it *so* carefully that all the ends were perfectly straight and the whole thing fitted together beautifully. Then she'd sharpen her pencil into the miniature box and when she'd finished, she'd close the little lid, screw the whole thing up in her fist, box and pencil shavings all mixed up together and throw the whole lot in what she and all of us then called 'the wacky B'. She did this over and over again through the Missionary Journeys of Saint Paul, through Other Faiths, for what seemed like weeks and weeks. Megan and Bella and I wondered if she could be mad.

'I mean,' I said, 'it's so pointless, isn't it? She spends ages and ages on it and then it's gone.'

'Mad,' Bella agreed. 'I don't mind that so much, but she's so ugly. All weedy and stringy with that mousey hair.'

Megan said: 'You can't dislike a person because of how they look. It's not fair. She might be really nice.'

'Ah, but she's not,' said Bella. 'So there. She's Harpic.'

'Whatever does that mean?' I asked. It was a new expression I'd never heard before. Bella in those days was forever saying things that I needed to have translated for me.

She giggled. 'Harpic is a toilet cleaner. It cleans round what they call the S-bend. Therefore, Prue Scott is . . . clean round the bend!'

I can remember how we laughed. Prue Scott went to secretarial college, I think. She's probably frightfully efficient and ordinary now and no longer makes those silly little boxes. If she could see me, she'd think I was the one who was Harpic.

THE BISHOP. 1821. Gallica. Upright bush. Clear
cerise open flower fades to grey-purple at edges.
The lower panes of the French window in the drawing-room are now completely covered by this rose.

Miss van der Leyden came into my room a little while ago. She sat beside me on a chair near my bed and told me that she was going back to Egerton Hall. I heard her sniffing. With my eyes closed, I imagined her wiping away tears with a little hankie edged with lace. Soon, she would be back in her own room at school, getting ready for the beginning of term, arranging for the laundry to collect all those candlewick bedspreads, mending the torn cubicle curtains, cleaning the cupboards where the bandages and sticking plasters and bottles of Virol and cod liver oil live. She leaned over me before she left the room and kissed me on the forehead. I could smell her violet-scented toilet water and feel that her face was damp from crying.

'Alice, ma petite fleur,' she whispered, 'j'espère que tu vas me pardonner.'

What does she want to be forgiven for? Does she really think she is responsible for my silence, my lack of movement? She probably thinks that if she'd said something different, done something else on the night of the party, all this might have been avoided. But everything happened before I went to her room. I went there to hide. I went there for comfort, peace. I wanted to get as far away as possible from the ground, from the garden.

Now Miss van der Leyden asks me to forgive her. There's nothing to forgive. I'm sorry she's leaving. I'm sorry I've made her sad.

Jean-Luc is the only young man I have ever met whom I would describe as 'beautiful'. Bella used to hold up pictures of actors and ask my opinion of them, and the best I could find to say was: 'Quite nice.'

'Alice, I could strangle you! Why are you so fussy?' she would growl, and grind her teeth at me.

I met Jean-Luc at my Aunt Lily's house in Eccleston

Square. His mother was a French countess and she and Aunt Lily were at finishing school together in Switzerland, years and years ago. Jean-Luc stood up to be introduced to me. Aunt Lily, who imagines she's still a debutante or a Bright Young Thing or something, wears a silk bandage affair tied round her forehead and smokes pink and blue and green Sobranie cigarettes, which look good enough to eat and far too pretty to go up in smoke.

'Darlings,' she crooned, 'you two are positively destined to be frightfully good chums! After all, Monique and I go back to before the Ark. Alice, this is Jean-Luc and don't you think he's a perfect poppet? Jean-Luc, this is the divine Alice . . . now we two ancient crones are going to show you into the study while we sip our G and Ts and dissect old friends.'

Jean-Luc shook my hand and smiled at me and blushed. I blushed too, but not because of my embarrassing aunt. I was used to her. No, I blushed because Jean-Luc was beautiful: fair and tall, with eyes the exact colour of the sky at twilight, between blue and mauve, and as I stared at him, I could feel him looking at me, and thinking I was beautiful, too.

We sat in the study that used to belong to Lily's late husband, Colin, who was my father's brother. Now I keep trying to bring back that conversation, to think myself into it again, to recall it. I can't really remember it, though, however hard I try. Part of the trouble was that we were talking French, and I was so worried about trying to get everything right that I couldn't concentrate properly. I told him about Egerton Hall, about my life there, and what I was studying, but all the time my mouth was making the sounds, I was thinking about how much I wanted to put my hand out and touch that hair, and about what it would be like if he were just to lean forward only a little in his chair and put his lips on my skin. Thinking this, I could feel a blush spreading up from my neck to cover my face, and at the same time, my stomach seemed to melt and squirm and tighten in a way I'd never felt before. He told me about his school, and about the military service he would be starting on his return to France. Perhaps, he said, he would be posted overseas. Would I consider writing to him? I said yes, of course, I'd love to. He took a notebook out of the inside pocket of his jacket, and I wrote my name and address in it.

'I haven't got a notebook,' I said, 'but there must be some paper here somewhere.' I found some old writing paper in a drawer of Uncle Colin's desk. Jean-Luc came over and stood beside me to write. Then he turned to me. (I do remember this. I don't remember other words, but I do remember this.)

'*Alice, je veux vous embrasser . . .*' he said, and I can remember thinking: he's calling me '*vous*' as though he hardly knows me. I couldn't even bring out the right words, the ones I wanted to say, in English, much less in French, so I just nodded. Then he kissed me. I've never spoken to anyone about that kiss, not Megan, not Bella, not anyone in the whole world. I couldn't describe it. I just knew I felt as if I had blossomed, as if every part of me were opening like a new rose. I don't know how long we stood there, drinking one another in, but Aunt Lily and Monique came giggling and clinking their glasses and we heard them as they walked along the passage, and sprang apart. Later, when we said goodbye, he kissed my hand.

That was the only time I've ever seen him. He used to write to me often, but just lately, in the last few months, the letters have tailed off. I haven't heard for four weeks now. I think he must have forgotten me. Perhaps he met someone else. Kissed someone else. Perhaps that one kiss means nothing to him any more. If you eat lots of delicious sweets, why should you even try to remember a tasty one you had months ago? The reason I haven't forgotten is because I consider Jean-Luc's kiss to be the only loving kiss I've ever had from someone other than my family. I used to dream about it, dream about him. One of the reasons I sleep so much is that I can sometimes be there for a while, in that study, close to him. Just lately, though, the Red Riding Hood dreams have started to come back.

Angus was in a dream I had last night. We were in the dining-room at Egerton Hall and I was at the top of the table because I was a prefect. I had to serve out the shepherd's pie, but as I handed out each plate, the person who took it was Angus. In the end, there was just me and six separate Anguses: three on each side of the table. The shepherd's pie had turned into something else – lumps of earth for the meat and where the potato should have been, grass.

'You can't eat here with such dirty hands,' I said to all the Anguses. 'Your hands are filthy.'

They didn't take any notice, but went on digging in the brown earth and green grass with knife-and-fork-sized trowels.

As soon as Megan came back, everything returned to what it was like before she left. I felt as though an important part of me that was missing had been replaced. I hated it while she was away. Every night, her empty bed in the Tower Room made me feel sad. Bella and I used to play a game of 'At this very moment Megan is . . .' and we'd think of all sorts of splendid and silly and downright impossible things for her to be doing. For a while after she'd gone, at least until the end of last term, everyone was talking about nothing else, gossiping, pretending they'd known all along about Simon and Megan, and making things up that we knew weren't true because Megan had told us so. We kept denying all this, Bella and I, but the more we denied the worse it became until all sorts of horrible stories were flying round the school: Megan and

Simon had been seen, half-naked, coming out of Chapel, Megan and Simon had been spotted in the pavilion during a lacrosse match, kissing behind the stacked-up cricket equipment, Simon had been seen with this or that member of staff in Egerton Magna, he'd been seen with his arms round Dorothy through the window of the stationery cupboard . . . all these rumours and much worse ones, ones that I can't even write down, began to circulate. Then, over the holidays, people forgot. Megan came back and smiled and said nothing. Dorothy, who'd been very chilly and sarcastic towards me and Bella, warmed up a little, although not much. She would nod her head in our direction if she saw us in the corridor. Maybe, we thought, by the time exams are here, she'll manage a smile.

Whenever we weren't working, or lying in the grass near the cricket field worrying about work we weren't doing, we would discuss the Grand Ball. This was the name Bella had given to my party, and for ages we used endlessly to talk about what we'd be wearing.

'Marjorie's being jolly mean,' said Bella. 'My whole life seems to be a series of quarrels and disagreements with my wicked stepmother.' She sighed and went on:

'I want absolutely acres of black satin – a huge skirt so that I can trail down all your staircases, Alice, looking frightfully dramatic. Or else very, very little material: a plain black sheath from neck to hem, with a long slit up the side and no back at all.'

Megan giggled. 'You'll look like a witch, Bella.'

'Don't you start!' Bella said. 'Marjorie said that. She also said, (and I doubt if I can do justice to her acid tones, but I'll try) "It'll be the very opposite of mutton dressed as lamb, darling. Too, too ageing for words."' Bella made a face. 'So I've given in. Compromised. I hate doing it, but there you are. Marjorie's paying after all. It's quite nice, actually.'

'Describe it,' Megan said. 'Go on.'

'Well,' said Bella, 'it's red. A wonderful, flaming, scarlet satin. And it's strapless. You should just see my creamy shoulders!'

'And are there yards and yards of fabric in the skirt?' I asked.

'Not really. It's quite discreet. Not straight exactly, but more tulip-shaped.'

'What's going to happen to sweeping down staircases?' Megan said.

'I shall have to confine myself to gliding gracefully across the parquet, or strolling elegantly over the lawns.'

I said: 'You will be banned from the lawns by my father if you're in your winkle-pickers.'

'I thought lawns were supposed to be pricked sometimes.'

'One hundred pairs of stiletto heels wouldn't prick. They'd . . . they'd . . .' I couldn't think of the right word.

'Churn up?' Bella suggested.

'Spoil?' That was Megan. 'I suppose that's putting it a bit mildly.'

'What about destroy?' I said.

We all agreed that Bella would have to wear flat pumps or be banished from the lawns altogether.

'There are gravel paths,' I pointed out. 'You could stick to those.'

Bella sighed. 'Enough about my dress. What are we going to do about Megan?'

'What about me?'

'Well,' said Bella, 'you simply can't wear that same old pink party dress again. Not to the Grand Ball.'

'I don't see why not,' Megan replied mildly. 'It still fits.'

'Don't you *want* a new dress?'

'I hate choosing,' Megan said, looking embarrassed.

'We'll help you, Alice and I. We've got exquisite taste, haven't we, Alice?'

176

'I have,' I said. 'I don't know about you.'

Bella and Megan couldn't stop laughing. I hardly ever make jokes, and they're so surprised when I say anything even mildly funny that it takes them ages to recover. When they did, we decided that we would go to London and choose Megan's dress during the few days before the exams when we were sent home to rest. Then it was time to go in for Prep. No one had talked about my dress, and even if they had, I would have changed the subject. I wanted it to be a surprise.

'I am,' Jean-Luc says in one of his last letters, 'beginning to forget English. I am also forgetting real French. I am learning Army talk, which is not like anything. I am eating Army food which is (I do not know the word in English) *déguelasse*. I am marching up and down in the sun. I have learned how a rifle is cleaned. *Sensat, n'est-ce pas?* I wish I could see you. Even for only half an hour. Thank you for the photograph. You are beautiful, but small and too far away. I think of you every day.'

Oh, I think of you, Jean-Luc, not only every day, but sometimes for hours on end.

The Empire Day Picnic on May 24th each year was an Egerton Hall tradition.

'It's a ghastly tradition,' said Bella, 'and someone ought to put a stop to it. Imagine: busloads of girls being driven to some remote corner of the countryside, or worse still, the seaside, and then being forced to wrestle with triangular cheeses in silver paper.'

'The hard-boiled eggs are nice,' said Megan.

'I squashed mine last year,' I said. 'Do you remember? We were at Pevensey Beach and it was freezing cold. I spent the whole of the picnic bundled up in my cloak. Anyway, I banged my egg against a pebble and squashed the whole thing.'

'Why can't they give us something different?' Bella

moaned. 'Those awful bread rolls gummed together with butter . . .'

'Marge,' said Megan.

'Sorry, yes, of course. Whoever heard of butter at Egerton Hall? Those terrible silver-wrapped cheeses and a rubbery tomato . . .'

'. . . and a packet of crisps and a chocolate biscuit,' I said, laughing.

On the coach, we planned the food for our ideal picnic.

'Cold chicken.' (Megan.)

'Asparagus.' (Bella.)

'Strawberries and cream.' (Me.)

'Champagne.' (Bella.)

'Prawn cocktail.' (Megan.)

'Chocolate cake.' (Me.)

'And,' said Bella, 'we wouldn't be having it in what the staff consider a leafy woodland glade, either. There's far too much wildlife. I really don't see why I should share every mouthful with droves of wasps.'

'It isn't droves,' said Megan. 'Not for wasps. You can't say "droves."'

'Don't be pedantic,' said Bella. 'I shall say what I like. Crowds of wasps, gangs of wasps, cohorts of wasps, clouds of wasps, bunches of wasps . . . whatever does it matter? I can't bear them anyway. I'd have my picnic indoors.'

'Then,' I said, 'it wouldn't be a picnic at all.'

'That'd be the best thing about it,' said Bella. 'It would just be a meal. I hate picnics and I love meals.'

PARVIFOLIA. 1664. Dwarf centifolia. Low twiggy bush. Small red flowers.
This grows beside the porch, and looks stunted, even though I know it's bred to be tiny. Its stems look like a bird's nest, all matted together.

My dress, the dress I wore to the Grand Ball . . . what have they done with it? Could my mother have given it to Miss van der Leyden to be mended? I never want to see it again. No one has spoken of it. My mother thinks, perhaps, that it isn't in the least important what happens to the dress, but it is, it is, and if ever I hear that it's mended or that it's being returned to my wardrobe, I shall cut it up with scissors into very small bits, or burn it, or maybe cut it up first and burn the bits after that. One way or another I would like it erased. Obliterated, annihilated, gone. When I think of it, all I can see is the way the fabric tore apart, ripped right through the hearts of all the flowers in the lace, and stains from sweaty hands all over the bodice, turning the ivory silk to grey, spoiling it for ever.

My dress . . . there had been a committee of aunts discussing it for months on end. It began last Christmas holidays at a tea-party given by Great-Aunt Hortense. Hortense isn't even a real aunt, only the mother-in-law of my mother's Aunt Fleur, and she looks like nothing so much as an elderly eagle dressed in lavender serge. On this occasion, Aunt Daphne, Aunt May and Aunt Myrtle were there from my mother's side of the family, and Aunt Daisy and Aunt Lily from my father's side had dropped in as well. The conversation turned to my eighteenth birthday, first to the day itself and then to the dress. They were all talking and talking around me and over my head as though I weren't there at all. Great-Aunt Hortense started. She said:

'If I were Emily, I would be very careful indeed about what I arranged. After what happened last time, I think I would keep the whole affair very quiet indeed.'

Aunt Myrtle said:

'That would be to play right into Violette's hands. Nothing would give her greater pleasure than to think we were all still fearful after all these years . . . I mean, did any of you actually *believe* her drunken babblings at the time?'

'I did,' Aunt Lily said. 'I've always believed it. I mean, I believe in ill-wishing anyway, and especially in this case.'

'*Tais-toi*,' said Great-Aunt Hortense, quite forgetting I was studying Advanced Level French. '*Pas devant l'enfant*.'

I ate another almond biscuit. It's more than time, I thought, that I found out some details about this ill-wishing that people had been hinting at for as long as I could remember. I decided to corner Aunt Myrtle on our way home and get her to tell me everything. Aunt Daphne laughed: 'Well, Alice has her artistic gifts from me and her beauty from Lily and her kindness from you, Fleur. If we are believers in those sorts of gifts, I think we have at least to consider . . . how shall I put it? . . . the other side of the coin.' Aunt May, who always looks to me like a sweet-pea flower that's been buffeted by a strong wind, with pale, wispy hair and a wafty sort of taste in frocks, said:

'So do you think Emily and William should make as little fuss as possible about this birthday?'

'No, no,' Aunt Daphne said. 'On the contrary, they should make as loud a noise as they can, I say. Be damned to Violette. Can you imagine the satisfaction it'll give her if we all go about feeling cowed?'

The others nodded. Aunt Daphne went on:

'Which means, of course, that we must start thinking about The Dress. Emily, as you know, has always said we could take charge of it.'

All the other aunts nodded and sipped their tea.

'I'd always imagined,' Aunt May said, as she began at last to cut the cake, 'Alice in the very palest turquoise, with frills. A frilled skirt. Possibly in tiers.'

'Pink,' said Aunt Lily. 'That's the colour for a young girl.'

'But pink can be so sugary and vulgar,' said Aunt Daphne. 'One has to be so careful to avoid looking doll-like.'

'I wasn't thinking of a *vulgar* pink, Daphne,' said Aunt Lily. 'Do credit me with a little taste. I meant, naturally, the very palest of pinks. The merest blush, that's all.'

Aunt Daphne sniffed to show her low opinion of pinks in general and Aunt Lily's pinks in particular.

'What about,' said Aunt May, intervening to smooth things over, 'yellow? Buttercup yellow chiffon? Alice would look sweet, don't you agree?'

No one really bothered to answer. Great-Aunt Hortense looked down the slopes of her nose. 'I,' she said, 'have always been an admirer of shades of mauve.'

'You can all,' said Aunt Daphne, 'say what you like, but the decision has already been taken. I have been keeping the fabric safe since the day Alice was born.'

Everyone turned to look at her. In matters to do with dress and style, we all listened to Aunt Daphne.

'Tell us,' breathed Aunt May. 'Tell us about the dress.'

'I have,' said Aunt Daphne, 'several yards of the very finest Italian silk, the colour of old ivory. I have also acquired a quantity of handmade Belgian lace. I envisage a simple style: high-waisted, the skirt of silk overlaid with the lace, and the lace rising like a kind of mist to surround the bare shoulders.'

Silence fell. Slices of Christmas cake lay unnoticed on plates as all the Aunts imagined how I would look. I imagined it too, and felt happy at the thought of it all: my dress, my party, my friends, my father's roses woven into a garland for my hair.

Aunt Myrtle said: 'Don't you think we ought to ask Alice for her opinion, Daphne? It is, after all, her special day.'

'Nonsense,' Aunt Daphne said. 'Alice will have the good sense to agree with me, won't you, child?'

Everyone looked at me as though they'd only just realized I was there.

'Yes, Aunt Daphne,' I said. 'I do agree with you. I think the dress sounds beautiful.'

I was so busy daydreaming about how I would look in June in my ivory silk dress that I quite forgot to ask Aunt Myrtle about what the ill-wishing could possibly mean. A fog had come down while we'd been in Great-Aunt Hortense's house, and we had to pick our way home carefully among the dimmed lights and the looming dark shapes of houses and traffic.

I never worried very much about having to wear school uniform. To me it always meant an extra few minutes in bed in the morning, because I knew what I was going to put on before I started. At home, it used to take me ages to decide. Megan doesn't think very much about clothes and would probably have been quite satisfied to wear uniform all the time. Bella, though, used to fume and rage every single morning, flinging on her shirt and tunic, tying her tie as though she meant to throttle herself, and keeping up a running commentary on what she would be putting on if she had a chance. As it was, she managed to make the skirt of her Sunday suit as tight as it could be without crippling her, her nylons were the sheerest you could buy, and on those occasions, like Saturday Night Dancing, when we were allowed home clothes, Bella's were the most flamboyant of anyone's. She was the first person in the school to get a pair of stiletto heels, and she wore them until they were banned for making pock-marks in the parquet floor of the hall.

'I don't see the point of living,' said Bella, white with anger, 'if all I can wear is Cuban heels.'

Two weeks after the beginning of last term, Miss Herbert sent me to the San. for a rest. She said I must be tired, worrying too much about the examinations, overwrought. She had come upon me walking around in my dressing-gown in the middle of the night. What she didn't realize was that I quite often did this. I like places at night when no one is there. I feel as though I can think better, seeing how things look in the near-darkness or the half-light, how they're transformed. I was in Study Passage when Miss Herbert saw me. She'd heard footsteps earlier on, as I'd walked past her door. At first, she thought I was sleepwalking. I mumbled something about looking up a passage in one of my text books and she frowned.

'Come and have a warm drink, Alice,' she said and took me into her drawing room. It was strange to see her in a woolly dressing-gown, with her feet in sensible, dark blue plush slippers. We'd often tried, Megan and Bella and I, to imagine Miss Herbert in her nightclothes, but it was hard not to think of her as being propped up against the pillows, still dressed in her good tweed suits.

She gave me cocoa that night and asked me if I was worried about my work.

'A little,' I admitted, and she nodded and then said she was going to send me to the San. for a couple of days, to rest. I was quite pleased. I'd been there once or twice before when I was ill, and I'd enjoyed the small treats we were allowed, like not having to wake up with the bell, and being able to listen to 'Housewives' Choice' and 'Music while you work' on the wireless. Sister, who looked after you when you were there, was kind but brisk . . . oh, I would enjoy the rest, there was no doubt about that, but I didn't know if lying around all day with nothing to do would stop me worrying. I've always worried about my work. There's nothing I do, nothing I write or draw or work out without also thinking immediately afterwards: did I do that properly? Should it have been different? Could it have been better if . . . and so on. I've tried to explain this to Bella and Megan and to my teachers over and over again, but although they say they understand, they don't, not really.

'It's like,' I said once, 'being at a crossroads and choosing a way to go and then wondering, all the time you're walking down that road, whether you wouldn't have got where you wanted more quickly if you'd taken another path.'

Bella and Megan laughed. Bella takes whichever road seems the most exciting and forgets about any other possibilities. Megan examines each road in turn, then chooses. If she finds she's on the wrong path, she comes back to the beginning and starts again. I wish I could be like them.

MADAME PLANTIER. 1835. Alba. Climbs high if trained up trees. Flowers open rich cream, turning later to white.
There are two rowan trees at the edge of the front terrace. The trunks of the trees are twined with woody stems. Rowan trees are supposed to bring good luck, but these are suffocating in the embrace of Madame Plantier.

It's a long time since I've walked about at night. Maybe tonight I'll creep out of this room when everyone is fast asleep, and see what the rest of the house looks like. Maybe I'll even step into the garden for a while. No one will ever know. It's very warm. No one will hear me. I'll be very quiet. My mother takes sleeping pills now, that the doctor gives her. My father drinks rather more than he used to, so that he, too, will sleep soundly. I know these things because my mother has told me about them. She sits for hours beside my bed, talking, and she talks quite freely because part of her believes I can hear nothing. She knows I'm not dead, she probably knows I'm not asleep when my eyes are closed, but it's as if I were absent, somewhere else, even though my body is stretched out on the bed in front of her eyes. I know I am hurting her, but I can't speak, and I can't move. No.

Dr Benyon comes to see me every few days. He checks my pulse and temperature and asks my parents about my diet. Last time he came the word 'consultant' was mentioned, and I also think I heard them say 'psychiatrist.' It seems that Dr Benyon has decided there's nothing very much wrong with me physically. I don't think he knows quite what's to be done about me. I think he wants some reinforcements. I don't care. Let them all come and stare at me. I shall lie here and allow myself to be looked at.

My mother came into my room at lunchtime with Aunt Fleur. It's the first time that Aunt Fleur has been to visit since the party. They whispered beside the bed. It's funny. My mother, I know, would give anything if I were to open my eyes and get up and speak and return to normal, and yet, whenever she's by my bed with somebody else, they whisper so as not to disturb me, not to wake me up. My mother even whispers when she's here by herself. Aunt Fleur has a very loud whisper. This is what they said:

Aunt Fleur: 'The poor lamb! How pale she is! Oh, it's dreadful, too dreadful! Is she . . .?'

My mother: 'We don't know. We don't know what she can hear. We don't know what she's thinking.'

Aunt Fleur: 'She's fretting, poor soul, and who can blame her? Oh, it's scandalous! Can't the Police do something?'

My mother: 'It's not a police, matter, Fleur.'

Aunt Fleur: 'I think it is. I think young men who go about doing what he did deserve to be locked up.'

My mother: 'I don't want Alice dragged through the courts. I . . . I don't think he will trouble us again. We are lucky it was not very much worse. It could have been . . . he could have . . .' (My mother's voice faded to nothing, then became firmer. She was making an effort to lighten the conversation.) 'The dress is ruined, of course.'

Aunt Fleur (taking out a hankie and wiping away a tear): 'Oh, the dress! How beautiful Alice looked in it. Even Hortense said so. She said to me. She said: "I think I may have been mistaken about the mauve."'

They've left the room now. I don't want to think about what they've said. When I think about it, a cloud of black floods into my mind. It's like stirring water that has a thick layer of mud at the bottom. When this layer is disturbed, the mud spreads everywhere, clouds everything and stains it dark. By tomorrow my head will be clearer. All the mud will have subsided to its usual place, and become a thick, oozing, slimy sediment in the very deepest part of my mind, until someone says something, or I think something that stirs it all up again.

I will write about the Ill-wishing very soon.

I've had the very worst Red Riding Hood dream I can imagine. Even thinking about it makes me shiver and I can't bear to close my eyes because then bits of it swim about in my head.

We were in the Tower Room, Bella, Megan and I. We were getting ready for bed, taking off our clothes and folding them on our chairs. Then we got into our beds. Megan said:

'Alice, would you mind brushing my hair?' and I said no, I wouldn't mind and I got out of bed and went to sit next to Megan, near where her pillows were. She leaned right forward so that I could give her hair a thorough brushing.

'It's long again, Megan,' I said. 'I like it better long.'

'I grew it especially for you,' she said. Her voice was funny. I brushed and brushed, amazed at how stubbornly it was braided together, at how much effort it took to separate the strands. Then I said:

'There, I've finished now,' and stood up.

'Thanks masses,' Megan said and leaned into her pillows,

but it wasn't Megan at all. The face under the hair was Angus's face: the thick lips and long teeth, the eyebrows that nearly met above the dark eyes, the tongue lolling in the mouth so that you could see how wet and red it was . . . and all crowned with Megan's hair. I ran to Bella's bed, frozen with horror.

'Bella,' I said. 'Look at Megan! Look what's happened!'

'Don't worry,' said Bella and she put her white arm round my shoulders as I sat beside her. 'It's only Megan.'

Then I looked again, and it *was* Megan and I felt a most wonderful relief. It must have been my imagination. I turned to Bella with a smile, and then started screaming and screaming to wake myself up, because in that split second that I looked at her, I saw she wasn't Bella at all. The face so close to mine was Angus's face and the arm round my shoulder was brown and covered in dark hairs and there was earth, brown earth under long fingernails.

Last night, because I was frightened of my nightmare returning, I left my room and went for a slow and silent walk around Arcadia House. The air outside was beautiful: somewhere between mauve and blue. It was two in the morning. Soon, it would be light, I thought, but I've still got time. I tiptoed downstairs and walked the full length of the house. I went into every room. All the flower vases were empty. In the dining-room, the drawing-room, the library and the study dust-sheets covered the furniture, as though no one was living there any more. The Den, the smallest and shabbiest room in the house, seemed to contain my parents' whole life. My father's pipes, some old newspapers, my mother's embroidery frame . . . I picked it up. It seemed to me that nothing had been added to the work since I saw it last. I couldn't see any letters for me anywhere, not from Megan and Bella and not from Jean-Luc. I hadn't really been expecting any. It was clear he had forgotten about me, and yet I'd hoped that somehow, somehow, a message would have reached him, through Aunt Lily and his mother. Normally, the Aunts knowing something would have been a guarantee that everyone else would know it a few hours later, but this? I don't think I've behaved badly, but maybe it's a disgrace having a niece who refuses to talk or get out of bed . . . people will say I've lost my mind. The Aunts are evidently keeping it dark, and when they turn their minds to secrecy, they're very good at it – almost as good as they are at gossiping and spreading stories.

I peeped through the glass door of the conservatory, but I didn't go in. All the succulents and cacti, all the plants in pots arranged around the white wrought-iron chairs and tables, seemed to have black leaves. I never did like the conservatory. The air in there was always thick with warmth and moisture, almost like a greenhouse, and you could smell the soil: a heavy, rich, brown smell flew up out of the pots and smothered me whenever I went into the room. The more elderly of the Aunts used to sit there for hours at a time, sipping tea among the creepers, like exotic old parrots in a jungle. My mother was in charge of watering these plants. She used to rustle between the flowerpots with a long-spouted watering-can in her hand, attending to each one in turn. Now, in the darkness, I was glad that it was impossible to see whether she was neglecting them.

The kitchen had hardly any food in it at all. No leftovers, no cakes in the tin, no store-cupboard filled with goodies from one of my mother's excursions to Fortnum and Mason's. It was obvious that my parents had no intention of entertaining in the near future. I opened the back door then and went outside.

It was that that made me cry: walking through the garden. Before last night, I'd have said that my father would have to be dead before he allowed such neglect to fall upon his roses. I didn't know, and would never have guessed, that all the careful, loving work that had gone into rearing them for years and years could have been undone in this short time. The summer had been warm, that was true, but still. I never expected such growth, so many stems knotted together, and twisting into strange shapes, so much decay, such brown petals and withered leaves, such a profusion of thorns. The climbers along the walls of the house were high and thick, clusters of pink and white and yellow roses beat their dying heads against closed windows. Bushes that had once been neat and rounded had spread, sending out rogue shoots along the ground. Anything that grew in a tub or an urn had spilled over and trailed its stems on the gravel. So many petals had fallen . . . Not one single rose had been looked at or touched by my father since the night of my party.

I went back to bed and cried and cried. I didn't go anywhere near the summerhouse.

I never knew there were so many tears! I went to bed crying, and this morning I've been crying since I woke up, because I didn't want my dream to end, ever. I saw Jean-Luc. I was at school, in Chapel, and for some reason sitting up with the Choir, to the left of the organ. All the Aunts were in the Parents' Gallery, in the front row, and Jean-Luc was sitting right at the end with his mother. He looked at me and smiled, all through the hymns and the prayers and when no one was looking, he signalled to me that we would meet outside after Matins was over. The guests left the gallery at the end of the service, and the Choir followed them. I could see him walking ahead of me through the cloisters. I began to run, and then he turned and smiled and came towards me and took my hand. I felt as though I were flying, flying . . . and then I woke up. I can close my eyes and see his face, but it's getting further and further away.

*

I feel better today. I want to write about The Ill-wishing. Now that Aunt Myrtle has told me all the details, I realize that if I'd only thought for a while, I could have stitched the story together for myself. I saw that for almost my whole life I've known parts of the tale, that it had been growing in me in the same way that a piece of grit in an oyster turns slowly, slowly into a pearl. Now that I see the pearl complete, I understand many things. I know that such curses are as rare as pearls. I also see why I'm here now, why I *must* be here. Such wishes are not to be trifled with, oh no. We obey them, we submit to them, they direct the course of our lives. I only began to understand this after my birthday. At first, I regarded it as yet another rather eccentric family story, and all through last term before the exams, I told Bella and Megan about it like a kind of serial.

I remember very clearly how it started. We'd gone in to Egerton Parva for our Sunday afternoon outing. Prefects were allowed to go into the village four times a term. There was a café there called The Old Forge which had low, dark beams, and horse brasses on the walls, and which served the most delicious Welsh rarebit and chips, and toasted teacakes with overlapping moons of butter melting into them.

'I think,' said Bella, 'that this must be what Heaven is like.' The corners of her mouth and parts of her chin were glistening and yellow. She licked her fingers and started wiping her face with a paper napkin. 'I love butter,' she announced, as if that were news. We were always having to stay behind after the Staff had left at breakfast, so that Bella could make raids on their table, bearing off triangles of brown toast and real butter to put on them.

'It's so unjust,' she would say, 'giving us marge and the Staff butter. I mean, we're the ones who are paying the fees. I think we should sign a petition or something.'

'Come on, Bella,' Megan always said, not really taking any notice, 'buck up or you'll be late for Chapel.'

Now, at The Old Forge, Bella looked around and said:

'I wonder if it's safe to have a cigarette?'

'Bella!' I was shocked. 'If anyone catches you, you'll be in awful trouble.'

'Yes, but do I care?'

'Of course you care,' said Megan. 'And even if you don't, we do. Besides, we don't want puffs of smoke blown in our faces.'

Megan was beginning to sound more cheerful. Part of the reason we'd decided to go out that day was to cheer Megan up. She'd heard from Simon that he was taking a teaching job in America.

'I wouldn't mind that so much,' Megan had said that morning, trying to look as though she hadn't been crying, 'it's that he thinks . . . he really *does* think . . . that I don't love him. He says I would never have come back to school if I'd really loved him. Nothing I write and tell him will convince him.'

Bella said, 'He'll discover how much he really misses you. Maybe you could go to America? Go there to university, I mean.'

Megan was very quiet. Then she said, 'I'm not sure if he would want me to. He's . . . he's quite angry with me. That's the worst thing of all.'

'What will you do, Megan?' I asked. I knew a little of how she felt. I hadn't heard from Jean-Luc for a long time.

Megan said, 'I'll wait. I'll do my exams and get on with my life and I'll wait.'

'Yes, but for how long?' asked Bella. 'I don't think I could manage more than a couple of months. Other men'd be catching my eye all the time.'

'My eye,' said Megan, 'doesn't get caught quite as easily as yours. I shall wait forever.'

She said it briskly, practically, as if she were saying: I shall wait till Thursday. I could see she meant it.

'I vote,' said Bella, 'we forget all about Love and soppiness of every shape and form and go and guzzle Welsh rarebits at The Old Forge. There isn't a heartache in the world that doesn't feel better after a pile of golden chips and a couple of scrumptious tea-cakes.'

Bella was right. We did feel better. By the time tea was over, we could hardly move.

'Let's walk back to school,' said Megan, 'otherwise I'll fall asleep.'

'Oh, Lord, really?' Bella groaned. 'Walking's such a bore!'

'No, come on, Bella, it'll be good fun,' I said. Bella looked unconvinced. 'I'll tell you a story.'

'You never tell stories, Alice,' said Bella. 'You paint pictures. I don't know if your story's going to be worth missing the bus for.'

'It is,' I said to her. 'I don't know if I can tell it properly, but it's about an Ill-wishing.'

'You mean a curse?' Bella looked happier instantly.

'They call it The Ill-wishing in my family,' I said.

'It sounds blissful! I'm mad about things like that. Who's had this malediction put upon them?'

'Me.'

Bella looked so shocked that I giggled. At that moment, she would have followed me to Timbuctoo, just to hear the story.

'Well,' she said, when she'd recovered, 'you'd better tell us all about it.'

So we set off along the road to school and I started to tell them about the Christening.

FELICITÉ PARMENTIER. 1894. Flowers open palest buff-pink and turn white.

I can see this rose to the left of the steps leading down to the first terrace. This year the white pompoms of the flowers are turning brown and withering very early.

'It all started,' I said to Megan and Bella, 'when I was born. I think the Aunts had given up any hope of my mother ever producing a child, and so, when they discovered that she was pregnant, they all began preparing for the event as if my mother were some kind of queen. It was wartime, as well, don't forget. Festivities were harder to organize. I mean, there were food shortages and no one gave much thought to luxuries.

'I first heard about my birth during a tea-party at my Aunt May's house. Aunt May is dithery. She's shy and tall and nearly pretty, but she has a faded look about her, somehow. Since her divorce (which happened before I was born) she seems to have started having slightly too much sherry during the long afternoons. That's family gossip. She's not what my father would call "falling down drunk" but spends a great deal of time in a state that's, well, a bit squiffy.'

'Squiffy?' Bella snorted. 'I like that. "I'm feeling a bit squiffy." I shall use it.'

'They also say "squiffed" in my family,' I continued. 'But squiffy or not, Aunt May's rather dingy little flat was part of the tea-circuit. Aunts would gather there every couple of months or so and my mother would always take me. Later on I came to realize that one of the main reasons for the tea-parties was so that I could be inspected; so that all of them could kiss me and finger my hair and clothes and turn me round and make me recite nursery rhymes I'd learned at school, and play silly little tunes on the piano. They were seeing, said my mother, how I was coming along.

'Well, that day at Aunt May's, Great-Aunt Hortense began to talk about my birth out of the blue. Maybe it was getting near my birthday, I can't remember. But she said: "I'll never forget the night Alice was born. It had been such a fine day. Then at five o'clock the clouds began gathering on the horizon. Daphne, Marguerite and I were at Arcadia House, doing our best for the layette. And, my dears, you cannot imagine how difficult it was, preparing for a baby in those dark days! We had cut up silk peignoirs to make dresses and robes, we had undone suitable cardigans and jumpers to knit into small jackets, we had all begun smocking and embroidering and quilting the minute we'd heard about the pregnancy, but just before the birth we were at fever pitch. Daisy had insisted we use her wedding veil of handmade Belgian lace for a christening robe, but I can still remember how she shivered and turned pale the day that Daphne first cut into it with her scissors. So there we were, stitching and snipping and talking and wondering and outside the sky was turning purple and the clouds seemed to lie so low over the garden that we could have reached out and touched them. William was with us. He was convalescing, after having been wounded in action. Emily, I recall, couldn't settle to anything. First, she tried to read and couldn't get comfortable, then we tried to persuade her into a gentle game of whist, but her attention kept wandering.

'I'm going out,' she declared finally. 'I'm going for a walk.'

'But it's nearly dark, dear,' Daphne said.

'And I can hear thunder,' Marguerite added, and William said:

'Let me come with you, dear.'

'No,' said Emily. 'I want to be by myself. I shan't be long.'

'Take a shawl, dear,' I can remember saying, 'in case it's turned chilly with all those clouds.'

Emily picked up a shawl and left. It wasn't too long after that that the clouds let fall the weight of water they'd been holding. I've never seen rain like that before or since. Sheets of it swept against the drawing-room window, torrents of it flattened the roses and pulped the petals where they fell on the gravel paths and the grass. A wind came up to lash the rain into even greater frenzies and lightning sliced and zigzagged through the sky – and Emily was out in this storm. William ran out at once to look for her, and although it was perhaps a mere ten minutes till they returned, the time seemed to stretch out for ever. We fluttered against the window-panes like so many moths, but it was impossible to see anything. At last, they returned. William was carrying Emily in his arms. Her shawl dripped on to the hall carpet and no one cared. Her hair was soaked, hanging down over William's arm like rope. Her eyes were closed and she was as pale as death.

'It's started,' William whispered. 'The baby's coming.'

We had all been, I realized at that moment, waiting like actors in a play for the drama to begin. Now that it had begun, we all moved to take up our positions, speak the right lines, play our parts. Marguerite came into her own. She had been a midwife, years ago, and began to oversee the boiling of water, the preparation of the bed and the warming-up and drying of poor Emily.'"

'Oh, Lord,' said Bella. 'We'll be at school in a minute. Do get a move on, Alice! Can't you even manage to get yourself born before we have to stop?'

'I'll try,' I said. 'Great-Aunt Hortense made it very clear that she was not one to watch an actual birth.

'"All that blood," she said. "A messy business at best, and far better left to those who know about such things. No, I stayed in the drawing-room with William (who really did pace up and down like someone in a play) and a few more of the cowardly among us. Outside, the storm had decided it was time for a climax and on the stroke of eleven o'clock . . . I remember the chime starting . . . lightning and thunder crashed together over the very roof of Arcadia House, so that the fabric of the building shook and the sound of the clock was drowned and the drawing-room was all of a sudden illuminated by the ghastly flare of the lightning. Then the thunder stopped, the last stroke of the clock fell into the silence and then we heard it, over the splashing of the wind and the rain: a baby crying. William ran from the room, just as Daphne ran into it, saying:

'It's a girl! And she's a beauty!' "

'At this point, Great-Aunt Hortense would turn to me and I would blush and not know where to look.'

'That's only the beginning, though,' said Bella. 'There's not been one sniff of an Ill-wishing, as you call it. You're a fraud, Alice.'

'I'm not,' I said. 'I'll go on with the story tonight.'

'You'd better,' said Megan. 'We're dying of curiosity.'

OLD BLUSH. 1752. Climber. Smells of sweet peas. Pale pink.
These roses grow around the trees near the kitchen garden and this year they're growing in such profusion that the poor trees seem to be choking.

Now, lying here trying to make sense of everything, I imagine the night of my birth, and apart from the rain and the storm, it seems familiar. I think I must have looked very much like my mother as I lay in my father's arms on the night of my party, after he'd found me in the summerhouse and brought me back. I cannot remember anything of how I felt then. Everything was black in my head and spinning and whirling and all the faces I could see were stretched and distorted. But when I think of my mother, brought in like that on the night of my birth, I can stand back and see her and the Aunts gathered round her, shocked into silence for once, and it reminds me of myself.

'But what I want to know,' Bella said on the evening of our walk home from The Old Forge, 'is *why* the dreaded Violette was so dreaded. It can't just have been for wearing black and living in Paris.'

'No, it wasn't,' I said. 'It goes back a long way . . . long before I was born. Before even my father was born. Violette is my grandfather's elder sister.'

'Yes, but what did she *do*?' Bella was sitting on her bed in the Tower Room, filing her nails.

'It wasn't so much what she did, exactly, although that did have something to do with it. It was more what she was.'

'Right,' said Bella, flinging her nailfile on to the chest of drawers and leaping into bed, pulling the cover up to her chin. 'I'm ready for my bedtime story now. Tell.'

So I told. I'm not sure I told it properly, or made Megan and Bella understand what it was about Violette that made her such a powerful force among the Aunts. It's hard to make other people understand how your own family works. You have to explain things that can't really be unravelled: old resentments, rivalries that go back to childhood, strange attachments and loyalties.

Violette is my father's aunt. When she was born, my great-grandfather was already a wealthy man. She was a difficult child and a peculiar one. She didn't speak at all until she was three years old, and then began to utter whole sentences, full of complicated words which her relations were sure she couldn't understand. When she was three, my grandfather was born and Violette hated him. Apparently (this is according to one or another of the Aunts) she used to try to murder him at least once a week when he was a baby.

'Quite natural!' everyone said. 'Her nose is out of joint. She's jealous of all the attention the baby's getting. It'll pass.'

And it did pass, or maybe Violette simply gave up in the

face of the battalions of maids and nannies and attendants of one sort or another who were ranged around the baby to protect him. When he was eight and Violette was eleven, he was sent away to school. Violette was furious. She had to make do with governesses who taught her how to paint in watercolours and read to her from the more ladylike pages of French, German and English literature. As a revenge she taught herself Latin, Greek, Mathematics, Philosophy, Chemistry and Physics.

'Subjects,' as Great-Aunt Hortense once said, 'which in those days were considered rather dangerous for young gels to excel in. A smattering of knowledge was one thing. No one could blame a young woman for that, but to make oneself as clever and well-educated as the men . . . well, that wasn't the done thing at all, it did lessen one's chances, do you see, of finding a husband.'

Still, Violette's education might have been overlooked if she herself had been different, but she was quite remote from the pretty, creamy-bosomed beauties of her generation. She was very tall and thin with a nose that dominated the rest of her face. She had a very white skin, and hooded eyelids over her eyes so dark that they were almost black. Her hair was brown, but she made it black, dyeing it to the colour and shine of patent leather. She wore it on top of her head in a complex arrangement of braids, like many snakes twined into a knot.

'And her clothes!' Aunt Daphne always raised her hands in horror as she described them. 'You can't begin to imagine! Huge, billowing purple, scarlet and black tent-like creations that just hung down and floated out behind her. You must remember, dear, she has no bust to speak of . . . and then those terrible flat, black shoes. Almost like a man's shoes . . . oh, she was the laughing stock of all London.'

'Except,' Aunt Myrtle once told me, 'that no one dared to

laugh. Anyone who *did* laugh, anyone who slighted her in any way, anyone she even suspected was saying things behind her back . . . well, let us just say that unpleasant things began to happen to them.'

'What sort of things?' I asked.

'Oh, one woman's hair fell out. One of her neighbours developed the most frightful skin complaint. Another woman she regarded as a rival fell over and twisted her ankle. Once, a house she was staying in caught fire just after she'd left . . . No one could explain that . . . there seemed to be no visible cause. All sorts of things happened and so Violette acquired a reputation.'

'As a kind of a witch, do you mean? A reputation for magic powers?'

'Well, people are amazingly silly, aren't they? They *will* look for supernatural reasons for things, as though intelligence, malice and a will of iron couldn't wreak enough havoc all on their own.'

When their father died and was found to have left his entire fortune to his son, my grandfather, Violette took up with the most unsuitable person she could find: a penniless painter of no fixed address and no family at all. They set up home in Paris, where he painted pictures no one seemed to want to buy, and she lay about in cafés, talking of revenge, muttering into her coffee and letting their studio turn into a hovel. Occasionally, one of the Aunts used to visit her and back would come reports of horrors: dishes left to pile up beside the sink until there wasn't a clean cup left to drink from . . . sheets that were grey with dirt . . . a roof that let the rain in . . . no inside lavatory. Oh, the Aunts would cluck and mutter and shake their heads. Violette, it seemed, had gone from bad to worse. But she had an obsession with the family and in particular with her brother's child, my father. No one knew how she kept up with events, not really.

'But she had her spies in London,' Aunt Myrtle used to say, 'who sent her things . . . the announcement of his engagement to your mother, the account of the wedding that was in the paper, the article about Arcadia House and the cutting from the *Times*, Alice, announcing your birth. That,' Aunt Myrtle paused as she looked at me, 'should never have been sent. No, indeed.'

I sometimes used to wonder how different things would have been in our family if my father had tried to include the dreaded Violette a little . . . sent her an invitation to his wedding, perhaps, involved her in the life of Arcadia House, tried somehow to make amends for her being so completely disinherited, even gone to see her in Paris. I said this once to Aunt Fleur when I was about twelve and I was helping her in the kitchen, cutting out leaves of pastry to decorate a pie.

'Try to appease Violette?' She laughed and wiped a hand white with flour over her apron. 'You might just as well try to make friends with a hurricane.'

BELLE DES JARDINS. 1845. White flowers. Palest pink shadowings and markings. Spoils easily in the rain.
The rose flowers along the drive. Its flowers are scarred with mildew this year.

The next day, I continued my story for Megan and Bella. We were walking round the grounds of Egerton Hall after lunch and before lessons started again for the afternoon.

'The night before my christening party,' I said, 'the Aunts had dinner with my parents and I was left upstairs in my basket with a new nursery maid to look after me. I just lay there in my beautiful, white basket, waiting. I was always, my mother says, good and quiet and peaceful and no trouble to anyone.'

'But you must have been told about it so many times,' said Megan, 'that you can tell us every word that was said at the dinner.'

'I know what they spoke about,' I said. 'They spoke about all the gifts they would have liked to give me, if they could give abstract sorts of things.'

'Like what?' asked Bella.

'Well, like beauty and wealth, and grace,' I said.

'I don't see,' said Bella, 'that you've done too badly in the gifts department.'

'No,' I said, 'I've been really lucky. Anyway, they took turns round the table, each one saying both what she would have liked to give me, and what she actually was giving me. Then my mother made a most extraordinary discovery. She realized that all the real presents symbolized the gift that each aunt wanted to pass on to me.'

'How do you mean?' Megan asked.

'Well, Aunt May wanted me to have intelligence, so she gave me a book . . . a beautiful, leather-bound edition of *A Child's Garden of Verses*. Aunt Daphne wanted me to be artistic and she gave me a painting. Aunt Ivy thought that common-sense was easily the most important quality a person should have and she gave me a set of building bricks. Then there was Aunt Daisy, who thought of grace, and she gave me a little statuette of a dancer. Aunt Lily, who wanted to give me beauty gave me a real pearl necklace.'

'What about Great-Aunt Hortense?' Bella asked. 'What did she think was a good gift?'

'Wealth,' I answered. 'She bought me some shares in something or another.'

Megan and Bella laughed. 'Just the thing,' said Bella, 'that every baby is absolutely longing for! What else did you get?'

'I had two dolls from Aunt Petunia, who wanted to give me friendship.'

'That,' said Megan, pointing at Bella, 'must mean us.' She laughed.

'Of course it does. Then Aunt Fleur gave me a kitten,

because she thought I should learn kindness. Aunt Marigold gave me a heart-shaped locket for love. Aunt Rose thought courage was a desirable quality in a person. She gave me a sweet little pair of shoes. I still know where they are.'

'Shoes!' Bella was scornful. 'I don't see how they can represent courage. What have shoes got to do with courage? Anyway, Alice, you're not a bit courageous, so that proves my point. The shoes were not a huge success as a present.'

'She could hardly have given a baby a set of duelling pistols,' said Megan, 'now could she? Anyway, shoes are for stepping bravely forward through life in. That's what I think she meant.'

Bella groaned. 'It's all that poetry you write, Megan. It makes you see anything you like as a symbol of something else. Just ask anyone if shoes equals courage to them and see what kind of answer you get.'

'That,' said Megan, 'is because most people lack imagination.'

I said: 'That was Myrtle's gift . . . imagination.'

'Don't tell me,' said Bella. 'Let me guess. Imagination was represented by a coal-scuttle!'

'No, of course not, stupid!' I said. 'She gave me a book to write in.'

'An exercise book?' Megan was horrified.

'Oh, no, it was beautiful. The leaves were edged with gold and the cover was soft, red suede. I wish I still had it. I wish it were still empty. I filled it up with drawings and now my mother keeps it with all my other baby things: the christening robe and the dolls . . .'

'. . . and the Magic Shoes of Courage,' said Bella. 'Come on, that's the bell. I can see we're not going to get any maledictions today.' She started running towards Egerton Hall.

'Hang on!' I called after her. 'I can't run as fast as you do.'

'Those Aunts,' she shouted back over her shoulder, 'forgot to endow you with speed.' She dashed ahead of Megan and her laughter was carried back to us on the wind.

BLUSH NOISETTE. 1817. Climber. Flowers in
clusters, cream shadowed with pink. Smells sweetly of
cloves.
This rose is growing on the wall under my window.
Green tendrils snake up the grey stone, feeling their
way towards my windowsill.

Last night I dreamed of a road and a car going along a road. I couldn't see anything at the side of the road, only an asphalt ribbon unwinding in front of the car, and no landscape anywhere. The car was big and square and black, almost like a taxi. I couldn't see who was driving it, but I knew it was a woman. I could see her hands on the steering wheel, her long, red nails. As the car drove along everything grew darker, and then I realized that it was travelling up the drive of this house. Then the car stopped and the driver got out, but the soft black folds of the clothes she was wearing blew up and covered her over, and spread and spread, blotting out everything I could see. When I woke up, my quilt had slid up over my face.

Bella is the least patient person I know, but Megan will wait and wait for something she wants for ages. Every day since she came back to school, I noticed her looking at Miss Herbert's pile of letters, trying to guess whether there was one there from Simon. I could see how she almost held her breath, because I did the same thing myself, waiting for letters from Jean-Luc which arrived less and less frequently. I knew that Megan was missing Simon, even though she never said a word. She used to stand by the window of the Tower Room for ages, looking down, but the scaffolding that was there in January had been taken away.

Bella is quite different. She always told us exactly what she was feeling and thinking whether we were interested in hearing it or not, and when she wanted something, she always had to have it 'immediately if not sooner' – that was her expression. She kept on and on at me, nagging me about the story, the story of the malediction, and it didn't matter that I had to do my French revision or go to the Studio for an extra hour of Life drawing. Bella couldn't wait. In the end she cornered me in my study, just as I was sitting down to do a French Unseen.

'Never mind that now,' she said, 'you can do that later. Megan and I are parched. Gasping to hear what comes next.'

'Can't it wait for tonight?' I said. 'I'll tell you tonight, honestly.'

'Now,' said Bella, closing all the books on my desk and settling herself down in the armchair. 'Tell.'

So I sighed deeply and told them. I think they were both a little disappointed although of course they were too polite to say so. They hoped for something much more dramatic perhaps, or maybe it's the way I told the story. I know that I think it's frightening, but maybe maledictions are less terrifying if they're not directed at you. Maybe it's easier to ignore them and say you don't believe in them if you aren't the person chosen for . . . whatever it is. I can write about it calmly now, because, in a way, it's over. No, that's not quite right. What was supposed to happen, happened, but for me it's still going on.

The weather was perfect for my christening: a warm August day full of sunlight. I know this because I've seen the photographs and they all show my mother in a hat with a wide, lacy brim, and shadows sharp and black in the glare, and all the Aunts shading their eyes as they look into the camera. Great-Aunt Hortense and Aunt Ivy have fans and

Aunt Daphne is wearing sunglasses. I'm there too, in my mother's arms, outside the church, with my christening robe reaching almost to her knees.

After the ceremony, there was a party at Arcadia House. No one took any pictures of the food, but I know that it was set out on the long, polished table in the dining-room on the very best crockery. Everyone came in their finery, and examined me and left presents and ate and drank and later walked about among the roses, admiring what was left to admire after my father had filled every vase in the house. By about five o'clock in the afternoon, all the guests had gone and only the family was left. They gathered round my cradle. Aunt Marigold said:

'I've never seen so many presents in my life. Aren't people kind? Our gifts will be quite eclipsed.'

'Nonsense,' said Great-Aunt Hortense. 'No one else can give her what we can give . . . and I propose we begin our little ceremony now.'

'Where's Marguerite, though?' asked Aunt Myrtle.

'She'll be here soon,' said Aunt Ivy. 'I think she's seeing to matters in the kitchen.'

'Let us start without her, then,' said Great-Aunt Hortense. 'She can be so tiresome . . . really, the whole thing will be quite spoiled.'

This is what I've been told: one by one they came up to my mother and gave her their gifts: the pearls, the painting, the book, all the other presents.

'I was so entranced,' my mother told me, 'that I never noticed. Well, you can imagine . . . it'd been an exhausting day. All those people and the heat and up so early in the morning and the food and drink on top of that. I can tell you, by the time the aunts began their little ceremony, I was reeling. I never saw the sky grow dark or the rain begin to tap and tap on the windowpanes, announcing the coming of a storm. Suddenly, though, we all became aware of a commotion somewhere in the house: shouting, doors slamming, footsteps running along the corridors towards us. Then the doors of the drawing-room were flung open and at that very moment the first bolt of lightning flared in the sky and seemed to outline in white and livid light the enormously tall figure that had burst into the room. She (oh, she was clearly a woman) had her arms outspread for an instant. She was wearing some kind of long, black, cloaklike garment and it seemed to us all that for a fraction of a second every fold and seam was fiery, charged with a kind of electricity.

'"I don't suppose for one moment," she said in a voice like razor blades covered in treacle, "that anyone was expecting me." Just as she finished speaking, there was a roll of thunder in the distance.'

I can see the silence and shock that followed Violette's entrance. I can imagine it. After a while, everyone returned to some kind of normality, some kind of social chit-chat: how are you? How is Paris? How long are you staying? Violette answered politely, said she was dying for a drink, took off her black cloak to reveal a black dress underneath. ('Ten years out of date,' said Aunt Daphne.) Then she turned to my mother and smiled.

'I believe, darlings,' she said, 'that you've all just had the most divine christening party. Is it true?'

'Yes,' my mother whispered. 'For my daughter, Alice.'

'Alice . . .' Violette rummaged in her pockets, produced a packet of French cigarettes and lit one. 'Alice,' she said again and blew a cloud of acrid smoke into the air. 'May I see her?'

'Oh, yes,' said my mother. 'Yes, of course.'

My cradle was on the other side of the room, in a corner. It had been put there so that I could sleep away from the voices of the chattering aunts arranged around the fireplace in sofas and armchairs. My mother says that walking across the carpet with Violette to where I was lying seemed to go on for ever and ever.

'How pretty!' Violette said, and turning to my mother:

'How naughty you are, Emily, not to invite me to the christening! And William . . . well, it's what I've come to expect, but still, I should have thought that an occasion like this . . . never mind.' And Violette turned and went back to sit among the Aunts.

'And have you all given little Alice the most marvellous presents?' she murmured, accepting a gin and tonic. No one answered. Violette laughed.

'The thing is, you're all too, too predictable. Too safe. I know precisely what gifts you've given. All the usual things I'm quite sure. My gift,' she smiled, 'is more original. Quite different, really. Don't you think Death an original gift?' The aunts shifted in their seats. My mother turned white. The thunder was getting nearer, crashing round the house, shaking the windows. My father said:

'Violette, I know we haven't seen one another for many years, but I must ask you . . .'

'Ask me what? To leave? Oh, I left long ago. Can you sense something, William? Trouble perhaps? Is that why you'd rather I weren't here, spoiling the fun? I'll go, don't worry, but not before I've given the baby, Alice, my little present.' She laughed. 'I wasn't really serious, William, only I *do* think that even a little scrap like this should have a . . . what shall we call it? . . . a *memento mori*. A tiny reminder that even the prettiest rosebud does wither in the end.'

She stood up and strode over to the cradle. My mother and father flew after her. Violette pinned a jet mourning-brooch to the edge of the shawl I was wrapped in.

'Oh, don't worry, darlings!' she said. 'Stabbing young babies is not my style . . . not my style at all. No, you shall have your Alice for a while yet, but I do think it's such a waste, growing old. Don't you? That's what I wish for Alice: never to grow old. Just one last, magnificent final fling and then out like a candle. At eighteen, perhaps? Yes, like a candle. Extinguished.' Violette began to laugh.

'Please,' said my father. 'Please, Violette, you've been drinking. You're not yourself. I can see that. I implore you.'

'Don't implore,' said Violette. 'I'm leaving. I only came to bring my little gift and I have.'

The Aunts began to wail and moan. Violette put her cloak on, paused at the door and looked at my parents.

'You should have thought,' she said quietly, 'to invite me to your christening. I have no children, any more than the rest of you. I might have taken Alice under my wing. Ah, well, it's too late now, I suppose.' She slammed the door behind her and as she did so, lightning and thunder met and clashed over the roof of Arcadia House. The storm was now directly overhead. My mother ran to my cradle, unpinned the brooch and flung it away from her as though it were alive and poisonous. It was at this point that Aunt Marguerite came back from the kitchen.

'I'm sorry to have been so long,' she said, 'only one of the little helpers from the village was so frightened of the thunder that I had to comfort her, silly goose. Whatever's the matter here?'

The Aunts told her. My mother, half-fainting with terror, told her. Then the discussion began. Long into the night the arguments raged. Violette was powerless . . . Violette could do anything she wanted . . . believe her . . . not believe her . . . Alice is doomed . . . Alice is no more doomed than the next person. Back and forth went the words, and the tears flowed. Then Marguerite spoke.

'Listen,' she said. 'I haven't given Alice my gift yet. I could wish for something that would cancel out what Violette has said. I could . . . soften it a little.'

'But what?' asked Aunt Lily. 'What can you possibly give that we haven't already thought of?'

Aunt Marguerite chuckled. 'You're all so fancy and high-falutin' that you've overlooked something.'

'I never overlook anything,' said Great-Aunt Hortense. 'I must have considered it and thought better of it.'

'It's the gift I was going to give Alice all along,' said Aunt Marguerite. 'I've brought a lot of babies into this world and I know what's important and what isn't. I shall give the gift of health. I was going to wish her a long life. I expect,' she looked around at the gaping mouths and wide-open eyes staring at her in amazement, 'that now, what with Violette's wish, there may be an accident or an illness, or something of that kind, but Alice will live to a ripe old age. That's my wish.'

'But were your mother and father comforted by that?' Bella wanted to know when I'd finished telling her and Megan the story. 'I don't know if I would have been. Violette seems to be a much more dramatic and forceful character than Marguerite. Surely her wish would have more power?'

'If you believe in the power of wishes at all,' I said. 'I don't know whether I do or not.'

'Well, you should,' said Bella, 'because everything everyone wished you when you were born seems to have come true.'

'Then so will Aunt Marguerite's,' I said. 'If I believe in one wish, I must believe in them all. I don't see why the dreaded Violette's should be stronger than anyone else's.'

Bella didn't answer. She didn't need to. I knew what she was thinking. Death is a bit of a trump card. It's hard to think of anything more final than that.

Aunt Marguerite's wish was stronger in the end, though, wasn't it, Bella? Megan? Here I am still, not quite fully alive, but not in the condition Violette predicted. A long way away from that.

BELLE AMOUR. Alba. Pale pink flowers. Distinct in its thorns. Scent has a hint of aniseed.
This rose is straggling over the gravel of the drive, which looks dreadful from my window. The pink petals are speckled with brown, as though they've been scorched.

The exams seem to have happened a very long time ago and almost in another place, a place I find I can barely remember now. They seem to be unimportant and when I think of them (which isn't often) I can't imagine how it was that they filled my life for so long. From before the time Megan went away, right up until my birthday, they were all I ever thought about when I wasn't daydreaming about Jean-Luc. I worried about them. I used to sit for hours, learning quotations, going over essays, trying to make sense of everything, trying to pack items of knowledge into my head. I felt I was folding clothes into a suitcase . . . there and there, I said to myself, that's learned, I know that, put that in the case and close the lid before it can fly out again. Depending on my mood, I either felt that my suitcase was pleasantly full of neat little packages of information, all ready to be unwrapped when the exams arrived, or else that something, someone had robbed me in the night and my whole suitcase was empty and echoing and I wouldn't be able to find one single thing to offer up on paper.

Before the exams started, we were sent home for a few days of compulsory rest. No one was supposed to take any work with them, but of course we did. We all became as ingenious as diamond-smugglers, hiding our notes where no one would think to look for them – in boxes of sanitary towels, for example. Some pieces of paper were really tiny and could be rolled up tight and put inside hair rollers. That was Bella's idea.

'Actually,' she said. 'I think they're right. I feel we *should* rest. Anything we don't know by now we'll probably never learn.'

These words terrified me. Oh, I thought, as we packed for the days at home, how I long for it to be over! How much I want the inside of my head to be clear again, swept clean. Now, of course, I feel differently. Now I would love to have the subjunctive of '*faire*' to worry about, and nothing would please me more than reciting lists of quotations as long as my arm. It would be restful to do that again, instead of what I'm doing now: I'm thinking over everything that's taken place in the last few weeks and while I'm doing that, I'm also waiting. I don't know what I'm waiting for, but something, something is coming towards me from somewhere, and I will know what it is when I see it, or when I feel it. Meanwhile, I spend hours and hours sleeping and dreaming, and when I'm not doing that, I'm watching the roses.

BLANCHEFLEUR. 1835. Bunches of palest pink flowers. Thorny growth. Very sweetly scented.
A tall vase in the study was filled with this rose on the night of my party. There are so many thorns along the stems.

Megan came to spend the days before the exams with me at Arcadia House. We had arranged to meet Bella in London one day, and we were all going to choose an evening dress with Megan.

'It's not going to be easy,' said Bella, taking a huge bite out of her Wimpy and slurping down some chocolate milkshake that was so thick it could barely travel through the straw. 'I don't know what style you are, Megan.'

'Something plain,' Megan said.

'But not boring,' I added. 'I think Megan should wear a dark colour.'

'Not too dark,' said Megan anxiously. 'I mean, not black, or navy or anything. It *is* June after all and not a funeral or anything.'

'You'd look lovely in black,' said Bella. 'It'd be tremendously chic, with your colouring.'

'But half the Aunts will be in black,' I pointed out. 'We don't want Megan mistaken for an Aunt.'

We must have gone into at least twenty shops. Megan was beginning to look desperate. We had turned down sequins, beads, chiffon, pleats, gathers, strapless, off the shoulder, halter-necked dresses in every colour of the rainbow. In the end, though, we found the perfect one for Megan. Even she had to admit it made her look beautiful.

'Not like a Scandinavian milkmaid at all,' said Bella. 'More like a water-nymph.'

The dress was made of taffeta in a colour that was neither blue or green, but both together. When Megan moved, the colours merged and blended in the fabric. The skirt was full, the bodice tight, and Megan's shoulders rose from the square-cut neckline like (Bella decided) 'newly-carved alabaster.'

'You'll put us all to shame,' she declared. 'Oh, it does make me furious to think of Simon missing this! He is quite, quite crazy.'

At the mention of Simon, Megan drooped visibly, just as though all her energy had left her. She turned to me.

'Alice, unzip this, will you please?'

I unzipped her lovely dress and she stepped out of it.

'You *are* taking it, though, aren't you?' Bella asked, and when Megan nodded, she said, 'Well, give it to me with the money and I'll go and get it wrapped while you dress.'

As soon as she had gone, Megan sat down on the little stool in the corner of the changing-room and looked at me. Tears stood in her eyes.

'He isn't coming back, Alice. I know he isn't.'

'How do you know?'

'I had a letter. Two days ago. From America.'

'You said that was a boring letter from your American pen-friend. Why didn't you tell us? What did he say?'

Megan sniffed and wiped her eyes and started pulling her skirt on.

'It just said he's accepted a job in the States for the summer. It said that maybe if he liked it there, he'd try to stay for longer. It said . . . well, I think what it was trying to say was goodbye.'

I couldn't think how to answer. Megan sounded normal again, but I could see she was still upset.

'Are you going to tell Bella?' I asked.

'Oh yes,' said Megan. 'Only not now.'

Megan told Bella in the Golden Egg Restaurant in Leicester Square. For once, Bella didn't make a joke about it. It was only later, when she was seeing us off at Victoria that she patted the paper bag that held Megan's dress and said:

'It'll be all right after the party. In this dress, you'll be gathering the young men up in bunches of six, like daffodils!'

On the train, Megan looked out of the window, and then at me and said:

'Bella's right, isn't she? I mean that would be the practical thing to do. I should look for someone else.'

'I suppose I should too,' I answered. 'I haven't heard from Jean-Luc for weeks and weeks. He must have forgotten all about me.'

The train clattered and shook through the outer suburbs of London.

'The trouble is,' I went on, 'I don't want to look for anyone else. No one else would be quite the same.'

Megan nodded. 'Exactly. That's exactly how I feel.'

I wonder what this dream means? I am wrapped in many,

many layers of newspaper, but I can still breathe and see. Someone is pulling the newspaper apart with their bare hands. Soon I can feel that it's all gone, and then I see him. It's Jean-Luc. In the middle of the dream I think: it's Jean-Luc. Why am I not embarrassed? I must be naked. Why aren't I blushing? Then I notice that he's gone. I go to the window of this room, my room. There's an aeroplane, no bigger than an insect in the sky. I go quietly back to my bed because I know the aeroplane is coming closer to me every minute and I know that Jean-Luc is on it. I felt happy for a long time after I woke up.

My mother used to bring in some embroidery with her when she came to visit me, or some crochet, but now she stares in front of her, or else she goes to the window and stares out of that. Her eyes are heavy, full of weariness.

'So why,' I hear Bella's confident voice in my mind, 'don't you put the poor old thing out of her misery and say something? It doesn't have to be brilliant. Just "Hello" would be a start.'

When I don't hear Bella, I hear Mighty Mack, who was Matron when we were in the Junior House. She had a very brisk approach to health and fitness. She was a founder-member of the 'pull-your-socks-up' school of medical treatment, and she would only provide medicines when exhortation failed. Sometimes I think: if only Mighty Mack would storm in here, clap her hands and say: 'Now, now, no more of this silly behaviour, Alice, please. A brisk walk around the lacrosse fields and a spoonful of Syrup of Figs and you'll be quite yourself again,' I would get up, dress, speak, and go about my life again. Maybe if I've failed any of my exams, I would be able to go back to school next term. But. But, but, but. What you don't know, Mighty Mack and Bella, what you have no idea of at all, is how hard I've tried.

Every morning, every single morning, I say to myself: today I'm going to get up, put on some clothes and walk out of my door and down the stairs to breakfast. And every morning I can't do it. I begin to sweat and feel faint as I think about it. By the time I reach the cupboard, my knees start trembling and my whole body sways and as I move to take a skirt from a hanger, I feel dizzy and have to go and lie down again. The truth is, I'm afraid to leave this room because the world outside my door seems threatening. I know Angus has gone. I know that he will never trouble me again, but the knowledge doesn't seem to help with the fear.

GUINÉE. 1938. Grows to fifteen feet. Darkest red of all the roses. Can seem almost black.
Guinée is curling itself over the wrought-iron gates at the bottom of the drive, lacing itself to the metal as though it were part of the design.

I eat everything my mother puts on my trays but I don't enjoy it. Often, I've forgotten in the evening what I've had to eat during the day. I just don't notice it. At Egerton Hall, my favourite food was rhubarb crumble and my best breakfast was tinned tomatoes and fried bread, but at school, of course, we thought about food a lot of the time.

'Just like in prison,' Bella used to say. Sweets and fruit sent from home were kept locked up in two cupboards just outside the Dining-Room and after lunch they were unlocked and everyone went to her labelled tin or brown paper bag and took out a little bit for that day: one apple, one orange and a bar of chocolate, say. Then great swappings would go on right up to afternoon lessons. Someone or another was always on a slimming diet and wanting to exchange a Mars bar for an apple. I often seemed to be the Prefect on Cupboard Duty. There was one more cupboard which was unlocked before supper. This one had in it whatever we wanted to spread on our bread and butter: jam or honey or Marmite or sandwich spread. Once there was a craze for chocolate spread, and another time pineapple jam was a favourite. After supper all the jars had to be locked up again.

We talked an awful lot about food, describing in detail every mouthful of the meals we'd had when our parents took us out. Things were slightly better in the Fifth and Sixth forms. We were allowed tins of biscuits in our studies, and four times a term on Saturday the Prefects gave Study Tea to a few girls from other forms. There was great competition among the Prefects to invite the pleasanter girls, and even greater competition among the lower forms to be asked to tea by someone they had a crush on. We made sandwiches and sliced cake and arranged biscuits on plates and pretended we were society hostesses. The guests came and gobbled them up and sometimes chatted happily and sometimes sat in adoring silence. Bella always had her guests in fits of laughter, imitating members of staff, or teasing Mary-Ellen, the irritating girl who shared her study.

CARDINAL RICHELIEU. Dark crimson flowers,
opening to deep purple sphere.
This grows near the summerhouse. I see it in dreams
and the flowers are almost black.

Yesterday, Aunt Lily came to see my mother. They stood at the foot of my bed and spoke as though I were not there at all. I was being lulled to sleep quite genuinely by the sound of their voices rising and falling when I suddenly heard Aunt Lily say:

'I've written to my friend Monique about poor darling Alice . . . perhaps she knows of a sanatorium in Switzerland or even Vienna. They can do such wonderful things in those continental places. They're much more sophisticated in these matters than we are. One should never give up hope.'

Oh, no, Aunt Lily, one never should! My heart leaped with the first fluttering of real joy I've had for weeks and weeks. Monique is Jean-Luc's mother. Surely if Aunt Lily tells her of my condition, she'll write and let him know, wherever he is? And surely if he knows that I'm lying here, he will come and see me? And if he does? I can't let myself hope too much. What if he thinks 'Poor Alice' and does nothing? What if he can't just drop everything and travel all the way to England?

'*Alice*,' he said to me the only time I ever saw him, '*je veux vous embrasser.*'

If he still wants to kiss me, if he wants to enough, then he'll come, however hard it may be for him. I know that if he comes, if he kisses me, I'll get up, out of this bed, out of this room, out of Arcadia House and into the world. The enchantment that has bound me here will be broken.

Aunt Lily's visit has even brought hope into a dream I had last night. I was umpiring a tennis match, something I've only done once or twice in real life. I called out the score in a loud, clear voice. Jean-Luc was playing but I can't remember who else was there. The net started growing, higher and higher, until it began to resemble a trellis with *Duchesse d'Angoulême* roses growing all over it. *Duchesse d'Angoulême* has nodding white flowers touched with very pale pink. I wanted to stop the game, but Jean-Luc kept trying to hit tennis balls over the net which now loomed above his head like a cliff.

'Game, set and match,' I called, but he continued to serve, and every time he hit one of the roses, all the petals fell to the ground.

At school, we had to do Prep. every evening, ready for the next day's lessons. I know that in day schools, pupils have to fit doing their school work into their home lives. For one thing, they have to decide when they're going to do it: should it be straight after getting home from school, or last thing at night when it becomes impossible to put it off any longer? We had all that organized for us. Special time was set aside every afternoon, and we'd sit at our desks in the J.P.R. and a prefect would sit in a big desk by the door and make sure that no one spoke and that everyone got on with their work. A girl called Janet Newsom was Head of House when we first came into the Senior School and her look was capable of turning me to stone, and not only me. Bella was always very rude about her behind her back and called her Hugebum quite openly, but somehow was always strangely quiet when Janet was taking Prep. Her bust looked to us as though it were trying to break out of her tunic and she had lots and lots of very square white teeth in an extremely pink face.

An awful lot of note-passing went on during Prep., and if the prefect was trying hard to work at her own A-level subjects, and was someone other than Janet, she used to let this pass, as long as no actual noise was made. Disruption of Prep. meant being sent out. Being sent out meant you didn't do your Prep., and if you didn't do it at the right time you had to do it during your free time, and therefore most people kept quiet. Of course, there were other ways of not doing Prep. You could write letters (me) or read books in brown paper wrappers (Bella) or write poems (Megan) but then you would get into trouble next day. We weren't very old before we decided that it was a lot less tiresome to do whatever we'd been set to do first, and go on to more enjoyable things later.

The reason I've been thinking all this is quite simple. I have to write about the party and I don't really want to. I think, I hope, that if I do write about it, as simply and clearly as I can, I shall feel as though a wound has been cleansed. Very well, then. Tomorrow I shall summon up Janet's ghostly presence and sit her in an imaginary prefect's desk in a corner of my bedroom. She will see that I don't shirk it. She will see that I get it done.

BELLE ISIS. 1845. Gallica. Pinkish-cream flowers.
Thorny stems.
This grows on the terrace. Am I imagining that the thorns seem longer, more curved, thicker on the stems now?

Three days before the party, the Aunts took up residence in the spare bedrooms. Two days before the party, vans bringing the food began to appear in the drive. A small army of men arrived one morning and started to put up huge pink and white striped marquees on the front lawn. The kitchen grew fuller and fuller of roast chickens, whole hams, sides of beef, smoked salmon and fresh salmon. Scarlet mountains of strawberries grew in the pantry, gallons of cream were beaten into snowdrifts and placed in the fridge.

'Keep well clear of Mrs Morris this morning,' Aunt May told me. 'She's making the mayonnaise and I dread to think what will become of us if it should curdle!'

So Mrs Morris was left to drip olive oil into egg yolks in the kitchen, while my mother and Aunts Myrtle, Petunia and Daisy took all the family silver out and gave it a good going over with the polish. Aunt Daisy also washed the glasses herself, thus deeply offending Mrs Moris's niece from the village who was helping out for the party and who considered it her place to be washing glasses.

Aunts Ivy, Daphne and Lily were busy with the dress. First it had to be tried on one last time, then final adjustments had to be made to the length and the fit. Then it had to be pressed very carefully indeed and left to hang outside the cupboard in my room wrapped in a long white sheet, so that no speck of dust should reach it.

Great-Aunt Hortense sat in the conservatory with a huge pot of tea and the guest list. As presents began to arrive, she would tick off the sender's name on the list and write next to it what they had sent. This was to enable me to write thank-you letters later. Here is one more thing I haven't done, one more burden for my mother. I wonder if she's written all those dozens and dozens of letters? It's something I've not thought about before.

Bella and Megan arrived on Friday afternoon, the day before the party. Aunt Daphne whisked their party dresses off to be pressed and hung up in their bedroom almost before they'd put their cases down in the hall.

Mrs Morris was icing the cake in the kitchen and the dining-room was already set for the party buffet, so for supper we had a picnic of sandwiches and salad and penguin biscuits on the terrace.

'I don't call this a proper picnic at all,' said Bella. 'No triangular cheeses.'

'You'll get a proper meal tomorrow,' said Megan, 'so stop complaining.'

'What I want to know is,' said Bella, ignoring her and biting into a beef-and-pickle doorstep, 'why all this fuss for an eighteenth birthday? Most people do this sort of thing when they're twenty-one.'

'You weren't listening when Alice told us about the malediction,' said Megan. 'This is a "let's defy Violette" party, isn't it, Alice?'

'How do you mean?' asked Bella.

'Well,' I answered, 'we're saying: here we are and I've reached eighteen with no mishaps, and just to show that we don't give a fig for curses, we're having the biggest and grandest party possible, and let's just see if any of your ill-wishing has any effect on us whatsoever.'

'Hurray!' shouted Bella. 'I get it. Pass another sandwich, Megan.'

'What about Violette, though?' Megan said. 'Has she been invited this time?'

'Oh, yes,' I nodded. 'You'll get to meet her at last, although she was a little enigmatic about when she'd be arriving. If I had to guess, I'd say, when we least expect her. Aunt Marguerite is in a frightful tizzy getting her bedroom ready. I don't think anyone wants Violette to find fault with anything.'

'Goody goody,' said Bella. 'I'm dying to see her. Has she sent you a present?'

'It's awful,' I said. 'I really hate it, only I think I shall have to wear it. It's a brooch, in the shape of a star, or a wheel or something. Anyway, it's got a lot of pointed bits sticking out all over the place, and what's more it's studded all over with tiny opals, which are dreadfully unlucky.'

'Do you have to wear it?' Megan asked. 'At the party I mean. Can't you say it doesn't go with your dress?'

I shook my head. 'We can't risk it. Even Aunt Daphne says so, and you can see how much it upsets her that the outfit she's been planning for so long won't be perfect in every detail. "We shall just," she says, "have to grin and bear it. It won't be too bad. We will pin it on to your sash. Just by the bow and then the bow will almost hide it. Oh, how typical of Violette to provide flies for any ointment she can get her hands on!"'

'I simply can't wait for tomorrow,' said Bella, stretching out on the grass and turning her face to the sun. 'I just adore getting ready for parties. That's the best bit of the whole thing. What time can we start?'

'Oh, first thing in the morning,' I said. 'We've got to do all the hairwashing and setting and things.'

'Not me,' said Megan. 'I hardly even have to comb mine. But I'll help both of you with your rollers and things if you like.'

'Now, Megan, don't be offended,' said Bella, 'but Aunt Lily is in charge of Hair. She is personally overseeing every curl and ringlet . . . oh, I can't wait! I shall be able to spend an entire day titivating.'

'I can't think,' said Megan, 'of anything more boring.'

'Wet blanket! Killjoy!' Bella began to pelt Megan with bits of pulled-up grass. 'Off you go to the conservatory and read a book or something if you don't want to chat to us while we're getting ready.'

'I never said I didn't want to chat,' Megan said soothingly. 'Just that it was boring to titivate all day long.'

'Well,' said Bella, 'I've raided Marjorie's dressing-table and brought along every cream and unguent I could find. We'll have such good fun! I wish it could be tomorrow right now!'

Bella was quite right. Getting ready for the party turned out to be wonderful. Speculating about how we would look, whom we would dance with, what they would say, was like imagining all our best dreams.

'It'll have to be a pretty amazing party,' said Bella, 'if it's going to live up to expectations.'

The day started with very long, highly-perfumed baths for all of us. We each bathed in turn, and whoever wasn't actually in the water was there simply to chat, so the whole process took ages.

'It's exactly like the Junior House all over again,' said Megan. 'Remember how we used to bath in groups of three?'

'I hated it,' I said, 'but I like this.'

'And we don't have to worry about modesty,' said Megan. 'Bella's bath has made such a fog in here, I can scarcely find the sink.'

'It's steam,' said Bella, who was almost completely submerged. 'Marjorie says it's awfully good for the complexion. It opens the pores and lets the skin breathe.'

'I like my pores just as they are, thank you,' I said. 'All this steam's making me feel so sweaty, I shall need another bath.'

At last, everyone was clean and powdered and had every pore they possessed thoroughly opened.

'And our fingers and toes,' Bella added, 'look like white prunes.'

We all went to my room. Aunt Lily then glided in and began fiddling with rollers and kirby grips and setting lotions. Bella, almost before she had sat down at the dressing-table, started to ask Aunt Lily all the questions I'd been too embarrassed to ask for days.

'Why isn't Alice's boyfriend coming tonight? You know, Jean-Luc, the son of your friend.'

'Alice's boyfriend?' Aunt Lily paused, tail comb quivering in her hand. 'They only met once in my house, as far as I know, and that was last year.'

'But didn't you know they'd been writing to one another?' Bella asked.

'No.' Aunt Lily resumed winding Bella's black hair on to enormous rollers. 'Alice, you naughty little thing! Why ever didn't you tell me? I wonder if Monique has any idea . . .?'

'No, really, Aunt Lily,' I said hastily. 'He's not really my boyfriend. Bella's exaggerating as per usual. I've just been writing to him now and then. It's very helpful to me' (oh, this was a brilliant idea! How quick of me, I thought, to summon it up at this moment!) 'for my written French.'

'Yes, I suppose it must be,' said Aunt Lily, losing interest now that Romance had been reduced to less than fairytale proportions.

'But still,' (Bella never could leave well enough alone and she continued her interrogation of Aunt Lily undeterred) 'he could have been invited. He is a friend of Alice's and hundreds and hundreds of people are coming she's never even laid eyes on before. He might have sent her a card or a present.'

'I'm sure he has,' I said, not feeling sure at all. 'I mean I did write and tell him. And I invited him to the party. It's just that sometimes things take ages to come from Africa, or even get lost in the post.'

'Fancy having to go all the way to Africa for your military service!' said Bella. 'It is a bit of a long way to come just for a party, I suppose. Oh, well,' Bella's glance met mine in the mirror, 'you'll just have to keep your eyes peeled tonight, and see what you can find.'

'Ugh!' Megan shivered. 'What a disgusting expression! Imagine having your eyes peeled. It's dreadful!'

'Right, Bella, you're finished,' said Aunt Lily. 'You next, Alice. Come and sit down here.'

I went and sat in front of the mirror and Aunt Lily began to divide my hair into dozens of sections waiting to be rolled up. I was to have it done on top of my head in some kind of knot, from which a waterfall of ringlets would tumble on to my bare shoulders. I peered at myself, trying to imagine what it would look like. Bella and Megan had been diverted for a while into a discussion about the staying-up powers of the strapless bra, so I was left alone to wonder who, indeed, if Jean-Luc were not here, would make the party a pleasant one for me.

SISSINGHURST CASTLE. Old Gallica. Dark red.
This rose has become entangled in the small gate of the kitchen garden, winding itself in and out of the spirals and scrolls of the black wrought iron. The edges of the petals are blighted.

The afternoon passed. We lounged about in our dressing-gowns, watching the chairs and tables being set out on the terrace.

'How divine!' Bella said. 'We get our food from the dining room and bring it out there. Lovely. Like something from a film.'

I saw my father walking about among the roses with Mr Harris, making sure that every flower was at its best. I knew that that morning, even before Megan, Bella and I had woken up, he'd been out picking hundreds of buds that were just on the point of opening. They were now arranged in vases all over the house. Now he was making sure that all the fallen petals had been swept up, and that any rose that showed the slightest sign of decay was snipped off and thrown away.

At about six o'clock, we began to put on our make-up. Bella was in charge of that.

'O.K. Megan, you first,' she said.

'Now don't go overboard,' Megan protested. 'Truly, I'll look fine with a bit of lipstick and just some powder to take the shine off my nose.'

'Shut up,' said Bella. 'You just have no idea how wonderful you'll look when I've finished with you.'

Megan didn't shut up. She moaned and complained like a child in a dentist's chair. Every now and then there'd be a wailing:

'Oh, Bella, not foundation! Why do I have to have that?' or 'That eyeshadow's too green' or 'You're hurting me . . . what if that brush goes in my eye?'

Bella didn't even bother to reply. In the end she said:

'There you are, Megan, take a look. And don't you dare to contradict me ever again.'

Megan looked. She grinned at Bella.

'Humble and grovelling apologies, oh wondrous miracle worker! Truly, I am transformed.'

She was. It was the first time I had ever seen Megan looking beautiful. She hurried away to put on her sea-coloured dress.

'You next, Alice,' said Bella, 'then me.'

'But I won't be able to tell how I look,' I said, 'because of the rollers.'

'Yes, you will,' said Bella. 'Aunt Lily is arriving to arrange the tresses in twenty minutes, so we'd better get cracking. I'm going to need ages and ages if I'm to look half as good as you and Megan.'

I try not to look in my mirror any more, because what I see there frightens me. I think: this is what I shall be like when I am dead. This is how my skin will be: grey and lifeless. My eyes will have these purple smudges all round them, and my hair will hang down sadly on either side of my face. All my life everyone has told me I am beautiful. I never truly believed them. Looking at myself today, I can see that I was right all along. On the night of the party, though, I came very close to beauty. Bella had put blue eyeshadow on my eyelids, and brushed the lashes with mascara. My lipstick was exactly the colour of the rose called *Celeste* and my cheeks glowed with what Bella called 'the merest whisper of rouge'. Aunt Lily had arranged my hair, and every separate ringlet caught the light.

'It looks,' said Megan, 'like burnished gold.'

'What it is to be a poet!' Bella said. 'I was just going to say it looked terrific.'

'And you both look terrific, too,' I said, and they did. 'Megan, you look like a proper sea-nymph and Bella, you look like . . . like . . .'

'Like Carmen!' said Bella and began to improvise a flamenco dance. 'Only I can't do this dance on such a thick carpet. Just wait till we get downstairs. Olé!'

Bella's dress was scarlet, with a skirt shaped like a tulip. 'I wanted flounces in tiers,' she said, 'and a black lace mantilla and comb, but Marjorie said it would be altogether too much.'

'Well,' I said, 'you look wonderful just as you are.' Bella's eyes shone. 'Oh, I know I do,' she said. 'Anyone I get my little

226

mitts on had better watch out. I feel positively dangerous. It's only a bit of a disappointment to me, Alice, that your parents didn't invite Pete and the band to provide the music. Then I could have sung in front of all your guests.'

'Knowing you,' Megan said, 'you probably will anyway.'

By the time I put my dress on, everyone else was ready. They gathered in my bedroom: Megan and Bella, my mother and most of the Aunts, and Miss van der Leyden. I felt like a mannequin in a window, being dressed for a display. No one said anything while the zip was fastened at the back, while the sash was tied and Violette's brooch pinned next to the bow. No one even dared to breathe, it seemed to me. Aunt Daphne fiddled with the lace of the skirt, pulled the satin sash a little to the left, and then stood back rather like (Megan said later) Michelangelo after he'd put the finishing touches to his statue of David. Everyone breathed again. Little shrieks of delight and exclamations of wonder rose into the air. My mother came towards me with tears in her eyes and kissed me. Megan and Bella hugged me and jumped up and down.

'You are without doubt,' said Bella, 'the Belly of the Ball.'

'"Belle", dear,' said Great-Aunt Hortense, 'to rhyme with "tell". Not "belly."'

'Oh, I know,' said Bella. 'It was supposed to be a joke.'

Great-Aunt Hortense looked at her without any sign of comprehension.

'Never mind,' Bella said. 'Alice looks wonderful. That's all I was trying to say.'

CRAMOISI SUPÉRIEUR. Climber. Red flowers in clusters.
The stems now form a closely-woven trellis outside the dining-room window, and the flowers look like spreading bloodstains.

For the first hour of my party, I felt as though I'd been transported to a magic realm that looked like the inside of a kaleidoscope. Every time I moved, every time I turned my head, the house, the guests, the jewels, the flowers, and the music shifted and settled into different patterns, each one more entrancing than the last. My hand was weak from being shaken, and I was dizzy from smiling and kissing and walking between one knot of people and another and thanking them for their wonderful gifts. The sunlight of early evening was still coming through the open windows, throwing ribbons of gold around the gigantic tubs of roses that stood in every corner.

'I don't know,' said Bella, 'how we're ever going to investigate the possibility of divine young men with this circus going on.'

'Aunt Myrtle says it'll thin out a bit later,' I said, 'when people go out into the garden and when they realize that there are drinks and music in the marquees.'

'I need a drink,' said Bella. 'I still haven't quite recovered from meeting the dreaded Violette.'

We giggled with relief that at least one ordeal was over. Violette had been standing with the other aunts in a corner of the drawing-room when my mother took me over to be introduced. Megan and Bella stayed close behind me. Violette was dressed in a dark purple robe that looked, Bella said later, like an exceedingly posh dressing-gown. When she kissed me, her lips were cool and a chilly draught seemed to spring up from her skirts and blow along my bare arms and shoulders, so that I was immediately covered in gooseflesh.

'You've turned out,' she said to me, 'exactly as I had expected . . .' and she laughed. 'I regret I cannot stay to see,' she smiled, 'how the party ends.' She turned to my father. 'You have cultivated here, William, a rose among roses. One that is ready, more than ready, to be plucked.' Then she raised one hand in the air and held it for a moment a few inches from my face in a scissor-shape.

'Snip, snip, snip,' she said and let out a thin, metallic sort of laugh. 'Oh, most assuredly, snip, snip, snip.'

The rays of the dying sun flashed white light from the rings on her fingers, and lit up her whole hand so that for one dreadful second – no, less than a second: a tiny instant of time but one that I remember now as though it had been branded on my vision – her arm seemed to end in a pair of giant scissors with their points ready to cut into my skin. Then the moment passed and everything was different.

Violette left soon afterwards, in a sweep of purple. A shiny, black car with darkened glass at the windows made its way up the drive. We watched it pulling up at the front door, Megan, Bella and I, from one of the drawing-room windows. Violette folded herself into the car, and it went down the drive again and disappeared. Everyone else was much too busy enjoying themselves to take much notice.

'When, though,' said Bella, 'did she arrive? I never saw her and your parents never mentioned it. Nor did the Aunts.'

'I don't know,' I said. 'She always seems to appear. And disappear. She sort of swoops down like a bird.'

'She *is* like a bird,' said Megan. 'Tall and beaky and with those dark eyes.'

'A kind of purple stork,' said Bella. 'Or an oversized crow or raven.' She laughed. 'But her eyes were strange. Did you notice, Alice?'

'Notice what?'

'That the pupils were almost yellow,' Bella said. 'I don't expect they were really. I should think it was just a trick of the light, but still, it gave me the shivers.'

Megan nodded. 'At least we know now why she's called "the dreaded Violette". I'm jolly glad she's gone. Now we can get on and enjoy the rest of the party.'

*

And, at first, I did enjoy the party, just as I had been expecting to. Bella ate too many strawberries. We went about making rude remarks to one another about other people's dresses.

'The Egerton Hall contingent,' said Bella, 'looks quite good on the whole, only I *do* think Roberta's lime green is a mistake, and why is Fiona wearing a sort of tartan scarf over her dress like an Order of the Garter?'

'It's because she's Scottish,' Megan said.

'No excuse,' said Bella. 'No excuse at all. I can't actually think why you invited all these people.'

'I had to invite someone,' I said, 'so I invited friends from school.'

'And lots of other people too,' Bella said, 'but Male Divinities are a little thin on the ground.'

'I don't know all that many boys,' I said. 'Most of these are from Aunt Lily's list of eligible young men about town.'

Bella sighed. 'They're all so respectable. So well-scrubbed. I'd like to meet someone really rascally and scandalous and flirt like mad. I think I'll go and make friends with the band.'

Bella walked off towards one of the marquees.

That was the last time I saw Bella to speak to. Later on in the evening, I heard her singing 'Moon River' with the band my father had hired to play for dancing. My attention was elsewhere at the time, and I had had a few glasses of punch, but I can remember thinking what a beautiful song it was and how Bella's voice suited it, streaming into the warm night like moonlight. Moon river, I thought fuzzily, such a lovely name . . . so lovely, so sweet.

I ask myself now, I have asked myself for weeks on end a question to which there is no answer: how was it that I didn't recognize Angus? How was it that the face that had filled my nightmares didn't immediately set off all kinds of alarm bells in me? Maybe it did. Maybe what I felt when I saw him standing under one of the apple trees – and I hadn't noticed him before – was a thrill of fear and I didn't realize that that was what it was. I have gone over and over this in my mind. I have gone round and round a central question until I am almost mad with uncertainty. The question I cannot answer is this: was it my fault? Was anything that happened my fault? I know it wasn't. They tell me again and again that it wasn't. My mother has clearly been advised by the doctor, told that she must emphasize this, must convince me of my own innocence, and when she sits by my bed, she recites like a poem, like a kind of lullaby:

'It wasn't your fault, Alice.
Nothing was your fault.
Nothing that happened to you was your fault.'

I believe her. Most of the time, I believe her, and yet I keep thinking: if only. If only I had recognized him. If only I had known. If only: the saddest words in the world.

He was different, quite different from what I remembered. He was very tall and strong and dark. You couldn't see his broad shoulders and muscles under the dinner-jacket, but you could tell they were there. His hands were hairy at the wrists, his eyebrows nearly met over his nose. His teeth were white and pointed in a longish face, but his mouth no longer hung open. Does he sound a little like a wolf? I suppose that I am not giving an unbiased description. If I'm honest, I have to admit I thought him handsome when I saw him. Dangerous looking. A little wild about the eyes, but definitely handsome. I felt angry that Jean-Luc had not even sent me a letter for my eighteenth birthday. I felt defiant. I felt a little giggly and silly because I'd had some punch. I felt I should be grown-up and flirt a little, and most of all (and I know this was a very peculiar sentiment in the middle of a party in my honour, a party crowded with my friends) I felt completely alone. Everywhere I looked there were couples dancing, talking, laughing, eating and I was on my own. Bella was singing and Megan had gone off with Marion Tipton and her boyfriend to find some more food.

Angus walked towards me across the grass. He came straight up to me. As he walked, he looked at me and I stood frozen, mesmerized until he was right beside me.

'May I,' he said, 'have the pleasure of this dance, Alice?'

I shivered slightly as my name was spoken. Did I hear echoes of long-ago hissing? That's what I think now. At the time I thought: the evening is losing its warmth a little.

'I don't think I know you,' I whispered.

'Of course not. How awfully rude of me. I'm Andrew Green. I came with the Hendersons.'

One of the names, I thought, from Aunt Lily's list of London Eligibles.

'How do you know my name?' I asked.

'You were pointed out as the birthday girl. It's an awful cheek on my part, I know, asking you to dance when there must be hordes of people clamouring to partner you, but you've been standing on your own for a while, so I thought I'd try my luck.'

He smiled and I felt a kind of squeezing around my heart. I thought I might be blushing. I said:

'There are no hordes at the moment. I'd love to dance.'

We went into the marquee where the music was. I haven't often danced with a man. At school, it's always girls we practise on, during dancing lessons or the frightful Saturday Night Dancing. Andrew – Angus – felt strange. I was aware

232

of how hard his body was under the suit. Heat seemed to flow from it. His hand holding mine seemed enormous. He towered over me. If I looked up and sideways I could see the line of his jaw, which was dark with the beginnings of a beard.

We paused between dances. I was hot from being so close to him. I drank more fruit punch, which tasted cool and sweet but which also made me silly and muddled in the head. If only. There I go again. If only I hadn't had quite so much fruit punch.

I relaxed. Instead of standing stiffly in the circle of Angus's arm, keeping my distance, not touching him except where I absolutely had to, I leaned into his body, felt myself dissolving round the edges. He said things into my ear, told me how beautiful I was, how soft, how white, how lovely, and all the time drew me closer and closer to him.

I could have stopped it. I could have pulled myself away. I could have run into the house, made an excuse, danced with someone else and I didn't. I liked it. There, I've said it and I feel as if I've dug out a splinter of wood that's been under my nail for a very long time. I liked it. Was I wrong to like it? Did my liking it give Angus some excuse for how he treated me later? I know, deep in my heart, that it didn't, but still the worry persists. I say: I liked it. That's a very bad way of describing how I felt and not quite true. I liked it and I hated it. I wanted it and was terrified by it all at once. I felt as if I were on a rollercoaster: I wanted to scream and be sick, my stomach felt as though it were going to fly out of my mouth, but I didn't want it to stop.

After many dances, we stepped outside the marquee. The night was starlit all around us. I could smell the roses. Angus kissed me quite softly on the mouth.

'Alice,' he whispered, 'where can we go? I want to be alone with you.'

He touched my hair and kissed me again. My heart was beating very fast. I felt dizzy and hot and a little ill.

'We can go to the summerhouse,' I said. My voice sounded thick and fuzzy to me.

'Then let's go there,' Angus said, and took my hand. As we walked down the gravel paths, people passed us. I heard the rustling of skirts coming towards me, vanishing behind me into the darkness. It was just as if they were ghosts: misty, insubstantial shapes drifting to the strains of music that came from a very long way off. My legs felt wobbly. Angus put an arm round me to help me.

'You'll feel better sitting down,' he said.

We followed the path across the back lawns, and made our way to the summerhouse. I went in first. There's a round, wrought-iron table in there and chairs with cushions on them. I sat down on one of these, suddenly feeling very weak. Away from the marquee lights, Angus was nothing but a black shape against the glass. I felt a moment of pure terror as he shut the door behind him. I closed my eyes. When I opened them, he was kneeling beside me, his head almost on a level with mine, but a little lower, so that I touched his hair with my mouth when I turned my face.

'Alice,' he murmured, 'oh, Alice, Alice please . . . please kiss me, Alice.'

He buried his face in my shoulder, saying my name over and over again. It was then, at that moment, that I realized exactly who he was.

I don't know how to write about what happened to me in the summerhouse. All these days of lying here, of writing everything down and saying nothing to anyone, I have dreaded this moment. I knew it would come. I would have to open a door, like a cupboard door in my head which I have kept very firmly shut, and look again at the monstrous thing hiding there in the dark. Sometimes I've thought: I can avoid it. I can exorcise it in one sentence. I can be brief, factual and to the point, like a police report: At approximately twelve midnight on the night of June 20th, the accused (for I like to think of him as in the dock, though he will never appear there) raped one Alice Gregson (18) of Arcadia House. There, I've written it and I hate it. It's a word that gives me pain when I think it, sears the page as I write, leaves a trail of anguish and sorrow in my heart when I think it – and which sounds like fingernails scraping a blackboard. But writing that sentence isn't enough. I need to go through it, at least the parts of it that I remember.

As soon as I knew who he was, I became ice-cold and began to shiver. The part of my brain that was still working properly said: be calm. You're no longer a child. Speak firmly to him. Apologize. Say you want to go back to the house. Be quite friendly, but make it clear that you're no longer interested. Talk your way out of this. Disarm him. Distract him. Suggest going to dance a little more. Finally, I said:

'I know who you are, you know.'

He laughed: 'When did you realize?'

'Only a moment ago. You've changed an awful lot.'

'I know. You'd never have danced with me if you'd known who I was. Go on. Admit it.'

(Lie, said a voice in my head. Be light. Be frivolous. Pretend you're Bella.)

'I don't know . . .' (fading away.)

'I do. Wouldn't come near me when we were kids.'

'You . . . you frightened me. You were so rough.'

'You don't mind that now, though.'

(Keep your voice full of laughter) 'You're not rough now. You're jolly sophisticated.' (Flatter him. Placate him.) 'And a jolly good dancer. In fact,' I stood up and pushed the chair away a little, 'I'd like to dance with you again. Shall we go back to the marquee?'

He laughed. It sounded like a growl in this throat.

'Oh, no, you're not getting away that easily. Oh no.'

'Why?' My voice sounded high and shrill in my ears. A squeak. A pathetic little mouse-squeak. 'What would you like to do? Would you like some food? There's strawberries.'

'I'd like,' he said, coming closer, gathering me in his arms, 'to nibble on you a little. Gobble you all up.'

I pulled away from him but his arms were strong, wouldn't loosen their grip.

'But I don't feel like . . .' I began. He laughed again, that hideous laugh that had nothing at all of pleasure or fun in it, only a threat of anger in it somewhere, a promise of pain.

'You didn't mind before,' he said. 'In fact, I got the impression you quite liked it. You're not going to turn out to be a little teaser, are you?'

'I don't know what you mean,' I stammered. 'I don't know what a teaser is. But I'm not one. I'm positive I'm not. No one's ever called me that before.'

'A teaser,' he said, 'is *exactly* what you are. You lead a chap on, and you flirt and toss your curls and smile and press yourself against him soft as a lamb, and you're happy to kiss him and maybe even let him touch you – above the waist, mind – but that's it. Not a step further. Well, that might work with the milksops you're used to, but I'm different.'

He smiled at me then . . . I could see his teeth in the light from the stars, and his breath burned my cheeks. I thought: I could scream. I will scream. Someone will come if I scream and take him away. I'll imagine he's a horrible hairy spider, that's all, and if I scream loudly enough, someone will hear and come and pluck him off my body.

I screamed. I screamed as loudly as I knew how. I didn't know, I never realized that there was so much sound inside me. But I shouldn't have screamed. It was a mistake. It made him very angry and he slapped me. He slapped me in the face. I cried out with the pain and fell back into the chair. He stood over me.

'I really shouldn't do that if I were you, Alice. No one will hear you, for a start, because we're so far from the house, and there's all that music and laughter, isn't there? Besides which, if you scream, I shall have to do something I'd really hate to do and which you'd hate as well. So don't make me, there's a good girl.'

'What,' I whispered, 'what will you do?'

His eyes glittered. He put his face close to mine and said:

'I'll cut you. I've got a razor in my pocket and I'll cut your pretty face. You wouldn't like that, Alice, now would you?'

'No.' I was beginning to freeze up, to turn to stone, starting at my feet. I closed my eyes, so that I shouldn't have to see him. I tried to think of myself as not being there, as being out of my body, as not being real. I tried to imagine I was not a person, but a marble statue. I tried to think: it'll all be over soon. Keep still and it'll all be over soon. If you keep still and don't move, he can't hurt you. Just keep still.

I kept still. I closed my eyes – oh, but I could still smell him and feel him: his hands crawling over my skin, his breathing coming faster and faster, rasping in his throat. He tore off my satin sash, and pulled me to my feet. I'm a rag-doll, I thought. I'm a nothing, a non-person. I flopped, lifeless in his arms. He laid me down on the concrete floor and it was hard and cold on my back. He lay down alongside me, breathing on me. His hands pushed at my dress. I felt his fingers close over my breasts. Then he pulled at my skirts. I heard tearing. I thought: I want to die. Please God let me die. Let me die now before anything else happens.

I didn't die then. I died later. I died as his full weight rolled on to me, died as I felt him crush me and cover my mouth with his, stopping the sounds that I could hear coming from me in spite of myself: the thin, bloodstained shrieks of a small animal in the teeth of a metal trap.

*

I must have fainted, I suppose. When I came to, I was alone in the summerhouse, on the dirty, concrete floor. After a long time, I sat up. My breasts were bare. I touched them and they were sore. My mouth felt bruised and swollen. When I looked down at my legs I burst into tears and was glad that it was dark. My knickers were still around one ankle. The skirt of my dress was torn. So were my stockings. My thighs were covered in slime, as though slugs had crawled over my flesh, leaving trails of blood. I don't know how long I sat there. Then I stood up. I could stand. I pulled my knickers on again and tried to find my sash, feeling about for it all over the floor. I found it in the end, but Violette's brooch must have sprung open and I pricked my finger on the pin. I held my hand against my skirt to stop the pain, and when I took it away I noticed the small spots of darkness my blood was making on the fabric. Help, I thought. I must get help. My mother. My father. Bella. Megan. I couldn't bear the thought of seeing anyone. I wanted silent, unquestioning, undemanding comfort. I staggered into the garden thinking: I'll go and find Miss van der Leyden. I found it hard to walk. I felt like a butterfly, pierced through the core by a metal pin. Impaled.

VIRIDIFLORA (montrosa.) 1843. Permanently deformed flowers. Petals: green scales, later tinged with red.
My father told me that this rose is a botanical freak, a curiosity. It grows hidden among the trees in the orchard.

The steps to Miss van der Leyden's room go round and round in a spiral. The light there is very dim. I could see my own shadow walking at my side. My long skirt, spread out behind me, looked like black wings on the wall. Miss van der Leyden was surprised to see me. She had already got into her bed, and when I came in, she got up and went behind a small screen that stood near the washbasin, to put her dressing-gown on, I think. As she was doing that, she chattered away: why was I leaving the party, she asked, and did I want tea . . . would I sit for a minute . . . and how sweet, how kind of me to spare a thought for a sick old woman when there was all that revelry going on below. I must have answered. I must have made some replies that seemed quite sensible, because otherwise she would have come out sooner from behind the screen. I can remember leaning against the chest-of-drawers. My thumb had begun to bleed again where Violette's brooch had pricked me. When Miss van der Leyden turned at last and saw me, her hand flew to her mouth and she screamed.

'*Alice, ma petite,*' she sobbed, '*qu'est-ce qu'il-y-a? Oh, quelle horreur!*'

Her voice was like a bell that woke me up.

'It was a man . . . Angus,' I muttered. 'He . . .' I couldn't go on, but what I had said was enough. I could see from her face, from the way it was dissolving, melting with anguish, that she knew, that she could guess what had happened. Suddenly, I found I couldn't bear it. I ran for the door and tore it open. Then I raced down the spiral staircase, down through the kitchen, out of the back door and into the garden. If only, I thought, I could get to the orchard, I could lose myself among the trees and no one would find me.

No one came looking for me for a long time. Miss van der Leyden, I learned later from my mother, had collapsed on the night of the party. She had, my mother said, fallen down the stairs. It must have been Miss van der Leyden who told my parents what she had learned, and even more importantly, the identity of the person responsible for the state I was in.

I don't know how long I spent in the orchard. I leaned against one tree after another. Roses grew round every single one of them, and I knew it. I simply wanted the thorns to hurt me. They made small holes in the fabric of my dress, tiny pinpricks in the skin of my chest and arms. I wanted some pain to distract me from what had happened, to take my mind over, to stop me thinking . . . thinking. I don't know why I went back to the summerhouse, but I remember wanting to destroy something, someone. I wanted to hurt. I wanted to cut and tear apart. The summerhouse was empty, of course. Someone had left a pair of shears there, though, and that was where they found me. I don't know how long I'd been there. I was cutting up the cushions into small pieces with the garden shears. I shall never forget my father's face when he saw me. I think they had been looking for me for hours. Even in the orchard, I think I heard my name being called. My father picked me up and brought me to this room. The party was over.

HEBE'S LIP. 1912. Damask. Semi-double flowers.
Cream edged with crimson. Flowers close at night.
This rose grows in a round bed on the back lawn. The dark edges of the petals seem dipped in blood.

At first, you say nothing because even forming the thoughts that are in your head into real words is terribly painful. Then you say nothing because you are protecting someone: your parents, everyone who loves you. You think: if I tell them this, they will think I am different, worse, defiled in some way. Then you say nothing because you've fallen into the habit of not speaking and it's easy to let a crust of silence form like a scab over a bleeding wound.

But writing this is a kind of talking and I feel: if only I had done it straight away, poured all the poison out at once, to my parents, Bella, Megan, then I would never have needed to lie here all these weeks under my blanket of misery.

At school, people were forever having poultices put on boils by Mighty Mack. Mighty Mack believed in poultices.

'They draw all the horrid substances out of the body, d'ye see,' she said, 'and leave the sore place empty and clean, ready to heal all by itself.'

That is how I feel now, having rid myself at last of this burden: empty and clean and ready to heal.

Everything will heal. That's what my mother said and maybe she's right. This morning I spoke. My voice sounded very peculiar, like a rusty hinge. I went to the mirror and stood in front of it. Then I said, 'Hello, Alice,' and a thin, pale stranger with wild red curls stared at me out of uncomprehending eyes and seemed to say, 'Hello, Alice,' at the same time. I was just thinking: 'I'll walk out now, walk downstairs to my mother, speak to her, tell her I'm feeling better . . . and then I heard my mother's tread on the stairs, and I fled back to my bed, to rearrange myself into the patterns of sleep she'd grown used to. I felt so angry with myself, so disappointed that I wasn't really better, that I nearly cried, all over again.

My mother said: 'Alice, Alice, if you can hear me, I've got news that will make you happy. A parcel came for you today. All the way from Africa. It's taken simply ages and ages, but here it is at last . . . a birthday present from your French pen-friend. It's very pretty. I'll put it here, on the bedside table with the letter . . .' She went on and on talking, and I waited for her to finish, and leave the room so that I could see what it was that Jean-Luc had sent me. He hadn't forgotten me. He hadn't forgotten my birthday. Oh, go, please go, I said silently in my head to my mother, over and over again. Please, please go.

When she left, I picked up Jean-Luc's present. It was a small antelope carved from a wood that shone like brown-yellow satin. The letter was not a letter, but more of a note:

'Heureux Anniversaire, ma chère Alice! Je ne pense qu'à toi. À bientôt. Jean-Luc.'

Je ne pense qu'à toi . . . I'm thinking only of you. *À bientôt* . . . see you soon. It was, I thought, a strange thing to put in a note. It was more the kind of thing you say to someone when you're going to see them tomorrow, or next week . . . Soon. Very soon.

> *BOURBON QUEEN. 1834. Pink and white clusters.*
> *Free flowering.*
> This rose, growing at the back of the house, has so
> much massed blossom this year that it looks like a
> cloud at sunrise, touched with new colour.

I haven't written in these pages for three days. There has been no time. Arcadia House is waking up, coming back to life again. The dust sheets have been taken off the furniture. My mother hasn't played the piano, not yet, but she has dusted and polished it and put back all the photographs that used to stand on it. I have seen her looking at it with longing. She will play it soon, just as soon as Arcadia House is back to normal. Mrs Morris is back in the kitchen. There is a new daily from Egerton Parva who dusts and polishes all day long. Curtains have been taken down and sent to the cleaners, and the hum of the Hoover fills the corridors. My father is not to be seen. He is in the garden from morning till night, tidying the roses, nursing them back to health, watering them, feeding them, cutting off all the dead heads, the tangled stems, the neglected, overgrown thorns. He has three men to help him.

I feel as though my life has begun again. Jean-Luc is here. He and I walk through the gardens. I have told him everything. I have spoken on the telephone to Megan and Bella. They have special permission from Miss Herbert to come and stay here next weekend. We have all passed our exams. When I heard the news, I had to think for a good few seconds before I remembered exactly what the word meant. I have 'B' for Art and English and 'C' for French. Bella has 'A' for English and French and 'B' for Spanish. Megan, naturally, has all 'A's. They are both back in Egerton Hall.

'You come back too, Alice,' Megan said. 'It'll be such fun. We could get the Tower Room again. I'm sure we could, if you came back. It's only for the University entrance.'

'No,' I said. 'I couldn't bear it. Not more exams. Not now. I'll come and visit you both. I'll take you out to The Old Forge.'

'What about University?' Megan said.

'I don't want to go to University. Not at the moment.'

Bella said: 'What will you do? We've been so worried, honestly, Alice. They wouldn't let us write. They said you were in a coma. Is that true. Were you?'

'In a way. I suppose a kind of coma. I don't know what I'll do. Go to France, perhaps, to meet Jean-Luc's family.'

'Lucky thing!' Bella cried. 'I've been in Paris almost the whole of the hols. It was fantastic, honestly! I can't wait to tell you about it. However did Jean-Luc arrive like that out of the blue? Were you expecting him?'

'I wasn't expecting anyone. Aunt Lily had told his mother and she had written to him. The army has given him special compassionate leave, just so that he could come. He'll have to go back in the end, of course, but not for ages yet. Not until Christmas.'

'How wonderful! Only are you O.K. now? Really?'

'I'm fine. I'll tell you everything when you arrive. I can't wait to see you both.'

I will tell them. I will also give them this notebook to read and because of that, I have left Jean-Luc talking to my father in the garden and come up to my room to finish the story.

The day after Jean-Luc's present arrived, I woke up very

early and stood beside my window for a long time, noticing how autumn had begun to creep into the sunlight, turning the first leaves on the trees, blowing the first frosty mists into the pale daylight. In the early morning noise carries a very long way. I heard a distant metallic shaking, like chains being pulled about, and I couldn't think what it was. I looked all round the garden and saw nothing. I opened my window to get a better view and the rattling iron noise was louder. It's someone rattling at the gates, I thought. Why are they doing that? I looked round the drive to see what was happening and the rattling stopped. Then I saw a head sticking up over the top of the gates. Someone was climbing over them. It's a burglar, I thought. It's someone come to rob us. Immediately, though, I knew it couldn't be a burglar. What thief in his right mind would rattle and shake the gates and then climb over them in broad daylight? The person started to walk up the drive. Then he stepped on to the lawns below the terrace and I recognized Jean-Luc. He made his way up to the house, through the overgrown roses. I could see him stepping over stems, pushing his way through the creeping tendrils of plants that had run wild into a mesh of green twigs, and crushing under his feet the fallen petals from flowers that had once been pink and red and cream and crimson, and were now turning into snowdrifts of a uniform faded beige.

When Jean-Luc reached the porch, I hid behind a curtain so that he shouldn't see me. The door was locked, of course. He knocked and knocked and no one came to open it. I saw him hesitate beside the hall window. It was open just a little at the bottom. The beigey-pink flowers and thorny stems of *La Vesuve* had crept over the sill. Jean-Luc carefully pulled them back and away from the wall. He looked around him. Could he feel my eyes following him? I jumped back into the room, the beats of my own heart very loud in my head. Then

I heard the noise of the window being pushed up, the squeak of the stiff wood. I lay down on the bed and closed my eyes. I thought: this must be a dream. Nothing is what it seems in a dream. In a moment, I shall wake up and none of it will have been true. I could hear Jean-Luc's voice now, calling softly for me.

'*Alice! Alice, òu es-tu? Alice, c'est moi. C'est Jean-Luc.*'

I tried to imagine where he was. Suddenly, I heard his footsteps on the stairs. I could feel him gently opening and closing all the doors along this corridor. I flew to the bed and lay down, arranging myself with my hands folded over my heart. Then he opened the door of my bedroom and silence fell all over the house. Did it take him two seconds or three to cross the carpet to my bed? To me those seconds stretched and stretched so that I could hardly bear the waiting. My eyes were closed, but I could smell him. He smelled of the garden, and damp cloth.

'*Alice*,' he whispered, kneeling down beside the bed. '*Alice, enfin* . . . wake up, it's me. It's Jean-Luc.'

'I know it's you,' I said, opening my eyes. 'I've been looking at you. Out of the window. I saw you climb over the gate.'

'I did not know how to come in,' he said. His eyes were even bluer than I remembered. 'But I knew I needed to see you, and now,' he blushed and looked away, 'now that I have arrived, I have nothing to say. I do not know what to say.'

'It doesn't matter,' I said. 'You don't have to say anything. I'm very happy . . . happy to see you.'

'Alice . . .' he said, and stood up and went over to the window so that I could no longer see his face. 'Alice . . . my mother has told me what happened to you. If I could pick up, carry away some of your pain, I would do it.'

'It's all right,' I said. 'Just seeing you again makes it all right. Don't let's talk about horrid things.'

He came over to the bed and sat down on it just in the way that Dr Benyon often sat. He took my hand.

'*Alice*,' he whispered, '*je veux te donner un baiser.*'

What silly things come into your head sometimes! What I was saying to myself at that moment was: he must like me. Last time he said that, I was '*vous*' and he's not using the more formal '*embrasser*'. Oh, he must like me a lot. Even after all this time. He thinks I am someone worth climbing gates and creeping through windows for, someone for whom he is prepared to tear roses from the sills, someone worth searching for.

He kissed me then.

Sometimes, when the weather turns hot, the roses need to be watered towards the evening. When I was very young, I had my own little watering-can, and my father used to let me help him. The dry, cracked earth around every plant always looked so parched, so thirsty, until my water poured on to it, soaking every root.

'Just the ticket,' my father used to say. 'Can't you almost feel them flourishing and growing?'

When Jean-Luc kissed me, that was exactly what it felt like: something hard and dry had softened and turned green.

He took both my hands and helped me get off the bed. 'Everyone has been so worried,' he said. 'They thought that . . . I don't know the dreadful things they thought.'

'I do,' I said. 'They thought I was . . . not normal. Mad in some way. I don't know. I think they thought I was hopeless. A hopeless case.'

'Then let us go down. Let us show them that you are again . . . yourself. Have you got a dressing-gown?'

I told him where it was, and he helped me to put it on. Tenderly, like a parent with a small child, he drew my arms through the sleeves, and tied the belt. Then he kneeled down and put on my slippers.

'*Voilà*,' he said proudly. 'Let us go and find your parents.'

Something (the squeak of the window, the whispers in the corridors) must have woken them up. They were standing at the foot of the staircase, looking up at me with tears of happiness in their eyes as Jean-Luc led me down into the hall.

Pictures of the Night

For Patty Cammack

World's End

'ONCE upon a time,' I said, 'I had a mother, but I killed her.'

Greg said, 'You're being melodramatic as usual, Bella. Try and get a little rest. What happened yesterday has made you think along these morbid lines, that's what it is. I don't believe you killed your mother at all.'

'She died when I was born though.'

'That's not the same thing, is it? You didn't mean to kill her. The intention wasn't there, so the whole affair becomes sad, of course, but not exactly lurid.'

'You're as bad as Megan and Alice,' I sighed. 'They're forever telling me off for exaggerating, making an exhibition of myself, being what you call melodramatic.'

Greg strummed a few notes on his guitar. He was sitting on the end of the bed, looking after me. Because of what happened yesterday, I'd been put in the best bed in the whole house, the one in Pete's room. All the others were out for some reason or other. Greg's fair hair flopped over on to his forehead, almost hiding his eyes. He looked cuddly, in spite of being over six feet tall. He'd folded his legs into strange shapes, to squeeze on to the small amount of space left over on the bed after I'd stretched my legs out as far as they would go.

'Who is Megan . . . What is she . . .' he sang, to the tune of 'Who is Sylvia?', and I kicked him through the blankets. He stopped singing and added, 'and Alice too, if it comes to that.'

'I keep telling you and you never listen,' I said. 'It's because you've always got your nose in a guitar. Megan and Alice are my friends at school, at Egerton Hall.'

'Oh, very la-di-da, I'm sure!'

'Shut up and pay attention. They are my best friends. We used to share a room called the Tower Room, but then last Easter term Megan ran away to London with Simon, the rather sweet laboratory assistant . . .'

'Did you report the story to the *News of the World*? You could have made a bit of money.'

'Greg, belt up! I'm telling you something. Megan came back to do her A-level exams. Can you imagine? Leaving the one you love and coming back to school? I can't. Simon went off to America in a huff.'

'When I go to America,' said Greg, 'I shall try and go in a plane. They're more reliable than huffs.'

'I give up.' I pulled the blankets over my head and pretended to be hurt. 'You're not a bit interested, so I'll keep quiet.'

'No, Bella, truly, I'm sorry.' Greg jumped off the foot of the bed and came to find my face under the covers. He looked very contrite. I said:

'If you interrupt me again, I'll never say another word to you. Not ever.'

As soon as I'd said it, I regretted it. Greg looked stricken, so I laughed.

'I don't mean it, Greg, only you're an impossible person to tell a story to. Just sit still and listen.'

And Greg did listen, because I told him about Alice, and about how she was raped on the night of her eighteenth birthday party, just a couple of weeks ago. That silenced him for a bit, then he said:

'Where is she now?'

'In her bedroom. She won't speak to anyone. She won't see anyone. Megan and I have just been told to wait till she gets better.'

'You could write letters,' Greg suggested.

'I have, but there's no point in sending them. She wouldn't be able to read them. Poor Alice!' I hated to think of her, in her room in Arcadia House. What if she wasn't really in a coma, as we'd been told? What if she knew what was happening and just thought Megan and I had stopped caring about her? I couldn't bear that, and so every now and then I would write to her, and put the letter in my suitcase. I felt sure she'd be herself one day, because I simply couldn't face any other possibility and I was keeping all the letters to show her I'd been thinking about her.

'I don't know,' said Greg. 'It's not a bit what I'd imagined went on in a girls' school. Running off to London with your lover isn't exactly school story stuff, and as for your other friend . . .' Greg looked at me. 'I don't know what to say. You must feel . . .' He couldn't find the right words and I couldn't help him. I closed my eyes.

What happened yesterday was very strange, or was I really being melodramatic? I don't care. Long live melodrama, say I, and passion and bright scarlet dresses and loud music and everything that isn't flat and dull and grey and little and ordinary. I hate ordinary things, and ordinary people bore me to death.

There's nothing ordinary about Pete and the band. I met them at a party in December 1961, which was only last year though it seems ages ago now. The party was at the Establishment Club which was *the* place to go, and that very evening they had taken me to another nightclub, where I sang with them for the very first time. Since then they've let me perform with the band now and again, whenever I could, and once or twice when I couldn't. Last February, I sneaked out of Egerton Hall to sing at a Valentine's Day ball and climbed back into the Tower Room up the same scaffolding that Megan's Simon used in order to reach her. Last holidays, I visited Pete's house a couple of times, but now I'm staying here. After what happened to Alice, I can't really face going home. The advantage of having a fantastically busy father and a stepmother who permanently wishes you as far as possible from where she is, is that you can stay away from home for ages. I haven't told them exactly where I am. They think I'm staying with an aunt of Alice's. Alice has thirteen aunts who are useful in all sorts of ways, and providing an alibi for me is what they're doing now. I write a postcard home every few days and phone occasionally, but Marjorie, my wicked stepmother, is so relieved to be rid of me that she'll accept any story I tell her. My father thinks Marjorie has the whole situation under control, and so he's happy too. It's an ideal arrangement.

I looked at Greg. He was deeply into a song he'd been working on for some days. There were scrappy pieces of paper all over the floor, and a pencil that had seen better days and had totally forgotten what a sharpener looked like, and Greg had slipped off the bed and taken up residence amidst all the chaos on the floor. From time to time he'd play a few notes on the guitar, and these little snippets of melody would hang in the silence for a few moments, and then disappear. I knew Greg would now be unreachable until he'd finished whatever it was he was writing, so I decided to think quietly back over everything that had happened since I'd come to Pete's house, here in this part of London where Chelsea ceases to be Chelsea and becomes World's End.

I like the name: World's End. It has a certain ring of doom to it, you've got to admit. In fact, the street is full of stuccoed houses fallen on hard times. Pete's house is tall and thin. I liked it from the very first time I saw it because it was the exact opposite of my house, and could have been specifically designed as Marjorie's idea of Hell.

There were three floors full of rooms, each one more cluttered and messy than the last. It reminded me of a doll's house, because all sorts of strange objects (a large stuffed bear, a tiger-skin rug, brass trays on gate-leg tables, the odd dragon-shaped kite, a marble urn, the propeller from an ancient aircraft) were dotted about all over the place, as though some giant child had been playing and left them lying about for the dolls to wonder at. As well as peculiar bits and pieces everywhere, there was all the mess you'd expect from seven men living together. That was how I'd expressed it to Megan, when I told her about it last term.

'I don't see any reason why men shouldn't be as tidy as women, do you?' she'd said.

'No,' I said. 'There isn't any reason, but this lot are amazing. I tease them about it. I say things like: "Didn't your mother ever tell you dirty socks go in a laundry basket?" and they just laugh and say: "What's a laundry basket?" Dave, whose mother died when he was quite young, says: "You can come and look after us. Teach us how to take care of ourselves," and Pete laughs and says: "Better yet, come and take care of us yourself!"'

'I can't believe you will,' Megan had smiled. 'You're not what I'd call the house-proud type.'

'I'm not, it's true, but honestly, Megan, in that house it's tidy it up yourself or risk vanishing altogether in a rising ride of garbage.'

Now that I'm staying here, I do try and make things as pleasant as possible. Megan and Alice would be astonished, but I enjoy the gratitude I get from Pete and the others. They are all so delighted with everything. Even quite a simple idea like gathering up all the waste paper no one wants off the floor and putting it into the dustbin was greeted like a major discovery the first time I did it, and really daring initiatives like running some hot water into a basin and washing a few dishes, well, I felt as though I'd just topped the bill at the London Palladium, I got so much praise.

I had the nicest room in the house, somewhere all to myself. That was an accident. The first time I ever found this house, no one was in. This didn't matter as it turned out, because the front door wasn't locked. Later, I discovered that it frequently remained open, because the stiff mortise lock needed oiling, and the old-fashioned keys were always getting themselves mislaid. It was the middle of the afternoon when I turned up, and the place was deserted. I knew the address, of course, but I'd come on the off-chance that they'd be in, and could give me a cup of tea. I'd been shopping in the King's Road, and felt quite worn out. I snooped around a bit, but only on the ground floor, and eventually found myself in a small room at the back of the house. There was a battered old chaise-longue in there, upholstered in moth-eaten puce velvet with sad-looking braid in a tarnished gold colour clinging here and there to the wreckage. I can remember thinking: I'll just lie down here for a moment and think what to do next, and then I suppose I must have fallen asleep.

When I woke up, hours later, darkness had fallen, and Pete and the boys were all standing round and looking at me. Waking up and finding them, all seven of them, staring at me while I slept was a bit of a shock, but I pulled myself together and sat up. They still looked quite alarming, all shadowy and enormous. Later on, I realized that this must have been because of the unusual lighting arrangements in the house. Pete hated any kind of fixture dangling from the ceiling and abhorred what he called 'chilly light' and the rooms were full of light bulbs in shades of red and yellow screwed into the tops of bottles that had been turned into lamps and then quite deliberately hidden behind other pieces of furniture. This meant that you could never see where the light was coming from and wherever it fell it cast long, medieval-looking shadows on the walls and ceilings. Reading in bed was out of the question, although Pete did have a supply of candles and cracked saucers. You could actually do it: take a candle and go upstairs from the kitchen singing, 'Here comes a candle to light you to bed'.

'But,' said Pete on the first night, 'I wouldn't recommend it. I reckon it's a fire hazard. Anyone still lively enough to want to read in bed can stay and do it in the kitchen. There's a decent-enough light in there.'

Of course, we never were lively enough. The music sessions went on till late in the orange dimness of the lounge or in Pete's room, where the darkness loomed in the corners and the shadows of the instruments danced along the walls.

That was after I had become a member of the household. On the first night, though, they led me down to the kitchen which was in the basement. Over coffee, I asked them if I could stay for a bit. They all said I could and seemed to take it for granted that the old chaise-longue was to be my bed, so that little room became mine, complete with a rocking chair with the seat missing, a couple of traffic signals, the odd car number-plate, two crash helmets and a drum kit.

'What about a cupboard?' I could imagine Megan asking. 'Isn't there a cupboard or a chest of drawers?' There isn't of course, but one can manage very well with open suitcases and garments draped over the back of the rocking chair. You never know what you can do till you try, as Marjorie has never tired of telling me.

Megan and Alice could never get the individual members of the band quite straight in their heads.

'You're not trying,' I used to say. 'Megan, you managed Alice's thirteen aunts quite well. I can't think why seven men is so difficult for you.'

There's Pete and Dave and Phil and Steve and Kenny and Harry and Greg. Pete's the leader of the band. He's thin and bearded and dark, and looks like a benevolent pirate. Harry's everyone's darling. Easygoing. Affable. Happy-go-lucky, with a round face and twinkling blue eyes.

'Girls love him,' I used to tell Megan and Alice. 'He sits there behind his drums and grins at them and they cluster around him afterwards wanting kisses and autographs.'

'And does Harry oblige?' Megan had wanted to know, and I knew what she was really asking.

'He's not my type,' I told her, 'but it would be very hard not to like him.'

They were all of them kind to me, and looked after me, but Greg . . . Greg loves me. I know that, although he hasn't actually said anything. Greg's eyes when he looks at me are full of devotion, and he's the one, who, from the first, spent every possible moment with me, always sat next to me at meals and took me about with him all over the place. Perhaps it's because he's the youngest member of the band, and only three years older than me. He has written songs for me to sing, he says, and he will show them to me soon.

It was Greg who took me to Jeannie's shop for the very first time. I suppose most people would call 'Aladdin's Cave' a junk shop, but it was full of treasures: old silk scarves and pieces of lace and jewellery and feathers and buttons and cushions in velvet covers and old uniforms and cracked records. I loved it from the moment I stepped into it, and I liked Jeannie, the owner, immediately. She is one of those amazingly glamorous slatterns with a face ravaged by time and alcohol and teeth practically ochre-coloured from too many cigarettes, but still tremendously vivid, alive. She has huge brown eyes, wears lashings of rouge and never puts anything on her body that you can actually identify as a proper garment, like a skirt or a cardigan or a pair of trousers. Jeannie just seems to be wrapped, or enveloped, in all sorts of pieces of fabric that are pinned or tied or held together somehow in an arrangement that manages to look exotic: strange and beautiful. All the floaty bits are always such colours: pinks and tangerines and saffron yellows and mossy greens and always, somewhere, different textures and surfaces of black: velvet, satin, chiffon or wool. Oh, I thought when I first saw her, she's like a sort of magic butterfly. That was one side of her character. The other was very practical. She always, for instance, wore slippers or gym shoes, saying that winklepickers were as bad for you in their way as binding up the feet in the old Chinese style. And she smelled extraordinary. I'm very knowledgeable about perfume, but these smells that hung about her shop were new to me.

'Oils,' she told me. 'Oriental oils. Patchouli, Bergamot and Sandalwood.'

She burned fragrant joss sticks in the shop so that the very air smelled magical. And she had a sense of humour, too. She told me her real name wasn't Jeannie at all.

'But,' she said, 'how can you have an Aladdin's cave and no genie? I changed it, that's all. Changed it to fit the shop. I ran a sea-food restaurant once. Down in Brighton, that was, called "Full Fathom Five" and guess what I was called?'

I couldn't guess. I suggested silly things like 'Shrimp' and 'Squid' but she waved her garments at me.

'Give over, Bella! You're not trying, are ya? I called myself Pearl then, didn't I? See?'

'Sea? North Sea? Irish Sea? Which sea do you mean?' I said and Jeannie shook with laughter.

'Ooh, Bella,' she shrieked. 'You are a caution and no mistake.'

I used to go to Aladdin's Cave almost every day, partly to see Jeannie and partly because there were always new goodies to be found there, especially in the boxes set out on trestle tables on the pavement outside the shop, where nothing cost more than a shilling. Greg usually came with me, but yesterday I was alone in the house.

'I don't like leaving you all on your own here,' Greg said. 'You be sure and lock the door now and don't open it to just anyone.'

'I don't know what you think's going to happen to me,' I said. 'No one even knows I'm here. Anyway, I thought I'd go down to Jeannie's shop for a while.'

'Don't be long then,' Greg said. 'And make sure you lock the door behind you when you get back.'

'You sound like my dad,' I told him. 'I'll be fine.'

And I was fine. I set out for Aladdin's Cave feeling very cheerful, and began rummaging happily through the shilling boxes as soon as I'd said hello to Jeannie.

I didn't really pay much attention to the woman who passed close beside me to go into the shop. I only noticed, in a half-hearted, absent-minded sort of way, that she smelt very faintly of 'Je Reviens' and that as she passed, a cloud spread itself over the sun and I felt, all at once, quite cold. She was inside the shop with Jeannie for about fifteen minutes and then she left. I got a better look at her this time. What struck me about her was that she appeared faded, as though she were a faint carbon copy of a real person. She wore grey and her hair was grey and she had most of her face hidden in a chiffon scarf. She was carrying a battered brown suitcase, and she walked quickly past me, and down the road. At the time, I could have sworn she didn't even look at me.

'Who's that?' I asked Jeannie.

'One of my suppliers,' Jeannie said. 'No one you'd be interested in. She brings me bits of lace and stuff.'

When I went home, I let myself in with my key, and slammed the door behind me. I forgot to lock it, of course. We all forgot, all the time, and no one ever troubled us. It wasn't as though there was anything worth stealing in the house. I went down to the kitchen to make some tea. I hadn't been there more than five minutes, when I heard someone in the hall.

'Hell-oo,' said an unfamiliar voice. 'Yoo-hoo! Is there anyone at home?'

It was a woman, and she was calling out to me, so I didn't feel at all nervous. She must be a neighbour, I thought, one I haven't met yet. I'd better go and see what she wants.

I walked up to the hall, and the first thing I saw was a white cat. It looked just like Snowflake, the cat I used to have when I was very young, the cat that my stepmother had claimed she was allergic to . . . I didn't want to be remind-ed of her, and I wanted this one out of the house. I said:

'Is that your cat?' to the woman who was standing in the shadows by the hatstand, and then I saw she was the one from Jeannie's shop. She even had her brown suitcase at her feet. I looked at the pretty, fluffy creature who by this time had run up a few stairs and was sitting there as though it intended to stay. I said, 'How did you know where I live? Did you follow me? And is that your cat?'

'That's no cat of mine, ducky. I'm what you might call

allergic to them. Must have crept in behind me . . . and yes, dear, I did follow you, cos I saw you at Jeannie's, didn't I, and I says to meself, Em, old girl, that child's a real beauty and if ever you had an ideal customer, she's the one.' The woman took a step forward and patted her suitcase. 'I've got stuff in here, dearie, that'll make your heart beat faster, and that's why I came after you, see? To show you . . .'

'Why didn't you show this stuff to me, whatever it is, when you noticed me in the shop? I don't like the thought of you following me, I must say.'

'Well, I'm very sorry, I'm sure, miss, but I meant no harm, honest. Only you've got to be a bit smart in my line of work, see. Seize any opportunity that comes along, like. And you being such a pretty girl, I thought: she'll love you for this, Em. She won't be able to resist what you've got to show her.' She patted the brown suitcase encouragingly and smiled.

I have to admit that I was tempted. There seemed to be no actual harm in her, although something in her manner, or her way of smiling, sent a shiver down my spine.

'Well, come in then,' I said reluctantly. 'Come down to the kitchen. I was just making some tea.'

'Oh,' said the woman (Em, she'd called herself). 'I can see that I was right about you, sure enough. Not only beautiful, but kind.'

She pulled a chair up to the table and sat down with her brown suitcase beside her. 'Two sugars, if you don't mind.'

I made the tea. The cat (oh, he did look like Snowflake! Who did he belong to? He wasn't one of the cats I'd seen wandering in the back gardens. I must ask Greg about him) came into the kitchen and jumped on to the windowsill.

All the time we were drinking our tea, the woman babbled on. I felt more and more uncomfortable, because what she was talking about was me, and my looks. She seemed to be gloating over them, but underneath the praise, the compliments, the extravagant comparisons she kept making between me and every famous beauty you can imagine, I could feel – this is the best way I have of describing it – a thick layer of dislike, of envy and even malice in everything she said. Clouds had massed in the sky and it was getting quite dark in the kitchen. I wanted to go and turn the light on, but to do this, I'd have had to pass Em's chair and this made me hesitate. Suddenly I wanted her gone: out of the house. Something in the way she drank her tea, the way she sat at the table was very familiar. I could hardly see her face in the dim light. I said:

'All my friends will be back in a minute. Don't you think you'd better show me what you've got in your case? That is, after all, why you came, isn't it?'

She stood up. 'It is! Of course it is!' she said. 'May I put my case here on the table?'

'Yes,' I said, 'and could you turn the light on, too, please? The switch is on the wall over there.'

She was obviously cleverer than I realized. She was quite right about the contents of her case. It had in it everything in the world that I most desired: exquisitely beautiful scarves and shawls and fans and jewels. I wanted every single thing. I said:

'You're right. It's all very beautiful, but I can't afford any of this. I haven't got much money.'

'Then let me make you a small present,' she said. 'After all, you did invite me in for tea.' She laughed and I thought: I've heard that laugh before somewhere, and then the thought left my head like a trail of smoke floating away from a cigarette.

'Oh, no, I couldn't,' I said. 'I couldn't accept a present.'

'I don't see why not,' she said, 'if it pleases me to give you one.' She pulled a wide pink suede belt from the whirlpool of laces and silks that frothed in her case and said:

'Come over here and let's try this for size.'

I went and stood in front of her. I was mesmerized, fascinated to see how I would look. I was wearing black trousers and a black polo-necked jumper. I stood in front of Em and raised my arms so that she could put the belt around my waist and tie the thongs of fine leather that held the ends together at the back. It seemed to take her rather a long time.

'It's a bit fiddly,' she said, 'this fastening. Good job I'm here to help you, eh?'

'Yes,' I said. 'Thank you very much.'

'Don't thank me, duck. It's made for you, that belt. There's no one else would suit it like you do.'

She left soon after that, and I was glad to close the door on her. I flew upstairs after she'd gone and stood in front of the only mirror in the house (propped up beside the window in Pete's room) to admire myself. I looked wonderful, and went to the window to see if I could still see Em in the road. There she was, down by the corner, gazing up at me. The thought came to me: that could be Marjorie . . . that's how she walks exactly. Well, I told myself, there's nothing strange about that. People often do resemble one another. I pranced about in front of the mirror for a while, enjoying how tiny my waist looked in my new belt. Then I thought: I'd better take it off, and I pulled it round so that the fastening was now at the front where I could undo it. It was laced up like a shoe, and I began pulling at the ends of the laces, thinking that the knot would fall open at once, but it didn't, and the harder I pulled the tighter the belt became and the angrier I felt. I'd seen a special chair in a museum once, long ago, into which they tied criminals, binding them to the back and arms by an intricate arrangement of leather straps. The more the prisoner struggled, the tighter the bonds grew, until they cut cruelly into flesh. This belt was like that.

'But it can't be,' I said aloud to myself. 'They're only skimpy little laces.' I gave them another tug, and then I found that I could hardly breathe. I knew what I had to do. I had to cut the laces. Pete's house is not a place where you can depend on finding a pair of scissors. I daresay I could have unearthed some if I'd turned the place upside down, but there wasn't time for that. I was beginning to feel faint. I stumbled down the stairs, thinking: I must get to the knives. I can cut the laces with a kitchen knife. That was the last thought I remember. I must have passed out then. When I woke up, I was lying on the floor of the hall with my head in Greg's lap. He was muttering softly and holding a wet cloth to my forehead.

'Oh, Bella!' he said when I opened my eyes. 'Oh, Bella, we all thought you were dead!'

I could hardly speak. I only said, 'Get my belt off, Greg, quickly. Please. Cut the laces.'

Greg didn't move. Pete ran to fetch the sharpest kitchen knife and at last the belt was off. I could breathe again. As I began to feel better, I saw that all seven of the band were gathered around me.

'You okay now?' Pete asked. I nodded.

'What happened to the cat?' I said. 'There was a white cat in the hall before . . . ' My voice faded.

'Haven't seen a cat,' said Steve. The cat must have slipped out with Em. Em. Did she know she was making the belt impossible to remove? Could she have wanted me to faint, or worse? It seemed extremely unlikely to me, and yet every time I've thought about it since, the whole thing seems to have been intentional, as though she meant to do me harm. I know all the objections to such thoughts. Why should a perfect stranger want to hurt me? I have gone over and over it in my mind since yesterday and the answer I keep returning to is this: maybe Em is not a stranger but someone known to me. She did, after all, remind me of Marjorie. Could it have been Marjorie herself, in some kind of disguise, or is that paranoia? How, I asked myself for the hundredth time, could Marjorie have found out where I really was, and then all of a sudden I had the answer. Armand, the hairdresser we both went to . . . he could easily have told her. I cursed myself for being too talkative, and for not swearing him to secrecy. I could imagine the scene perfectly. Marjorie saying, 'Oh, I hardly see Bella these days, now she's so grown-up,' and Armand, right on cue, answering: 'Oh, but she was 'ere last week, and full of the beans, with Pete and the crazy loony house in World's End, I think she say . . .' and Marjorie would mutter: 'You're only young once,' or something similar, and then she'd walk the streets of World's End and once she'd come across Aladdin's Cave she'd know (because she knows me very well) that I would go in there all the time . . . the rest is easy. After all, Jeannie hadn't said how long Em had been one of her suppliers.

'Greg,' I said. 'Greg, listen. I think my stepmother is trying to kill me.'

Greg looked up from his guitar. 'I like that,' he said, smiling. 'That's a good one, even for you. Fancy a cup of coffee, my poor little tragedy queen?'

'You're hopeless,' I said. 'You have no imagination. Yes, I'll have a coffee. While you're making it, I shall fester and lurk. So be quick.'

I could hear Greg chuckling as he took the steps down to the kitchen in great flying leaps.

I didn't ask what he'd done with the pink suede belt, but I never saw it again.

This is a story my father used to tell me over and over again when I was a little girl. It's about my mother. When she was pregnant with me, he took her to see *Gone With the Wind* at the cinema. My mother loved going to the pictures better than anything. They would sit and hold hands and know that when the ruched silky curtain went up, when the darkness fell, the white screen would glow with light and they would be transported into an enchanted land where women were always lovely and perfectly dressed, and where one could tell the difference between a hero and a villain immediately, just by looking at them. When *Gone With the Wind* appeared, it was a sensation. This film was longer, more colourful, bigger in every way than any other picture anyone had seen. The American Civil War raged, the city of Atlanta burned, Tara was destroyed, people loved and lost and loved again, and towering over everything were the hero and heroine: Rhett Butler and Scarlett O'Hara.

It was wintertime when my parents saw the film, and the ground was covered in snow when they came out. They walked round to the car park at the back of the cinema. At one point, my mother slipped a little and put out her hand to prevent herself from falling. She wasn't badly hurt, but the tips of her fingers were slightly grazed. When they reached the car, my father tied his white handkerchief round my mother's hand.

'Just like those poor wounded soldiers in the film,' she said.

They drove home through the black night.

'Look at that snow!' my mother said. 'How white it is! Vivien Leigh looks wintery, doesn't she . . .? all that lovely white skin and hair like the night.' She laughed. 'I'd like our baby to look like that,' she said, turning to my father. 'Hair like the night, and skin like the snow, and lips as red as the blood on this hankie.'

When I was a little girl and my father was telling me this story, he'd always take me over to the mirror and show me my own face. The mirror always said the same thing, and I'd repeat the words silently in my head as I looked at my image in the glass: 'Hair like the night, skin like the snow and lips as red as blood.'

I resemble, of course, not Vivien Leigh at all, but my mother. It was only to be expected. As my father used to say to me until Marjorie came along:

'Your mother was more beautiful than any actress. And you are just like her.'

That was before his second marriage, before Marjorie.

Some people say they can remember being in their mother's womb, but I take that kind of statement with a couple of hefty pinches of salt. I think I can remember the three years between when I was two and when I was five, but it may just be that my father has told me so often about everything we did that it's become vivid to me in retrospect. Still, if anyone ever asked me to describe what life was like before my father's second marriage, I'd have all the answers.

We lived in a big, comfortable, shabby sort of house with a big, comfortable, shabby sort of garden around it. My father is a doctor. The only respectable rooms in the house were his surgery (to the left of the front door) and his little waiting room (to the right) with its hunting prints on the wall and its shiny copies of *Punch* and the *Illustrated London News* on a small table by the window. We didn't have a proper receptionist then. Mrs McBride, who kept house for us and cooked for us, used to stick her head round the door and call the patients into the surgery one by one.

My father must have been busy. Doctors are always busy. And yet, I remember flying kites on Wimbledon Common. He would put me on his shoulders and run and run and I'd cling on to his hair, and the wind would lift the bright orange diamond of our kite up and up until I was sure it would touch a cloud, and all the time he'd never stop running and the green earth would tilt and fall away, far, far below me, and every minute I felt as though we were going to run right off the edge of the turning world. I remember that. I also remember being pushed on the baby swing in the park, and squelching along to the shops in my wellington boots, hoping my father was going to buy some liquorice all-sorts for us to share on the way home. I even remember the bedtime songs. Every night, he would sing three songs: 'Bye bye blackbird', 'When the red red robin comes bob-bob-bobbin' along' and 'Golden Slumbers'. Then he would say:

'Would you like two more?' and I would nod and he would do his encores, always the same songs in the same order: 'Over the Rainbow' and 'If you were the only girl in the world'. By the time I was three I could sing all of them perfectly and would give concerts in the waiting room almost daily. The patients loved me. So did Mrs McBride. So, more than any of them, did my father.

Before his second marriage, there was always music playing in our house. My father loved jazz and taught me how to find my way through the woefully wailing saxophones, the silver trumpets and the syncopated rhythms of the piano. Then I listened to the voices. I heard the blues: Bessie Smith, Leadbelly, and most loved of all, Billie Holiday, Lady Day, with a gardenia in her hair and songs that yearned and swooped and lodged themselves in the dark corners of my heart. I pretended to be her. I tucked a dead chrysanthemum (the nearest thing I could find to a gardenia) behind my ear and sang along to all her records.

Alice and Megan can never understand why I'm so mad about music. Alice's mother plays the piano, but the way I listen to Radio Lux under the bedclothes mystifies them. They keep up with all the latest songs, because simply being a friend of mine is an education in pop music. I'm always singing and they're always listening, but their hearts aren't in it. They simply cannot see what I see in Elvis, for instance. Alice thinks he looks horrible, with 'thick, blubbery lips' as she puts it, and his music is 'too noisy'. Megan thinks he's a little ridiculous. She doesn't actually say so, but I can tell. She finds him funny. When she and Alice mention the name of one of his songs, I can hear the inverted commas in their voices as they say the words aloud.

I love Elvis because he came along to help me when I particularly wanted to annoy Marjorie. He was louder and more dangerous-looking than Buddy Holly. I stuck posters of him all over my bedroom at home and played his records at full blast on my portable gramophone. Marjorie winced and frowned every time she came into my bedroom and found me gyrating to the pounding rhythms of his guitar. Thank you, Elvis, I used to think, and cherished him for being everything Marjorie couldn't stand: wild and slightly greasy and the possessor of a Pelvis that upset her very much.

One night when I was four, my father went to a Fancy Dress dance at the Bridge Club and met Marjorie. He fell in love with her from the very first moment he saw her, shimmying away in a beaded 1920s-style gown that clung to every bit of her. I mustn't let my present feelings for Marjorie obscure the truth about her. She is very beautiful, even now, and in those days her loveliness was the kind that made people, men and women, stare after her in the street. She was – is – as tall as my father, and a sort of goldy-brown colour all over. Her hair is tawny and thick, and she has always worn it in a page-boy bob to just above her shoulders. Her clothes tend towards the golden, too. Shiny fabrics and velvety ones, softly draped and clingy, are what she likes: silk jersey and crêpe and evening dresses made of satin that slide over her body like licks of gloss paint.

My father thought she was wonderful. He brought her to the house and *I* thought she was wonderful. She used to stand me on the padded stool in front of my own mother's dressing-table mirror and pat my nose with fluffy puffs of sweet-smelling face powder. She used to hang chains around my neck and let me clop around the house in her high-heeled shoes. She let me open her handbag and take out her ruby-studded compact and her lipstick and pretend to use them.

She made gradual changes in the house. She changed the pictures in the waiting room. She tidied up – oh, not by herself, but she saw to it. Mrs McBride vanished and was replaced by Mrs Deering, a thin-faced, sour woman who for the most part kept herself to herself.

My father told me when I was five what was going to happen.

'There's going to be a lovely wedding party,' he said, 'and you shall be the only bridesmaid. Then after that, Marjorie will come and live here and she'll be your very own new mummy.'

'And we'll have such fun together, darling, won't we?' added Marjorie, crushing me against her fragrant bosom. 'The very first thing we must do is decide on the dresses . . . yours and mine.'

It was the happiest day of my life. The next few weeks

were most tremendously exciting. I trailed around everywhere with Marjorie: to the dressmakers, the shoe shops, the jewellers, the florists, and everywhere we went, everyone would make a fuss of me and give me little presents and kiss me.

Very occasionally I take out the photograph album with the wedding pictures in it, looking to see if there's any sign at all there of Marjorie's dislike of me, or of my feelings towards her. My dress was very pale blue, I remember, and I had a little coronet of pale blue flowers on my head. The cake had four tiers. Marjorie wore a dress in oyster satin, very closely draped round every curve of her body, and there were quite a few of those. My father's eyes are fixed on her in every single picture. I don't know who took the photographs, but it seems as if I was trying to attract his attention. I'm smiling very winsomely, straight at the camera. Everyone looks blissfully happy, just as though bad thoughts, unhappiness and jealousy were only to be found somewhere else. Not here. Never here.

I don't think I realized, then, that Marjorie would be with us the whole time. I think I thought that she would go back to her own house to sleep. I said so to my father one day and he laughed.

'But she's my wife now, Bella darling. I love her.'

'You said you loved me.' (I know I must have been pouting as I said this. I was tearing up my toast at the time.)

'I *do* love you, Bella. I love you best in the world, you know that. *Do* you know that?'

'Yes,' I said, 'but what about Mummy?'

My father sighed. 'I did love Mummy, but she would want Marjorie to look after us both now that she's not here any more.'

My father was right. Marjorie did look after us. The house was redecorated. The garden was landscaped. A receptionist was installed in the waiting room behind a desk. Later on, my father's surgery was moved to another part of London altogether because, as Marjorie put it:

'Seeing patients in one's own house is too, too A.J. Cronin for words.'

I didn't know it then, but soon discovered that A.J. Cronin wrote books about Scottish doctors whose one desire was to help the poor.

Marjorie arranged flowers in large and (I thought) rather ugly vases all over the house. Women with jewellery that rattled came to play bridge and take tea. We hardly ever went for walks or flew kites. My father was too successful, and in any case, by then I was too old to be put up on his shoulders, and too old to be sung to at night. There were no more bed-time songs.

People don't realize, I think, quite how much little children notice. I knew, right from the start, that my father enjoyed the way Marjorie snuggled against him when they kissed. He liked her to lean round him as he sat at breakfast, and kiss him on the mouth and rub her blouse against his shoulder. I could see that he liked touching her, and it didn't surprise me at all. I liked touching her too. Her skin was smooth and silky and she smelled lovely. I told Megan and Alice once that I'd wanted to learn French ever since I heard the beautiful names of Marjorie's perfumes said aloud: 'Je Reviens' and 'Arpège' and 'Jolie Madame' and my favourite, 'Vent Vert' which, she said, meant Green Wind.

She had the most wonderful underwear I'd ever seen. It was, all of it, lacy and delicate and slippery, and it lay quietly in her drawers until the moment came for dressing, when it would unfold into foaming waves of peach or white or black against Marjorie's skin.

'When I'm a big lady,' I used to say, 'I'm going to have things exactly like that.' But years later, when we went to Daniel Neal's, in order to kit me out ready for Egerton Hall, I nearly wept with rage, right there in the shop. All those horrid thick cotton knickers and beige socks and hideously scratchy liberty bodices filled me with despair. I looked at Marjorie as if to say: help me. You know I loathe this. Help me not to have to go to a place that makes you wear knickers like these. Marjorie, though, had started to hate me long before I went away to school and the only expression to cross her face was a smile of undisguised triumph.

Maybe I'm being melodramatic again, and half of it is in my own mind, but this I do know. Marjorie's attitude towards me changed when I was seven. I can pinpoint the very day: it was the day of my first visit to Monsieur Armand's hair-dressing salon, Chez Armand. Up until then, Marjorie loved me in the way that someone loves a pretty doll. She liked dressing me up in lovely clothes. She even enjoyed draping me in her own jewels and scarves and spraying me with perfume from the cut-glass bottles lining the dressing-table. When it came to matters of style or make-up, she was a talented teacher. There are things she said then which had the force of moral rules for her: you must never wear a white blouse over black underwear, you must never wear high-heeled shoes with trousers, you must never wear a cardigan over a cotton dress, and you must never be seen in your dressing-gown after ten in the morning unless you were ill, and you must always, always assume, every single time you left the house (even if you were just popping down the road to post a letter) that on this occasion you would meet someone of the utmost importance, like the Man of Your Dreams or a Crowned Head of Europe. You also had to take it for granted that every time you left the house you were going to be the victim of an accident and doctors saving your life would furrow their brows in deep distress if your vest was less than pristine and ditto, naturally, your knickers.

When I was seven, Marjorie decided that I looked wild.

'Look, darling,' she said to my father one night. 'Bella's turning into a little ragamuffin. You don't want to be a little ragamuffin, Bella dear, do you?'

'No,' I answered, a bit doubtfully. Secretly I thought a ragamuffin sounded rather nice, like a tastier version of a muffin.

'Tomorrow,' Marjorie continued, 'I shall take you to meet Monsieur Armand, my divine hairdresser, and we'll ask his advice. Monsieur Armand always knows exactly what to do. And won't you be glad to be rid of all that messy hair? To say nothing of the time we shall save, not having to plait it every morning before school.'

I thought: she never does plait it, anyway. It's always Mrs Deering who does it.

Stepping into Chez Armand was like walking into the heart of a rose. The carpets were pink and soft, the chairs were covered in pink velvet. I was very impressed when a pretty lady put some cushions on a chair and lifted me on to them. She then covered me with a pink sheet, so that only my head was showing. I giggled and said to Marjorie:

'My head looks like a black cherry on top of a pink blancmange.'

Marjorie wasn't listening. She was smiling and waving at someone she knew on the other side of the salon. I didn't care. I was looking at the enormous mirror in front of me. It had the most wonderful golden frame carved with roses, long, trailing ribbons, leaves, little vases, a musical instrument I'd never seen before, and at the very top, a couple of chubby naked babies who made me smile. I realized, because of their wings, that they were meant to be little angels, but they still struck me as fat and funny, flying about at the top of the mirror with not even nappies to cover their bottoms.

After a while, Monsieur Armand arrived for The Consultation.

'Mais *elle est tellement mignonne*!' he exclaimed. I didn't know at the time what this meant, but I gathered he liked me, because he kept blowing kisses at my reflection in the mirror.

'Well, yes,' Marjorie said, a little shaken by all this ecstasy, 'but she does look rather untidy, don't you think? What should we do?'

'Perhaps,' Monsieur Armand considered carefully, 'a little fringe *comme ça*, and just below the ears like that?'

'That sounds very nice,' said Marjorie and pulled up a velvet chair so that she could follow every snip. My black hair fell on to the pink sheet like feathers. I didn't like it at first: the horrible, softly crunching sound the scissors made as they closed on my hair. But after a while, and soothed by Monsieur Armand's gentle murmurings and his strong hands turning my head first this way then that, I began to relax and enjoy myself.

'When I'm a grown-up lady,' I told Monsieur Armand, 'I shall come in here every single week to have my hair done just like Marjorie.'

Marjorie leaned forward so that her head was reflected next to mine in the mirror.

'What do you think, Armand, do I need a trim? Or perhaps a set?'

'Reassure yourself, Madame,' Monsieur Armand smiled at her. 'You are looking . . . how do you say? A picture. Perhaps a set in a day or so?'

'I'll make an appointment on the way out.'

'*Voilà!*' He turned to Marjorie with a flourish, to show her the result of his labours on me. 'Do you not think this is *merveilleux?*'

'Oh, that's very nice,' said Marjorie. 'Thank you so much, Armand.'

'Thank you,' I said. 'I think it's lovely.'

'You are going to become . . . how do you say? . . . the competition for Madame Lavanne, *n'est-çe pas?*'

Marjorie was almost silent on the way home. My father was very pleased with my new hair-style.

'You look simply lovely, Bellissima!' he said and kissed me. 'More like your mother than ever. It quite takes me back!' Maybe his words were less than diplomatic. Marjorie became even quieter.

'Ooh, the little pet!' said Mrs Deering when she saw me. 'Doesn't she look a picture?' Mrs Deering was a glum woman usually and this uncharacteristic enthusiasm reduced Marjorie to total silence.

At the time, I didn't really notice that Marjorie was in a sulk. I was so excited that I could hardly tear myself away from the mirror. I was sitting at Marjorie's dressing-table and gloating, when she came into the room and saw me, and started shaking.

'I don't know whose dressing-table you think this is, young lady,' she said in a wobbly voice, 'but I'd rather you didn't use it from now on, d'you hear?'

I jumped down from the stool and started to make my way to the door. I'd never seen Marjorie like this. She went on:

'It's mine. It's *my* dressing-table, and you're to keep away from it, do you understand?'

'Yes, Marjorie,' I whispered, nearly at the door. She was coming towards me now. She said:

'Haven't you got a mirror in your bedroom?'

'Yes,' I whispered.

'Then bloody well use it in future!' She pushed me a little roughly out of the door and banged it behind me. I felt icy all over. I wanted to run and tell my father, but I knew that I mustn't do that: it'd only make things worse. I wanted to open the door and run to Marjorie and ask her what had happened, and why she wasn't being nice to me any more and what had I done to stop her liking me, and wasn't she going to be my mother any longer? At the same time, I wanted to hit her and hurt her and break every single bottle on her dressing-table into tiny pieces and cover her carpet with broken glass. I did none of those things. I just stood there, paralysed, and then I heard a strange noise coming from inside the door. It sounded just like . . . but it couldn't be, because grown-ups never cried, did they? I looked through the keyhole and saw Marjorie staring into the mirror and howling like a child, tears running down her face and into her neck and she wasn't even bothering to wipe them away. I ran to my own room and closed the door and didn't come out again until supper-time.

Marjorie looked fairly normal during the meal, and spoke fairly normally too, but we knew, both of us, that something between us had changed that day.

What I still think of as The Snowflake Campaign started soon after our visit to Monsieur Armand's salon.

Snowflake was my cat. By the time Marjorie came to live in the house, she was already a grown-up, sedate sort of cat, much given to flopping about on carpets and curling up on the quilt on my bed. She padded about the house, looking wistfully at Mrs Deering as she cooked, or sat for hours on the windowsill in my bedroom, remembering her younger days, when she used to chase squirrels up into the trees with great abandon. She was white and fluffy, with eyes the colour of boiled gooseberries. I loved her. My father had given her to me for my second birthday, and he loved her too. She slept on my bed, usually quite placidly by my toes, but in winter I'd often wake up and find she was occupying half the pillow.

Marjorie never seemed to mind Snowflake, although I don't think she was ever mad about her. She never seemed to stroke her, Mrs Deering and I fed her, and really, I would have said that Marjorie hardly knew Snowflake was in the house. Then, one morning, The Campaign began. Marjorie arrived at the breakfast-table dabbing her eyes with a lace-edged hankie.

'I cannot seem,' she said to my father, 'to stop my eyes watering. Do you think I could be allergic to something?' My father munched toast rapidly and answered, not even looking at Marjorie properly:

'I expect it's all that muck you put on your eyes, dear. Mascara and what-have-you. Terrifically delicate things, eyes.' Marjorie stabbed at the butter and took the severed lump on to her plate. Her hand, I could see, was trembling but her voice was as sweet and clear as the Golden Shred marmalade she was busy applying to her toast.

'I hardly think so, Robert. I have, after all, been wearing this make-up with no ill-effects for years and years.'

'Then perhaps,' said my father, 'it's a slight cold coming on. Or even hay fever. There's a tremendous amount of hay fever about this year.'

'If you want my opinion,' said Marjorie, 'I think it's the cat.'

She always called Snowflake 'the cat'. I thought: how would she like it if Snowflake, or anyone else, for that matter, called her 'the woman'? My father pushed his chair away from the table.

'We'll talk about it tonight, darling. I have to rush now, truly. Though I can't imagine who would want to be allergic to poor old Snowflake, what?' He laughed.

'People do not choose, Robert, what they are allergic to. The reaction simply happens, whether you want it to or not. As a doctor, you should know that.'

'I do, my blossom, I do!' My father blew kisses in the general direction of both of us as he left the room. When he'd gone, Marjorie turned to me.

'Why, Bella dear, are you looking at me like that?' she said.

'I'm not, Marjorie,' I said quickly. 'Honestly, I'm not.' I bent my head and looked very closely at my plate. But I *was* looking. I had seen two things. Firstly, that Marjorie's eyes were now completely non-inflamed, and secondly, that Snowflake had come silently into the room and was now asleep behind the fruit bowl on the sideboard, within about two feet of where Marjorie was sitting.

For the next couple of weeks, she sniffed and coughed and wiped her eyes and assured my father (who was meanwhile treating her for hay fever) that Snowflake was the cause of her increasing discomfort.

I never imagined my poor cat was in any danger. They waited, my father and Marjorie, until I was safely at school, and then they murdered her. Oh, I don't mean they cut her throat with a razor or anything like that. No. Of course not. They simply took her to the vet, and she was put to sleep.

That was how my father told me, when I came back from school at lunchtime.

'We had to put her to sleep, lovey,' he said. 'She was making poor Marjorie ill.'

'But couldn't she just have gone to live somewhere else? With another family?' I wailed.

'No, Bella, she would have been very unhappy. Cats grow attached to their houses, their territory, you know. It's better this way.'

'Then why didn't you say you were going to do it? I never even kissed her goodbye! You're cruel and horrible and I hate you both.'

'Bella darling, don't say that! We didn't tell you because we didn't want to make you unhappy.'

'But you have!' I shrieked. 'You *have* made me. Very, very unhappy. I'm not going to stop crying. Not ever, so there.'

I did stop crying. Of course I did. Everything calmed down after a while, as it always does. But I have not forgotten that day. If I'd believed, really believed that Marjorie was allergic to cats, then maybe I would have been more sympathetic, but I think, even after all these years, that she made it up. She did it to hurt me. I don't think allergies had anything to do with it. After all, she has always worn her leopard-skin coat with no ill-effects. Poor leopards, killed to make coats for people like Marjorie! And poor Snowflake, now only a smudgy white blur in a few tiny photographs in my album.

Marjorie became subtle after a while and so did I. She realized quickly that my father loved the idea of the two of us being the best of friends, so that was what she pretended to be. Everyone admired her for it. Everyone was taken in by it, except me. Oh, she let me go back to sitting in front of her mirror and trying on her clothes and make-up, and she made a point of helping me to choose my clothes, and I, for my part, tried hard to annoy her without the whole thing becoming too obvious and thus calling the attention of my father to the sad fact that we were not, as he would put it, 'getting on'.

Visits to the hairdresser continued, of course, and each time we went, Marjorie would ask Monsieur Armand, sometimes in a roundabout way and sometimes straight out, which one of us was the more beautiful. For a long time, Monsieur Armand twisted and turned his replies into complicated knots of words that always worked out as the message Marjorie wanted to hear: there's nothing to choose between you. Then, one day when I was ten, she caught him off guard.

'Tell me truly, Armand,' she said after a particularly successful session with the scissors and rollers, 'how does the competition look now?' I was reading the *Tatler* in the velvet chair next to Marjorie's. Monsieur Armand looked across at me and then back at Marjorie's reflection in the mirror.

'You will 'ave,' he said with a shrug, 'to . . . as you say, I think . . . look to the laurels.'

Marjorie's anguished stare nearly shattered the glass. We left the salon quickly. I knew better than to ask Marjorie herself what 'look to the laurels' meant. Later that evening, I asked Mrs Deering. She said:

'Well, it's like a championship, you know. You got the laurels as a prize, see, and if someone coming up was going to be even better, you had to jolly well look out, make sure this other person didn't win your laurels off you. Do you understand?'

I understood very well indeed. It meant that Monsieur Armand thought I was going to be prettier than Marjorie. And Marjorie, although she couldn't really hurt me, was from that moment deeply against me. She would never show it, but I knew. And although Megan and Alice don't believe me, I'm of the firm opinion that she tried to lose me at the Harrods sale.

'No one,' Megan said, 'takes a child to Harrods and deliberately loses her. It's ridiculous.'

I suppose she may be right, but I still remember how terrified I was.

We had gone up to Knightsbridge on the top of a number 73 bus. I loved it up there, seeing the whole of London spread out below me, and I loved Harrods. It smelled just like Marjorie's bedroom, only more so. It was always crowded, and most of the people were much taller than me, so that I felt that I was walking through a forest where the trees were moving about all around me. There were ladies in fur coats and gentlemen in suits all coming and going at great speed up and down the aisles. I must have been a nuisance to Marjorie. I must have slowed her down. I wanted to look at every single thing.

'May I stay here while you do the shopping, Marjorie?' I asked, when we reached Perfumery, my favourite department. Marjorie looked all around her, worried, as though dangerous kidnappers were hiding behind every marble column.

'I'm not a baby,' I said. 'I'm ten. I won't get lost. I'll stay here all the time.'

'Well, please see that you do, Bella. I shan't be long. I have to go to the Food Hall and the lingerie department, that's all, and then I'll come back and fetch you. I shan't be more than half an hour or so.'

'Oh, thank you,' I said, and she strode off to the Food Hall without a backward glance. After she had gone, I wondered how I was going to know when the half-hour was up. Then I had a brilliant idea. I asked the pretty lady behind the Revlon counter what the time was.

'It's eleven o'clock,' she said, and smiled.

I pottered about happily among the lipsticks and creams for what seemed like ages. I asked the pretty lady the time again, and she said:

'It's quarter to twelve.'

Marjorie was late. I wasn't really worried. Marjorie was often late. I found a little stool and sat down to wait. At half-past twelve I began to worry and at one o'clock I started to cry. My pretty friend came out from behind her counter to ask me what the matter was.

'It's Marjorie,' I sobbed. 'She's left me here. She's forgotten all about me.'

'Who's Marjorie?'

'My stepmother,' I said.

'She'll be back soon. You dry your eyes, love.'

'But she said half an hour and it's two hours. I want to go home.' I started howling in a way that simply wasn't done at Harrods. Someone called the Floor Manager came and took me into an office and I phoned my father in his surgery. I had never done such a thing before.

'I'm coming for you at once, Bella,' he said on the telephone. 'Stop crying and wait for me.'

I stopped crying and turned my attention to the milk and biscuits the Floor Manager had brought me.

My father hugged me at first, but later, in the car going home, he became angry when I told him the truth. I'd calmed down completely by then.

'However did you manage to get yourself lost?' he asked.

'I wasn't lost,' I said. 'I was exactly where I said I'd be. Marjorie forgot about me, that's all. I expect she wanted to lose me altogether.'

I think my father would have smacked me then, if he hadn't been driving the car. As it was, he flashed a furious glance in my direction and said, in the coldest voice I'd ever heard him use to me:

'Don't you *dare* say such a wicked thing, Bella! Apologize at once. I'm deeply, deeply ashamed of you. How could you even think such a thing?'

'I'm sorry,' I muttered. 'I shouldn't have said that.' Well, I certainly shouldn't have said it, but I wasn't in the least sorry. I knew I was right. We arrived home to find Marjorie in floods of tears, babbling on about how I'd wandered off and how she couldn't find me, and didn't know what to do, and how she'd run home in a panic and oh, poor love, how dreadful it must have been, and all the time she was weeping and clasping me to her bosom and saying how love-ly it was that everything had ended happily and on and on and on. But she didn't fool me, not for a moment. I could see right through to the coldness at the heart of her, and I knew, I could feel in the way she stroked my hair that some huge, hidden, iceberg-like part of her was deeply sorry that I had ever been 'found', as she put it, and brought home.

'And that's why,' I used to say to Megan and Alice, 'I was sent to Egerton Hall, don't you see? So that she could be rid of me. It was supposed to be a kind of exile. I could easily have gone to school round the corner from our house, but Marjorie wanted me far away.'

'But you like it here, don't you?' Alice said. 'It's not a bad kind of exile, is it?'

'Not bad at all, but the point is, Marjorie wouldn't care either way. I'm not where she is, that's the main thing. She likes to think of this place as set in the middle of a forest. That's what it said in the prospectus, anyway. She likes to pretend that I'm really hidden away. She was a bit disappointed when she saw what the real forest looked like!'

We all laughed then. Our forest, out beyond the school boundary (which we call The Rim of the Known World), *is* a bit of a joke. It's a scrubby sort of place with too few trees to score more than about four out of ten in a Sinister Forest Test. Still, it was the best Marjorie could do, and she approached my departure for Egerton Hall with more enthusiasm and pleasure than I'd seen her display in years.

I've been in bed thirty-six hours, which was about twenty-four hours longer than necessary, but I'm fully recovered now. Pete decided that we should have a special meal as a celebration of the fact that I was now well enough to cook it.

'I did all the shopping,' said Steve. 'I expect to be let off all the cooking and washing up.'

'Expect away,' I said. 'They'll rope you in.' Steve was a plump, dour sort of person, who didn't say much unless he was pointing out some grievance.

'Look at me,' I said. 'I'm not grumbling and I've got to fling together a delicious forgetti Bolognese, as Harry calls it, for eight people.'

'But you're a girl,' said Dave.

'And a trainee knife-thrower to boot,' I said, 'so I advise you not to make remarks like that in this kitchen when I'm around.'

'You are not,' said Pete to Dave, 'to fluster the cook. Gallons of gallant suffragette blood run in her veins, and if you're not good and polite she will dash off and chain herself to the nearest railing and then you can forget about forgetti, Bolognese or no Bolognese.'

I set about chopping onions and peppers and mushrooms

and soon the kitchen was full of fragrant steam rising from my saucepan.

Phil, a lanky man with a rather thin, high voice and toffee-coloured hair in a sort of mop-shape, had been sent down the road to the off-licence to get some bottles of wine. This was because the meal was a celebration. On non-celebration nights, they all drank beer and I generally had to make do with milk or water.

I doled out the spaghetti to everyone. 'Being mother' was what Dave called it.

'Not mother,' I grinned at him. 'Table Prefect. And if you don't behave yourselves, you can come and see me in my study after supper. I could give you Automatically Minus Two.'

'Ooh,' said Harry, 'that sounds lovely! Is it the name for a new sexual perversion?'

'No, stupid. You have Minus House Points and Plus House Points and at the end of term the House with the most points wins a cup.'

Kenny said, 'How too, too Malory Towers, darling!' and stretched his arms languidly above his head, and everyone laughed and said: 'Jolly hockey sticks!' and 'St Trinian's!' and I ignored them and continued to dole out spaghetti.

'Shut up and eat your supper,' I said.

'Only if you swear to tell us what you all got up to after Lights Out, treasure,' said Kenny. I stuck my tongue out at him, and tossed a piece of bread at his head, but it missed and hit Dave instead. We all started giggling then, and Phil and Steve began to suck up individual strands of spaghetti.

'You're nothing but a bunch of silly kids,' I said, 'and you're the ones who are going to have to clean up this mess. Greg and I have things to discuss.'

Wolf whistles, shouts of 'Hello, hello, what's this then?'

and hoots of one kind and another greeted this remark. Greg turned redder than the Bolognese sauce and said:

'I've written a couple of songs for Bella to sing. We want to rehearse them, that's all.'

'Well, ducky,' said Kenny, 'I've heard plenty of euphemisms in my time, but rehearsing's a good one, I have to admit.'

'When I get my hands on you, Kenny,' I smiled, 'you'll have to think of a euphemism for strangling.'

Kenny laughed. 'Can't think of anything in the world more titillating than being manhandled by a public school-girl. I can hardly wait, darling. Do come over here and start.' I ignored him and finished my spaghetti. Greg smiled at me gratefully. I had succeeded in diverting everyone's attention from him, so he could listen to the banter quite happily.

There always was a lot of chatting and laughter at the table, but it struck me as I watched them that these seven supposedly grown-up men, living in suitably beatnik disorder, actually had as many rules and regulations governing their meals as we had at Egerton Hall, even if the table manners that went with them left something to be desired. They did a great deal of slouching about, loud laughing, chucking around of bits of bread, and passing salt and pepper pots across your face when your spoon was an inch away from your mouth. Still, every one of the band had his appointed seat at the table, and I had to learn which mug was whose very quickly because no one would dream of taking even one sip from somebody else's.

Phil, Dave and Harry did the washing-up. On the table, the candle we'd stuck into the Chianti bottle to be extra festive had burned down to its last inch, and the green glass was encrusted with opaque white blobs and bobbles and streaks of hardened wax.

Monday morning and the house is empty and everything is slightly different after the weekend. Megan came to stay for a couple of days, and now she's gone there's a chance to think. While she was here, we were too busy talking. I only told her briefly about the pink suede belt – I'd almost begun to think I'd imagined it, anyway.

'We'll take turns,' I said. 'You can have the chaise-longue on alternate nights.'

'It's okay,' said Megan. 'My sleeping-bag's probably more comfortable, especially if I lie it on top of a folded blanket or something.'

'I know,' I said. 'That's why I want to alternate. In a previous incarnation, this chaise-longue was used as a kind of rack by the Spanish Inquisition.' We started to giggle. I said:

'It'll be just like the Tower Room, but with fags.'

'Oh, no, Bella. Not fags. You know I hate the smell.'

'The whole house reeks of smoke, though. What will you do?'

'Suffer, I suppose. But I'm going to make you hang out of the window in here. I don't see why I should have smoke puffed right in my face.'

I wasn't really listening to her. I said:

'It won't really be like the Tower Room. Alice isn't here.'

'No,' said Megan, and then, 'Do you think about her a lot?'

'All the time. You?'

'Yes,' said Megan. 'I feel sick when I think about it. I feel cold and terrified.'

'I don't. I feel hot and angry. I feel I'd like to hit someone very hard. Him, preferably.'

I meant Angus. I couldn't even remember exactly what he looked like, except that he was dark and had eyebrows that met above his nose. Megan shook her head as if to clear it of terrible thoughts, and sat down on a reasonably clean bit of floor. She said:

'I like this house. Dorothy would have fifty fits if she could see me.'

I laughed aloud. Dorothy was Megan's guardian, a frosty, stuffy sort of person. I said:

'What about Marjorie? She'd have a hundred fits if she could see me. It's super fun that you could come. And extra super that it's this weekend. You can come to The Dance.'

'What dance? You never said anything about a dance. I haven't brought a dress.'

'You don't need a dress. You're coming with us. You can be like one of the band. Your blue skirt'll be fine, and that silky blouse. We can go down to Jeannie's and pick you up a piece of glittery jewellery, if you like.'

'I don't like. Honestly, Bella, you might have told me! I don't even know if I want to go to this dance. Where is it?'

'It's being given in this amazingly posh enormous house in Cheyne Gardens. A twenty-first birthday party for the Hon. Roderick Maxton. Everyone who is anyone will be there: the Jeunesse Dorée, the Bright Young Things, the Crème de la Crème . . .'

'You're trying to camouflage the fact,' said Megan, 'that this is actually some kind of debutantes' do, and the place will be crawling with chinless wonders, ninety per cent of whom will be called Nigel.'

I laughed.

'You're quite right,' I said. 'Thank goodness we're going with the band.'

Megan said, 'But what I don't understand is how the band, who all look so disreputable, get themselves invited to play at such a party.'

'Ah, well, that's Greg's doing. He and Miss Rilly Maxton used to have what Pete calls "a Thing". She used to be his girl-friend, and she's the Hon. Roderick's sister, so, of course . . .'

'Whatever kind of name is Rilly?' Megan wanted to know.

'Short for Amaryllis, wouldn't you just know it? She's actually quite pretty, but definitely the sort of person who looks as though she's just on the point of turning into a pig, like the baby in *Alice in Wonderland*. She's pink and healthy-looking and her nose turns up. I think I shall put it slightly out of joint when she realizes how Greg feels about me. According to Harry, who is an expert on these matters, Rilly still thinks Greg is (and I quote him) "hers".'

'Oh, well, if there are to be dramatic jealous scenes,' said Megan, 'then I'm quite looking forward to the occasion. By then I will have got used to the band myself. I was quite overwhelmed by them this morning. I felt like a nice, juicy bone in the midst of a bunch of over-eager puppies.'

It was true. They had all (apart from Greg, who stood alone outside the group, smiling) patted Megan and grinned at her, and pressed cups of coffee, cigarettes and biscuits at her, and pulled out chairs for her and jostled to be near her. In the end, I had to shoo them all away, or I would never have had a chance to talk to Megan myself.

'They were just excited, that's all,' I explained. 'They'll have calmed down by tonight. And when they're playing, when we're on – well, they'll take no notice of you whatso-ever. You could be doing the dance of the seven veils and they wouldn't even glance in your direction. They get swallowed up by the music.'

'Even Greg?' Megan asked and winked at me.

'Greg especially,' I said. 'Although I'm going to sing two of his songs for the very first time tonight, so he might just look up to see if they're okay.'

*

The Maxton house – they would probably have preferred it to be called the Maxton Residence – was huge. There was a flight of steps leading up to the front door, with fat white columns holding up the porch. We arrived before the guests, and Lady Maxton was all of a twitter.

'Vernon,' she trilled to a butlerish sort of person, 'these are the young people for the cellar.' She turned her hostess smile on us.

'Darlings, I do admire your costumes. Too, too Bohemian for words. Vernon will show you your "spot", as darling Roddy calls it. You'll never believe how the cellar's been transformed. Magic on the part of Belinda Sowersby – do you know her?'

We all trooped down to the cellar behind Vernon. I said to Megan:

'Costumes, indeed! What a cheek! These are the same clothes most of them have been in all day. I know for a fact that Kenny hasn't changed his shirt since Thursday. Bohemian, I ask you!'

The cellar had been made to look as much like a sleazy nightclub as Belinda Sowersby, whoever she was, could manage. There was a space for dancing, tables with red and white checked cloths on them, red light bulbs everywhere and candles stuck in bottles all over the place.

'Are we allowed to wander about, then?' I asked.

'I don't see why not,' Pete said. 'But be back here by twelve ready for work.'

'We'll stick out like sore thumbs,' said Megan as we came up from the cellar into the house.

'I don't care,' I said. 'I'm only looking.'

Rilly Maxton was in peacock blue satin, and Jennifer's Diary would undoubtedly refer to her in the next issue of *Tatler* as 'resplendent'. She did her best to corner Greg, but he slunk off and hid in the cellar and pretended to make last-minute adjustments to the microphone.

The house was full of dresses. Skirts in fondant colours, in soft, rustly materials, wispy chiffons and lustrous satins, stiff crinolines in glittery taffeta, moved in and out of doorways and round and round the dance floors, and every exotic flower of a skirt was tied, it seemed, to a black-and-white stake: a partner in evening dress. We made our way to where an enormously long table was spread with all the things which, as Megan put it, 'were our best fantasies at school'. We walked the length of this table, plucking vol-au-vents and legs of chicken and smoked salmon sandwiches from the plates as we passed. A sedate sort of orchestra (three elderly men in penguin suits and a white-haired lady in beaded aquamarine at the pianoforte) were squelching out Victor Sylvester imitations in the ballroom, which was about the size of a small cathedral, though more elaborately decorated.

Soon it was what Megan called 'Cinderella time' and we went down to the cellar again. It was packed. Couples were crowding the dance floor, all the girls in their pretty flowers of dresses by this time twined round their black-and-white men, clinging to them, making their arms into soft tendrils to bind round necks and waists. Music poured into the spaces around them, golden and sweet like treacle. Inhibitions had melted in the candle flames. Everywhere, couples were kissing, oblivious of the rest of the world.

I started out by singing some smoochy standards. Then, towards the end of my set, I sang one of the songs Greg had written for me:

> Pack your bags
> and all your money
> don't forget your jewels,

honey.
We're going to ride
that dazzle train
right into love
and back again.
Tell the guard
just where you're goin'
hear that lovesick
whistle blowin'.
Grab your sweetie,
hang on tight,
love train's goin' to
run all night.

The upbeat rhythm, the change of pace after all the smoochiness, made everyone pay attention. Even the most drowned of the kissers came up for air and looked at me. No one danced as I sang it, but on the reprise, someone started clapping to the beat, and everyone else joined in. When I finished the applause was deafening. I looked at Greg. I'd felt him smiling at my back all the time I'd been singing, but now his eyes were glittering most suspiciously.

'He was,' Megan told me much later. 'He was nearly crying as you sang.'

Pete jumped up and raised his hand for silence.

'Thanks, folks! We're glad you liked that song, because it was written by Greg, there on the guitar. Let's hear it for Greg!' (Another burst of applause.) 'But we've lost that loving, melancholy mood, it seems, so to bring it back, here's Bella again with another song by Greg. Quite a different one, this is. Take it away, Bella!'

I sang 'Turn your face' then and the words filled the air like smoke:

Turn your face,
turn your eyes,
turn yourself
to me.
What do you see,
tell me,
what do you see?
I see white birds flying
high into the blue.
I see all my sweet dreams
never coming true.
I see all your loving
walking out the door,
I hear goodbye words
you never said before.
You've met another someone
but don't you realize
you've got pieces of the past
pieces of my fantasies
pieces of my love for you
forever in your eyes.

'Greg,' I said to him as I stepped away from the microphone, 'thank you for those songs.' I could see he wanted to say something, but couldn't find words. He seemed to be reaching out for air. I said:

'When it's time for your break, let's have a drink.' He nodded and turned back to his guitar.

Later on, Greg and I had a glass of wine each, sitting at one of the tables. Suddenly, I felt a surge of tenderness and affection for him sweep over me. I put my hand over his.

'Greg, the songs are beautiful. Everyone really loved them.

I loved singing them.' Greg smiled and said nothing. Now, a tape recorder was playing 'Body and Soul'.

'Come,' I said, 'dance with me. It's ages since I danced with anyone.'

At first, he stood very stiffly, slightly away from me. I could feel the tension running all down his arm as it circled my waist. It seemed as though he'd stopped breathing. I said:

'Greg, this is like dancing with a suit of armour! What's the matter with you? I'm not made of china. I shan't break, you know.'

I deliberately put both my arms around his neck and moved my body close to his. I could feel tremors running through him at first, and then he stopped trembling and bent his head so that his mouth was buried in my hair. I closed my eyes.

Greg was very warm. I could feel his breath touching my forehead. I felt sleepy. I felt safe with his arms around me. I snuggled in closer to him. I felt so cosy there, so comfortable, so full of what I think must have been a kind of gratitude for his kindness, his love, his beautiful songs, that I lifted my face to his and kissed him very thoroughly on the mouth. It was as though I'd turned a tap, flicked a switch, opened the lid on a box of feelings that Greg had been keeping carefully hidden.

'Oh, Bella, Bella,' he said, almost sighing, and then he kissed me: my mouth, my hair, my neck where it met my shoulders: hundreds of kisses and words muttered under his breath so that I could hardly hear them. I caught 'so much'. I heard 'never' and 'always' and my name over and over again, and his arms were around me, unhesitatingly this time and tight, as if he never wanted to let me go.

*

'But do you love him?' Megan asked me the next afternoon. She had left her sleeping-bag. I was still on the chaise-longue.

'I like him. I like the way he makes me feel when he kisses me. He comforts me, just by being there. He makes me feel safe, cared for. I don't know. Would you call that love?'

Megan came over and sat on the end of the chaise-longue.

'I don't know either,' she said. 'But I think if you have to ask the question, then it may not be.'

'I don't care.' I grinned at her, feeling as though everything in the world were suddenly lit up. 'Even if it isn't love, it feels jolly nice. So there.'

'Then,' said Megan, 'you can tell for certain that it isn't love. Love means torment and anguish and suffering.' I jumped off the chaise-longue and pulled a face.

'That's a lot of flummery and flannel put about by the Romantic poets and I don't believe a word of it!' I ran up to the bathroom singing 'I'm in love with a wonderful guy' at the very top of my voice.

So now Greg and I will be considered A Couple. I don't know what I feel about this. I laughed it off with Megan, but in my heart of hearts, I know – I think I know – that what I feel for Greg isn't love. It isn't what the poets mean by love, it isn't what Elvis and Buddy Holly and Billie Holliday and all the songs mean by it. The truth of the matter is, I'm rather ignorant about Love and Sex and everything that goes with them, except in theory. Oh, I was considered (am still considered, probably) the expert on such matters at school. I have had a reputation since the Junior House for being daring, precocious, adventurous. I was the first person in the class to be kissed properly. I read all the juicy books first, and was quite clever about picking up the clues the writer let slip about the disposition of limbs, etc. etc. The truth of the matter is, Megan knows what there is to know and I only imagine it, and the irony is, I can't interrogate her about such matters, because I'm supposed to know already. In any case, Megan would find it hard, not so much to put what she felt into words, but to give a good, practical account of what actually happens: who does what and for how long and what does it feel like, when you get past all the grunting and heaving and melting and so forth that goes on in books? I shall have to find out for myself, I suppose, and the reason I know that what I feel for Greg isn't love is this: at the moment, anyway, I do not especially want him to be the one to teach me.

'But why ever not?' I imagine Megan saying. 'He's so handsome and sweet and he loves you so much.'

I don't know why not. Kissing him is very pleasant. He looks after me. He is devoted to me. Perhaps that's what's not right about it. I feel affectionate towards him, tender, concerned. I like stroking his hair. I've thought and thought about it, and decided that I am fond of Greg in much the same way as I'd be fond of a special pet. I do not feel swept off my feet, breathless, anxious, tremulous, in despair, and so I suppose I am not in love. If I had a proper mother, I'd ask her: how will I know when the real thing happens to me? I cannot tell what my real mother would have said, but Marjorie would trot out clichés from the latest magazine article. I can hear her now: 'Love will hit you when you least expect it.' She would probably start paraphrasing 'Some Enchanted Evening', which is a sort of National Anthem for believers in Love at First Sight. With a hey and a ho and a hey nonny no!

Later that week, over breakfast, Pete suddenly put down his paper and looked at all of us slouching round the table in various stages of undress. He said:

'Well, I can't think why when I look at you all, but I had a chat with Matt Quinton yesterday, and he's fixed up an engagement for us in Paris.'

Everyone who was eating stopped at once. Greg said:

'Paris? Are you serious? When?'

Pete laughed. 'Quite serious. There's a place in Montparnasse called Club Sortilège. Matt's dad is part-owner. They're offering us one spot per night. Money's not great, but it's Paris, so who cares, eh?'

'When is this?' I said.

'Next week. Can you make it, Bella? What about your folks? Will they mind?'

'I'll fix it,' I said, already composing in my head a suitable tissue of lies for the benefit of my father and Marjorie. 'Have you got an address I can give them? Parents always find that tremendously reassuring, for some reason.'

'That's the best bit,' said Pete. 'Free accommodation, and guess where?'

'Let me try,' said Kenny. 'What about wrapped in old copies of *Le Figaro* on top of the Metro gratings?'

'Close,' said Pete. 'It's an artist's studio.'

'What about the artist? Where will he be?'

'On holiday. Beside the sea.'

'Don't know what the world's coming to,' said Kenny. 'Time was when your artist would be slowly starving to death over a nice cosy glass of absinthe. Now they're traipsing off to the seaside like common or garden trippers. And does anyone speak French?'

'I do,' I said. 'I did it for my A-levels.'

'Thank goodness for that,' said Phil. 'The rest of us haven't got two sentences to rub together.'

I stood up feeling excited, feeling elated. I said:

'I'm going to write to my father.'

Dear Dad and Marjorie,

By the time you get this, I shall be in Paris. A friend of Alice's Aunt Daphne, who lives there, needs someone to take care of her studio for a couple of weeks, so Megan and I and another friend from Egerton Hall (Marion Tipton) will be staying there and looking after things. I'm delighted because I can consolidate my spoken French before the University entrance exams next term. This is the address: 4 Rue du Texel, Paris 14ième, France. I shall telephone if I can, though I don't know how easy it'll be, and if you could possibly see your way to sending me a cheque of the plumpish variety *by return* I'd be very grateful.

Lots of love,
Bella

I phoned Megan that night to say goodbye. I knew she couldn't come to Paris with me, because she'd already arranged to go to Scotland with Dorothy, but Marjorie needn't know that. Having Megan as part of the trip would give it, in their minds, the stamp of respectability. Safety.

'Write to me,' Megan said on the phone. 'Write to me every single day.'

'What about plunging myself into Parisian life?'

'Plunge first,' Megan laughed, 'and write later!'

Paris

Paris *the something of August, 1962*

To my dear Megan, roaming in the Scottish gloaming, *Hoots mon* and other appropriately Caledonian greetings! I have this image in my mind of you and Dorothy, standing on top of a high mountain (purple) gazing at some lochs (steel grey) in the distance. There are even, I think, some deer around. I expect the truth is she's dragging you to every stately home, art gallery and place of historical interest within miles.

I, on the other hand, am seeing a Paris far removed from the well-beaten tourist track. Not for us the Eiffel Tower, the Louvre, Les Invalides, etc. Where we are, you'd hardly know they existed. We are on the Left Bank, living La Vie Bohème with a vengeance and the most exciting thing I've seen is the back of someone who might have been Jean-Paul Sartre, the famous Existentialist Philosopher, and then again, might have been Just Anyone. I shall never know, but he was taking coffee at the Deux Magots, and he did look quite lugubrious and philosophical. I asked Greg and Phil, who were with me at the time. Phil wasn't sure if it was Sartre, and Greg wasn't sure he knew who Sartre was anyway.

I know you wanted lots of stories about my thrilling Parisian adventures, but it's been very quiet so far. I wouldn't say boring, because Paris is far too beautiful ever to be that. Really, every street corner looks like an Impressionist painting. Alice would love it. I think of her a lot, because thinking is one thing I do do plenty of, mainly in cafés. That's where I'm writing this, as a matter of fact, both because at the studio there is no clean surface on which to rest paper (see under studio, later on) and because sitting here in the sun and just writing the odd sentence and then looking up and watching all the people go by for a bit and then taking a sip of coffee is so wonderfully easy and leisured, I can't quite get over it. You can sit here all day long if you want to, as long as you keep buying the occasional cup of something. It's heaven. I try to remember what bells sound like, what having to get work done on time means, what teachers are . . . they all seem to belong to another life altogether. As for seeing things, well, there's not much going on in life that I can't see just by looking up from this page. Quite enough to fill a whole series of novels. Here are some examples at random:

1) A respectable woman dressed in a grey suit and navy hat, rather like Matron when she's putting on the style, knocking back the brandies as though they were medicine. She has a wedding ring on. I deduce her lover has let her down. He has found someone else, rather like
2) the American lady in bright colours, flashing teeth and diamonds at the waiters. She is on the lookout for a gigolo . . . I never believed there were such things outside stories by Somerset Maugham, but there's
3) a German couple hung about with cameras and with maps spread out in front of them on the table. They are talking earnestly. They will cover every square foot of Paris or die trying.

I could go on, but I shan't. It's as good as a theatre any day.
I am alone because the others have gone to do various

things I'd rather not do: chat to the management at Club Sortilège about our appearances, visit cathedrals, etc. or walk about for hours in this heat. Greg has said he will come and join me later and I daresay he will if he can remember the name of the café. If not, he will roll up at Rue du Texel when he's hungry, like a cat who turns up only when it's supper-time.

4 Rue du Texel . . . well, if this is what an artist's studio is like, I'm not a bit surprised that they die of consumption all over the place. It's hot now, so cholera is the more immediate danger, but the place has a glass roof and no visible heating system, so it must be hell in winter. It's not exactly heaven now, though traipsing down a little alley beside the house to an unspeakably filthy lavatory at the back must be even worse when it's cold. I refuse to describe this lavatory. All I can tell you is I am a recent convert to the chamber pot, quite a few of which we found in the studio when we arrived. We puzzled about them at first, but very rapidly discovered what a boon they were. There is also a shower that would not be featured in Homes and Gardens but we use it just the same. I close my eyes when I'm in there.

On to slightly less sordid things. The artist and his wife who have gone off to the seaside did not believe in housework. They hadn't even washed the dishes before they left. The first evening we all worked flat out to make the place fit to live in. You should have seen the band! I stood over them and made them mop and sweep and stack all the paintings neatly against the wall, and turn the mattress on the one available bed (mine, up on a little raised platform affair built above the main room) while I set to in the kitchen washing all those horrible dishes.

They, the band, divided the studio very carefully

between them, and I noticed that each instrument had its own special place. It may seem to an outsider as though these men live in total chaos, but if you look closely, it's quite clear that each one has his own territory, like a cat, and that the others respect all the boundaries.

'The sheets are full of holes!' I said to Harry, as he was helping me sort out the contents of the linen cupboard.

'Probably him and his family,' he answered, pointing to where a tiny mouse was peeping out from a hole in the skirting-board.

'How do you know,' I whispered, 'that he has a family?'

'Mice aren't often bachelors,' Harry said. 'And in France you get all sorts of reductions for large numbers of children. It's what they call "*une famille nombreuse*".'

'Not too *nombreuse*, I hope,' I said. 'I'm not going to jump on a chair and shriek at the sight of one little creature, but I don't know that I want entire families scampering over my toes as I sleep.'

'I'll set up my drum kit and blast them,' said Harry. 'They won't know what hit them.'

After a few hours of back-breaking labour, the place looked almost normal. All the sleeping bags, lilos, etc. were lined up in the middle of the floor. There are two big, ugly, squashy sofas . . . the men are all playing Musical Beds so that everyone gets a turn. I'm the lucky one, upstairs on the only real live mattress. It is a double bed so it seemed only fair that I should offer to share it (on a strictly chaste feet-to-head basis, you understand) but everyone gallantly said they were fine, and they were not in Paris to sleep, but to burn the candle at both ends, etc. etc. and that thank you, yes, they would avail themselves of my bed in groups of two or three for little naps when I was out in cafés and so on. It wouldn't surprise me if a couple of them weren't there now, having a short siesta.

Up in your Scottish fastness of clean linen and high moral tone, I can imagine you saying: 'Ugh! How can you bear to sleep in someone else's sheets?' I can see Alice wrinkling her nose in disgust and shuddering delicately. She would, I know, sit up all night on a hard chair rather than bed down in linen someone else had been sleeping on. Well, I've learned not to be so squeamish. For one thing, I know and like all these people and they are all reasonably clean, because I remind them to shower. For another I'm so intensely grateful that this bed is free of bugs and other creepy-crawlies that grubby sheets are as nothing to me. Thirdly I'm usually too tired to care about anything when I fall into my bed at dawn. Did I forget to mention that? It's very important. We don't get to see the morning, and most of the afternoon has gone by the time we get up for breakfast. This is because we are on so late at Club Sortilège. It's a bit like being on the night shift.

But the nights here are magnificent. I never realized there were so many different kinds of light. Perhaps that's why Paris is called 'La Ville Lumière'. The best light of all is in cafés at night, around lamps which seem to shine yellow. You can almost see the brush strokes fanning out all around each one, just in the way Van Gogh painted them. Out in the streets there are the neon lights of course, and lots of them are pink or green or blue and turn themselves on and off in a beautiful dance-like sequence. Then there are the headlights and tail-lights of all the cars whizzing around at high speeds, the warm light that spills on to the pavements through the café windows, and the chilly light shining out of shops closed up till the morning. The only light that fails to come up to scratch is our light in the studio. It's about sixty watts and very depressing. Luckily, we're hardly ever there at night.

It's nearly time to repair to our favourite restaurant 'A la Chaumière' for what most people think of as supper, but what I suppose is a kind of lunch for us in this topsy-turvy existence.

A bientôt, as they say over here,
Bella

*

A few days later on in August, 1962

Dear Megan,

Another dispatch from the City of Light! Life at 4 Rue du Texel has settled down to a nice routine, but Greg is looking sulkier and sulkier. This is because (he says) he has less and less time alone with me. I try to point out that living in bunches of seven (or eight if you include me), is not conducive to privacy, and that we are sort of alone for part of the evening, on our money-making venture.

Greg and I have started busking round the cafés in the early evening and very lucrative it is too. He plays the guitar and I sing all sorts of songs and then we pass round a hat. We go to big cafés like the Dôme and the Coupole and all the tourists think we're terrific and fill our hat with notes and coins. This means that we can (all eight of us) afford a slap-up meal with wine each night before we go off to the club at about midnight. Any spare cash gets divided up between Greg and me, and yes, I *will* afford a cake one day. Meanwhile, it's good fun and you see some funny things. Guess who I saw the other night? I'm sure it was her. The Dreaded Violette! – Alice's sinister great aunt. I'd recognize those eyes anywhere. She was right at the back of the café, hidden in the shadows, all draped in rusty black floaty bits and pieces, but those eyes shone out like a beacon. I don't know if she remembered me from Alice's party. In any case, I noticed it was coins and not a note she put into the hat. I daresay she's not all that wealthy. The man she was with (her husband, could it be?) was a scraggy, bearded creature dressed in shades of brown. They had a chessboard set up between them. He was concentrating on the game and she wasn't. She was moving her head this way and that, raking the half-dark-ness with those eyes, for all the world like a lighthouse shining out across the water, turning and turning. I'm sure it was her.

So that's the routine. We sing for our supper among the well-heeled tourists, then we have our supper, then we go along to Club Sortilège and sing all over again, for our breakfast, I suppose you could say, but it's not much money and there are eight of us.

The really blissful part about it all is the singing. I've never done so much of it in my life, and quite honestly, Megan, I feel so wonderful while I'm doing it that I wish there were a way I could go on and on doing it for ever and never stopping. The way it makes me feel is impossi-ble to describe. The music swells up somewhere in your head (but also partly in your stomach) and then you open your mouth and are conscious of this tremendous noise vibrating all through your skull and pouring out of your mouth just carried along by your breath . . . oh, it's a mazing! A really marvellous feeling. The great advantage it has over every other activity I can think of is that it takes up your whole attention while you're doing it. I get completely, totally absorbed. I never find myself thinking in the middle of a song: 'I wonder what's for dinner?' or 'What shall I wear tomorrow?' The song I'm singing has taken up all the available space in my mind and body. When the singing is over, it's as though I'm literally coming down to earth. Landing, after a flight that took me out of the real world.

But anyway, you do not want philosophizing or meditations on music, you want solid information, so I'll continue . . .

Club Sortilège is a funny sort of place. You could easily miss it altogether if you didn't know it was there. It's just a hole in the wall with steps going down to a cellar. There's a small neon sign saying Club Sortilège and an arrow pointing the way outside on the wall, but the electricity has failed or something so all you've got is an arrow flashing on and off in a half-hearted fashion. The Club is bang in the middle of the Red Light district and yes, there really are what Miss Clarke would call 'Ladies of the Night' in fishnet tights and skimpy blouses tottering around and leaning against the walls in extremely uncomfortable-looking high-heeled shoes. No one seems terribly interested in them. They come into the club from time to time for a drink and a rest and once they're sitting at a table and chatting and have kicked their shoes off they really look quite ordinary and tired and sad and old, some of them. Not at all glamorous or dangerous or exotic. If Alice could see them, she'd say they looked like the women Toulouse-Lautrec painted. They like coming to the club because it's very cosy and homelike. It sounds a strange thing to say about a nightclub, but it's true. I think I was hoping it would be full of wicked gangsters and their molls, but if the people who come here are part of the criminal underworld, then they're on their best behaviour

on account of Monsieur and Madame de la Pompière
running the place in respectable French bourgeois style as
though it were their home, which I suppose in a way it is.
Madame de la P. is known as Madame (logical, *n'est-çe
pas?*) and is enormous. Tall, and with what everyone here
refers to as a '*belle poitrine*' i.e. a bosom of positively
Gargantuan proportions. They say she was once a dancer
at the Folies Bergères and jiggled herself about clad in not
much more than a feather or two . . . imagine! She rules
the Sortilège empire (a kind of whitewashed cellar with a
bar at one end and a bandstand at the other, and scattered
chairs and tables in between) with a rod of iron. What she
says goes and she says it very loudly and very quickly.
Monsieur, her '*pauvre petit mari*' (that's what the Ladies of
the Night call him when she's out of earshot, which isn't
very often), seems henpecked but contented enough. He
works behind the bar and listens constantly to Edith Piaf.
Have you ever heard her songs, Megan? If there's such a
thing as a record shop in your porridge-bespattered
wilderness, get you thither at the double and listen to this
amazing singer who is like no one else at all. Greg knows
all about her. She is incredibly small and thin (query:
could this be part of the attraction for Monsieur? A
creature so different from Madame?) and has led the kind
of unhappy life a novelist would never dare to invent:
horrible childhood, drugs, alcohol, and truly ghastly men
trampling all over her. And she sings about all of it – oh,
it's enough to make you cry and break out all over in
goosepimples. Listen to 'La Vie en Rose' and 'L'hymne à
l'Amour'. If only I could sound like that. I shall buy some
of her records while I'm here and you'll be able to hear
them back at Egerton Hall. I imagine a Scottish record
shop stocked entirely with eightsome reels and many

moving renditions of 'Loch Lomond' but I'm sure that's not fair.

As well as the whitewashed cellar that makes up the club itself, there are various rather squalid little dressing-rooms-cum-lounges where the artistes can sit about while they're getting ready to perform. There's an unspeakable lavatory (question for the Oxbridge General Papers: how can a culture that has given us Racine and Baudelaire and Edith Piaf be so cavalier about the state of its lavatories? Discuss while holding a scented handkerchief to your nose) and a kind of cupboard which is home to Margot, an all-purpose maid and dresser and clearer-up of things. Luckily, Margot doesn't come out of her lair too often. She gives me the creeps, I can't think why. She's always quite kind, but there's a mothlike softness and wispiness about her that I can't stand, as though she might crumble if you touch her. Maybe it's her clothes. They're wafty and grey and grubby and drift about like wings. Also, she reminds me of someone I don't wish to be reminded of: that awful Em who gave me the pink suede belt in London. The resemblance is so strong that I actually asked Margot if she had relations in England. She just looked vague, so I shut up and now I try to keep out of her way as much as possible which is hard because she feels she has to help me dress. Madame herself decided on the very first night that I was not eye-catching enough. Perhaps she had a point. I was in black from head to toe, in best Parisian Existentialist style, complete with my hair hanging over my face, white lipstick and thick black eyeliner.

'*Mais c'est affreux!*' said Madame when she saw me and I have to concede she may have been right. She dragged me off to her private room and began flinging open drawers and cupboard doors, and in the twinkling of an eye every available surface was heaped with ostrich feathers, spangles, sequins, satins, laces, frills, flounces, lamé, brocade and all in blistering colours like cerise and peacock blue.

'It is necessary absolutely,' said Madame (I'm translating, of course), 'to make the dazzling impression.'

'Yes,' I said. What else could I say? I'm a great one for dazzling impressions myself, as you know, but sequins and feathers? I really didn't quite see how I was going to escape, but at last, after trying on outfit after outfit of the utmost hideousness, I found something I liked and which I now wear on stage every night. It's a dress, which already puts it way ahead of some of the things I tried, e.g. little skirt and bra sets, and things with no skirt at all at the front and a very long train affair at the back. The dress is red taffeta, low cut and very tight over the bust showing every inch of my '*belle poitrine*' with frills around the neckline. It keeps on being tight right down to my hips and then it breaks out in a sort of mad rush of flounces down to below the knee.

'It has the air,' said Madame, 'completely Spanish.' I know exactly what she meant. I could have gone straight on stage as Carmen. All I needed was a black mantilla on my hair and a rose clutched between my teeth and I'd have been ready for a Fandango. But I liked the way I looked, so I thanked Madame profusely and worried privately that perhaps the band would refuse to play with me dressed as I was. But no, they were enchanted, and made me turn around so that they could all admire me.

'That dress,' said Harry, 'could knock a chap's eyes out at twenty paces!'

'Phew! What a scorcher!' said Kenny and everyone else

whistled. Not Greg, though. He was miserable, I could see. He didn't say anything about it then, but I cornered him afterwards and he admitted it. He didn't like me looking so good for fear someone else would run off with me! I managed to convince him that the Red Dress bore no resemblance to the magical Red Shoes which made the poor girl in the story dance until she dropped down dead. I told him I was still me, and all the scarlet flounces in the world wouldn't turn me suddenly into a lustful and debauched creature, so he should stop worrying. Aren't men silly? It's true that the set went very well that night, so Madame clearly knows her stuff. I can't believe, though, that she *ever* fitted into my dress, even a hundred years ago.

Till next time,
Yours dazzlingly,
Bella

*

Paris, *later in August '62*

Oh, Megan, Megan, something awful has happened and something wonderful! Or maybe it hasn't happened. Do I sound totally mad? I feel mad. For the first time in my life I can understand *why* people want to write poems etc. and string together all the most wonderful and resplendent words they can find. It's all to do with *LOVE*. Oh, Megan, I've found it! I've found it! I know what it feels like now and I always will, but I can't ever have it . . . oh, I could cry and scream and tear my clothes, I feel so miserable. And yet I'm happy because I know what it feels like at last. I'm making very little sense. I realize that. I shall take a deep breath and make myself as calm as I possibly can and tell you the whole story, from the beginning.

I have to say one thing before I start. I've never been a believer in all this Dante and Beatrice stuff. I've had no time for stories about people who just glimpse someone once on a bridge or something – isn't that where Dante saw his beloved? – and are in thrall to them for ever, without so much as a word being spoken. It's always struck me as a lot of Romantic poppycock, thought up by male poets of the lyrical tendency. That's what I thought before this morning. Now I'm here to tell you that Dante and his ilk knew what they were talking about, and in fact may not have put the case quite strongly enough. I know this, because I have undergone just such an experience, and I don't think I'll ever recover.

This is what happened. I'm terrified to write it down in case it's like a dream and just putting it into words robs it of some of its magic.

Last night, from about ten o'clock, the Sortilège was very crowded. There was a party in from the Sorbonne: foreign students, most of them, who had come over to Paris for a spot of French language and culture during the summer hols. Lots of them were American. You could tell at once – I don't quite know how. Perhaps it was their height or their clothes, or their very good teeth, or it might have been something to do with their loud exclamations about everything in American accents. I caught gems like: 'Gee, they have a band here . . . let's stay and hear how they sound . . .' from where I was sitting, near the bar, and I felt irritated. It was as if they were willing us to be not-so-hot, saying to us: impress us if you can. We're from the kingdom of Jazz, Elvis country, Buddy Holly land.

'Don't flare your nostrils like that, Bella,' Greg said. 'We'll show them. We'll do "Suitcase". That'll sort them out.'

I laughed. 'Suitcase' is an amazingly fast, jazzy, upbeat number that takes every scrap of energy and breath in my body. I also sing it very loudly, so that it just about takes the roof off the room I'm doing it in.

'Is the Sortilège built for it, I wonder? Won't the place just cave in?'

'Let's risk it,' said Greg, 'and then we'll follow up with "Sleeping" to calm them down.'

So that's what we did when it came to my set. I blasted them with a few gentle verses of 'Suitcase':

Look at this suitcase, full of stuff
does it look like a heart to you?
Let me tell you, enough's enough
and I'm unpacking, baby, it's true.
Out they go
the hugs and kisses
dates and wishes
promises and I love you,
photographs
and lots of laughs
and memories
that make me blue
all your cheating
all your lying
all my sighing
and my crying –
from now on
I'm butterflying!
Out goes loving

turtledoveing
I'll go jazzing
razzmatazzing.
I'm tossing out
the things you gave me
the necklaces
and rings you gave me
taking off
the wings you gave me
when we flew
when love was new –
Baby, I'm grounded now
yessir.
Baby, I'm grounded now.

The song goes on in this vein for three minutes with Harry doing his utmost on the drums. You can imagine the effect. Just as I was taking a bow (and I have to hand it to the American contingent. They were very enthusiastic applauders) I glanced towards the steps leading down from outside and I saw him. I couldn't stop looking at him, Megan, because he was the most beautiful person I had ever seen in my life: tall and dark and with eyes the colour of aquamarines. He came to sit at a table quite near the front, and I heard everyone say: 'Hi, Mark!' and 'Look, Mark's here!' and so I knew his name. I just gazed and gazed at him, until Greg said:

'Bella, what's the matter? What's wrong? Aren't we going to do "Sleeping"?'

'Yes,' I whispered. 'Yes, we'll do it.' My mouth was dry, and I could hear my heart beating in the very centre of my head, louder than the drumbeat. I started to sing, and I sang it for him, for Mark. The spotlight grew smaller and smaller until I could sense it on my face, and the rest of the club was in semi-darkness. As I sang the words, I could feel them flying up out of my mouth and into the air and wrapping themselves around this man, this Mark, like a caress. Oh, I meant every one of them, Megan.

> My eyes were closed
> before I looked at you.
> I was asleep
> when you came in.
> Then there you were
> and when I looked at you
> the world inside my heart
> began to spin.
> My heart was ice
> before you melted it.
> I was asleep
> and feeling blue.
> Now here you are
> and when you look at me
> the sweetest dreams I have
> are filled with you.

Don't you think it's significant, that we should have decided to sing just that song and at just that moment? It seems to me as if it was Meant, part of some great plan, although I know you'll probably be giggling at such a far-fetched suggestion. Anyway, I sang, and as I did, I knew Mark's eyes were on me, and when the song was finished and the lights came on again, I met his gaze and didn't look away. Not for a long time. The look just stretched out between us like a thin, silver wire, vibrating, quivering, and I could feel him drinking me in, every bit of me, consuming me there where I stood, scanning my face as though he had to learn it quickly, immediately: learn it by heart to keep it for ever. I looked back at him, until Greg said:

'Right, Bella, that was great. Come and have a drink.' He took my hand and led me over to a table far away from the one Mark was at. I could feel the disappointment rising in me, making me feel sick. I wanted to tear my hand out of Greg's and run to the table down by the dance floor and sit next to Mark. You're being stupid, I said to myself. He's with a whole gang of his friends. You can't go barging in there. Maybe one of those fresh-faced, sparkly-looking young women is his girlfriend. He was only looking at you like that because he liked the way you sing. Lots of people like the way you sing. It doesn't mean anything really. It's just a kind of spell that is broken as the last note of the music dies away, that's all. You can imagine what kind of gloomy thoughts I was having, Megan, without me telling you. Then, I noticed a flurry of chair-scraping and goodbyes being called out and I saw that Mark's party was leaving. I couldn't bear it. They were going . . . he was going and I'd never see him again. He actually began to make his way up the steps when quite suddenly he turned and came back to where I was sitting with the others. I think it was the force of my longing directed at his back that made him return, made him come and speak to me. He said:

'Excuse me, Miss, but could I have a word with you?' I was too overcome to speak. I nodded and stood up and we walked over to a corner near the staircase.

'I just wanted,' he began, and hesitated. 'I just wanted to say how much I enjoyed your singing. It was terrific.'

'Thank you,' I said.

He shook his head. 'No, I don't just want to say that. That sounds as lame as hell. I'm sorry. I don't know what to say, and that's the truth. I'm leaving Paris on the six a.m. flight tomorrow and I'll be back in Medical School in Boston in a couple of weeks. Otherwise . . .' He let the word hang in the air.

'Otherwise what?' I said.

'Never mind,' he said. 'Only I want you to know . . .' he looked around as if searching for the right words, 'that I'll always remember you. Always.'

I blushed. I said, 'I don't even know your name.'

'Mark. Mark Eschen. I have to go now . . . they'll be back and drag me off if I don't.'

'Okay,' I said. ''Bye.'

''Bye,' he whispered and ran up the steps. At the top, he looked back and it seemed to me as though he made some kind of movement that might have been a kiss. I think he made the shape of a kiss with his mouth. I groaned, because the pain I felt, the loss I felt, was so terrible. He was here, with me, within my grasp and I'd let him go. He doesn't even know my name, I thought. He knows nothing about me, nothing about where to find me. I should have gone with him, jumped on the flight to Boston, not let him out of my sight. As it is, all I have to remember him by are his name and the memory of his eyes on my face, and a half-blown kiss in the dark that may not have been a kiss at all.

I went back to where the others were chatting and sat down in a daze. Greg was looking sad and sulky.

'What've you done with your Stage-door Johnnie, Bella?' Phil said. 'He was properly smitten, wasn't he?'

'He's going back to America tomorrow,' I said. This had a remarkable effect on Greg. It was as though a cloud had floated past the sun. He started smiling at everyone and immediately put an arm around my shoulders. I hardly noticed. You can't be sad at losing him, I said to myself. You've only exchanged a couple of sentences with him. You don't know him. But 'sad' wasn't the word for what I felt. It was more as though I'd been struck by lightning. I felt shaken. I felt as though I would never be myself properly again. I had loved him. That was what had happened to me. Only for a few minutes, it's true, but oh, Megan, with such intensity, such longing! Of course I realize that I will probably never see him again, so that's that.

There you are. Not much of a story, is it? But my dreams are so full of him, Megan, and because I've never really known him, I can make him into whatever I choose. I sing every song for him now. Greg says, 'You're singing better than ever,' and I feel so guilty! Poor Greg! What shall I tell him? I think I'll have to tell him the truth eventually, but I don't want to hurt him and I will. Who invented love, Megan? Didn't they make a dreadful *mess* of it? Why can it almost never be all right? Oh, I could weep! Pay no attention to me. I'm raving and incoherent. I'm sure you remember what it's like. Perhaps next time I write, I'll feel a little more normal.

Tons of love,
Bella

*

Paris, *Summer '62 etc.*

Dear old Megan,
A couple of days have passed and although the first delirious babblings have subsided somewhat, both in my

breast and (it is to be hoped) on paper, I am still haunted by the knowledge that somewhere in the world Mark – isn't it a wonderful name? – is walking around, alive. I see his face in dreams and my thoughts turn to him quite a lot, but I shan't bore you with that. Unless something exciting is happening in any romance, I do think people should keep quiet, don't you? All that pure undiluted feeling and yearning is terribly tedious for everyone else. So as I've nothing more to report on that front, I'll go on to other things.

Club Sortilège is as usual. I'm getting quite attached to the old place. A white cat has adopted us. One of the Night Ladies must have fed it or something and now it hangs around the stage door, and occasionally even comes in and takes up residence in one of the dressing-rooms. This is okay, except if Margot finds it. She doesn't like cats at all, and flicks at it with a duster, and hisses at it and the poor creature runs for its life and skulks behind the dustbins outside. Why do all the cats I see look like poor Snowflake? Is it that they're the only ones that catch my eye? It's mysterious and that's a fact.

There's not really very much news. Life at the studio is okay. We are just about keeping our heads above the surface of the chaos. I'm not sure what I'm doing wrong. Perhaps eight people is more than the place can take, but it is very hard to keep it looking decent. Things do lie about so, and if you're not careful, they'll engulf you. That's what it seems like to me. And in spite of the fact that I do hardly any cooking at all, there's always stacks of washing-up. Another mystery; life is full of them.

People like my singing, so that makes me happy. We are *un succès fou* at the Sortilège and I have to do encores every night. Madame thinks it's the red dress and I'm sure she's right.

I'm not feeling myself today, Megan, and it's because of a quarrel I've had with Greg. It happened the night after I'd seen Mark, so I suppose my nerves were jangling, or something. At least that's my excuse, but I should never have . . . well, let me start at the beginning. Greg was pestering me, asking me what was wrong . . . why was I different . . . what had he done, etc. etc. I tried to say nothing. I pleaded tiredness, but he went on and on. In the end, I couldn't bear it another moment. I said:

'I'm sorry, Greg, I'm sorry to have to tell you this, but I'm in love with someone else.'

As soon as the words were out of my mouth, I wished I hadn't said them. Poor Greg looked stunned, wounded. He said:

'You can't be. You haven't . . . where did you meet him?'

'Last night at the club.'

'That guy?' (He relaxed a bit.) 'I saw you both . . . you only talked to him for about three minutes and then he was gone. How can you be in love with someone you hardly know?'

'Oh, I know all I need to know about him,' I said.

'I don't believe it.' Greg laughed. 'You're not letting me anywhere near you because of someone who just happened to be there last night while you sang?'

'It wouldn't be fair to you,' I said. 'Leading you on when I don't really love you.'

Oh, Megan, I said it, and he looked . . . he looked as though all the separate bits of his face were going to disintegrate.

'You don't love me,' he whispered. 'I thought . . .'

I tried to backtrack. I tried to make it better and only

made it worse. I muttered about different kinds of love, and always being his friend and loving his music. I chattered on and while I was chattering, Greg, I could see, was just smouldering, getting angrier and angrier every moment. We were the only ones in the studio and we were in the kitchen. I'd actually persuaded Greg to help me with the washing-up, which meant he had all the ammunition ready to hand for when he lost his temper. I didn't realize he was losing it until it was thoroughly lost, if you see what I mean. He started very quietly, muttering into the dirty water and then got louder and louder until by the end he was yelling at me:

'Jesus, Bella, I don't know what you want. I mean, what else was I supposed to do? I thought, when you first came to the house, I thought you liked me. You *did* like me. You said you did and you bloody well behaved as though you did, or have you conveniently forgotten that, eh?' He turned round and snarled at me. 'I think . . . you know what I think? I think you've lost your mind, that's what. I don't think it's true, any of that stuff you said, because I think you *do* love me, and the rest of that waffle, all the bit about the mystery man at the Sortilège is just made up, rubbish, total *bullshit*! You sing my songs as though you mean them, don't you?' His voice subsided a bit at this point.

'Of course I mean it,' I said. 'I love your songs, you know I do. Don't you know that?'

'Well, that proves it then. Those songs are me. The best bits of me. If you love them, you love me. It's logical.'

'It's not a bit logical. I admire you, of course, for being able to write the songs, but it doesn't follow at all that I love you. Oh, Greg, I'm only trying to be honest with you.'

This was when he saw red. He actually picked up cups and saucers from the draining board and started flinging them round the room.

'Who the hell asked you to be honest, eh? Who gave you the right to go tearing into people with all this truth?' I didn't answer. I was cowering behind a chair. Greg shook his head and looked around him as though he'd suddenly come out of a dream.

'Oh, God,' he said, 'look what I've done now.'

He started going round the floor of the studio picking up the pieces of broken china and tears were just pouring down his face.

I said, 'Greg, don't cry. I can't bear it. It's better if you yell at me.'

'I can't help it,' he said. 'I can't stop.'

'Please, Greg,' I said, crying myself now. 'Please stop. I don't mean to hurt you, but I can't lie to you and I can't help what I feel.'

I sat down at the kitchen table and began to cry as I haven't cried since I was a small child. I bawled. I howled. I sobbed. I screamed. And the tears just poured and poured out of me. As I cried, I could feel that I was weeping about everything: everything I'd never properly wept about all through my life: I cried for sorrow for Alice and for anger at that animal who hurt her and I cried for the loss of my cat who'd been killed and I think for the first time in my life I even cried for my mother. And of course, Greg tried to stop me, and I pushed him away and said:

'Let me cry. It's good for me to cry.'

'But how are you going to be able to sing tonight? Your eyes'll be like two slices of boiled beetroot.'

That made me laugh in the midst of my tears. Greg found a bottle of wine and poured us a drink.

'What do my eyes look like?' he asked. 'Men aren't supposed to cry.'

'You shouldn't cry for me,' I said. 'I'm not worth the tears.'

'You are,' said Greg, 'to me.'

'I'm really sorry,' I said, hiccuping from the after-effects of all those tears. 'I really am. I didn't mean to hurt you.'

'Never mind,' said Greg. 'I'll get over it by the time I'm forty, I expect. But I still can't believe what you told me. About that bloke last night at the Sortilège. Is it true?'

'Yes,' I said, 'it's true, and that's the last time I'm ever going to see him.' I started crying again.

'Bloody hell, Bella,' said Greg, 'don't begin all over again or we'll all drown!'

I stopped in the end. Well, you have to, don't you? The show has to go on, doesn't it? Thank heavens for eye make-up, that's what I say, and for Madame's red dress, which, as they say in all the best fashion magazines, 'attracts the eye towards the bust line'. Fortunately my breasts are not transparent, or the entire clientele of the Sortilège would have been able to gaze at my bruised and bleeding heart.

Yours, expiring in a Paris studio
from impossible dreams of love,
　　Bohemian Bella

*

August 25th, 1962

Dear Megan,

I know that people say 'I wish you were here' all the time, but I really mean it, and really do wish it, and the thought that I won't see you until almost the beginning of next term is truly ghastly. I need you. I need to tell you things. So much has happened and it would be such a relief to have you to discuss it with. As it is, I have to limit myself to this rather inadequate means of communication. That is the one thing – the only thing – I am looking forward to next term: chatting to you again. I *think* I'm dreading the thought of going back to Egerton Hall, but that may well be because since arriving here the whole of my normal life seems to have no more reality than the painted backdrop of a pantomime seen long ago. I blame all this foreign travel. I am not myself. Even these long letters aren't like me, are they? But there's such a lot I want to tell you . . . two things mainly. So here goes.

Our time here is almost at an end. I feel nostalgic about this café, and this table, even before I've left it. I also have the impression that everything has changed and become steadily darker since I first wrote to you. It was only two weeks ago, and already the letters I wrote then seem to belong to another life and to have been written by a 'me' who was altogether bouncier and more optimistic. I think I must be still not quite over what happened on Thursday night, the day before yesterday. The doctor at the hospital who put the stitches in said that I was lucky to avoid blood-poisoning. Don't be alarmed, Megan. I'm telling this the wrong way round. I'm okay really, but my energy has been sapped and I don't seem to have my usual enthusiasm. Oh, things are different!

The truth of the matter is, ever since seeing Mark and having the row with Greg, I've been in a foul temper. I am impatient with everyone because nothing seems worth doing any more. It scarcely seems worth walking around in a world without Mark in it – no, don't worry, I'm not in the least suicidal, just furious that a certain combination of features should have brought me to this *silly and undignified pass*. I'm livid with myself. I hate the sort of person I've become: given to weeping for no good reason, and fantasizing my way through some of the daylight hours and most of the night-time ones.

I was a little unnerved on Thursday night even before we got to the Sortilège. This was because I had seen the dreaded Violette again, and this time there was no mistake. She actually spoke to me. Greg and I had been busking. I was taking the hat round. I hadn't noticed her, right at the back of the café, all by herself.

'You don't remember me,' she said, in that terrible, rusty voice. 'I'm Alice's Aunt Violette.'

I looked at her properly then. That was a bit of a shock as well. When we saw her at Alice's party she must have been all done up. She looked quite different now, all thin and pinched and white in the face, and oh, Megan, so dreadfully old! The skin round her mouth was puckered into lines, there were hundreds of wrinkles round her eyes and her neck was leathery and scraggy like a chicken's. Her eyes blazed at me. I found I had to turn away. She put a hand on my arm while she was talking. It looked like a claw, or the talon of a bird. The nails were painted such a dark red that they seemed almost black.

'Of course I remember you,' I said and smiled my most charming smile. 'We met recently at Alice's party.'

'Alice . . .' said Violette. 'How is Alice now?' I wondered briefly who had told her about Alice and how much she knew. I decided she couldn't know everything, so I said:

'She's a lot better now, I believe. The doctors are very pleased with her progress.'

'Really?' Violette looked at me and frowned. 'That's not

what I heard at all.' She stood up, towering above me, gathering the folds of her robe or cloak or whatever it was closer about her. Then she leaned down and whispered in my ear:

'I hear she's knocking,' (she rapped with a bony, ring-encrusted hand on the marble tabletop), 'knocking at Death's Door.' She laughed a hideous laugh, and wound her way between the tables, waving goodbye to me as she went with her skeletal fingers, a kind of death's-head grin on her face.

I made Greg buy me a drink after that. I was shaken and upset, and couldn't help worrying about Alice. She *will* be all right, Megan, won't she? I really couldn't bear it if she isn't.

Anyway, you can imagine that after such an encounter I wasn't in the best of moods. Thursday night, our second-to-last performance (and my last, although I didn't know it then), had been talked about for days. It was to be a Gala. All this meant was that the Ladies of the Night were encouraged to drag their gentlemen friends in, Monsieur and Madame invited every elderly reprobate they could think of (and assured us that some of them were real live music critics), drinks were more expensive than usual, the floor had been swept, and Madame herself was the centre of attention in diamanté-studded grey satin, like a sea lion ready for a Hunt Ball. It had also been decided, before I arrived in my less-than-Gala mood, that a special effort was to be made to improve on the red, flouncy dress. Madame herself came into my little dressing-room to tell me her decision. She was herding poor Margot into the room ahead of her, as if she were a small child who need-ed to be told where to go. Margot was in her habitual moth-grey bits and pieces, Gala or no Gala.

'Sit yourself there, *chérie*,' Madame said to her, and then turned to me. 'You are going certainly to excuse me for interrupting you,' she began.

'But naturally,' I said, trying hard to smile.

'I have been considering what one must do to give you the air Gala . . .' I nodded and hmmed non-committally. '. . . and at first I thought that it would be a question of the addition of a few jewels, simply . . .' (oh, well, I was thinking, if it'll please the old bat, I'll doll myself up in a couple of strands of glass beads . . . why not?) '. . . but then I decided that that would not walk well at all . . .' (please remember I am translating exactly from the French!). 'One has need, I think, of a coiffure.'

I knew what she meant by that. I didn't need a translation and neither will you. We both know that a coiffure is to a hairdo what champagne is to Lucozade, and that what Madame had in mind was the kind of arrangement it takes about half an hour to create. I said:

'But I haven't the time for a coiffure, and besides, it's ten o'clock at night. All the salons have been closed for hours.'

A look of triumph which would not have disgraced Napoleon at Austerlitz crossed Madame's face.

'But it is for this that I bring Margot!' She leaned towards me, and the whalebones in her corset could be heard creaking. 'Margot, who has only been working here for a few weeks, is nevertheless known to me as a veritable artiste of the hair. She will transform you . . . you must believe me.'

'Oh, I do, I do! But surely it will be a lot of trouble . . . surely I could just put it up like this . . .' I indicated a French pleat with my hands. I hated the thought of those pallid fingers fluttering round in my hair. Margot, too, it has to be said, was sitting in her chair looking distinctly unkeen on the whole idea.

'No, no,' Madame said, in a tone which signalled the interview was nearly over. 'Absolutely not. Margot will create you here a masterpiece.' And as though to silence any further reservations I might have had, she produced her trump card. Turning to Margot, she said:

'Show her the comb. She will not be able to resist.'

She smiled at us both and swept out of the room. Margot was scrabbling about, meanwhile, in the folds of her skirt. Then she stood up and came to stand behind me, so that I could see her in the rather spotty mirror. It's typical of Club Sortilège that they have light bulbs all round the mirror in best Hollywood style, and only half of them are actually working. It's enough light to see by and not enough to be cruel: an ideal arrangement. Margot held up what was in her hand, and showed it to me in the mirror. I gasped. The comb was thickly encrusted with obviously false but still blindingly twinkling gems in all the colours of the rainbow. The whole thing should have been hideous, but was curiously attractive. I can't explain why, but all of a sudden I wanted nothing more than an elaborate structure on the top of my head, anchored into place with that magnificent comb. I could just see myself under the follow-spot, with the comb bouncing tiny arrows of coloured light into the dark corners of the cellar.

'It's lovely!' I said to Margot, trying to be friendly, trying to inject some kind of warmth into my voice. Was I going to have to chat to her? I cringed at the thought. Whatever could I say? I'd never found it difficult to talk to Armand. He was always so ready with delightfully appetizing morsels of society gossip, and, of course, we used to discuss Marjorie at great length. Fortunately it became clear as Margot began to comb and pin my hair that she, too, preferred to work in silence. I watched as the coiffure began to take shape, thinking how vulnerable I felt. This person I hardly knew had the power to transform me. She could make me beautiful, but she could also, if the whim came upon her, put her hands into the recesses of her garments and pull out some scissors and cut every bit of my hair off. She could make me hideous. For a moment I felt a tremor of fear, but the sight of her, heaping one curl on the next so carefully and daintily, was strangely hypnotic. For a second, I felt my eyelids droop, but I was woken, brought to myself again, when Margot spoke.

'Now,' she said, 'we must fasten the comb. It will feel a little tight at first, but do not worry. It is for the security, you understand. So that it should not fall.'

She pushed the comb into my hair, driving the teeth through the spirals and loops she had fashioned, and twisting it a little before pushing it into position. I winced at the pain. It felt as if all the hairs around the teeth of the comb had been pulled too tight. After a bit, I thought, I'll get used to it. I smiled at Margot in the mirror and said:

'Thank you so much. It looks very nice. Very Gala.'

Margot simply nodded and gave a half-smile and then left. I looked at myself more carefully in the mirror. Even in this dim light, the jewels on the comb shone with a heart-lifting radiance. All of a sudden I felt strangely elated. Even the thought that I might never see Mark again seemed to be romantic rather than depressing. I was slightly dizzy, as well. Perhaps I should have eaten something with the drink Greg had bought me earlier in the evening. I should send someone out to get a sandwich. As soon as I thought that, I felt sick. Then the sickness passed and I felt weak. Straight after the show tonight, I promised myself, I shall go to sleep and not wake up until I'm quite rested. What the Club Sortilège needed, I decided, was someone like Matron. She'd make sure that all the artistes kept sensible hours and didn't let themselves get run down. I smiled to think what Matron would say if she could see me dressed like this, ready to go on and sing in front of a whole lot of strangers in a Paris basement.

Just then, Greg stuck his head round the door and said: 'We're on,' and I stood up.

What happened next, the whole sequence of events from the time I went on stage (Thursday midnight) until about lunchtime on Friday is like a dream. Some parts are clear and sharp. They stand out in my mind like pictures hung on a white, white wall. Some of them do not make sense, but they are vivid, brightly coloured. All the rest is space: misty and white, and in the space sometimes I can hear voices, and sometimes the voices blur and become thick and unclear.

Mainly, I remember the pain. As I sang the first couple of songs, it seemed as though the whole room was moving further and further away from me. Even the people at the tables right beside the stage looked as though they were at the wrong end of a telescope. I could sense the light pouring out from the jewels in my comb, but instead of dazzling the audience, I felt as if it was burning small holes in my scalp, and that the teeth of the comb were embedding themselves deeper and deeper in my head . . . they will go down and down, I thought fuzzily, and bore right through my scalp and through my skull and into the soft parts of my brain. That was the last thought I can recall with any certainty, and then a great wave of blackness broke over my head.

The next clear picture is of looking down at my hand,

lying on a red blanket. My hand is being stroked by Greg's. There is a bright line of light moving across a window. I've been told by Greg that Madame sent immediately for an ambulance, the moment I collapsed on to the stage.

'What happened to the comb?' I asked Greg today.

'I don't know. I suppose it must have fallen out somewhere. We were all too worried about you to bother about it. The doctor wanted to see it, after you'd told them you had holes in your head . . . but it was too late by then. The Sortilège would have been closed.'

That's another picture: the doctor frowning at me. Pressing his lips together and shaking his head. They had to shave a tiny bit of hair off, Megan. Luckily, no one can see it, because I can comb the rest of my hair to cover it up and of course it will grow back. Still, sometimes I imagine the small patch of shaved scalp to be as wide as a desert, and those pinpricks that caused me so much pain looking like wells brimming with blood.

'This comb,' I remember the doctor asking me, 'could it have been contaminated? Poisoned? Do you know where it was kept before it was used in your hair?'

I shook my head then. Later I asked Greg:

'Why did he mention poison?' and Greg said:

'Apparently, your reaction was very extreme. Not what he would have expected, he said, from what was after all quite a superficial injury.'

I came back to the studio to rest. The doctor absolutely forbade me to go on stage last night for the final performance. I was quite relieved. Greg said:

'I'll stay with her. You can manage without me, too.'

'But what about the paying customers?' said Pete. 'It's bad enough that Bella's off without losing you as well.'

'Yes,' I said, feeling better by now. 'Pete's right. You ought to go.'

Greg looked stubborn and said quite harshly:

'I don't give a tuppenny damn about the paying customers. I'm staying here and looking after Bella, and if you don't like it, tough.'

'Okay,' Pete said, clearly taken aback by Greg's uncharacteristically firm statement. 'It's okay. It can't be helped. I'll explain . . . to everyone. Any messages, Bella?'

'Say goodbye for me,' I said.

When the others came back after the last performance in the early hours of Saturday morning, Greg and I were already asleep. They'd arranged the dress over the back of the chair, so that it was the first thing I saw when I woke up.

'Madame said you should keep it,' said Phil. 'She actually made a joke. She said it no longer fitted her, and until she got her figure back, the dress was yours. Don't you reckon that counts as a joke?'

I did. I was very touched, and burst into tears to think of Madame's kindness. Then I remembered the comb. I said:

'Did anyone find the comb?' and they all shook their heads. Kenny said:

'I asked about that. Everyone claimed not to have seen it, but one of the Ladies . . . Lizette, is that her name? the redhead . . . told me later that she'd seen Margot throwing something small wrapped in newspaper into the outside bin. She also said she saw that white cat sniffing around there, and that Margot stamped her foot at him and he ran away.'

'Oh, well,' I said, 'good riddance to the comb, anyway.'

I haven't told Greg this, nor any of the others, but

sometimes, Megan, I wonder whether everything isn't linked together in some way. You're going to think I'm crazy, I know, but in my worst moments I can convince myself that it's Marjorie who's at the bottom of everything. Ever since she tried to lose me that time in Harrods, I think she's wanted me gone – out of her life. Sometimes I think she'd be quite pleased if I died. Do you remember how I choked on one of her apples, a couple of terms ago, and had to go to the San? Then the belt and now the comb, and also the fact that Em and Margot are so *like* Marjorie in so many ways, and the white cats I keep seeing – are they some kind of warning? Some sign? You will think I'm still delirious, I know. And I also know exactly what you'll tell me. I know all the reasonable explanations for everything. Marjorie is jealous of me. Marjorie is quite capable of trying to make my life difficult. She doesn't especially care if she doesn't see too much of me – but the rest is in my mind, a figment of my over-active imagination. Em and Margot looking like one another and like Marjorie is only a coincidence. The belt and the comb are accidents, and the cats are separate white cats, of which there are plenty in the world. They are of no special significance. It's exactly like Alice's story all over again: did what happened to Alice come about because the Dreaded Violette wished it to be so, or for other reasons? The truth is, we'll never know and our answers – my answers – depend on what time of day it is. During the bright and sunshiny daylight hours, I'm as rational as the next person, but waking from a bad dream and staring through the dark in the long hours before morning, I believe my worst fears are true. I believe everything.

So there you are, Megan. Another chapter in The Paris Adventures of an English Schoolgirl. Tomorrow night, we are coming back to England. I may manage one more letter. There is still something I have to tell you, something important. Maybe I should wait until I see you.

Enigmatically yours,
Bella

Dear Megan,

I've thought and thought (for about twenty minutes, truly! It proved to be the most tremendous effort. My poor little brain is quite rusty and out of practice) about whether I should write to you about this, or wait until I see you. In the end, as you can see, I've decided to write. My reasons are:

1) I want to get it off my chest.
2) I don't think I could find the right words if I had to tell you face to face. I'd be embarrassed.
3) There's nothing much else to do for the next few hours before the train leaves. All the others are lying about reading, playing cards, etc. and Greg is working on a new song . . . I bet I know what it'll be about, but I digress.

Okay. Here it is then. Last night I let Greg make love to me. (Oh, I *am* glad I'm writing this and not saying it! I'm blushing just from setting the words down on this piece of paper.) I feel guilty towards poor Greg for not loving him properly, completely, in the way I *know* I would be capable of loving Mark, but at least I have made him happy and I have to admit I'm not miserable either. In fact, it's done quite a lot to cheer me up and I recommend it as a cure for all kinds of ailments, including lingering pains in the head caused by stitches after an accident with a comb. It's also made me realize that I have to put Mark right out of my head and consign him to the category of Adolescent Fantasy, along with Elvis, Buddy, Marlon Brando and all the other heroes who are not real people in my mind, but almost fictional characters whom you can idolize and dream about without there being any real danger of hurting yourself. You remember I was still in a very woozy state on Friday evening. The doctor had given me some painkilling pills which not only dulled the pain but also made me feel fuzzy round the edges, like a picture that's not been coloured in terribly neatly. By about six o'clock, all the members of the band had gone out to one place or another. Phil and Harry had made some soup from a packet and left instructions with Greg about heating it up and giving it to me at regular intervals to build up my strength.

So, at about eleven o'clock, Greg said:

'I've got some soup here,' and came upstairs with a bowl in one hand and a spoon stuck into his belt. 'Phil says I'm to give it to you. Do you think he means I have to spoonfeed you?'

'No,' I said, 'I'm sure he doesn't. I think I can manage. Just help me to sit up a bit. Can you pile these pillows behind my back?'

'Okay,' said Greg. Suddenly, I was very hungry, and I started spooning the soup up quite enthusiastically.

'I feel much better now,' I said.

'Well enough to hear a song I've just written?'

I nodded again, because my mouth was full of soup. Greg ran down the rickety stairs to get his guitar. He started playing the introduction on his way up.

'I could stay and play it down there,' he said. 'Like a kind of serenade . . .'

'No, I want to hear it properly,' I said. 'I love the beat.'
And I did. Under the sheet, my feet were already
tapping to the rhythm: what I always think of as a driven,
pushed-through-a-saxophone-with-great-force kind of
rhythm, the kind spangled dancing girls strut their stuff
to, and even take their clothes off to . . . typical nightclub
music.

'It's written,' said Greg, 'in honour of your red dress.'

> I've got my red dress, sugar
> and my high heels on
> and I'm turning all the lights on
> till my blues are gone.
> Making that darkness
> turn so bright,
> I'm gonna sing my sorrows, honey
> Clear out of sight.
>
> Don't want no sad pictures
> no, no, no,
> don't want no
> never, no, never
> don't want no sad pictures,
> sad pictures of the night.
>
> Don't want no dark snaps, baby,
> cos everything's all right.
> Just want a lit-up set of memories
> yeah
> yeah
> a floodlit set of memories
> to bring the good times back.
> In my pictures of the night,

I'm gonna lose the black.

'That's fantastic,' I said. 'That's my very favourite of all your songs. Can I learn it tomorrow?'

'Whenever you like. I'm sorry you couldn't get to sing it at the Sortilège. But there'll be other gigs, won't there? In London?'

I nodded. I didn't know how often I would see Greg and the others next term. I think they'd quite forgotten there ever were such things in the world as schools, universities, exams, etc. I didn't blame them. I'd practically forgotten myself. I just said:

'Greg, do you remember what I told you in London?'

'What's that then?'

'That I thought my stepmother tried to kill me . . . do you remember, when my belt wouldn't come off?'

Greg laughed. 'Oh, right! I'd forgotten that . . . you doing your "I am a Gothic heroine" routine. I thought you were a bit . . . I don't know . . . delirious at the time. What with fainting and everything.'

'You're going to think I'm even more delirious now then.'

'Why?'

'Because I'm sure . . . almost sure . . . that Margot meant that comb to harm me last night, and that in some way . . . don't ask me how . . . I don't know how . . . Marjorie was behind it. No, okay, I'm not going to say another word. I can see you think I've taken leave of my senses. I take it all back. Feverish babblings, that's all. Just the sickness talking.'

'I should hope so, too.' Greg looked relieved. 'That would *really* be crazy, Bella. We'd have had to send for a doctor with a Viennese accent at least three inches thick!'

I kept quiet about my suspicions after that. Of course Greg was right, and yet I couldn't shake off what I felt deep down: that in spite of the fact that there was no visible connection between Marjorie and Margot, it was Marjorie's malicious intentions guiding the whole incident.

Anyway, I decided to change the subject.

'It's ever so nice of you,' I said, 'to miss the last night at the Sortilège and stay and look after me.'

'I like looking after you,' he said and blushed. 'I'd like . . .'

'What would you like?' I grinned. I was flirting with him, Megan, I knew I was. I had a very good idea of what he would say.

'I'd like to look after you always,' he muttered, so quietly that I could hardly hear him. I put the bowl (empty now) on the floor and leaned forward to wind my arms around him. Just suddenly I was full of affection for him, felt like hugging him and stroking his hair. So I did hug him, in a cuddly sort of way, and he began to shake. That's really the only way to describe it, Megan. He was trembling, and his lips were burning hot. I could feel them on my hair and my mouth and my neck and soon, before I knew what was happening, he had undone my pyjama buttons, and had buried his face in my breasts. It's not that I wasn't enjoying all this. I don't want you to think of me as entirely cold-hearted. I liked it. I didn't care if it went on for ages and ages, but at no point did I ever lose control of myself. I mean, I even found myself wondering if Greg had ever done this with Rilly Maxton of the porky thighs. I'm sure that's not how it's meant to be, is it, Megan? I can remember quite clearly thinking: 'it's going to happen soon. I'm not going to say no. I'm going to let

Greg undress me, make love to me. I shall know how it feels'. I was taking an almost scientific interest in what was happening. Part of me seemed to be detached, watching the antics on the bed from a spot near the ceiling somewhere. I thought at one point: 'This will hurt. I'm sure it's supposed to hurt the first time' but it didn't hurt at all. Maybe that was because of all the painkillers I'd taken for my head.

I think afterwards we must have fallen asleep for ages. I woke up and Greg was still asleep next to me. I could see him quite clearly in the moonlight coming through the glass roof above my head. I touched his shoulder and his back, and it felt so soft and smooth that I was quite surprised. I don't know what I thought a man's back would be like – all hard and armour-plated like an armadillo's perhaps – but it made me feel sad all at once to think that they were just like girls in so many things, especially when they were asleep. I think in some ways they are even more vulnerable than we are. Greg cried last night, Megan. Real tears. He kept saying how happy he was and weeping and weeping. My neck and shoulder were quite damp. I felt strong by contrast. I have a kind of power over him now. I know that, and it worries me. What will become of him if I ever leave him? This thought made me feel cold in the middle of a hot August night, and immediately I began to scheme, to think of various ways in which I could distance myself. Perhaps I should say it was a mistake? I could say I wasn't feeling quite well, that we must draw a line under all this before it was too late. I fell asleep pondering these weighty matters. Then (it must have been around dawn . . . the studio was empty . . . the others must have gone to Les Halles to eat onion soup or something) Greg woke up and began kissing me again, and it was even nicer the second time. I decided not to say anything for now. Am I being utterly beastly, Megan? Am I immoral, enjoying it so much without actually being in love with the person? Oh, I wish I had you here to talk to! We will have tons of things to discuss when we meet. Till then, I should stop writing and start packing. We leave Paris in an hour. The caravan moves on!

Lots of love,
Bella

Egerton Hall

Hip, hip, hooray! We have all of us, Megan and Alice and I, passed our exams! The envelope was waiting for me when I came home from Paris. My father had prudently decided it should await my arrival, rather than surprise me while I was abroad. I was glad of it, because it distracted him from interrogating me too closely about my time in France with Megan and Marion Tipton . . . I had almost forgotten the story I had told before setting out for Paris. Anyway, I have done rather better than I expected, and almost before the envelope had been opened, the siren voices began and the upshot of it all is, I'm back at Egerton Hall, ready to sit the exams for Oxford and Cambridge, just before Christmas. I knew all along, of course, that I would be coming back if my results were satisfactory, but it has been so easy, over this long summer holiday, to forget about work and school altogether and turn one's attention to a kind of deliciously lazy sentimental education, which is much pleasanter, that I've let the whole matter of my future slide entirely out of my head.

I'd also got out of the habit of being at home, under the same roof as my father and Marjorie again. My bedroom seemed quite suddenly very small and wrongly decorated, as if some sweet little girl lived there. I'd chosen the wallpaper and the fixtures and fittings myself, so that there was no one I could blame for anything. But had I ever really wanted a dressing-table with white net frills round it? Or a puffy eiderdown covered in burgundy satiny material? As Miss Herbert would have said in our Latin lessons: '*horresco referens*' – I shudder to relate.

'It's lovely to have you back, dear,' Marjorie said to me as we were having a drink before dinner on my very first night at home. I was considered grown-up enough for a small sherry. 'Your father has missed you.'

You haven't, I thought. You've been delighted that I wasn't here.

'And so have I, of course,' she went on. 'You must tell us simply every detail.'

'Oh, it was wonderful!' I gushed. 'We went everywhere: the Louvre, Les Invalides, Notre Dame, even Versailles.'

'But not, alas, to the launderette.' Marjorie shook a finger waggishly at me. 'I've never seen such piles of dirty clothes.'

There was no answer to that. I took a sip of my drink and made an attempt to change the subject.

'I saw one of Alice's aunts while I was there . . . Violette.' Marjorie's brow furrowed.

'Poor Alice!' she said. 'That was a dreadful business. Have you any news of her?'

'Yes, she's very much better, thank you,' I said. Marjorie was hardly listening, still shaking her head as she contemplated that 'dreadful business'. I knew she hadn't given Alice a moment's thought all summer long. I said:

'Do you know someone in Paris called Margot Duboisset?'

Marjorie looked puzzled.

'I don't know a soul in Paris, Bella. You know that.'

'I only asked because . . . well, she looked a little like you. Not as pretty of course, and much older, but there was something.'

'No,' Marjorie shook her head, 'I've never heard of her. How did you meet her?'

'Marion knew her. We went to visit her a couple of times . . . at her flat . . .' (Let it stop, I was thinking, let me change the subject quickly. This lying is harder than I thought. I won't ask about Em.)

'I expect,' Marjorie said, 'you'll be eager for school to start again.'

I was about to make some remark about missing Megan, when I remembered just in time that she was supposed to have been in Paris with me. I made a mental promise to myself never to lie unless I really had to. I said:

'Yes, it'll be fun to see the old place again.'

Marjorie smiled at me and I smiled back, but we had both been speaking in code. She meant: 'I'm longing for you to go, longing for you to get out of this house', and I meant: 'Anything is better than being here with you, even going back to Egerton Hall.'

Just before school started, though, Megan and I went to Arcadia House to spend the weekend with Alice. She is thin now, thinner than she ever was, and her skin is practically transparent, but oh, it was lovely to hear her sounding normal, and being almost exactly like she was before her long . . . I don't know what to call it . . . her long absence from me and Megan. Jean-Luc was there too, and he is completely besotted with Alice, and she flourishes under his gaze like a flower in the sun, so Megan and I feel very happy and also, I think, a little envious.

Arcadia House, which we used to tease Alice by calling the Castle Next Door, was in the process of being restored to its normal state. The gardens, especially, looked terribly neglected and Alice's father seemed to be out in them the whole time we were there, overseeing the care of the roses as his helpers pruned, trimmed, tended and watered all day long.

Megan and I planned to leave Arcadia House on Sunday evening, so Sunday lunch was a farewell celebration.

'I feel like lying down on the nearest bed and sleeping till supper-time,' I said. 'I knew that second helping of apple pie was a mistake. I can hardly breathe, I'm so full.'

'Come for a walk then,' said Alice. 'It'll make you feel better, and in any case I want you and Megan to do me a favour.'

'I can't think of anything I'd rather do less,' I said, 'but this favour sounds mysterious enough to intrigue me. Why can't we do it indoors?'

'You lazy thing,' said Alice. 'You just don't want to move. You can't do this favour inside. It's special.'

So, with me moaning and groaning and Alice and Megan laughing at me, we went into the garden. It was a very warm afternoon. The sun was only visible as a yellow blur behind thin cloud, and the air was heavy. I noticed that on the trees a few of the leaves had begun to turn red and brown. Summer was nearly over. We made our way round the side of the house and over the terraced lawns at the back.

'We're going to the summerhouse,' said Alice. 'We're going to do a – I've forgotten what you call it – one of those ceremonies where you shoo ghosts away from a place.'

'An exorcism,' said Megan. 'Why do we have to do an exorcism here?'

Alice had reached the summerhouse and was opening the door and stepping inside. She turned and looked at Megan and me, standing outside on the grass. She said:

'Because this was where it happened. With Angus. I haven't dared come near here since my party, but I feel . . .' She blushed. 'I feel if you two come in here with me I won't be scared of the place any longer. I'll have some different memories.'

We stepped inside. I sat on a wicker chair and Alice and Megan sat very close to one another on a sort of garden bench.

'Are we supposed to say anything special?' Megan said. 'A prayer?'

'No,' said Alice. 'Just being here is enough. Just talk naturally.'

'Whenever someone tells me to talk naturally,' I said, 'I can't think of a single word to say.'

Alice laughed rather nervously and looked around. She said, rather in the manner of a hostess making conversation:

'Do you still want to go to Oxford, Bella?'

I said:

'I'm not sure any more. Everyone's been persuading me for so long. Megan, you're the worst.'

'It'll be lovely,' said Megan. 'You'll see. Nothing but pleasure every minute of the day.'

'Listen to her,' I said to Alice. 'She always paints these wonderful pictures of us lying around in punts under willow trees with young men of the utmost desirability, or else we're going to balls in flouncy dresses, or acting and singing in all those college productions. She never mentions lectures or tutorials or writing essays for hours on end.'

'Work,' said Megan, 'has never been any trouble to you, Bella. You'll just sail through all of that and hardly notice it.'

I said, 'That's all very nice and fine, but I'll tell you what really persuaded me in the end. It wasn't the teachers or you or my dad. It was Marjorie.'

'Marjorie!' Alice looked puzzled. 'Isn't it rather unlike you to do something Marjorie wants?'

I laughed. 'Well, she says things like: "Think of the fun! Think of the people you'll meet! Oh, it'll be splendid!" but even as she's enthusing away like billy-o, I can hear a thin, greenish sort of tinge of envy in her voice, and that made my mind up for me. The way I look at it is: if Marjorie is going to suffer pangs of one sort or another because I'm at university, then that's a good enough reason for trying to get in.'

'Besides,' said Megan, 'I might be there too. Alice, if only you'd come back as well, we could all be together for another three years.'

Alice shook her head. 'I'm not clever enough. And I hate exams. I hate them much worse than you two do. I shall try and get into Art School, I think, but next year.' She looked down at her hands. 'I have to do what the doctors call "taking it easy" for a bit. I'm going to France to meet Jean-Luc's relations, and then I'll come back and do a secretarial course or something.'

'And you can come and meet us,' said Megan, 'wherever we are and whatever we're doing.'

'Greg,' I said, 'is sulking because I'm going back to school. He thinks that singing his songs for ever to twenty people in a dark cellar should be the height of my ambition.'

'And isn't it?' Megan said. 'Won't you sing with the band again?'

'Of course I will,' I said, 'but only when I can. I've told them that next term is out of the question, at least until the exams are over, but you never know. I might not get into either Oxford or Cambridge and in that case I may very well decide to become a singer. But,' I added, 'there's not a lot of money in it.'

'The band could become amazingly famous,' Alice said.

'And then again,' I said, 'it could remain amazingly obscure!'

We went on talking and talking through the afternoon, until the shadows of the trees lengthened on the grass, and Megan said:

'This bench has become jolly hard, all of a sudden. I think we should go in.'

'Yes,' Alice said and stood up. 'It's getting late, if you want to get back to London tonight.'

Then, suddenly, a silence fell in the summerhouse. Don't they call that an angel passing over? I thought: here we are, all three of us sitting together, talking, and it may be for the very last time. This picture I could see of me and Megan and Alice in the summerhouse was laid over count-less other images that came flooding into my mind of us lying about on our beds in the Tower Room, sprawling about in the grass next to the cricket pitches, walking together around the Rim of the Known World, sighing over our homework in the JPR – all of them in the past, gone for ever. I was going to say something, something about my feelings, but I didn't in the end. I felt sad, though. There were Simon and Jean-Luc to think about now, and I had a kind of vision of Alice in the future sitting in this garden with children playing around her. It would never, never be only the three of us ever again. This, I thought, this is the end of my childhood.

On the way up to the house, I asked Alice:

'Did we do it? Did we exorcise all your bad memories?' She smiled and said, 'Maybe. I hope so. I won't know until the next time I go in there. But I hope so. And thank you.'

'There's nothing,' said Megan, 'to thank us for. I wish we could have made it never happen. I wish we could have done more to help you through it.'

Alice shook her head. 'No,' she said, 'don't talk about it any more. It's over now. Finished. Done with. And nothing but nice things to look forward to from now on.'

'Right,' I said. '"Happy ever after" – that'll be our motto. Let us drink a toast to this motto in tea!' Megan and Alice both laughed, but we did it anyway. We went into the kitchen and solemnly raised our teacups and banged them gently together.

'Happy ever after!' we said in unison, and burst out giggling as though we'd made the funniest joke in the world.

Now Alice is in France with Jean-Luc, and Megan and I are back at school. Not in the Tower Room, alas, but in two single rooms next door to one another, which they think is more fitting for such grown-up girls.

Every time I come back to Egerton Hall, as every term begins, I'm amazed at how distant this place is from the real world. I feel like someone who's travelled at the speed of light from one planet to another. The world of boarding-school is so removed from anything else that it's easy to forget what has just happened to you in another place. Perhaps I'm two people: home Bella and school Bella.

Megan has gone to help Matron do Weights and Measures. She volunteered. Miss van der Leyden has retired. That is what we have been told, and I imagine she must have gone back to Belgium. She was ill last spring, and what happened to Alice affected her deeply, so I hope she's better now. Alice is not here to miss her. I never had anything against the old thing, but was never one of her special favourites. Now, both Megan and I are in the very strange position of being the senior girls in the House, and yet having no real authority. Head of House, Second Head, Games Captain: these offices with their attendant obligations of list-making, supervision of people at all sorts of inconvenient times, etc. etc., are taken by girls in the second year Sixth. They've let us keep our Prefects' badges and the privileges that go with them, which is all I care about. We are allowed to go out on Saturday afternoons four times a term at least, and that's something. I can't help feeling we shouldn't be here at all. I said so to Megan this morning.

'I feel,' I said, 'like Gulliver, or something. Too large for this place. All those little first-formers look like ants to me. I feel I've grown up over the summer, Megan, and it's pathetic, after everything that's happened this hols . . . don't you feel like Alice in Wonderland this term? As if everything's very small and you're growing and growing and pushing against the walls, longing to escape?' Megan thought a bit about this before she answered. You could even say 'she considered'. She does a lot of that and I do almost none. Talk first, think later is more my philosophy. Anyway, Megan considered, then said:

'No, actually, I feel I've got smaller. Not physically, but next to the work that has to be done. I mean, up until last term, we always knew exactly what we had to do. This Oxbridge stuff is a bit of an unknown quantity, really. I mean, exams are all very well, but then there are those awful interviews. If you pass the exams, of course. Everyone says it's really the interviews that count, and I shall be tongue-tied, I know I shall.'

'Rubbish,' I said. 'You will impress everyone with the depth of your learning and the maturity of your calm exterior. I, on the other hand (if I pass the exams, as you say), will sizzle and dazzle and bat all available eyelashes etc. I will wear a very short skirt and very high heels.'

Megan giggled. 'Miss Herbert will never let you leave Egerton Hall looking like that! And anyway, it'll all be wasted. They'll all be female dons interviewing you.'

I sighed. 'How sad! I *did* imagine distinguished chaps with greying hair and mortar boards . . . I hoped to bring stirrings of youth and beauty into their crusty old hearts. Never mind! Even for ladies, I see no reason to lower one's standards of dress. You, Megan, are an innocent. I never said anything about leaving Egerton Hall in my outfit. Oh, no!'

'What then? Buck up and tell me. I've got to go and help with Weights and Measures.'

'Poor old you,' I said. 'You have clearly never heard of that quaint, old-fashioned custom: Changing in the Ladies' Room at Victoria Station. Should we go to our interviews together, I will show you how it's done. You, too, Megan, can sizzle and dazzle with a bit of help from me.'

I could hear Megan giggling in the corridor as she disappeared in the direction of Matron's room. Rather her than me. All those skinny kids in school vests and dressing-gowns. There's a craze for quilted nylon at the moment, I've noticed. It's always in ghastly pinks and blues and lemon yellows, and a particularly nasty shade of minty pale green. Ugh! The truth of the matter is I'm fed up to the back teeth with school and all its doings. I feel as if my entire life has been spent at Egerton Hall. I know, I know, every single argument that Megan and all my teachers and my father and everyone else puts to me about the value of education is obviously right and that's why I'm doing it, but I don't see why it has to be hedged in with rules and regulations. I feel ludicrous in my school tunic and that's that. I feel lumpy and the wrong shape for everything. My feet feel as though they belong to someone else, and I get a shock every time I catch a glimpse of them in these terrible, clomping lace-up shoes.

All through school, we've dreamed of food, and now joining the food dreams are the clothes dreams. My nights are filled with images of the red dress I wore in Paris, and I think: was that really me? The same person I am now? I long for wickedly beautiful patent-leather winklepickers with dangerously thin, high heels, skin-tight drainpipe trousers and floating, silky-feeling blouses. I have fantasies of chiffon scarves around my neck, and enormous pendants dangling on the fronts of fluffy jumpers in the rich, dark colours of antique jewels. Then, after all these dreams, I wake up when the bell goes (another horror, another indignity – all of us ordered about all the time as though we were in the army) and just looking at my bra hanging on the back of the chair depresses me. I made the mistake of saying so to Megan. She looked quite astonished.

'It's a bra, Bella. Only a bra. It's designed to stop you from wobbling about all over the place. How can it possibly depress you?'

'I give up,' I answered. 'I do, honestly. If you think all a bra has to do is stop you from wobbling – and I *do* like the elegant way you put that, I must say – then you've got a lot to learn.'

I tried my hardest to look enigmatic and superior so that Megan would beseech me for further enlightenment in the matter of Bras: Their Meaning and Function, but she only shook her head as if to say, 'Poor Bella! All worked up about such trivia . . .' and pointed out to me that if we didn't get a move on, we'd be late for first lesson.

I blame Dorothy. I can't say I've given that much thought to her underwear, but it's quite likely to be armour-plated. How could poor Megan ever discover all the delights of luxurious lingerie with such a person to set her an example? There are occasions (rare, admittedly) when I'm quite grateful to Marjorie for being the kind of woman she is.

I'd never realized how much time we used to spend simply having lessons when we were in the lower forms. Hours and hours on end were taken up, it seems, walking along the corridors from one classroom to another, and listening to teachers doing their bit in turn. It's all quite different now.

The day has become a kind of tundra, a flat, dull expanse only broken up by the odd meal and the odd class. These hours, stretching from breakfast till supper, Megan and I and the other Oxbridge entrants are supposed to fill usefully. When not actually being taught, we are supposed to be in the library reading what everyone and his uncle has said about every single one of our set authors. We are also supposed to read 'more widely' which really means anything even vaguely relevant to our subject.

'It's altogether too much,' I moaned to Megan. 'One can have a surfeit of even the greatest literature. Although I notice that you don't have trouble filling your day.'

'That's because,' Megan said, 'I write poems whenever I feel bored.'

'I can't write poems,' I said.

'Bet you can,' Megan said. 'You've never tried.'

'I sort of feel that if I can't be Rimbaud I'd rather not bother.'

'Then write to Alice,' Megan said.

'There's nothing to write *about*,' I grumbled. 'I'm not doing anything interesting. Alice doesn't want to know about imagery in Leconte de Lisle and Théophile Gautier. Even I don't want to know about it, when you get right down to it.'

'But I've seen you writing,' Megan said. 'You must be writing something.'

'If it's a toss-up,' I answered, 'between my innermost thoughts or an essay on "The Alexandrine is the perfect metre for Classical Tragedy. Discuss," then innermost thoughts win every time. In any case, it's addictive, isn't it?'

'A bit like talking to the perfect listener.' Megan nodded absently. Half her mind was on something else. 'One who never answers back or contradicts you.'

There is nothing for it. I am going to have to translate a chunk of Henry James into French, after first of all (as Megan rather wittily put it) translating the passage into English that normal people can understand.

A letter has come from Alice. Megan and I raced off to the study with it after breakfast. Now I shall have to answer her. Goody goody!

Dear Megan and Bella,

You are lucky to hear from me at all, because I am having such a wonderful time that I find it hard to tear myself away from what's going on even for a few minutes. But my heart goes out to the two of you, still there at Egerton Hall, working away for still more awful exams, and I think I should try and cheer you up a bit with a letter. It'll give you something to look forward to at breakfast if I start writing to you regularly.

Jean-Luc's family live in a castle! It's only a little castle, but it's by a river and it's got turrets and spiral staircases all over the place and there are vineyards all around it and the sun is still shining even though it's September.

He's got a *huge* family. Not as many aunts as I have, but any number of extra little branches of the family tree who keep appearing when you least expect them. *Grand'mère* (as he calls his mother's mother) is a terrifying old bony creature with a pince-nez and black clothes who stares all the time and pinches the tops of my arms and makes 'tsk'ing noises like the witch out of Hansel and Gretel, waiting for me to get plump so that she can eat me! His other granny is fat and jolly, thank goodness, and much given to kissing me and calling me '*petite poupée*'.

Jean-Luc and I do an awful lot of visiting. I think I'm

361

being scrutinized by the whole family, to see if I come up to scratch. When we can get away from relations and three-hour-long meals, we go for swims in the river and walks through the countryside. I shan't describe the meals. It'd be cruel to poor old you, still having to endure marge on your toast and rice pudding at least once a week.

I'm so happy, Megan and Bella, that I sometimes feel a bit guilty. I wish you could be here too, though, and I'd really love a letter. It'd be almost like a chat. I'd like to know what's going on at good old Egerton Hall. I miss it sometimes, much more than I miss Arcadia House. I suppose that's not so surprising, since my recent memories of home aren't all that entrancing.

Someone somewhere is preparing an enormous something-or-other for supper. I can smell fresh herbs and wine cooking slowly. Enough! Stop! I can hear you cry, so I shall torment you no further. Back you go to your soggy cabbage and gristly meat . . . Do write soon if poss.

Tons of love,
Alice.

P.S. Can you find out Miss van der Leyden's address? Matron would know, I'm sure. Many thanks.

Chère Princesse Lointaine,

I wish you weren't so 'lointaine', I do honestly. Still, Megan and I are both thrilled to bits that at long last you are living where you belong, i.e. in a castle. I'm writing for both of us, because Megan is in a *total tizzy* and cannot put pen to paper.

Alice, on no account are you to turn the pages to see *why* M. is in this state. That would be cheating.

There is no news. All we ever do is work, work, work.

Nineteenth Century now, all Romantic and Decadent stuff. Baudelaire is *tremendous*, full of sex and drugs and booze and the joys of living life to the full. I'm in love with Rimbaud, as you know, and apart from that, it's not too exciting.

Which brings me to my story. Last Saturday, Megan and I decided that we could bear Egerton Hall not one moment longer, so down we went to the Old Forge for a comforting guzzle. We had the usual. (Let me list it for you, Alice dear, in case the pots-au-feu and the tartes have addled your brain): Welsh rarebits, chips and teacakes. Remember? Doesn't it just make you want to rush back here tomorrow? Anyway, where was I? Yes, imagine M. and me sitting in the gloaming of the Old Forge, quietly tucking in and for once silent, absorbed in our munchings. We're sitting at that table right in the corner, under the sloping bit of the ceiling. Megan's facing the restaurant and I'm opposite her with my back to the door. After a few minutes' worth of chewing, I look up at Megan because she's making a funny noise in her throat, a cross between choking and gasping for breath.

'You've gone completely white, Megan,' I say. (She looked so dreadful that I quite forgot my chips – imagine!) 'Whatever's wrong?' She says nothing, but just sits there staring at the door. Honestly, Alice, it was just like Macbeth seeing Banquo's ghost. She even pointed a trembling finger over my shoulder. So I turn round to look at what she's seeing, and guess what? There's Simon, standing by the door, staring back at Megan in a pretty Macbeth-ish way himself.

Well, I can see at a glance that if Simon keeps standing there, no one can get in or out of the door, so I make a decisive move. Megan, I know, if she's left to her own devices, will just continue sitting in a trance with her fork clutched in her left hand, like Excalibur or something. So I wave and shout:

'Yoo-hoo! Simon! Come over and sit down,' or something equally discreet and elegant. Megan wakes up out of her daze to scold me for being embarrassing, but my shout has the desired effect and soon Simon is sitting with us. He declines Welsh Rarebit and chips and teacake (what devastation Love can wreak!) and orders tea. Megan stops eating altogether, which doesn't worry me. I just finish everything on her plate while they gaze into one another's eyes. Well, gazing has its place, I'd be the first to admit, and far be it from me to be a Preventer of Gazing. Still, I feel a little information wouldn't come amiss, so I start the ball rolling, conversationally. I say:

'I thought you were in America. Megan said you'd got a job.'

Simon says:

'I was never really happy there. As soon as I got there, I was thinking of ways of coming back. I've got a job here now, in a school near London. It's not much, but it's a start. At least I'm getting paid.'

I say:

'That's wonderful! Isn't that wonderful, Megan? Simon's going to be living in London.'

Megan is still silent, still staring at poor Simon as if her eyes could gobble him up and to be fair, he's looking a trifle gobbly, too. Then he says:

'Megan, will you come for a walk with me? Just for a bit? Please.'

Megan still can't bring herself to speak, so I answer for her.

'What a good idea!' I say, noting that the teacakes we

ordered have arrived at the table. 'Go on, Megan. I'll see you back at school. You've got ages. Till six o'clock.'

Megan nods at me, and they walk out of the Old Forge together. I'm so intrigued by what they might do when they get on to the pavement that I stop eating for a full five minutes and crane my head to look out of the window. What can I say, Alice? For the whole time I'm looking at them, they are absolutely *welded* together, starting at the mouth and carrying on to their knees. Welded and entwined. I was thrilled, Alice, I can tell you. I never knew Megan had it in her to stand on a public street *in her Egerton Hall uniform* kissing a man!! In the end, they separated themselves and began to walk away. I ate both teacakes, as a kind of celebration.

Megan arrived back at school at six o'clock, looking like a rosy sleepwalker.

'Where did you go?' I asked.

'For a walk,' Megan said, and then the bell went. I know you think I'd have interrogated her, Alice, asked her what happened, wanted to know details, etc. etc. but I didn't. I was good. You'd have been proud of me. I just felt happy that Megan was happy again, and I was content to leave it at that, only *the best is yet to come*. At about midnight that night, Megan came into my room.

'Are you awake, Bella?' she whispered.

'No, I'm sleeptalking,' I said.

'I'm sorry, only I've got to tell someone . . .'

'Tell,' I said. 'Tell at once.' I was sitting bolt upright by this time as you can imagine.

'It's Simon,' said Megan. 'He's asked me to marry him.' I fell flat on my back and pulled the covers over my face. I had an instant awful vision of Megan leaving the next morning, all dolled up in orange blossom and tulle, and me grinding along here with the exams all on my own. I said:

'What did you tell him?'

'I told him I'd think about it.'

I started laughing then and couldn't stop. Honestly, Alice, can you imagine a more Megan-ish answer??

Anyway, the long and the short of it is: they are Back Together Again, and Megan is Blissfully Happy, and you may or may not be a bridesmaid very soon. Watch this space for more news.

Do you realize I should have been working instead of scribbling all this? If I fail these exams, I shall blame you. All your fault for not being here, Where the Action is.

Megan sends her love and says she will write soon. She has read this letter and shaken her head over it. *Tant pis!*

Loads of love,
Bella

P.S. Write soon.

I am finding it increasingly difficult to concentrate on my work. It's not that the work is uninteresting, but other things keep happening that push it to the side of my attention. I have only to immerse myself in something or another and wham! there's an event. Megan's announcement of Simon's proposal was like that. We have talked of little else since then and Megan veers between wanting to leave school this very minute and fly to Simon's side for ever and ever, and saying things that sound altogether too much like the sensible advice dished out by women's magazines, e.g: 'If he really loves me, then he'll wait for me.'

'That's all very well,' I said, 'but how long can he be

expected to hang around waiting? The whole three years that you're at university? I call that a bit much.'

'Well,' Megan blushed, 'perhaps it is. Maybe I won't get into Oxford or Cambridge. Then I could go to London University, so as to be near him. Maybe I should do that anyway. What do you think?'

'How about Simon looking for a job at Oxford or Cambridge so as to be near you? Do you think he'd consider that? It's funny, isn't it, how we, the women, are always ready to drop our plans at a moment's notice to fit in with men. Do they ever do the same for us?'

'Gosh,' said Megan. 'I hadn't thought of it like that. I could ask him, I suppose. But are you allowed to go up to Oxford and Cambridge if you're married?'

'I've no idea. You needn't marry, of course. He could get a flat and you could be in your college and no one need ever know he's more than your boyfriend . . . though I don't know quite what's supposed to happen to the droves of admirers we were both going to have. I suppose I shall have to cope with them all by myself. Ah, me, a sorry pickle indeed!'

'I feel sometimes,' said Megan, snapping her books shut with an irritation I'd never seen her show before, 'that I'd like to take every single one of my notes and essays and snip them into a million pieces, toss them out of the Tower Room window and let them all drift down over the grass like snowflakes. I'm fed up to the back teeth with all this . . .' She made a gesture that took in the study, the books, and also, it seemed to me, the whole school and her past life. 'I'd like to be someone whose life is straightforward.'

'No, you wouldn't,' I said. 'That'd be too boring for words. All the people with straightforward lives are sitting about longing for complications, for a bit of interest.'

'I know,' said Megan. 'I know. Don't take any notice of me. I expect I'm just tired.'

It's easy to feel tired. We are both working so hard and trying to learn and memorize so much that it's a wonder we don't collapse under the strain. I have these mad fantasies at times, imagining what Rimbaud and Baudelaire and people of that ilk (who were all busy, busy, busy living life to the full, drinking and taking drugs and plunging, as Baudelaire put it, into the depths of the Abyss to find the New) would think of uniformed British schoolgirls writing neat notes about their poetry and considering the meaning of all their soul-shattering experiences. It's quite surreal. And all this cramming is not useless. Not at all. One learns fascinating things, such as this: the poet Gérard de Nerval used to tie a silk ribbon round the neck of his pet lobster and take it for walks along the streets of Paris. I find I can hardly remember the streets of Paris and I was there only weeks ago. The other day, Megan let me read all the letters I wrote her during the holidays, and I found it strange. Did I really feel that strongly about Mark? I realize with a bit of a sinking of the heart that I'm not Dante-and-Beatrice material after all. It's frightfully disappointing. It would have been deeply romantic to come back to school and go into a decline. Matron would have found no cure for such a state. I could have gone and wept at her door, in my own version of the 'Song of Songs':

'Stay me with Syrup of Figs, comfort me with Bovril, for I am sick of Love!' Alas, I think what's wrong with me is I'm too practical. I've managed to banish Mark almost completely from my thoughts. The front of my mind is always full of *now*. I'm not a bit like Megan and Alice who can both somehow manage to focus on their beloveds with a startling tenacity, whether they're there or not. On several occasions, it's true, I've woken up after a dream in which I knew I was on the edge of seeing his face again, but somehow it's always turned away. These dreams are unsettling. I have had to walk along the dim corridors for a bit to calm myself down. Egerton Hall has a special look about it at night. It's what I think of as a hospital look. The passages are lit by dim bulbs under antiseptic white lampshades. The flexes hang from the ceiling at intervals, and from my bedroom to the bathroom at the other end of the corridor, I can count four lights. The glow is pale and bluish and although the doors of all the rooms are closed, I know there are hospital-type beds in each one, with white-painted metal bedheads. It was worse in the Junior House. There we slept in dormitories like open tunnels and there was one light just outside each end. I hated getting up in the night to go to the lavatory, walking past the dark, curtained opening of each cubicle. I used to fix my eyes on the brightness at the end of the tunnel and walk towards it swiftly without turning my head either to left or right. Part of me, the normal, daytime part, knew that it was friends of mine in bed and asleep in every cubicle, but the night-time is a great transformer. I couldn't be sure what had replaced them in their beds with the coming of the dark. I remember this now and think what a silly child I used to be. The night is my favourite time of all now, when the bells have stopped and so have the voices of hordes of noisy girls, and the clever words of the teachers are put away till the morning.

Très chère Alice,

I think I have been indirectly responsible for one of the most exciting moments the school has seen since Megan and Simon ran away. Last Sunday morning when we all filed into Chapel, who do you think was there, right in the front row of the Gallery in the usual all-black get-up? You'll never guess in a million years so I'll tell you. It was

Greg. Every head was turned to look at him for sixty per cent of the time at least, and you could hear the Juniors twittering and giggling and wondering whose he was, so to speak . . . could he be a Brother? If so, then whose? He'd shaved for the occasion, and his hair had obviously just been washed and flopped over on to his forehead in a way perfectly designed to fill the daydreams of pewfuls (pewsful?) of fourteen-year-olds for months to come. Perhaps I have been taking him for granted, Alice. His eyes are somewhat spectacular, I have to admit. Or is it that being closeted away from all male company has this effect on me, as well as on those silly little girls?

I realized at once, of course, that something very important must have happened to bring Greg down to Egerton Hall. I spent most of the service worrying about what it could be. He was waiting for me outside Chapel when we came out.

'Hello,' he said. 'Bet you're surprised to see me, aren't you?'

'Yes . . . I mean, I'm delighted, but you might have warned me.'

'It was spur of the moment. I had the use of a car. Can I take you out of this place?'

'We'd have to go and find Miss Herbert.'

'Do I have to come? Can't I wait by the car?'

'No, I think she needs to see you. Make sure you're respectable.'

'Oh, Lord!' Greg groaned. 'If I'd known I'd have to meet a teacher, I'd have stayed in London.'

I dragged him off to Miss Herbert's study. She was chatting to some parents, so we waited by the polished table in the Front Hall. When Miss Herbert finally emerged, Greg was showing an enormous interest in the grandfather clock by the stairs. Well, I introduced them and he hummed and ha'ed and shuffled his feet, but he did manage a reasonable facsimile of a smile at one point and honestly, Alice, I could see Miss Herbert thaw out before my very eyes. She put her hand up to her bun and patted it in a way that was almost flirtatious. She smiled back at him. I think, though I'm not quite sure, that she referred to us as 'you young people', sounding positively benevolent.

'She's rather nice,' said Greg as we disappeared down the drive at high speed in a dangerous-looking little red thing he swore was a car, and it came to me with a bit of a shock that she, too, must have been young once. Do you remember how we used to invent a love-life for her, when we were in about the Upper Third? Anyway, I digress. Where do you think we went? Three guesses. Right first time: the Old Forge.

I said: 'To what do I owe the pleasure of a visit from you?'

'I've got some news,' Greg answered, 'so I thought I'd come and tell you and get out of London for the day at the same time.'

'First things first,' I said, and smiled over his head at the waitress. 'I heartily recommend the Welsh Rarebit. The teacakes are good, too. Also the chips. They do very good chips.'

'But it's only half past eleven,' said Greg. 'On normal days I wouldn't even be getting up yet.'

'You are a dissolute jazz musician,' I said, 'but I am a healthy English schoolgirl. It's hours and hours since breakfast. If you prefer, I can refer to this as an early lunch.'

He sighed. We ordered Welsh Rarebit and chips for me, and a cup of coffee for him.

'Right,' I said. 'Tell me all the news.'

'Well,' said Greg, 'the thing is we've been asked to do the cabaret at a twenty-first birthday party in December. This friend of Roddy Maxton's heard us at his party and is willing to pay us bundles of money on condition that you're with us. You will do it, Bella, won't you? He's taken quite a shine to you, this Ackworth chap.'

'Gosh,' I said, shovelling in the chips, 'that sounds great. Is it after the twelfth or will I have to climb in and out of school like I did for the Valentine's Day thing?'

'It's the fourteenth, so that's okay,' Greg said, 'only there is one tiny drawback.'

'Go on, tell me. I shan't collapse.'

Greg sighed. 'It turns out that the Ackworth family are patients of your dad's. I'm afraid that he's invited to the party and so is Marjorie.'

'I've changed my mind,' I said. 'I think I will collapse after all.' I grinned. 'No, I don't really mean it. I haven't any objections to singing in front of Marjorie. In fact, I'd quite enjoy it, if you want to know the truth. And there'll be crowds of people there, so we won't have to speak to them or sit with them or anything. Where's it being held, this do?'

'At a nightclub in Pimlico called The Glass Menagerie.'

'It sounds frightfully exclusive. That's because I've never heard of it.'

'I've never been there either,' said Greg, 'and we aren't going to get a chance to rehearse there until the morning of the party, but I gather from Phil that it's weird. A weird place.'

'Whatever do you mean?' I asked.

'I'm just repeating what Phil said. He said the decor was surrealistic and when I asked him what he meant, he shook his head and said, "Weird, man, really weird." And Rilly says . . .' Greg blushed and I looked at him, hard.

'Have you been seeing the Pink Marshmallow of London Town while I've been slaving away over a hot textbook?'

'No, no,' Greg stammered. He was still blushing. 'She and Roddy just came round one night for a drink. Honestly, that's all it was.'

'It's okay. Only don't go on protesting too much or I shall decide not to believe you.'

'No, please, Bella. Please believe me . . .' he said.

'All right,' I said. 'I'll believe you if you order me a toasted teacake.'

After the teacake, Greg drove me back to school, and we managed a very loving smooch in the front seat of the car before I got out. I wonder if anyone managed to see us. They must certainly have heard the car coming up the drive, gone to the windows to have a look, and then counted the minutes until I got out and wondered feverishly exactly what was going on in there! Tee, hee!

It's taken me ages to write all this. Please make sure you write back.

Love,
     Bella

The examinations are over.

It came to me in a rush right in the middle of my Spanish Translation paper that I had no desire whatsoever to spend the next three years reading texts in foreign languages, and putting down my thoughts about them in yet another long series of three-hour examinations. This revelation terrified me, and I continued with the Spanish Translation paper and all my other papers without saying a word to anyone, not even to Megan. She, I know, is dreaming of extending our time in school together for another three years. How can I tell her that the thought appals me? I have decided to say nothing and hope for the best. Most people, it has to be said, don't even get as far as an interview. I shall have to keep my fingers crossed. Now that the papers are over, I find it difficult to know how well or badly I've done. I suppose if I were really serious, I would have withdrawn from the whole examination, or sat at my desk and written nothing, but I couldn't do that to my teachers, who would have been so upset. As it is, if I don't make it to the interviews, they can mutter darkly about prevailing standards, bias among the markers, etc. etc. I haven't given any thought at all to what I could do instead of going to university. Personally, I'd be quite happy to go on singing with the band and leading a Bohemian existence in London, however uncomfortable such a life is sometimes, but what (if I don't become famous, which is more than likely) would I live on? It would be good to discuss this with someone, but Alice isn't due back here till the end of the month, and Megan . . . I daren't tell Megan any of this.

'Well,' said Miss Herbert, 'this has all come to pass in a very satisfactory manner.'

Megan and I, sitting in front of her desk on the two upright chairs reserved for parents being lightly grilled about their offspring, nodded politely.

'It is, perhaps, regrettable that you will be travelling to different destinations, but we must not be churlish. One interview each at Oxford and Cambridge is very creditable. Very creditable indeed. You may travel as far as London together on Monday afternoon and spend Monday night . . .?'

'At my parents' house . . .' I put in.

'Precisely. At the house of Dr and Mrs Lavanne and the next morning you can set off to your respective London termini.'

'Could we possibly leave on Monday morning?' I asked. 'I'd love to get my hair done in the afternoon.'

Miss Herbert's expression and tone did not alter, but a twinkle of amusement crossed her face.

'Naturally, I cannot imagine a place at one of our great universities being casually handed out to someone who appears for her interview . . . how shall I put it? . . . inadequately coiffed.' She stood up, thus telling us that our little interview was over.

Outside Miss Herbert's door, Megan said:

'Are you really going to have your hair done?'

'Certainly,' I said, 'what did you think I'd be doing?' From Megan's blush, I knew at once.

'You thought I'd rush straight round to Greg's for a spot of slap and tickle, didn't you?'

'Well . . .'

'Just because you're spending Monday night chez Simon . . .'

'Ssh . . .'

'It's all right, her door's closed. Anyway, there'll be no chummy changing into clothes in station loos together, will there? I call it a bit of a swizz. I don't know that I want to go to Cambridge, especially not without you.'

'Oh, Bella, not that again! Why not?'

'There's so much else I'd rather be doing than studying things and learning stuff and putting it all pointlessly down on paper.'

'You'll feel better,' said Megan, 'once you see the place. I'm sure you'll love it.'

'No, you're not,' I said. 'The only thing you're sure of is that *you'll* love it.' That's a different thing altogether.'

'Oh, for heaven's sake,' said Megan. 'They may not offer a place to either of us. Let's not quarrel about it.'

'Let's not,' I agreed. 'Let's talk about Armand's instead. Are you going to come with me?'

'No, I think there's very little he can do to my hair.'

'He could trim it,' I suggested.

'I think I'd be bald if he did,' Megan laughed.

'But you don't mind if I do, do you?'

'Certainly not,' she said. 'I shall be otherwise occupied.'

'I'll bet you will be.' I laughed and we went upstairs together to sort out garments with which to bewitch those who would be interviewing us.

Armand's salon was as delicious as ever. This, I thought, must be a little what Paradise is like. Whatever is worrying you, whatever troubles you may have in this chilly, grey November world outside, you simply hang up along with your outdoor coat in the cupboard by the entrance. Then you put on the rose-pink robe and at once peace and contentment settle around you.

'Mam'selle Bella! It is such a long time!' Armand was gratifyingly pleased to see me. 'No one has seen you. Madame Lavanne, she has stopped speaking of you almost completely. You 'ave been, how do they say? Living it up?'

I laughed. 'Whatever gave you that idea? I've been stuck at school with my head in a book for nearly three months.'

'Aah, le midnight oil! *Je comprends*. It is for that that you have the eyeshadows under the eyes.'

'Well, that's all over now. I doubt very much if I shall study anything more taxing than the *Tatler* ever again.'

Monsieur Armand said: 'And here he is, the new *Tatler*,

376

just for you. You will sit and study him while I comb out Madame La Contesse, then I will focus on you all my attention.'

The *Tatler* was full of girls who looked like Rilly Maxton popping out of strapless ballgowns and showing overtoothy grins to the cameras. None of the men looked at all desirable. I was so bored by the whole magazine that I nearly missed it. At first, I glanced at the page (a party in a castle in Scotland) and turned over, but some whisper, some half-glimpsed something made me turn back. I looked at each picture more closely and there it was, right in front of my eyes, at the very top of the right-hand page, on the right-hand side. At first it seemed to be like all the others: a photograph of some revellers in evening dress, but one of the faces was the face I had almost (but not quite) forgotten about, the face I'd first seen in the Club Sortilège in August. I felt cold. My heart started beating very quickly. The print under the photograph swam and danced before my eyes. Left to right, the Hon. this and that, Lord so-and-so, Viscount Thingummy, and then, in very clear black letters: 'Mr Mark Eschen, of Boston, U.S.A.' I stood up and walked over to where Armand was combing out the Countess or whatever she was. I said:

'Armand . . . Armand, please, please can I cut out this photo? Please. It's got someone in it that . . . that I saw once.'

Armand smiled at the Countess in the mirror and murmured something in her ear. Then he picked up his scissors.

'Which photo, *ma petite*? This one? *Voilà*. I cut for you.' Snip, snip went his scissors then he handed me the tiny scrap of paper and pointed straight at Mark.

'*Celui-là, n'est-ce pas?*' he said.

'However did you know?' I was amazed.

'About what you will love,' he said, 'I know a great deal.

This one, *par exemple*, is not your beloved.' He indicated a foxy-looking chap with a bristly moustache.

'Quite right, Armand, you're very clever.'

Later on, when he was combing out my hair, he said:

'So tell me the story. Where did you meet this so handsome young person?'

'I've only met him once. In Paris. He came to the club where I was singing. That's all.'

'But it is so romantic! If he saw you, this young man, if he spoke to you, then he loves you . . . *C'est très simple.*'

It was only when I passed a newsagent's on my way to Sloane Square Underground that I realized I could have bought my own copy of the magazine. I'd been too busy saying to myself, over and over again: he's not in America, he's here. He could be on the same tube; he could appear at any moment! Of course I knew he wouldn't, but it made me feel better to know that at the very least he was on the same side of the Atlantic as I was. I imagined Armand nodding his head knowingly. Lovely Armand! He was very kind to me, but what a lot of nonsense he talked from time to time!

Dearest Alice,

Will this letter reach you, I wonder, before you leave France and come back here to us? I don't suppose it matters, as I can easily tell you everything all over again.

Megan and I are back from our interviews, and we feel more out of place than ever. We are literally just hanging about the school killing time until the dreaded telegrams come or don't come. They send you one if you've got in, and if you haven't you just have to wait until the time for getting them has run out and then call it a day. It's not so bad for me, as I've decided . . . well, I'll tell you everything.

Before I start on my story, you should know that Megan has fallen in love with Oxford, and came back all starry-eyed and ready to throw herself off the nearest cliff if she doesn't get in, so keep your fingers crossed. She has decided that she and Simon will become engaged, and he has undertaken to wait for her until she takes her degree. It must be Love! Meanwhile, he will look for jobs in or around Oxford. They will announce their engagement at the party I've already told you about, the one given by Rilly Maxton's Rich Friend, in that club called The Glass Menagerie. It goes without saying that you are invited. December the fourteenth (my goodness, that's only ten days away . . .) at eight-ish. I'll give you the address nearer the time, but I know it's in Pimlico, just off Lupus Street somewhere.

Back to my interview. I have to say that I most likely didn't see Cambridge at its best. The weather was dank and misty and cold and the college was miles out of town, but still, I looked around the place and came to the conclusion that Seats of Learning are not my cup of tea. Everyone was very kind at the college, which is a red-brick, ivy-clad sort of building, but it's so exactly like school inside that I was quite downcast. As soon as I sat down to supper in what looked like a larger version of the Brontë House dining-room, I knew I couldn't possibly spend the next three years of my life in such a place. By that time I'd already had chats with two scholarly ladies, who had been most kind. I can hardly remember anything of what I said. I was just aware of my heart sinking further and further into my boots. There was to be one more interview after supper, then a night in one of the rooms and then back to London on a train in the morning. Actually, I was quite looking forward to this after-supper interview because it was with Madame Séverine Drouet, the person who wrote that book on Baudelaire . . . do you remember? I was quite excited at the thought of meeting a real live writer, and she was wonderful. Very chatty and friendly and Parisian. I found myself telling her all about my time in Paris, the singing, everything. She listened. She made us coffee (after being extremely rude about the college coffee), she told me about her early days as a student in the Sorbonne, and just as I was on the point of saying good-night and leaving, she looked me straight in the eye and said:

'You have no desire whatsoever to come to Cambridge. Am I right?'

I couldn't think what to answer, Alice. Honestly, I was so embarrassed. But don't you think it was clever of her to know? I couldn't lie. I said:

'No. No, I haven't. But I'm ashamed to tell anyone.' She stood up and I stood up and she walked with me to the door. Then she kissed me on both cheeks.

'*Adieu, ma petite*,' she said. 'Everything will turn out for the best. You will see. I am not at all worried about you.'

All night I lay awake, wondering what she meant. I've come to the conclusion that I won't be offered a place at all and that she will somehow have seen to it. Or maybe she just meant that I wasn't up to the standard anyway . . . it doesn't matter. Either way, I shall have to think of something else to do. You are very lucky to have your Art. Maybe I'll come to secretarial college with you after Christmas while I think what to do.

See you very soon,
Tons of love,
Bella

My letter never reached Alice. I forgot to post it when I got back to school, and on the Sunday after Megan and I returned from our interviews, Alice herself came down to Egerton Hall to take us out for the day. Her appearance in the Visitors' Gallery caused a sensation. All the flocks of juniors who had been devoted to her and had thought her lost for ever couldn't stop whispering and pointing. The Staff tried frowning at them, to quell them a little, but you could see they were half-hearted about it. Alice looked so lovely in a plain blue dress with a black headband holding her hair back from her face that even the Chaplain, I thought, found it difficult to pay attention to the service. After Chapel, we had trouble getting away for our lunch at the Old Forge. Walking through School Corridor was like a Royal Progress. Alice stopped and talked to everyone and smiled and smiled and said yes, she was very much better now, thank you, and Megan and I walked behind her like ladies-in-waiting, fending off those who seemed simply to want to touch her.

It was a huge relief to be out of school and sitting round our usual table in the delicious semi-darkness of the Old Forge. I said:

'Don't anyone dare to say: "It's just like old times." I'll kill them.'

Alice smiled. 'But you've said it!'

'So I have,' I answered. 'So now we've got that over with, thank goodness.'

'It was very strange,' Alice said, 'being back at Egerton Hall. It seems like such ages since I was there.'

'It's us you should feel sorry for,' I said. 'We're like Souls in Limbo now. Neither really at school, nor properly out of it. No more lessons. No more Prep. We just float about, like wraiths, don't we, Megan?'

Megan nodded. 'It's ghastly. We go round and round the

Rim of the Known World on these endless walks, and then we come in and supervise something or other: sit with forms while Staff get on with writing reports – that sort of thing. It's awful. And of course, we wait. Next week we'll know if we've got in.'

'You'll get in,' I said to Megan, 'and I shan't.'

'You don't know that,' Megan said. 'You don't know at all.'

I said nothing and settled in to eating my Welsh Rarebit. Then Megan said:

'You should have seen her, Alice, when she got back from Cambridge. She was like a Fury. Her hair was practically standing on end, she was so cross.'

'What about? What happened? Do tell,' Alice said. I noticed she had hardly touched her food.

'Eat up like a good girl,' I said, 'and I'll tell you.' Alice obediently speared a chip and began nibbling it.

'It was Greg,' I said. 'It all happened while I was having a milkshake, and I could cheerfully have chucked it into his lap, I can tell you.'

'What's he done?' Alice asked. She had finished Chip One and was just about to embark on Chip Two.

'He came to meet me at Liverpool Street and he was supposed to spend a pleasant hour in my company . . . please bear in mind that I am the Light of his Life and his Muse and Constant Inspiration . . . before putting me on to the train at Victoria. So we went into a Wimpy Bar and I ordered my usual treat – one of those chocolate milkshakes that's so thick it can hardly make its way through the straw – and we settled down to discuss arrangements for this twenty-first birthday party on December the fourteenth, and things like whether there would be time for rehearsals, etc. etc. Now I'd noticed, right from the second I saw him at the barrier at Liverpool Street, that all was not well. He kept not looking at me. He held my hand a bit on the tube, but as if he didn't quite want to, if you know what I mean. As if it embarrassed him. Then at the Wimpy Bar, he kept fidgeting and squeezing the plastic tomato on the table. He was making me feel nervous and angry, so I said:

'"Tell me what's on your mind, Greg. You haven't once looked me straight in the eye."

'He looked at me then and looked away at once. He muttered something I didn't hear. I said:

'"Say that again. I didn't hear it."

'He said, "I asked you whether you loved me. That's all."

'Well, I just sat there, quietly turning the colour of the plastic tomato Greg was still prodding in a desultory fashion. I laughed weakly and said:

'"That's a bit of an unexpected question in the middle of a chocolate milkshake."

'"Nevertheless," he said.

'"Nevertheless what?"

'"I want to know the answer," he said.

'Now I was the one to do a bit of looking away. I fiddled with my straw. I sucked on it a bit and managed to persuade a trickle of chocolate into my mouth. I knew I had to tell the truth. I knew I had to be honest even at the risk of hurting Greg's feelings. So I said:

'"No, I don't love you. Not properly love in the way you mean." Then I went gabbling on, trying to soften the blow. "But I'm frightfully fond of you, and I do think you're terrifically good-looking and I love singing your songs." I ended rather lamely, really, by saying, "I like you absolutely masses and masses."

'"But you wouldn't call it love?"

'"No," I said. "I wouldn't call it love. Why ever do you want to know so badly?"

'"Because there is someone. Someone who truly does love me."

'I felt relieved and mildly irritated at the same time. If Greg transferred his affections elsewhere, I would be free . . . free to dream about the face in the *Tatler* photo hidden deep in my purse. Big deal, I thought. I said:

'"Is it anyone I know?"

'"It's Rilly Maxton."

'"You told me she and Roddy had just come round for a drink . . ."

'"That was weeks ago. Things have . . . developed since then."

'"Really?" I said. "I suppose they must have."

'It wasn't the most brilliant thing to say, but I suddenly felt furious and jealous and even more livid with myself because I knew I had no right whatsoever to be jealous. It was just the thought of him kissing that pig-like face. I stood up with as much dignity as I could muster and said something like:

'"I hope you'll be very happy, but I've got to go and get my train now." We left the Wimpy Bar. Greg was much happier after his confession, but I was seething. Just before I got on to the train, I couldn't resist torturing him a bit. I said:

'"Maybe you'd like Rilly to sing at the party instead of me. How would that be?"

'He looked so stricken, turned so white that I instantly took pity on him.

'"Don't be ridiculous, Greg," I said. "Of course I'll do it. For old times' sake, etcetera."

'I got on the train and began to feel miserable, cross and sorry for myself. What was to become of me? I didn't want to go to Cambridge and now I didn't particularly want to live with the band in the house at World's End, and I certainly didn't want to stay at home with Marjorie and her comments and suggestions for ever.'

My narrative must have enthralled Alice. She had finished almost all her food without even noticing what she'd done. Megan said:

'She arrived back at school white-faced and tight-lipped and when I asked her what was wrong, she burst into tears and we were up half the night discussing Life and What Beasts Men Were, etcetera, etcetera. It was just like the good old days.'

Alice said, 'But if you honestly don't love him, Bella, you shouldn't really care.'

'I don't "really care", as you put it. I just feel peeved, and piqued and put out. It's not so much that I want him as that I resent Silly Rilly having him. I mean, I keep thinking: what can she give him that I can't? That's what I want to know.'

'Love,' said Megan, and Alice nodded her agreement.

'What about glamour, excitement, passion, uncertainty, danger? Not to mention Divine Beauty and Unquenchable Talent?'

Alice and Megan shook their heads.

'Not a patch on Love,' said Megan. 'If she really loves him, that's it. She'll get him.'

'She's welcome to him,' I said. 'They will have the most frightfully pink children, if they ever get married. I vote we order our teacakes and talk of happier things.'

I had half-expected the last days at Egerton Hall, the very end of my school career, to be marked by some excitement, but everything happened much as it had always happened in the past.

I found the whole thing a bit of an anti-climax. There was

a flurry of drama when Megan was told of her Oxford place – the Head even declared that there would be a half-holiday next term to celebrate – and murmurings of sympathy and understanding from all the staff who had taught me, who seemed personally wounded by my failure to gain entry to a Cambridge college.

My face, those last few nights at school, was quite stiff from smiling brave and cheerful smiles all day long.

'Thank goodness,' I said to Megan, 'for such things as the Carol Concert to take people's minds off us for a bit.'

'I'm feeling quite strange,' she said, 'leaving this place. You must remember, I've lived here since I was eleven, during the holidays, too. I'm dreading saying goodbye to Dorothy. I shall tell her the truth. She surely can't mind about me living with Simon now, can she? Not if we're actually announcing our engagement?'

'You'd be surprised,' I said. 'I expect she'll always mind, in some part of her. But I shouldn't think she'd dare say anything, not now that you've got into Oxford. She'll just do some inward festering, I expect, much like Marjorie, who will suddenly be faced with the prospect of me in her house again. You should think yourself lucky you've got Simon to go to. Oh, I could kick that Rilly Maxton for ruining the World's End house for me! I really loved it there.'

'Couldn't you stay there anyway?' Megan asked. 'There's tons of space. You need hardly ever see Greg, surely?'

'No, but I couldn't bear to cross the threshold knowing The Pink One is ensconced on my chaise-longue, most probably. No, I shall stick it out with Marjorie until some-thing more interesting presents itself.'

The last morning came, and then the last night. My trunk was full of uniform for the last time. I lay in the dark in my narrow school bed looking at it and thinking: I wish I could heave it out of the train window and into the river on the way in to London. That was the traditional thing to do with a school hat and tie, and mine, I had promised myself, would be first out of the window.

'This time tomorrow,' I muttered to myself,
'where shall I be?
out of the gates
of misery . . .'
I said all the verses I could remember. The last one before I fell asleep was:
'No more beetles
in my bath,
trying hard
to make me laugh.'

'But what,' said Marjorie, taking a delicate spoonful of apple crumble and holding it for a moment in front of her face, 'do you propose to do with your life?'

I waited till I could see her elegantly chewing before I answered.

'I'm not going to do anything till the New Year,' I said. 'I've got the party in a couple of days, and then I'm going to float about and think. Perhaps I'll apply to go to drama school. I'd like that, or I could do a secretarial course, like Alice. Or perhaps a Famous Producer will hear me at this party and make me rich and famous.'

Marjorie turned a little pale.

My father said:

'You don't want to badger the poor girl, my dear. She's had a lot of strain, what with the exams and the disappointment over Cambridge. It'll be a pleasure to have her at home again, as far as I'm concerned. You take all the time you like deciding what to do. We've seen little enough of you, these past few months.'

Marjorie was having some difficulty, I could see, in finishing her apple crumble. It appeared to have glued her teeth together. In the end, though, she did manage some semblance of a smile and said:

'Of course, Bella, you must stay just as long as you like. It'll be quite like the old days!'

'Yes,' I said, 'yes, it will.'

I was thinking: that's what I'm afraid of, and already casting about in my mind for some way of escaping. I had only been here one day, and already the walls were closing in. My apple crumble kept sticking to the roof of my mouth, and nearly choking me. I had to keep taking sips of water in order to get it down at all. Home sweet bloody home, I thought. Let me out.

Marjorie, who was obviously as delighted as I was at the prospect of having me permanently in residence, made a valiant effort to steer the conversation towards pleasanter things.

'Rosemary Ackworth tells me that your friends . . . the musicians . . . are providing the cabaret at Graham's twenty-first birthday party. Now at last we shall hear you sing.' She smiled, as though uncertain whether this was going to be a pleasure or not. 'And Rosemary has asked me to give a dinner party before the dance. Could you possibly come to that, or will you be with your friends?'

I thought of Pete's house, of the band preparing for the party, of Rilly Maxton quite possibly spread all over my chaise-longue.

'Could Megan and Simon come too?' I asked. 'And Alice? Then we could all go on to this nightclub together . . . The Glass Menagerie or whatever it's called.'

'What a frightfully good idea!' said my father. 'I shall feel as though I've come down to Egerton Hall to take you girls out for a slap-up lunch at the Royal George. It'll be quite like old times.'

'Yes,' I said. 'And thank you both. I'll let the others know.' It wouldn't be like old times at all, not one little bit, but whatever happened, at least Megan and Alice and I would be able to face it together.

There was never any question about what I would be wearing to sing at the Ackworths' party. It had to be Madame's red dress – to remind me of Paris, to remind Greg of me and what I had been to him, to remind me of possibilities in my life whose existence I had practically forgotten, and above all to say: there's one in the eye for you, respectable upper-middle-class London, with your princess-line taffetas and your boring old pastel colours!

I'd taken out the dress, and hung it on the back of the door. It could have done with a spot of dry-cleaning, I suppose, but I'd left it too late. I'd ironed all the flounces as best I could, and that would have to do.

As I got ready that evening, I remembered what fun it had been, preparing for Alice's party, only six months ago. Now I couldn't summon up any pleasurable feelings at all.

'In fact,' I said, grimacing at my reflection in the dressing-table mirror, 'you will be smiling though your heart is aching, even though it's breaking, etcetera, etcetera.' I struck a silly pose to cheer myself up. 'The show must go on! On with the motley! Calloo, callay!' I said, and began to decorate my eyes with black lines which would not have disgraced Cleopatra herself. Then Marjorie half-knocked at the door and came in without being asked.

'Bella darling,' she said, 'I was just wondering what you

were going to wear. I can't decide, so I've come to make sure we don't both pick the same colour, or something awful.'

I pointed to the back of the door. Marjorie stared at the dress for a full thirty seconds. Then she turned round to face me.

'But Bella,' she said, 'you can't possibly wear that.'

'Why not?' (Oh, my hand was very steady with the eyeliner brush! I could feel the distant rumbling of a row coming nearer and nearer.)

'Well, for one thing it's filthy.'

'No one'll notice.'

'Of course they'll notice. Have you really learned nothing from me in all these years, nothing about style or fashion, not to mention personal hygiene?'

'There's nothing wrong with my personal hygiene,' I said, 'and as for style, I like that dress. That *is* my style.'

'But it's tarty, Bella. You'll look cheap and tawdry.'

I turned round on my stool and gave her my full attention. I could have avoided what happened next. I could have said something conciliatory and calming, but I didn't want to. The urge to let out all the feelings I'd been bottling up over years was overwhelming, and I felt a thrill of excitement as I opened my mouth, like the sickening lurch of pleasure and terror at the start of a roller-coaster ride. I said, very slowly:

'No, Marjorie, you're wrong. I've worn that dress many times before, and I look terrific. Vibrant, alive, sexy, dangerous, sparkling, beautiful and above all YOUNG. It shows off my white skin with not one wrinkle in it, my breasts that don't yet need the assistance of an architect-designed bra. It flatters my 24-inch – yes, 24-inch – waist, and my black curling tresses. And you can't bear it, Marjorie, because you're not young any more. That's true now, but it hasn't always been. You were young once, too, and more beautiful than I was, and even then you weren't happy. You couldn't face the distant possibility of growing old. You've done everything in your power to hurt me, and I don't care what you say now . . . I don't believe you.'

'How dare you!' Marjorie hissed as I was drawing breath. 'I've been like a mother to you all these years . . .'

'Rubbish,' I shouted, losing all control. 'You have *not* been a mother to me. Nothing like a mother. That's just . . . just *bullshit!*'

Marjorie stiffened and turned to ice.

'It's no more,' she said, 'than what I expect from you . . . a vulgar word like that. Mixing with the kind of people you mix with . . . tatty musicians . . .'

'Get out!' I screamed. 'Get out and leave me alone!'

'It may have slipped your mind,' she answered, 'that I have a dinner party starting in two hours' time. For your father's sake, I would ask you to control yourself and act in a respectable manner.' She smiled at me frostily. 'We have managed this charade very well for many years, Bella. Let us try and bring it off just once more, shall we?'

'You admit it,' I said, exhausted by my outburst. 'You admit it was a charade.'

Marjorie said only: 'I hope you'll be all right at the dinner party. All this shouting will probably have given you a headache.'

'I shall take an aspirin,' I said stiffly.

'In the bathroom cupboard,' Marjorie said, and left the room.

I *did* find some pills in the bathroom cupboard, and took two, even though the packet looked unfamiliar. Then I caught sight of myself in the mirror over the sink. I suppose I must have had tears in my eyes, because the reflection I saw in the glass was fractured, as though my face had been broken up into tiny, glittering pieces.

Whatever they were, the pills must have worked. Everything looked very small and distant to me, as though the dinner party were happening at the other end of a telescope. Megan and Simon and Alice were sitting far away from me. I don't know what I said to my neighbours at the table. I can't remember any of the food. There was not a sign of it on my skin, but I felt as though I'd been repeatedly beaten, as though my whole body were nothing but one enormous bruise.

'You must try some of this, darling,' Marjorie said. 'It's very strong, of course, but absolutely scrumptious.' She handed me a glass full of golden liquid. I took a small sip, and my mouth was filled with the fragrance and taste of apples.

'What is it?' I asked.

'Calvados,' said Marjorie, 'from Normandy. It's a liqueur made from apples.'

I took another sip, but it went down the wrong way, and I began to cough and splutter. From a great distance, I could hear Alice saying:

'Look, Megan! Bella's choking . . . oh Megan, what shall we do?' and because I felt so dizzy I didn't know whether she really did say it, or whether I was remembering the scene that Sunday evening at Egerton Hall, when I'd had a piece of apple stuck in my throat.

'I'm fine,' I whispered after a moment. 'I'll be all right now. Really.'

The band were waiting for me at the Glass Menagerie. It was an extraordinary place.

The tables were black and made of plastic shaped into hands on top of arms that grew out of the floor. The walls were white and hung with huge, disembodied blue eyes and pairs of dark crimson lips.

'Let me explain,' said Phil, who seemed well up in Surrealism, or whatever this was. 'We are in a zoo. A menagerie. We are the animals. Those,' he pointed to the eyes and lips, 'represent the world looking at us, and that,' he nodded to a cage made of glass and thin gold wire which was hanging from the ceiling above the heads of the crowd, 'is a menagerie within a menagerie. That's usually occupied by a dancer, but tonight as a special treat, you are going to be the main attraction.' He beamed. 'We reckon it'll knock them all sideways, you singing your songs from that cage.'

'Well, roll up, roll bloody well up! All the fun of the fair! Bella Lavanne as part of a circus!' I shook my head in disbelief, but it still felt as though it were full of cotton wool. And I didn't care. I didn't care about anything. If they wanted songs sung from a glass cage, well, that was fine with me. I wanted the evening to be over. The taped music was so loud you couldn't hear yourself think, and more and more people were arriving all the time. Squeals of idiotic laughter cut through the noise here and there, and the temperature was rising.

'Do let's find a table, darling,' I heard Marjorie say to my father. 'I should never have worn these new shoes. Every step I take is absolute hell. I don't know how I'm going to stagger through the rest of the evening . . .'

My father chuckled. 'I shan't say, I told you so,' he laughed, 'but I did, didn't I?'

'Oh, really,' Marjorie snorted, 'I don't know how you can be so heartless. I feel as if these shoes have been soldered to my feet with red-hot irons, and that's all you can say!'

A waitress came round with drinks. I turned to Megan and Simon, who were standing beside me.

'Bring your champagne,' I shouted over the din, 'and you, Alice. Come upstairs for a moment. Come outside.'

'We'll freeze to death,' Megan shouted back.

'Only for a minute,' I yelled. 'We have to do this properly. Don't let's lose sight of the fact that we are celebrating your engagement.'

We pushed and struggled through the crowds. When we got outside, the air was inky-blue and icy. The silence sparkled in our ears. We breathed the night in. I caught sight of a white cat disappearing round a corner and I shivered. Don't be silly, I said to myself. London is full of cats. Why shouldn't some of them be white?

'Ladies and gentleman,' I said, 'I give you a toast: Megan and Simon.'

They all drank, and I drank too, and then we solemnly hugged one another.

'Ladies and gentleman,' said Megan, 'I give you another toast: Alice and Jean-Luc, an absent friend.'

'Alice and Jean-Luc!' we cried and Alice's eyes began to glitter suspiciously. Simon raised his glass, and looked at me.

'I'd like to propose a toast to all three of you: the Egerton Hall girls – Megan, Alice and Bella.'

I thought that was sweet of Simon. It made it less obvious that there was no one whose name could be said in the same breath as mine.

'Can we go back in now?' asked Alice. 'I'm so cold.' We laughed, and made our way downstairs.

'It looks,' Alice shouted from halfway down the stairs, 'like one of those pictures of Hell by Hieronymus Bosch.'

'Yes,' I answered, 'only the music's louder.' I noticed Rilly

Maxton dancing with Greg. A blissful smile played over her porky features.

'I'm not in the least jealous,' I said to Alice, 'but how *could he?*'

'She's not bad,' Alice said. 'Be fair. And she loves him. She's . . . buxom, that's all.'

'That's quite enough, I should have thought. Oh, well,' I sighed, 'I suppose I'd better go and get ready for my big moment. Harry's waving at me.'

I walked towards the dance floor. The glass cage had been lowered, ready for me to step into it.

'What about a microphone?' I said, and Pete answered:

'There are mikes concealed in the corners, here and here. You'll be fine.'

I walked into the cage and the doors closed behind me. Then the whole thing was slowly lifted into the air. Looking down, I could see the seven members of the band, much smaller suddenly, and, there were Megan and Alice and Simon, and over at one of the tables, Marjorie and my father and a few brave souls of their generation, suffering among the young. There was the faithful Rilly, near the edge of the dance floor, her generous bosom making what looked like a bid for freedom from the confines of her bodice, which was two sizes too tight. The rest of The Glass Menagerie was faces: whitish circles bobbing up and down in the semi-darkness. The spotlight was on me. I put out my hand and touched the glass. How strange, I remember thinking. Before I touched the glass, it was as if nothing but clear space surrounded me. I was a bird: an enormous scarlet bird flying high, high above everyone. Now, because I was aware of the invisible walls, I felt imprisoned, crushed, unable to breathe. Greg's words from the very first time I ever sang with the band came back to me. 'You're a trouper, Bella,' he'd said.

'That's what you are. A real trouper.' I blinked tears out of my eyes. Troupers didn't cry. Troupers sang even though ghastly tragedies had happened, were happening in their private lives. Remember Edith Piaf, I told myself. Sing like her. Be as tough as she was. The first few bars of the introduction to 'Get me out' hit me like a blast of fresh air, and I thought: what a good song to start with. That'll get everyone's toes tapping. I began the first verse:

> I'm in a prison
> that you can't see,
> bars of love
> surrounding me.
> Let me out!
> Get me out!
> Take this cage
> away from me.
> My poor old heart
> just wants to be free . . .
> Let me out!
> Get me out!

The last few bars of the first verse reached my ears and sounded very peculiar, as though they'd been stretched and distorted. I kept on singing. I thought I kept on singing, but all the words became jumbled in my mouth, as though they were sticky toffees I'd been sucking, caught around my teeth. I stopped and looked down at the pale discs of faces below me, all of them turned towards me to see what I would do. I remember thinking: I must be very ill. I am seeing things. There's Mark. There, at the edge of the crowd, pushing his way through towards me. I am going to close my eyes, and when I open them, he'll be gone. He is a dream. He is my dearest wish. I remember closing my eyes. I remember nothing but the dark, nothing but falling through miles and into a black lake of silence.

Now, now that it's all over, fragments of what happened next come back to me, like pieces of a jigsaw puzzle that I have to fit together. First, there was a voice, saying, 'Let me through. Let me through. I'm a doctor.'

'But you're not a doctor,' I said to Mark, later.

'No, but I will be,' he answered, 'and I wasn't going to let anyone touch you. No one. Not before I'd reached you.'

'So what did you do?'

'I gave you mouth-to-mouth resuscitation,' he said.

'The kiss of life,' I sighed.

'If you feel like being romantic about it.'

'I always feel like being romantic.'

Mark grinned. 'I'd noticed.'

'You don't seem to mind,' I said.

'I guess I could get used to it,' he said. 'With practice.' Then he kissed me, and another piece of the jigsaw floated into my thoughts: lying there on the floor of the glass cage and seeing very close to my face someone looking at me with eyes the colour of aquamarines. I think I said something silly like, 'What are you doing here?' and he said (I'm sure of this because it struck me as very funny, even then), 'I'm a friend of the Maxtons.' I giggled weakly and said, 'No, I mean, why aren't you in Boston?'

'It's the Christmas vacation,' he said, as though that explained everything.

I have some clearer answers now. Mark has a Scottish grandmother whom he visits every Christmas.

'You will meet her,' he said, 'when we go up there next week.'

'Am I coming with you?' I asked.

'I'm never letting you out of my sight again,' he said.

'That's very high-handed of you. I might have plans of my own.'

'Have you?'

'Yes,' I said.

'Okay,' he sighed. 'Let's hear them.'

'I plan,' I said, 'never to let you out of my sight ever again. I thought I'd lost you.'

Mark smiled. 'Not me. I knew I'd find you.'

'How did you know?'

'I would've turned this dinky little island of yours inside out looking for you, is how.'

'You didn't even know my name.'

'I would have described you to the Maxtons. The Maxtons know *everybody*.'

I started to laugh. 'Everybody who is *anybody*,' I said, and Mark joined in the laughter.

'Stop,' I said. 'I'm out of breath.'

'We'd better practise that kiss-of-life thing again, right?'

'Definitely right,' I breathed, and closed my eyes.

Now, I am sitting in the buffet at King's Cross. Megan and Alice will be here in a moment. So will Mark.

Yesterday, I went to say goodbye to Pete and the band. I took them each a pair of woolly gloves as a Christmas present.

'A different colour for each of you,' I said, 'so that you don't get them mixed up.' I smiled at them, all sitting at the kitchen table in their usual places, each with his own special mug in front of him.

'We wish you luck in Boston, Bella,' said Greg. 'They won't know what's hit them. And you can come back and sing with us any time. We'll miss you.'

'And I'll miss you,' I said. 'All of you.'

I left the house quickly and walked down the dark street without looking back.

I can see Megan and Alice through the window. Soon, they will be waving goodbye to us, to me and Mark, as we leave for Scotland on the overnight train. Tonight, I thought, tonight my happy ending will begin.